VAMPIRE EMPIRE

BOOK THREE: THE KINGMAKERS

CLAY GRIFFITH & SUSAN GRIFFITH

VAMPIRE EMPIRE

BOOK THREE: THE KINGMAKERS

an imprint of Prometheus Books
Amherst, NY

Published 2012 by Pyr®, an imprint of Prometheus Books

Cover illustration © Chris McGrath
Cover design by Grace M. Conti-Zilsberger

Inquiries should be addressed to
Pyr
59 John Glenn Drive
Amherst, New York 14228–2119
VOICE: 716–691–0133
FAX: 716–691–0137
WWW.PYRSF.COM

16 15 14 13 12 ⸱ 5 4 3 2 1

Library of Congress Cataloging-in-Publication Data

The kingmakers / by Clay Griffith and Susan Griffith.
    p. cm. — (Vampire empire ; bk. 3)
  ISBN 978–1–61614–674–0 (pbk.)
  ISBN 978–1–61614–675–7 (ebook)
  1. Vampires—Fiction. I. Griffith, Susan, 1963–

PS3607.R5486K56 2012
813'.6—dc23

2012019306

Printed in the United States of America

Dedicated to all our readers, stalwart champions all.

Thank you.

CHAPTER

Nightfall draped over No-Man's-Land like a burial shroud. Men huddled in freezing, wet trenches and stared into the darkness, terrified of what would erupt from it.

Horror.

Death.

Vampires.

Elbows and rifles rested on the ever-crumbling dirt banks. They stared across the plain at the vague shape of their distant objective, the town of Grenoble, surrounded on all sides by the moon-white Alps. Frigid rain had flooded the trenches and the tramping of thousands of soldiers' feet churned the ground into ragged mud, now iced over from the freezing temperatures. Extremities were victims of frostbite. Every tenth man was already sick, dying, or dead. The only thing that gave them courage as they huddled and shivered in the black and dirty ice was that a legend stood among them.

Unaffected by the bitter wind blowing through the hand-hewn trenches of dirt and rock, the Greyfriar stood tall and straight, looking into the ebony maw around them. He wore a dark uniform, but from a different age. He sported the short tunic of a Napoleonic Era rifleman with its intricate piping. His grey trousers and high boots spoke of a long-lost dragoon. Over it all, he wore a heavy cloak. His hand rested on the hilt of his rapier. Even though it was the dead of night the Greyfriar wore shaded mirrored glasses and a Bedouin head wrap concealing his features.

He had walked out of the darkness from a solitary patrol, the only one of them brave enough to wander the wasteland alone. He was the Greyfriar, the mysterious swordsman of the north. He was the consort of Empress Adele. And he could hear whispers from the soldiers, about him and about the empress they loved, as he strode the line.

Colonel Raheem Roxton weaved through the mass of men and mud until he reached the swordsman's side. The colonel's broad shoulders were hunched and his hands were stiff. His face was streaked with dirt and camouflage paint. "Are you on your way back to command?"

"No, not yet," replied Greyfriar.

"You must enjoy our company then, for I doubt you're lingering here for our moldy rations and rampant dysentery."

"No." His voice was quiet yet insistent. "You are about to be overrun."

Roxton went pale. "What do you mean? You saw them?"

"Yes, they will be here very soon."

The colonel went down the line, yelling for a runner. The men around Greyfriar stared up at him with frightened, blackened faces. The swordsman stood on the fire step, a step cut at the bottom of the trench to allow the men to crest the top. He stared toward the city.

A lone prayer was whispered as a man near Greyfriar pulled out a cross. The men around him made crude comments.

"Give it a rest, Curwood."

"That cross didn't do Matthews any good."

"Maybe you should wrap that round your gun barrel to improve your aim."

Curwood ignored them while the Greyfriar felt discomfort rise from the words and object of faith. This man's belief forced Greyfriar to slip farther down the line. Curwood endured the glares of his fellow soldiers as they assumed even the famous Greyfriar was embarrassed by such trivial superstition in this world of steel and steam. Prayer hadn't saved the world when the vampires rose up 150 years ago, so why would it protect a terrified man in battle?

Greyfriar continued to walk down the trench, letting as many men see him as possible. If his presence brought them some semblance of courage, then it was worth the effort before death was upon them.

He stiffened abruptly. Leaping out onto the bank in a single flex of his legs, he landed effortlessly on its lip, ignoring the slick and precarious ice. His gaze was fixated into the pitch black.

Men leaned deeper onto the muddy rim and readied their weapons, straining to see or hear what the Greyfriar had, but everything was silent and still. His dark grey cape fluttered in the wind, billowing out over their heads.

"They are coming," he told them.

The phrase swept down the trench as rifle bolts clacked and tensions rose.

Colonel Roxton climbed out laboriously, slipping and grunting, to stand beside the Greyfriar. "How many?"

"Thousands," the swordsman replied, crossing his arms to draw both a rapier and a cutlass from their scabbards with a scraping hiss.

"Are you sure? I can't see a blasted thing!"

"Yes." The rapier pointed above them to the north. "There."

As if on cue, flares lofted into the sky about a mile ahead of them, where a brave patrol was scouting. With each phosphorous burst, the darkness receded and hundreds of black shapes born of nightmares were silhouetted briefly before the night swallowed them again. There were so many drifting shadows they nearly blotted out the flashes of light. Precious seconds passed before cannons opened up miles to their rear, near command. The boom of the guns vibrated the ground and the soldiers' breastbones. The artillery pounded the sky in a hailstorm of shrapnel, but Greyfriar could see that they had already lost their chance. Most of the vampires were inside the range of the cannons and they would soon be in the trenches, slaughtering with tooth and claw. The big guns couldn't adjust fast enough against such a swift adversary.

Greyfriar turned to Roxton. "Make ready. They're here."

Out of the darkness erupted fanged monsters. A wave of vampires dropped from the sky. Men screamed as they met an enemy that many had only read about but all feared. The screaming was lost in the terrible roaring of the artillery, but it could be seen in the soldiers' faces.

The men fired wildly into the air, but the enemy was already among them and rifles were better used as truncheons. There was a scramble for trench weapons as savage hand-to-hand combat commenced. Bone-crushing maces and spiked clubs lifted and fell, short swords thrust at shapes, but still the troopers were hard-pressed to hold back the advancing wave with such crude instruments.

Greyfriar rushed forward, leaping over the trench and into the air. His rapier slashed through pale flesh and limbs. He twisted in midair, landing on the precarious lip of the hollowed-out earth. Claws snagged his cloak, ripping it from his back. He spun and the steel blade sliced through the top of the skull of the nearest vampire. His cloak and the beast dropped to the bloody dirt.

More creatures settled to the ground around him, fast, darting, but his swords were blinding and they tore through the enemy, a blur even to vampire eyes. His blades arced back and forth, both in front and behind. With a graceful spin, he swept his cutlass low and forced the vampires up and back. One vampire dove at a human below him in the trench, and Greyfriar's cutlass struck deep, wedging itself in the vampire's shoulder, preventing the killing stroke, but only just. The vampire turned on him, pulling the cutlass from his hand, its razor-sharp claws slicing forward with intent to gut him. Each blow landed on Greyfriar's rapier, and for a moment he struggled against the onslaught. The vampire came at him with its dark power surging hot. Greyfriar matched the enemy's incredible speed. The two combatants battled in a macabre dance.

Then the creature vaulted away, executing an immense leap that brought it onto another soldier. Vicious claws sliced into the human. Greyfriar couldn't save the man as two more vampires challenged him.

A wave of fire boiled so close that Greyfriar was momentarily blinded. He felt claws rip across his hip. The heat from the nearby flamethrower separated Greyfriar from the cadre of vampires circling him, his adversaries consumed by the hot flames. The heat drove him back also, but it only gained him a brief respite.

Four vampires hurtled out of the returning darkness in a calculated rush, two from the air and two from opposite sides. Greyfriar raised a pistol, and the crack of the shot split the air. The first vampire was flung back into the dim night, its face gone. Greyfriar ducked under the swipe of the second one and it sped past into the trench, falling upon a human. Greyfriar swore and swung his rapier. It sung as it moved in a wide arc. One vampire pulled its attack at the last minute, but the blade caught the second one across the throat. Red spewed forth, black as ink, and was lost in the mud at their feet. Its clawed hand clutched its weeping throat and it fell to its knees. Greyfriar kicked the dying creature to the ground and raced forward toward the escaping one and drove his sword point into the heart of his enemy, twisting it violently. The vampire convulsed once and then fell face forward as Greyfriar yanked out his weapon.

The smell of blood rose up in his nostrils. It was everywhere.

The first break of day spilled over the crest of the mountain, but there was no cheer from the men. Those still alive fought on, seeing their horrific adversaries now in the thin light of day. The battle was going poorly, but the Equatorians refused to give up. They knew they were trapped.

Greyfriar darted forward to fight with a circle of men trapped outside the trenches. Vampires swarmed the soldiers, who struggled to retreat and re-form their square as comrades dropped. The men's weapons were trained up and out to cover ground and air.

The vampires pulled back, lifting into the sky and floating back toward Grenoble. Humans stood shocked for a moment, and then men slumped to the ground. Some laughed and some wept as soft snowflakes began to fall.

Black smoke drifted across the sea of blood-soaked mud and dying flesh. The morning light shone on the wet earth covered with corpses so thick that it was difficult to recognize each sullied shape.

Greyfriar walked along the edge of the trench. His mouth grew grim beneath his headwrap. This was not glorious fighting. This was not heroic adventure. This was slaughter. Thousands of dead humans stretched out around him. He had saved only a handful.

He spied the man called Curwood, still alive, huddled in the mud, clutching his cross and a broken mace. His comrades lay dead around him. Perhaps the rest of the company shouldn't have been so quick to discount the power of faith.

The shaking soldier looked up with streaks of blood on his face. "I fought them, sir. Fought for the empress."

Greyfriar gave the young man a quick nod. "Well done. You will have the chance to fight again soon."

The war with the vampires was dragging into its fifth month. And the humans were losing.

CHAPTER 2

OILY SMOKE AND thick fog the colors of blood and snow engulfed Grenoble. The city was situated on the confluence of two rivers, the lion and serpent, the Drac and the Isère. To the right of the lion, a huge human army huddled on the rolling countryside south of the city, now largely stripped of trees. The sprawling camp was hemmed in by the river on the west and by steep mountain cliffs on the other side.

In the frozen filthy trenches, numb fingers clutched steel weapons as the breath of men hung in the air, mixing with the smoke drifting over the machine-gun nests whose guns had just stilled. Eyes were raised overhead, scanning the grey sky for the slightest hint of shadows.

General Mehmet Anhalt emerged from his command bunker dug deep into the frozen earth. He was relatively short and stocky, but moved with vigor and agility. He was Gurkha, olive-skinned and clean-shaven, reserved and calm. He wore a heavy wool coat over a uniform, tattered but kept pressed as sharply as possible, with mud-caked boots and a peaked helmet whose khaki wrap was showing wear.

Anhalt made his way through the trench system, eight feet below the surface of the hard ground. Some stretches of the trenchworks were covered with metal sheeting or rough wood planks to help shield the soldiers from the claws of the enemy, but most of the network was open to the sky. Even in the thin morning light, the muddy gashes were places of unhealthy shadow and stench.

Anhalt's helmet bore the scarab badge marking him as the holder of the revived title of *sirdar*, lord commander of the Imperial Equatorian Army, and commander in chief of the Grand Expeditionary Force in Europe. He strode past infantry troopers, some of whom stood and saluted, while others merely stared or nodded a greeting while continuing to smoke or preparing meager breakfasts while huddled around makeshift braziers trying to warm themselves. He hopped onto the fire step next to a young man, trembling either from the cold or nerves, with his head down on his arm. The boy looked up wearily and his eyes widened at the unexpected sight of the general standing next to him. Anhalt saw fear in the boy's face, and not just the reasonable fear of war. The trooper was drenched in terror.

No matter how strongly the command staff had attempted to indoctrinate the soldiers that the enemy was nothing more than a subspecies of humanity, bloody myths and spook stories crowded the Equatorian mind. Lectures in the sunbaked camps of Egypt were one thing; grey shadow creatures flitting unnaturally through the icy air of Europe were quite another.

Anhalt placed a hand on the trooper's shoulder, and through the khaki tunic more suited for desert service than the Alpine winter, he felt the roughness of chain mail. Many troopers wore mail, akin to the knights of old, because it afforded some protection from the claws of the vampires even though it hampered movement and agility. The general exchanged a brief smile with the young man, who stilled his trembling and stared with renewed resolve over the battlefield.

Through his field glasses, Anhalt saw that a light blanket of wet, heavy snow lay everywhere, partially shrouding bodies, both human and vampire. The eastern light was just appearing over the mountain peaks, illuminating the aftermath of another long, bloody night of fighting.

Anhalt dropped back into the trench and moved quickly toward the artillery command on the eastern flank of the sprawling Equatorian encampment. He eventually climbed out of the man-made canyons onto level ground where lines of eighteen-pound cannons were placed, surrounded by sandbags and earthen bulwarks. He approached Colonel Eugene Mobius, who sat outside a tent, sipping a metal cup of steaming tea. Mobius rose and saluted sharply. He was a tall, thin man with close-cropped brown hair and a long jaw. He rotated a shoulder, which made his chain undershirt clank and grind. He was a capable soldier, and directed the artillery units with much discipline and rigor.

"We gave them a thrashing they won't soon forget," Mobius proclaimed loudly, more for the morale of the men within earshot than for the sirdar. They both knew that they had barely held their line under the last vampire assault.

Anhalt merely nodded, his expression giving no indication as to his disposition. He climbed onto a berm thrown up in front of the cannons, and stared at the distant mist-shrouded roofs and steeples of Grenoble, which were beginning to glow orange in the rising sun. On the scarred plains between the glistening city and Anhalt's icy observation post, ghostly shades of trench-coated soldiers drifted across the field, searching for dying or dead companions.

Colonel Mobius joined him and said, a bit more quietly, "Our odds would improve, sir, if we could pound the bloody beasts to soften them up."

"You've read the Order of Battle, Colonel. And we've discussed this at length. An artillery barrage will do little more than waste ammunition and kill the humans we are trying to liberate. Vampires can easily rise above your falling shells."

Mobius scowled. "I'm more concerned with safeguarding the humans in Equatorian uniforms than those wandering Grenoble."

Anhalt turned to his officer with eyes smoldering. He did not deign to reply because he knew that, despite his words, Mobius wasn't trying to imply that Anhalt didn't care about his troops; the artillery colonel was outspoken and not always with clear forethought. As long as Mobius kept it between the two of them, Anhalt could absorb a little potential insubordination under such harsh conditions.

Mobius spat onto the ground, undeterred by his commander's clear anger. "I can't conceive why we're so concerned for these near-men. They're nothing more than herds. It's a known fact."

"The Northern Reports say otherwise. You read them."

"I did. They were required for command staff. But can those reports be believed? The General Staff didn't place much stock in them."

"Our empress wrote them. Therefore, we trust them completely. Is that understood?"

The colonel muttered, "The empress isn't out here, is she?"

"Damn it, Colonel!" Anhalt drew close to the startled officer. "When you have endured a quarter of the hardship and horror that Her Majesty has, I would welcome your opinion on it. Until then, you had best keep your snide comments related to the empress to yourself, certainly in my presence."

The colonel stared at the ground. "I understand, Sirdar. It's simply an option. It's said that the Americans aren't so careful of what they blow up. It's said that Senator Clark is rapidly gaining ground against the vampires in the old United States."

"Gaining ground is simple. Holding ground is difficult. And I do not care how Senator Clark and his American Republic fight their war. Their way is not the Equatorian way, which was made clear when our empress refused to marry the senator last year. Our empire pursues other options. That's the end of it." Anhalt's tone made it clear that discussion was at an end. He would brook no further argument on the matter, so Mobius wisely let it drop.

Abruptly, the whitening sky darkened as vampires darted out of the cold and miserable mist. Shouts of alarm went down the ranks as soldiers raised weapons and prepared to answer the attack yet again.

Colonel Mobius shouted, "Man your guns! Look lively! Shrapnel shells!" Crews scrambled to the cannons, and his arm rose and fell with each resounding order of "Fire!"

Flak peppered the sky, concussion and shrapnel pushing back the vampires momentarily. Only those creatures that took a direct hit fell to the ground in pieces, while the rest continued their attack.

"Get some men on the shriekers." Anhalt pointed to several two-foot brass boxes mounted nearby on rough wooden poles.

Mobius shook his head. "They're broken or frozen up. Haven't worked for days."

The men outside the perimeter struggled back toward the lines with the wounded and dead. But the vampires were too many and too fast. They dropped out of the sky and fell hard onto the backs of those who had been brave enough to step out into No-Man's-Land. Soldiers died instantly in a shower of blood and bone. Those remaining ran harder. Those who carried the dead abandoned their fallen comrades and helped with the wounded, desperately trying for safety. As the terrified men closed the distance to the trench line, machine-gun nests added to the din of artillery. The spray of bullets ripped many vampires to pieces.

"Battery Four! Adjust azimuth twenty-one degrees!" Colonel Mobius shouted with field glasses pressed to his eyes. His voice boomed as loud as his artillery. For those beyond its reach, others repeated orders down the line. Gunners paused to wheel their barrels up, unable to see the new wave looming in the distance. The double-barrels of the eighteen-pounders rhythmically churned out shell after shell.

"They're still coming," Mobius informed his superior, gesturing toward the city where shapes continued to swarm out from the Bastille fortress lost in the white fog of winter high on the rocky cliffs of the Chartreuse mountain range just behind Grenoble.

There was a moment of silence before General Anhalt ordered, "Use the combustion flak."

Mobius's eyebrow rose and he swallowed hard. "The wind is light enough. I suppose it's either that or be overrun."

"We will not be overrun."

"Yes, sir."

Word was passed down the line, and special bright brass shells were brought up. They were loaded in place of the normal shrapnel shells. Scrawled on the casings were pictures and slogans depicting the death and hatred of vampires. "Suck This!" "Back to the Grave!" "From Empress Adele, Greetings!"

Also brought up were fifteen long wooden poles that each held a slender warhead. The warheads were rocket-shaped and contained black powder for propulsion and a generous amount of combustible oil. They had a range of about two miles, were notoriously inaccurate, and the men handled them gingerly because they also tended to explode prematurely.

The Fourth Battery resumed its barrage, lobbing the new shells high to explode over the battlefield; but instead of vicious metal fragments, they spewed a yellow fog that hovered like a gaseous blanket. The wind was light, so the gas cloud remained relatively steady over many square miles between the Equatorian lines and Grenoble.

The vampires didn't seem to care as they darted in and out of it, unafraid, laughing almost.

Anhalt nodded and Mobius commanded, "Fire rockets!"

The artillerymen standing beside each of the slender poles applied fire to the ends and the rockets began to sputter. Tails wiggled for a couple of seconds, and then they darted along the length of the poles and up into the sky.

The first rocket flared too high and exploded in a dazzling display of red flame, but none of the sparks made it to the slowly drifting gas. Another rocket went wild and slammed back onto the bleak field tumbling this way and that, propelled forward along the ground in a frenzied dash toward an unknown target. Luckily, it didn't swing back toward the trenches. Finally a third rocket hit nearer the mark, just short of the cloud, but flame caught the edge of the yellow haze. The atmosphere ignited with a loud whoosh. The flames billowed out and over the vampires floating near the cloud. Anhalt watched as the shroud of fire roared above the field. Waves of heat washed over the soldiers, fanning cheeks and exposed skin, making them red and prickly.

At least a hundred vampires were caught in the firestorm. Their screams echoed in the howl of the flames. They writhed and dropped from the sky like charred bits of smoldering ash.

Soldiers cheered.

Abruptly the wind altered, bringing a rush of ice crystals down the side of the looming mountain to their right. The flaming gas cloud shifted and began to descend toward the Equatorian lines with a sickening lurch.

"Take cover! Take cover!" Anhalt shouted as he ran toward a bunker.

Gunners ran for covered trenches. Soldiers in open holes and ditches, far away from protective warrens, drew fire-retardant tarpaulins over their heads or simply pressed face-first into the frozen mud, praying that they'd survive without burning or suffocating.

Anhalt stopped at the door to the bunker, guiding soldier after soldier ahead of himself. The looming wall of heat sucked the very air away. Anhalt listed dizzily as he waved a stumbling straggler past. He ignored shouts, spying another band of soldiers running madly toward him. He knew they weren't going to make it, but still he urged them on. The sky grew red. He could smell his own hair burning. Just before the flames fell, he was yanked inside and the steel door slammed shut before him. A roar boomed and the door rattled with such force that screws and hinges shook loose. Vibrant heat filled the underground narrows.

The man gripping Anhalt's arm stumbled to one knee, so the commander pulled the man deeper into the damp tunnel.

"What do you think you were doing, man?" said Anhalt, leaning the cowled figure back against the dirt wall.

"I will ask you the same question," was the unsteady reply from Greyfriar, who lifted a shaking hand to his mask to ensure it was still in place.

"The wind shifted. I had to get my men under cover." Anhalt shook his head angrily. "I left some of them behind."

Greyfriar straightened, feeling his strength flood back into his limbs as the heat abated. "You should have entered first. You are the war chief."

"I am no more important than anyone else here."

"Adele would disagree. She told me to look out for you."

Anhalt gave a smile. "Funny. I've been charged with the same thing. With you."

"Then we both have our work cut out for us." Greyfriar glanced back toward the steel doors, which glowed red around the edges.

"Damn infernal weapon," Anhalt muttered. "We caught them unaware, but we'll be lucky if they fall for it a second time."

"They won't."

Anhalt regarded Greyfriar again. "Were you injured?"

"You make it challenging, but no. I'm fine."

Anhalt could almost see the toothy smile of the vampire behind the cowl.

He would have never expected humor to be part of the creature's repertoire. He was finding that many things he thought about vampires were gross misconceptions. He wondered how many of his officers and men would feel the same way if they knew Greyfriar's secret. Few enough, he suspected.

Greyfriar said, "I'm lucky. I was coming in from the northern lines when the screams of those, what do you call them, rockets, gave me warning. Though they set my teeth on edge."

"So long as it bothers you," Anhalt whispered, "then we know it bothers them as well. Hopefully now they'll be wary enough to buy us a day or two of peace."

Colonel Mobius ran up, wide-eyed and exhilarated. "By God, that was a close shave!"

"Quite." Anhalt patted out a glowing smolder on his coat, nonplussed. "As soon as it cools down out there, check the damage. Let's pray our miracle weapon hasn't cost as many on our side as theirs."

"Yes, sir."

"Find me when you've finished."

"Yes, sir." Mobius departed.

Anhalt started deeper into the underground bunker complex, with Greyfriar falling into step behind him. The dirt corridors were as crowded as a tenement in the worst neighborhoods of old Alexandria. He saw men huddled in every recess, breath misting, eating scarce rations from tins.

Greyfriar asked, "Still no word from Field Marshal Rotherford?"

"None." Anhalt struggled to keep annoyance out of his tone.

Greyfriar was too polite to notice. "Perhaps the weather has proved difficult for him as well."

Anhalt grunted. The war strategy that had been crafted for more than a year had to be hastily changed before operations even began. First, the American allies were no longer available due to the collapsed union between Empress Adele and Senator Clark. Second, intelligence from Greyfriar indicated that Cesare had brought the clans of Munich and Budapest together into an effective alliance. To draw off these powerful clans, the Equatorians split their army and sent five divisions to invade the Balkans, aimed at Budapest.

Meanwhile, General Anhalt's army landed in Marseilles in early fall. His opening gambit was to split his elements of the Grand Expeditionary Force to form a pincer attack on the dangerous clan at Lyon at the outlet of the Rhone Valley. Field Marshal Rotherford's overpowered column, nearly a corps in strength at over thirty thousand men, had departed Marseilles for St. Etienne in early October of last year, while Anhalt took his lighter Second Division, close to fifteen thousand men, up the Gap toward Grenoble. According to Greyfriar's scouting, the road to St. Etienne was open, and the city lightly defended. It was expected that St. Etienne could be secured easily, and Rotherford would then detach part of his force eastward with haste to join Anhalt for an attempt to take the more dangerous Grenoble. The goal was to create an operational cordon sanitaire, militarize the Rhone Valley, assault Lyon, and then stage further operations into central France.

However, nothing went quite as planned. The weather turned savage sooner than expected. Resupply from the coast was haphazard. Anhalt's frozen camp below Grenoble was cut off from land and air communication in December, and lay trapped for nearly a month as the vampires drew a net tighter. The few airships he'd had on the advance north were grounded or destroyed now. His men were freezing, sick, and dying, desperately low on food and ammunition. No reinforcements had come from Rotherford to the west.

Anhalt could only speculate what had happened to his brother officer. It was certainly possible that Rotherford's divisions had met with heavier resistance at St. Etienne than expected. He could still be engaged seizing his objective, or perhaps had even been thrown back toward the coast.

Though he didn't wish to, the Gurkha couldn't help but consider another reason why a relief column had failed to show. General Rotherford had been loud in his displeasure about Anhalt leapfrogging over more superior officers, such as Rotherford himself, to take command of the Imperial Army. He had made no secret of his opinion that Anhalt was an officer of limited command experience, as well as the author of the so-called Ptolemy Disaster last year when Princess Adele had been captured by the British vampire clan. Yet, General

Anhalt had been declared sirdar, that grand old Egyptian rank, and given the greatest army Equatoria had ever mustered, only because he was the pet of Empress Adele.

Anhalt put aside his speculations and turned his attention back to Greyfriar, who was studying the men in their tight confines. The vampire seemed continually fascinated by humans. It was the damnedest thing.

A familiar face appeared in the chaos. The stern ebony visage of General Luteta Ngongo from Katanga stopped and saluted. "Sirdar." He offered a polite nod to Greyfriar.

Anhalt returned the salute and led him into an alcove reserved for officers that had a simple stove. "You don't seem happy, Luteta." It couldn't be the extreme cold, despite the general's knee-length kilt and light shirt. Ngongo was used to operating his Mountaineer regiment in the sleet-driven wastes of the Rwenzori Mountains of central Africa.

"I fear I have nothing good to report. My Mountaineers returned from our latest scouting expedition yesterday." He held up a chart of the local Alps. All the tactical maps were based on old nineteenth-century documents, and were of limited use. "We could find no safe route to the west. The few passes that looked promising were either blocked or swarming with vampires. They are not suitable for retreat."

"Did you lose many men?"

"More than I'd like." General Ngongo tossed the chart on a rickety table and bent over it with a scowl. "I'm sorry, Sirdar. I will re-form my men and go out again tomorrow. There is another possible candidate farther to the south."

Greyfriar noted, "If the vampires keep attacking every day, which they will, you won't have enough ammunition or food to support a retreat."

Anhalt strode to the makeshift stove whose coals were long unlit and cold and, therefore, so was the coffee. Fingers stiff with bitter chill brushed the tin pot aside in annoyance. He tipped his khaki helmet back. "We can't retreat. We can't wait. We have only one choice now. If we are going to die, let's take the fight to them."

Greyfriar said, "It will be a bloodbath to storm the city as weak as we are."

"An attack on Grenoble is a desperate gamble, but we are quite desperate."

"If I may, Sirdar," Ngongo offered without waiting for permission, "I agree with you. I'd prefer to move forward. I'm frankly tired of wading through the hip-deep snow. Better to be killed with a loaded gun in your hand than crawling on the frozen ground."

Anhalt regarded his colleague before turning to Greyfriar. "You spend a great deal of time among the enlisted men. What would you say is their general feeling? Wait for relief or fight?" The general waited with his back rigid for the answer he knew was coming.

"They would choose to fight. I sense there is little they won't do for Adele, but the conditions are draining their enthusiasm for the war."

"Well, that's surprising," the sirdar grunted. "Very well. Our path is clear. Victory or death."

CHAPTER 3

SIRDAR GENERAL ANHALT convened a meeting of his General Staff in a freezing dirt-walled room. Present were the commanding officers of the various units of the Second Division of the Imperial Expeditionary Force: Colonel Mobius of the artillery brigade; Generals Khalifa and Dikkha, both recently elevated to the command of the two regiments of foot; General Ngongo of the Katanga Volunteer Regiment; Greyfriar; and General Anhalt himself. They were a somber group, but resolved. All knew they were likely facing the issuance of copious death certificates.

The sirdar surveyed his officers. "Gentlemen, we know the situation. We are out of time and will not survive long languishing here. Therefore, we must take Grenoble now. General Dikkha, General Khalifa, feed the men as well as possible. Then form your regiments in their entirety for the assault. All weapons and ammunition are to be served out." He looked at Colonel Mobius. "Shortly before dawn tomorrow, your artillery will bombard the perimeter of the city and demolish the old walls, taking care to avoid as much of the core of the city as possible. Our eighteen-pounders are not optimal for taking down fortifications, but I trust you will do your best. Once complete, all infantry forces will go over the top and move into Grenoble to engage the enemy. I have unit orders to pass out later."

Anhalt paced in front of the several mediocre maps of the area. He pointed at the Bastille high above Grenoble. "General Ngongo, your Mountaineers will depart today and move into position above the fort. Take the Dyula mercenaries with you for skirmishers. We have a small store of shoulder rockets, which are yours. When operations commence in the valley, you will storm the Bastille, where the clan lords tend to reside."

The Katangan officer nodded in grim agreement.

"Gentlemen, we have reached the point where there are no options. We have no air cover. We are laboring to get some shriekers into operation. The combustion flak is far too dangerous to our own men. There is little gain to be had from devising clever tactics. We cannot succeed through stealth or misdirection; the creatures are over us, spying at all times. Our only advantage is brute strength. Sheer firepower. We must bring firearms to bear at a distance. And, if that fails, steel at close quarters. We must simply come to grips with the enemy in a set battle, and kill more of them than they do of us. That is the end of it, gentlemen. It is us or them."

The officers sat mute. They all understood.

General Ngongo regarded Greyfriar, who leaned in the frigid corner, long legs stretched out in front of him. "And you, my friend, what of you? You are the mysterious ranger. Battles and armies are not your usual place. What mysterious role will you be playing in this maneuver?"

Greyfriar chuckled. "I'll find something to keep me busy. If your Mountaineers manage to reach the king of Grenoble, you will find me there waiting for you."

A commotion outside made them pause in their strategizing. The door opened and a red-faced lieutenant ran in, saluting quickly, and then blurted out, "We are under attack, sir. The Highlanders of the Fifth report they are hard-pressed from the south." General Khalifa, commander of Constantine's Fifth Regiment of Foot, stood in alarm.

Anhalt frowned bitterly at the news. "Damn them. I had hoped that the combustible flak would have deterred them for a few hours at least. Send word to Second Luxor to move up and reinforce. Have units of the Mombasa Askaris stand by to rotate in." The lieutenant acknowledged and departed.

"General Khalifa, you'll want to get to your units. Gentlemen, we'll reconvene at a future time. Carry on." Anhalt rose to his feet and his officers followed suit, trailing him out and departing for well-worn duties with their commands. Greyfriar fell into step beside Anhalt.

"Where are you going?" the general asked the swordsman.

"To join the fight, Sirdar."

"Then I'll take the long way," Anhalt remarked with a cynical grin. "Perhaps seeing a legendary folk hero will boost morale."

"Just try not to set me on fire and I'll be fine."

Despite himself, Anhalt laughed at the vampire's droll reply. Heaven help him, he found Greyfriar an amusing companion.

They emerged topside to a land charred black. Tentacles of smoke coiled up from the ground, and fires still burned in various areas. The rough coughs of soldiers echoed through the wasteland, and weary men scrambled for their positions. The distant popping of gunfire came from the south.

Anhalt and Greyfriar grabbed a transport, a light halftrack rumbling along the rutted paths between trenches and crude blockhouses. Its steam-driven pistons fired madly as the small treads struggled for traction on the churned muddy ground. Anhalt crouched on the edge of a front seat next to a driver suddenly nervous to find the sirdar in the cab, and Greyfriar clutched a bracket and hung perilously on the running board. The camp around them seemed to be in a chaos of men and machines and horses.

"They only have to wait us out," Anhalt shouted over the rattling vehicle. "Why attack so soon? Do vampires have no patience? You said time means nothing to them."

Greyfriar shrugged and offered blandly, "Vampires are also prideful and sadistic. They don't like being challenged."

"Oh really?" Anhalt displayed an expression of mock incredulity. He swore the swordsman was grinning behind his cowl.

Greyfriar said, "They can wait, but if they think they have the advantage, why hesitate to strike you down?"

"Do you think we are so susceptible?"

"No. You will not be easy prey until you are unarmed."

"Do you think they suspect a final push is coming?"

Greyfriar paused before nodding. "Perhaps. You're backed into a corner. They would be foolish to think you would just welcome death. Maybe their increased assaults are meant to forestall your attack, or simply to drain your ammunition."

As they drew close to the southern trench lines, which were festooned with pikes sharp against the sky, they heard gunfire rattling and, amazingly, men cheering. Hundreds of vampires were visible in the air, but they were pulling back, a much different scenario than Anhalt had anticipated. He leapt from the moving truck into a slimy mud hole. Greyfriar alighted gently next to him. They dropped into a trench where a young captain noticed their arrival and tried to tidy his torn uniform with bloody fingers. "We have the buggers on the run, sir!"

"I find that unlikely," was Greyfriar's reply, much to boyish Captain Hereghty's affront. "Something else must have caught their attention."

Anhalt climbed onto the fire step, shouldering in between soldiers who waited at the parapet with rifles ready, firing pointlessly at the vanishing vampires. He studied the retreating mob. It was clear the vampires were no longer interested in the rear lines of the Equatorian army. The creatures were rising into the low clouds rolling off the mountains to the south.

Suddenly, the rumble of cannons echoed through the valley.

"That was not our artillery," Anhalt exclaimed, hope springing in him for the first time in weeks.

"A ship's cannon, sir! I'd stake my life on it!" Hereghty shouted. "Reinforcements have arrived! Rotherford has broken through!"

Eager words of salvation immediately started leaping down the line, and the counterattack was resumed on the retreating vampires with more vigor. Soldiers forgot their cold, forgot their hunger, and forgot their illness in a rush of mad exhilaration.

Greyfriar suddenly jerked upright, and his head pivoted to the southeast. Anhalt took immediate notice. "What is it?"

"She's coming."

"Who's coming?" Anhalt followed the swordsman's gaze with a rising sense of dread. "Flay?"

"Adele."

"Here? She wouldn't come here." There was a sudden silence as the general contemplated what he was actually saying. "Damn it! Of course she would."

In the southern distance, the shadowy shape of an airship suddenly dropped out of the clouds, her descent rapid and foolhardy. Swarms of vampires surrounded her. She was a brig, and both Anhalt and Greyfriar immediately recognized the vessel. *Edinburgh*. No doubt, Anhalt's old friend and military colleague, Aswan Hariri, captained her. It didn't surprise him that Adele would have contacted Hariri for a mission so reckless. The man was more pirate than soldier, but his skill with a ship was unprecedented. Raucous cheers resounded down the line at sight of the brig, but began to fade as seconds passed and no more ships appeared out of the clouds. A single ship, and a small one at that. No fleet was coming to their rescue. Soldiers suddenly stood transfixed with dismay.

Vampires abruptly sloughed off the brig in great numbers, plummeting dead to the ground like swarms of dying birds. Soldiers watched amazed, pointed, and then resumed cheering.

Abruptly Greyfriar's tall frame reeled backward.

Anhalt turned. "What's wrong?"

"She's using her geomancy to burn a path to us. I can't go any closer." His words were low and clipped. He was clearly in pain.

Anhalt felt nothing, but he understood that vampires were susceptible to some skill the empress possessed. He looked to the south, trying to discern what was happening. The staccato of machine-gun fire echoed, cutting through vampires still rising to intercept the brig. Already more creatures clung to the wooden hull of *Edinburgh*, crowding over the dirigible from which it was suspended. Scores of them were attacking the sail-crowded masts that extended from the sides of the dirigible. The black shapes were everywhere. Anhalt's chest tightened with fear for his empress. The small vessel could hold no more than a company of soldiers. By sheer numbers, the enemy would overwhelm them.

"Go to her!" Greyfriar commanded Anhalt. "Help open her way!"

The Gurkha general shouted to Hereghty, "Captain, we must secure the ground beyond our lines! Come on, form ranks and stand ready. Quickly now! Not a second to lose!"

Orders were relayed and men gathered at the edge of the trenches, clinging to their rifles and swords and pikes. Faces blackened with dirt and grime stared into the frozen land beyond their trenches where vampires rose and fell, swarming the little airship. Officers adjusted caps and tarbooshes and turbans. Swagger sticks swung smartly under arms with calls of "All right, lads! Look sharp now. Up and out. Mind your heads at all times."

Captain Hereghty saluted Anhalt. "Ready, sir."

"Very well," the general snarled with pistol and Fahrenheit saber in hand. "Over the top!"

Whistles blew down through the trenches and machine-gun fire ceased. After seconds of silence, another whistle blew, only to be drowned out by the animalistic bellows of a thousand men as a khaki wave poured up onto the ground. Rifle fire commenced, popping across the field. Men ran and shot. Blades swung. Pikes jabbed at figures floating overhead. Some men stopped to execute burned vampires wriggling in the dirt.

General Anhalt could barely catch his breath from the excitement of the flood surrounding him, shouting and fighting. He yelled exhortations to the brave soldiers around him, even as his eyes searched the sky for the empress's ship.

Edinburgh tacked hard over and then righted in a strange maneuver. It had lost most of its forward momentum; there was no chance of outrunning the swarming monsters. No doubt, Captain Hariri was attempting to shake the creatures off, but those that lost their grip only veered back into place like black flies rising briefly from a disturbed carcass.

The ship was low enough and at such an angle that Anhalt glimpsed the deck. He saw the familiar red jackets of the White Guard, Adele's household troops, in a tight square around a lone figure, unmistakably a woman whose long auburn hair blew wildly in the wind. Their weapons snapped and flamed, bringing down any vampire that dared come close. The brig continued to rush toward Anhalt, sweeping so low now that the mooring lines dragged the ground.

Edinburgh made one more hard tack and then, without a sound or fanfare, the vampires clutching the airship or drifting in the air around it burst into flames. Anhalt heard their horrible and satisfying screams as hundreds of bodies dropped like burnt cords of lumber.

Soldiers on the ground pointed up with shock.

"Look! It's the empress!"

"What in the name of hell is she doing here?"

"She *is* crazy like they say! Bless her!"

Then the ship was past and Anhalt turned to race after it like a child chasing an escaped kite. Troopers on the ground dodged charred bodies of the enemy crashing to earth while others grabbed hold of *Edinburgh's* lines. Soon great clutches of soldiers were scrambling after the mooring lines, as well as the legs of their comrades who were being dragged by the slowing airship. Aboard the brig, airmen frantically furled sails and vented buoyants. The ship lurched to a halt just inside the trench line of the vast Equatorian camp.

Once the brig was secured to makeshift mooring stakes, a gang-plank descended. General Anhalt started to lope up, but he was met by Empress Adele striding down. She smiled wide, enhancing her Persian features. Her expression was open and friendly, an odd combination of girlish enthusiasm and mature intelligence, even wisdom. Her hair was unencumbered and went chaotic in the wind. She was lovely, but not stunning. Still, she exuded a personal authority that demanded attention.

She wore simple traveling clothes. A long corduroy skirt topped leather boots with a heavy Madras blouse, a thick fur-lined coat flying open over it all. She had her Fahrenheit khukri dagger, a gift from her late mother, shoved into her belt.

The lanky form of a hard-eyed army captain was close at the empress's elbow. Her White Guard in their khaki helmets, red woolen tunics, and blue trousers with white gaiters crowded behind her like a protective scarlet cloak. Anhalt had once commanded the esteemed White Guard. He knew these men well, particularly their new commander, Captain Shirazi. They were a select core of the regiment, the most loyal and toughest men who had accompanied him last summer deep into Africa with the exiled princess Adele. This group had bonded into a distinct unit, fanatically dedicated to the empress. They came to refer to themselves as the Harmattan, the fearful red wind of the Sahara. Adele couldn't go far without her loyal Harmattan swirling about her.

The general's stern demeanor didn't alter as he backed up so the empress could descend the gangplank, though it didn't seem to faze her. Her stride continued steady and measured, her expression remained regal, her head held high. She was every inch an empress and no longer the exuberant young girl he remembered.

Troopers who were gathering around the ship in great numbers began to chant her name. Adele inclined her head to the ranks, but he knew she was listening for only one voice among the multitudes. Her eyes scanned the gathering crowd, holding a trace of disappointment. Anhalt regarded her, his mouth a hard line. His right arm snapped up into a salute that he didn't release until she nodded. Then he dropped to one knee before her, head bowed. The whole battlefield around them followed suit in a rattle of arms and mail.

Anhalt heard Adele's breath quicken at the magnitude of her people's loyalty. He was proud that there was no sign of a haughty demeanor in her, only genuine gratitude for the troops' respect and adoration.

"Rise, Sirdar," Adele said, extending her arm.

General Anhalt took her hand, and immediately felt weakness in it. "Your Majesty. Are you well?"

"I am," she replied warmly, noting his expression of concern. "It is so good to see you, my old friend." She scanned the crowd again and her voice held a trace of anxiety, "Where is Greyfriar?"

"He could not attend you." When her concerned eyes darted quickly to him, Anhalt shook his head. "He is well, Your Majesty, merely . . . indisposed."

Adele breathed a sigh of relief.

"Your arrival is most unexpected." He raised a chiding eyebrow at her, then at the captain of the Harmattan. "And most foolish."

There was a collective gasp. The gathered soldiers' surprised looks darted between the general and the empress. Adele stared sternly at Anhalt, but then after a moment laughed loudly, throwing her head back in delight. "Only you would be cross at me for saving your life."

"Perhaps next time you could just send the ship without escorting it yourself."

"Now where's the fun in that?"

"The Empire cannot bear your loss, Your Majesty."

"Of course not, Sirdar," she conceded with a sobering nod, "but in this case, *my* presence was necessary. It was the only way to break through the enemy lines and reach you. And to bring you supplies."

He bowed and smiled at her. "Then you are most welcome."

Captain Hariri came down the gangplank with desert robes flying, and clasped Anhalt warmly. "Just like old times, eh? But colder."

The general grunted. "You really should at least try to resist going along with the empress's schemes."

"I only follow your voluminous previous examples, effendi."

Anhalt regarded Adele with a scowl. "I should have never introduced the two of you."

"Adele!"

The empress spun toward the familiar voice, her entire demeanor swiftly altering from a woman in charge to a woman in love.

The tall figure in grey strode to her, his long hair blowing wildly along with the ends of his head wrap. Adele ran to him but immediately halted as Greyfriar stiffened in his tracks, exhaling a sharp hiss of pain. He took a halting step back from her.

Adele's face showed her own anguish. The geomancy still echoed in her veins.

"My empress," he said, bowing low to her, not out of duty to crown, but out of reverence for the woman herself.

Anhalt observed the doomed pair. It had been months since they had last seen each other, and now they were held apart by the very power that had saved their lives. She could easily hurt Greyfriar, even kill him as she had the vampires swarming around her ship. Every time she practiced geomancy, she put him in danger. With time, so long as she didn't use her geomancy, she would revert back to normal. Until then, they could only stare at each other across a distance of a few feet.

"I'm so glad to see you," Adele said. "How are you?"

"I am quite well. And you are very lucky."

"Really, I won't be scolded by both of you. This was the only way. Admiral Moffet has been trying for three weeks to break through the Gap with little result other than mounting casualties and three lost frigates. We feared for you."

Anhalt waved them to follow him out of the icy wind and away from the ears of the men. "Your Majesty, shall we step out of the bitter cold into the merely frigid?"

Instructing Hariri to begin unloading *Edinburgh*, Adele accompanied Anhalt and the trailing Greyfriar into the tunnels. The Harmattan fell into step around them. They made for the deepest section, heavily fortified for the command staff. Once inside the rude dirt-walled situation room, with Shirazi and the Harmattan guarding the closed doors, their council resumed.

"What of Rotherford at St. Etienne?" Anhalt asked.

Adele responded, "He succeeded in taking the town, but since then he has been hard-pressed by sizable packs. Communication is sparse. Little word comes or goes from his command now."

Greyfriar asked from the farthest corner of the room, "What packs are attacking him? St. Etienne was a small clan. They shouldn't be able to match a force the size of Rotherford's."

"We don't know," the empress said, rubbing her gloved hands together to fight the chill.

"I don't understand," the swordsman muttered. "Something is wrong. Something is happening I don't know about."

General Anhalt furiously stoked a coal stove into a faint orange warmth. "Nevertheless. We will withdraw from Grenoble to reinforce St. Etienne. Now that the way south is clear." He offered a nod of gratitude to Adele.

She hesitated a moment and then smiled. "I have a better option."

Anhalt's lips pursed, knowing that he wasn't going to like this alternative. Neither would Greyfriar, judging by the way he crossed his arms, and by his next response.

"No," he said.

Adele threw up her hands. "You haven't even heard my plan."

"I know it involves you doing something dangerous, otherwise you would not be here. I cannot believe that your government allowed you to come on this errand."

"Well, Commons was told I was going to Damascus to tour a factory. What they don't know won't hurt them."

Anhalt asked, "You are planning something dangerous, aren't you?"

"No, of course not. But I was thinking I would enter Grenoble and destroy the clan there."

Anhalt and Greyfriar both exploded.

"Absolutely not!" the latter shouted.

"You are no longer a defiant princess!" Anhalt roared. "You are the empress! The sovereign of Equatoria. You cannot be seriously considering—"

"I am deadly serious." Adele's brown eyes darkened like a desert storm. "My foolishness with Senator Clark delayed us for so long. Our army is bogged down because of *me*! I will do everything that is within my power to lead a victorious campaign without the further waste of lives!"

Greyfriar stepped forward and grabbed her arm. Smoke rose from his gloved hand, but he did not relinquish his grip even when Adele attempted to pull away. "This was not your fault! Winter was always going to be a factor."

She retorted, "We had a better chance taking this city in the heat of the summer! Do you deny that?"

"No, but even so, no monarch fights on the front lines."

"My father did!" Adele pulled her arm from Greyfriar's smoldering hand. Her expression softened at the pain she caused.

"See reason, Your Majesty," Anhalt interjected. "There is no rationale for placing yourself at risk."

"There is every rationale," Adele said. "I'm here and we must take Grenoble. It has the greatest clan in southern France, save Lyon. We dare not bypass it."

Anhalt saw so much of the late emperor Constantine in Adele, in her words and her stance. She was as bold and uncompromising as he on matters close to her heart. If Adele thought she could prevent more bloodshed, she would not hesitate to sacrifice herself.

"How do you propose to take the city?" Greyfriar asked.

Anhalt turned on him. "No! Do not even ask! This matter is closed."

Greyfriar's cold, mirrored glasses regarded him. "We can no more control her now than we could before she was empress. She will do as she pleases the moment we turn away. It's better to be at her side protecting her."

Anhalt's fists trembled at his side. "I beg of you, Your Majesty, don't be so foolish."

Adele stepped up to her former protector, her voice softening. "My dear colonel," his old rank an endearment rather than a criticism, "I am no longer a silly girl playing at games. I have the ability to break this stalemate and I intend to use it. I can save lives here and now."

There was a knock on the door and Adele gave permission to enter, eager for an interruption. Captain Hariri swept into the small room, his face beaming. Clearly, he was happy to be back in the thick of action.

"The supplies have been unloaded and secured," he said with a bow. "Your special diversion is being readied, my lady."

"Excellent." Adele turned back to Greyfriar and Anhalt, her eyes sparking with mischief. "Gentlemen, I didn't come alone."

CHAPTER

"**E**ACH OF YOU must kill ten of them."

Flay's order spread through the gathered vampire packs in a hissing whisper that, if the humans at St. Etienne could hear, sounded like wind in the desiccated night-shrouded trees. There was much excited chatter and cackling as the horde shifted restlessly waiting for the command to attack.

Flay was tall and pale with long black hair braided straight down her back. She exuded strength, with a fury that seemed barely contained by her long scarlet frock coat and buff knee breeches. As was typical, she was bare breasted under the unbuttoned woolen coat. She pointed a long finger at her counterpart, the war chief from Lyon, Murrd. "Take four of your packs and come at the enemy from the south. I will storm their north with the main force."

Murrd nodded, his bald head shining in the night.

"Primary targets in this attack are the beasts. Horses. Oxen. Kill them and the humans are hamstrung. They have some mechanical wagons, but not enough to carry all their large guns and their food. Airships should be damaged on the way out only. Do not be distracted by them. We will destroy them in time."

"Yes," said Chambrai, the Lyonnaise sub—war chief, with a hint of mockery. "Flay will use her human troops to fight their airships."

Flay moved swiftly and caught Chambrai by the throat. In a spray of blood, the young Lyonnaise dropped dead. The packs froze in surprise. The Lyon vampires stood gaping at the body of their colleague, and then turned to Murrd for reaction. Flay went back slowly without apparent concern, content with her response to an underling's slur. She had no intention of letting some little cur from Lyon make snide comments about her because she had once been commanded, against her will, to lead the fanatical human Undead.

Murrd looked at his deceased lieutenant and nodded to Flay. "We're ready, War Chief."

"Excellent," said Flay. "You are also tasked with striking the center of the city. If you can locate the human war chiefs, kill them. Take out all the large guns you can. We will spread across the front and kill. Now, go."

Several Lyonnaise packs lifted into the night air with their chief.

Flay waited for them to vanish into the starry sky. It was a cold and breezy night. She could hear rustling and voices from the Equatorian camp beyond a low rise.

Flay had known the humans' war strategy from the beginning thanks to Cesare's spy in Alexandria, and she had authored the counter-tactics. First, the vampires had sent the Undead to damage the port facilities at Marseilles to limit the number of troops and weapons that the humans could pour into the battlefield in the opening months of the offensive. Flay did not harry the humans' landing, knowing the Equatorians would be eager to gain ground before winter set in. She lulled them into a sense of ease with every uncontested mile they marched, and even allowed them to take St. Etienne with token resistance.

Now, Flay had surrounded the sadly unprepared Equatorians with the full force of the Lyonnaise packs, along with St. Etienne reserves and a British spearhead. As soon as she had obliterated the army at St. Etienne, she would crush the Equatorians faltering at Grenoble. Flay would suffocate the grand Equatorian invasion in the mouth of the Rhone Valley, and Cesare would voice his praise.

Blood would spill.

Flay screeched and rose. The packs followed, filling the sky with thousands. She loved the sound of the wind fluttering the clothes of vampires around her. She hadn't led an army so large since the Great Killing. Since the slaughter of Ireland. Since the battles beside Prince Gareth.

Below was the northern edge of the ragged Equatorian camp. The hard winter earth was scarred by a network of trenches and earthen bastions. In the distance were the yellow lights of St. Etienne itself, and several airships hovered in the sky over the town, lashed to buildings. In the darkness, soldiers huddled around small fires, shivering in their too-thin coats. The flames would impair the humans' night vision, which was poor in any case.

Gunfire came from the south as Murrd's forces struck. Sleepy disturbed voices rose from the trenches below. Flay whistled commands that sent the vampires plummeting on the unprepared men, and confused murmurs turned to screams.

Flay's vision went red. Bodies wrapped in overcoats stirred. Rifles swung clumsily. Soldiers scrambled for long-handled pikes, ducking and plunging the blades toward the sky. Flay struck, and cloth tore and blood flowed. Stunned eyes stared out from under khaki helmets. *Vampires*, someone screamed and then died. Questions were shouted. Pistols rose. Swords flashed wildly.

Lithe figures leapt along the edges of the trenches, dropping to strike, then springing up into the air, dodging blades, and falling on others farther down the line. Soldiers flailed around in the dirty pits, firing in all directions, and swinging pointless steel at vague shapes.

Flay slashed at a man and hit something hard. She saw a glimpse of chain mail on the man's chest. The man's head had no armor, however, so he was soon dead. A bullet entered her shoulder without great effect. She spun and smashed another soldier to the frozen ground before bounding high into the air to scout the situation again.

Thudding blasts filled the air, and shards of metal whizzed past Flay. She saw the flaming of the humans' heavy guns. A vampire to her right disintegrated into bits in midair. Flay followed the flashes back to the ground and dove like a stone, slamming into the three men operating a cannon. They shouted and reached for weapons. A short sword slashed at her. She struck once, twice, three times. All the men fell to the frozen mud.

Flay turned to see a young man, a boy really, staring at her from under a comically outsized helmet and coat that draped over him. His unsteady rifle pointed at her. He fired one shell after another and disappeared behind a curtain of white smoke until the trigger clicked empty. Flay stepped toward him.

The boy dropped the rifle and raised his hands. "Don't. Please. I surrender."

She laughed. Her first swipe nearly took the flesh from his face. He tried to ward her off, and called for his mother. Then he was dead. Flay drank briefly from him, and found the lingering terror delicious. All around her, vampires huddled over bodies. She kicked several and urged them back into the fight.

A bright light caused Flay to flinch. A flare, and then another. The humans were finally sending their star shells overhead to illuminate the battlefield. Gunfire sounded regularly now, as well as the brutal staccato of machine guns and the repetitive boom of small cannons. A few vampires dropped from the sky, hit by the barrage. Others crouched low against the ground and scuttled like bugs.

Flay vaulted from trench to trench, killing with each hand. Then she felt a sharp edge push into her brain. She grabbed her head, but there was no wound. It was a sound that assaulted her. *Shriekers*. She had first experienced it when an American ship attacked the Tower of London. The sound was coming from a nearby airship where crewmen turned the crank on a machine that spit out a horrendous high-pitched wail. She wasn't damaged, but was disoriented. Vampires staggered, and one fell victim to a soldier's pike. Several more shriekers started up from other airships or ground stations around the camp.

Flay screamed commands that were only partially heard over the mechanical din. She fell back, and her packs started to draw away with her. They had done enough damage for now. Humans were easily surprised, but after the initial wave of shock and terror, they were quick to their guns and knives. Sustaining the attack now was unnecessary, and would expose the packs to concentrated fire. Vampires had the advantage of speed and mobility and surprise, as well as the ability to attack at night. Flay's tactic was to hit the humans, kill as many as possible in a short time, then withdraw to come again when she felt it was useful.

Her mission was to destroy this army by holding them in place and winnowing them away. If they attempted to come out of their defenses and move in force, either toward Lyon or to the relief of forces at Grenoble, Flay would cut them to pieces. Human armies could do two things relatively well—move or fight. They found it difficult to do both at the same time. They had too many things to carry.

Flay knew she would have to destroy the shriekers. Plus, the machine guns and shrapnel cannons were dangerous. Over the last 150 years, the humans had improved their claws. They could kill better now, but they still died easily.

She landed beyond a low hillock, out of sight and beyond the range of human weapons that continued to chatter, wasting ammunition since most of the vampires had withdrawn. That made Flay smile. The whine of shriekers was a dull hum now. The packs surrounded her; male and female celebrated their slaughter with bloody mouths while sharing stories of their kills. Flay allowed it; she would count her losses later, but she doubted it would be a high number. The wounded would still be dragging themselves back from St. Etienne for hours to come, unless they were unlucky enough to be caught by human soldiers hunting for them.

"War chief!" Murrd shouted as he settled beside her. "A success!"

"You killed their commander?"

"Their cowardly war chief must have hidden deep inside, but I struck several of their officers. Still, we killed thousands of their men, and left thousands more crippled. And I killed hundreds of horses myself."

Flay rolled her eyes at his inflated figures. "Hardly the stuff of epics."

Murrd laughed. "The humans will surely retreat. The Equatorians are nothing to us now."

"Idiot." The British war chief lifted off into the clean cold air as the Lyonnaise stared after her with shock and insult. She growled to herself as she watched the celebrations of the vampires. They didn't understand. She knew how to win this war if only they would listen to her. But she wasn't sure whether her words held the same authority with Prince

Cesare in London as they once did. The prince was a politician, not a warrior.

If only Prince Gareth ruled London.

Flay thought of Gareth and clenched her fists without thinking.

Gareth the traitor.

She still could barely believe that moment in the crypt below Alexandria when she discovered that her most hated enemy—the Greyfriar—was actually Prince Gareth. It wasn't just implausible; it was impossible. A vampire using weapons, wielding swords and pistols. A vampire helping humans.

Flay had returned to Britain after that event, unsure of her path. She had told Gareth that she had some sort of cunning scheme, but that was just to freeze him so she could escape. She had no idea what to do with the incredible information. It had to have some value, some use.

Flay had once tried to cajole Gareth into striking down his brother, Cesare, and taking his rightful place at the head of the clan. He had rejected her, which clearly had to do with his twisted obsession with humans and particularly with the wretched princess, Adele. Flay couldn't pretend to understand it.

Somehow, Flay would find a way to save Gareth from whatever madness had gripped him after the Great Killing and drawn him into isolation from his people, leading to his lunatic life behind the mask of the Greyfriar. Flay smiled at the thought of his gratitude once he shook his head clear of the spell Princess Adele had placed on him.

The Great Killing had, in many ways, been a disaster for vampires. They had grown soft and lazy like humans. And some, like Gareth, had gone insane.

This war would save them all.

—⁓—

Prince Cesare sat in a spotless wooden chair in the corner of a dark chamber beneath Buckingham Palace. He was well dressed in an impeccable grey suit and shined black shoes. He was short and lithe, with close-cropped hair and a sharp face. His blue eyes stared hard with no movement. Cesare was a thinking creature, and liked any who might observe him to know he was always in thought.

The only potential observer whose opinion mattered at the moment was mute. Across the room lay the body of Cesare's father, King Dmitri, dead for more than six months now. The king was thin and desiccated, having rotted away what soft fatty tissue he had possessed when he died. Now he was a leathery thing, empty eye sockets open and strained mouth agape as if struggling for one last breath. Cesare watched the human bloodmen slaves straightening the king's bedclothes. A dead human lay on the stones, his blood having been drained into a grate in the floor. An unfortunate victim was brought in every few days to be killed and drained, and then carted out by the bloodmen. It was an amusing fiction that Cesare maintained to imply that the king was still feeding. No one yet knew Dmitri was dead. With the exception of a few human slaves, only Cesare attended him, it was assumed out of extreme loyalty. The king's condition was to be hidden until it suited Cesare to announce his death.

And certainly no one needed to know that Cesare himself had murdered his father.

"How did you manage it?" Cesare asked Dmitri's body. "All these allies, all these clans with their pathetic quibblings. You were one of the kings of the Great Killing. Was it this much trouble? I'll admit, I have more respect for you now."

One of the bloodmen indicated the dripping sacrifice.

"Yes, yes." Cesare waved his hand. "Take it away."

The king's meal was dragged out and the door shut, leaving father and son alone.

"I'm a war king now too. Perhaps once I get affairs settled here, I will visit the front. I may even lead an attack." Cesare rose and crossed to his father's bedside. "Oddly enough, I've enjoyed these months we've spent together down here. But it will have to end soon. I'll have to use your death for my benefit. That's something I learned from you, planning, calculating, staying ahead of your enemies, and your friends too. Never trust anyone, as you trusted Gareth. And he deserted you in the end."

Cesare patted Dmitri's dead arm with cold comfort. "What to do about Gareth? I know I should kill him, but that would create trouble now when I need it least. I don't want some of the old clan lords getting their backs up about who is or isn't the proper heir. You always favored Gareth, but he is unsuitable to be king. There's something false about him. No one else notices, but I smell it. He's all artifice. I'm real, Father. You'd see that now if I hadn't killed you. I'm your true heir, and I will unite the clans in a way even you could not. You'll see. I mean, where is Gareth now? Here we are, in a war for our survival, and he is nowhere to be found. What sort of king would he make?"

There was a solid pounding on the door. The prince exhaled in annoyance at being interrupted in conversation with his father. He shouted, "What is it?"

"Lady Hallow to see you, my lord," came the muffled voice of his chamberlain, Stryon, who always waited outside.

Cesare said, "Very well," at which the door opened for him to exit and then closed behind him. Several of his vicious retainers moved in front of the door. They had constant orders to allow no one to see the king except Cesare. The prince went quickly to his conference room, a massive ballroom with festering old chandeliers cluttered with bones. The floors and walls were clotted with dried blood from decades of feasting. Lady Hallow rose as Cesare entered. Her slender figure bowed with a rustle of her scarlet gown. The moonlight reflected in her blonde hair, and her blue eyes gleamed in the dark.

Cesare boldly let his eyes rove over her. "I hope you bring me good news from the continent."

"Word of your skill and imminence is spreading among the clans. King Lothaire of Paris is prepared to join the Grand Coalition of the North. And he will bring several notable clans with him."

The young prince smiled and relaxed. "That's excellent. Excellent. I've received messages from Flay at the front that, with additional packs, she can destroy the humans utterly. How quickly will the Paris packs move south?"

Hallow's lustrous features went stiff. "It isn't quite so simple, my lord. King Lothaire is eager to be a part of the new era, but he made it clear that he will only ally himself with a king. He demands to meet with your father."

Cesare replied coldly, "He realizes that my father is indisposed and I speak for him?"

Hallow inclined her head with a wan smile. "I tried to make him understand. He felt it would be injurious to his prestige, which is tenuous at best, if he appeared to be subservient to a prince."

Cesare sneered. "Lothaire is an idiot. He's always been an idiot."

"He was always a close friend of Prince Gareth's," Hallow said hesitantly. "I suppose there is no way you could ask your brother to intercede?"

The prince glared at her. "No."

"Merely a suggestion."

"Even if I knew where Gareth was, he plays no part in the future of this clan. Did Lothaire say anything about Gareth to you?"

"No, my lord."

Cesare continued to stare at her. "Are you sure, Hallow? Did Lothaire mention that he would deal with Gareth, but not with me?"

"No, my lord. Prince Gareth never came up at all. King Lothaire knows that Gareth is in virtual exile."

"So, Lothaire wants only to treat with a king? And then his packs will be mine? With them we can win the war."

"Yes, my lord."

Cesare paced, his compact form dwarfed by the large room, with his footsteps ringing in the expanse. Finally, he paused. "Very well, then I must announce with great sorrow the passing of King Dmitri."

Hallow started. "My lord?"

"Yes, His Majesty has expired. It's all a terrible shock."

"When was this?"

"Earlier today. Tomorrow. Last month. Really, what does it matter? I say the king is dead, and so he is. I will call a coven for the next full moon to name the new king. Then we can draw Paris into the Grand Coalition and get on with the war before damned summertime."

"What about Prince Gareth?" Hallow asked.

"What about him?" Cesare asked sharply. "I'll send a message to his chamberlain in Edinburgh. Baudoin is the only person who ever knows where my brother is."

Hallow said in a measured voice, "Are you sure you want him here in London?"

"He's the eldest son. Tradition demands he open the coven, and it becomes sticky for me to be crowned king without him here to agree." The prince extended his claws and admired them. "What are you saying, Lady Hallow? What would you have me do with Prince Gareth?"

"Kill him, my lord. Now."

Cesare laughed at her sudden ruthlessness. "Why should I? I'm not afraid of him. Are you?"

"Yes, I am. Kill him."

"I'm alarmed by you, Hallow. You and Gareth were quite a pair once. Everyone expected you two to be the future king and queen."

"That was long ago."

Cesare nodded sarcastically. "Yes, apparently you're quite over him now."

"I am your servant, Prince Cesare. And as your servant, I beg you to kill Gareth."

The prince strolled to Hallow and took one of her slender alabaster hands. "You seem so frightened of him. He would never harm you. Not you, of all people."

"I'm not afraid for myself."

Cesare rubbed her hand slowly. "I'm touched by your concern. Or is it merely distress for your own future, since you're attached to me now?" Hallow began to protest, but he continued, "I must admit, I'm a bit annoyed. Do you think me so weak that my brother could take me whenever he chooses? He is isolated and despised; I will finish Gareth when it suits me. I want him to see me crowned king. He must witness it." He began to crush her fingers in his grip. "And once he has seen me take my place as leader of the clan, only then will I kill him, with my own hands. Just as he deserves."

Hallow said, "As you please, my lord. But I felt compelled to give you my honest opinion. Gareth is dangerous."

"He may have been dangerous once, but no more. I have become the greatest leader since the Great Killing, and I'm not even king yet. All the clan lords, and several foreign kings, owe allegiance to me. Gareth lives alone in a castle surrounded by cats and humans. I almost feel badly for him." Cesare kissed her abused hand and released it. "No. He's no threat to me."

Hallow nodded acceptance. "Very well, my lord. Condolences on the passing of His Majesty, King Dmitri. He was a great king."

"Yes, yes," Cesare muttered.

"Will you require a funeral for His Majesty?" she asked.

"A funeral?" Cesare frowned in annoyance, but then he smiled. "I suppose so. Yes. We should make note of the passing of such a mighty sovereign, and the ascension of his successor. Even so, I want a swift interregnum. I must deliver new packs to Flay as soon as possible."

"Do you truly believe she can push the humans back?" Hallow asked.

"If Flay says she can, then she can."

The ambassador pursed her lips. "I have found her to be resistant, even insubordinate."

Cesare turned away, uninterested in Hallow's complaints.

"I need your support, my lord," she said more forcefully. "I am your liaison to the allies. She is merely war chief. Her years here with you in the palace seem to have convinced her she is your chosen. Is she?"

The prince turned back. "You are my right hand, Lady Hallow. You have helped forge the Grand Coalition. Flay is useful for now. She is an inveterate warrior, and we are at war. But I will make it clear to her that you are the master of the alliance. She is to bow to you in all things."

"I am grateful." Hallow nodded, satisfied. "If it's possible to make anything clear to Flay."

Cesare shook his head with dismay. He didn't want to see strife between his chief lieutenants, political and military. He needed both of them. He required Flay more at the moment because there was no finer war chief, but he would need Hallow in the long term because she would make an extraordinary queen. Not only was she beautiful and brilliant . . . She had once been Gareth's.

"One final thing I want you aware of," Cesare said to change subjects, "is the disposition of the Undead."

Hallow regarded Cesare with disapproving eyes. Clearly she disdained his human troops. Just as clearly, to him, she didn't have the vision to grasp their revolutionary importance.

Only Cesare had the genius to play on the old mythology that vampires were undead humans risen from the grave. He had convinced huge numbers of humans in the north that if they died in service to their vampire masters, they would rise to join the ruling class. Over the last few years, preparing for a war with the free humans that he feared would come, he had forged legions of so-called "Undead." He had sent them on a suicide mission to destroy half the Equatorian fleet at Gibraltar. He had sent them in massed attacks to damage the precious port facilities in Marseilles and other cities that the Equatorians needed to invade Europe. Those Undead assaults had contributed to the desperate situation that the Equatorian forces now found themselves in with fewer troops and less materiel and little air support. Now Cesare had new uses for his human legions.

He said, "The Undead are serving two purposes for me now. With the growth of the clan alliance, you know that I have found it useful to place humans around the capitals and camps of our allies, and our potential allies."

"Why must you use humans as spies?"

"No one suspects their food. They can move unnoticed, and they may hear things that would be useful to me. Don't worry, Hallow, you shouldn't have to speak to them directly. I have vampire agents in place across Europe. I would hate for you to sully yourself."

Hallow couldn't quite hide her sneer. "You realize it is likely these Undead spies will be killed? Just in the course of a normal day's feasting. They are just humans."

"Let them die then. I'll replace them." Cesare gave Hallow a light touch meant to reassure her that he was quite sure of his course. "Now, my other duty for the Undead is in the south. The operations of the Equatorian army have created a chaotic situation in the Rhone Valley, with refugees everywhere. I have sent hundreds of Undead to insinuate themselves into those human streams and create chaos where they can. But more, I have chosen certain Undead who have been sent into Equatoria." He glanced up, annoyed at Hallow's questioning expression. "Do you have some quibble with this strategy too?"

"Suicidal missions are one thing, my lord," she replied, "but I don't like arming humans. The Undead are clumsy at best and potentially traitorous at worst."

"Traitorous? Don't be ridiculous. They'll do anything for me. They want to be me."

"Don't the Undead wonder why they've never seen any of their colleagues return as a vampire? How long before they start to question this?"

"They've already created a complicated set of ideas to explain away the inconsistencies in their doctrine. Humans are good at that. For them, it's all about faith."

The female continued to listen to her prince, trying to hide her doubts but failing.

"You must have faith too, Hallow. I know what I'm doing. I don't use just the Undead. I have an Equatorian traitor who is serving me. With his assistance, Undead infiltrators are tasked with certain important duties inside Equatoria."

"Such as?" Hallow asked suspiciously.

Cesare bared his teeth in a semblance of a grin. "Killing Empress Adele."

The ambassador nearly rolled her eyes and asked with slight sarcasm, "How many times are you going to attempt to kill that girl?"

"Until she's dead!" Cesare shouted violently, then squeezed his hands into fists and snarled, "Until she is dead."

CHAPTER

FIFTEEN METAL MONOLITHS shaped in human form stared down with empty black eyes at the three people gathered before them. The iron men towered twelve feet, standing silently in a line, as wind-driven snow piled onto their steel shoulders. One of the great suits of armor had its chest-cavity hatch open, revealing the complex controls enabling a man to operate the mechanical anatomy. The White Guard had formed a wide cordon to keep the curious away from the camp's new arrivals.

"This," Adele announced, "is our newly formed Galahad Battalion."

Anhalt took in the motionless army a moment. "Galahads?"

"So I dubbed them," Adele said. "They're like giant knights."

"Yes, I see," the general commented, stuffing his hands in the pockets of his greatcoat. "Majesty, you well know that we tested these land tanks two years ago, but the General Staff decided against buying them from the Katangans. They are difficult to keep fueled, so their range is limited. And they proved wildly unreliable."

"That was my father's General Staff, who were not always the most progressive of men. The Katangans have improved these tanks enormously. They are much more maneuverable now. In addition, I've brought experienced Katangan drivers whom King Msiri has seconded to our army. Given my limited needs for them, these machines will serve our purposes."

"And your purposes are?" Greyfriar stared at the machines with curiosity.

"A diversion of sorts," Adele said. "Each carries a flame thrower, fifty-caliber machine guns, and explosives." She gestured to Anhalt, who stood thoughtfully with a thumbnail to his lips. "You need only to occupy the vampires' attention long enough to allow me to do what I must."

"What can you hope to accomplish alone that my army has been unable to do for the past months?"

"The Bastille above Grenoble is located on a dormant rift. I intend to activate it, like I did in the Mountains of the Moon."

Anhalt cast a sharp glance at her.

Greyfriar pointed out the obvious. "The city is riddled with my . . . with vampires."

"And the city is also intersected by dragon spines, ley lines. So long as I stand near them, I can walk into the central fort undetected."

Her two colleagues regarded her dubiously.

"Geomancer." Adele pointed to herself.

"Mamoru has taught you to do this? To hide from vampires?"

"Yes. Apparently he says I'm quite good at it."

"Madness!" Anhalt shouted. "You cannot survive alone at the mercy of thousands of vampires!"

"She will not be alone," Greyfriar said quietly.

Now it was Adele's turn to be outraged. "Oh no. You can't go this time. I can't protect *you*. I won't have you die in Grenoble." Her voice lowered to a whisper. "Not after nearly killing you in Africa. Only humans will survive what I'm going to do up there."

"I'm the only one who can safeguard you to the rift in case something goes wrong. Once you're there, I will leave you to do what you must."

Anhalt exploded at Greyfriar. "I can't believe you're agreeing to this?"

"It would give us Grenoble, and we both know she is more than capable of protecting herself against vampires."

Adele said softly, "General, I know you fear for me. And I understand your argument that I am the empress and, therefore, irreplaceable, but at heart, I am still Adele. My people remain more important to me than the crown or my own life. In order to win this battle and move forward, everything that can be done must be done."

The conviction in Adele's eyes outweighed any counterpoint General Anhalt could muster. This was not about law or protocol or any sense of reason. This was an attempt by Adele to safeguard her people.

Anhalt let out the breath he had been holding, the fire in his eyes fading as he faced Adele. He nodded his consent. "I do not pretend to understand what it is you do, Majesty, and if I could take this burden from you, I would."

Her hand reached out to touch his shoulder. "Have faith."

Anhalt laughed humorously. "I have faith in you. It is the magic I cannot see that worries me."

"Then trust me," Greyfriar said. "I know what she can do, and it is terrifying and powerful. But it won't stop me from standing beside her."

Adele opened her mouth to protest once more, but Greyfriar stared at her. His cold, mirrored glasses betrayed nothing, but it was enough to still her protests. She whispered, "I would be grateful for your company."

"So be it then," Anhalt said, disheartened but realizing his private concerns fell flat in the wake of winning the war. Only determination remained in all of them now. "We'll throw everything we have at Grenoble to draw the vampires down from the Bastille."

"We'll name it Operation Bengal." At Anhalt's frown, she replied, "I promised Simon I'd name something after him. I can't disappoint him."

"Yes, your brother, the prince of Bengal, would appreciate that. Just so long as it isn't named Forlorn Hope. Isn't that the usual name of something so foolhardy and reckless?"

"I've heard that survivors of such hopeless operations get to name their reward?" noted Greyfriar.

Adele laughed. "And what riches would you ask for?"

Greyfriar replied without hesitation. "For you to finally show me your library in Alexandria."

Adele reached out to touch his arm. "I know we haven't had much time since my coronation and the start of the war. I'll grant your wish. The moment we return home."

He nodded and then commanded, "Come with me." With a turn of his heel, he strode toward the gangplank to nearby *Edinburgh*. Adele followed, her heartbeat building. They marched up onto the deck, and with the crews' heads pivoting to follow the pair, they disappeared down the companionway. There was a lone glow from a chemical lamp in a recess of the wall. Greyfriar held the door to their old cabin and she entered.

The moment the door closed, he grabbed her arm and pulled her to him in a deep embrace. She crushed against him, her mind filled only with the desire of him. His leather glove held the nape of her neck and tilted her head up as she pulled the cloth from his sharp-featured face so he could kiss her. His long dark hair brushed her cheek. She thought only of the long days and nights without him, filled with worry and want. His rough, desperate touch spoke the same.

Then she realized smoke was rising between them. She tried to pull back. "No, it's too soon. I'm hurting you."

"Hardly," he whispered hoarsely, refusing to let her go. He drew her back to him and captured her lips.

She couldn't refuse him. The need in both of them filled the room, though Gareth never demanded or forced more. She often thought about pushing their relationship, particularly when they were about to rush headlong to their possible deaths. Which seemed frequent.

The rise and fall of Gareth's chest against her felt as steady as the tides of the earth. As always, they lived in the space of a moment, forgetting their fears and the bittersweet taste of reality. Soon they would be in peril again. These fleeting moments together were all that was allowed them.

—◈—

Medieval spires rose above Grenoble, grey shapes in the milky sky. The city was frozen in time, still and serene, but not for much longer. Adele glanced at the man beside her, a man who always liked the shadows, and now stood in a world that had turned stark white.

Adele's breath formed in front of her in misty clouds. Snow was falling and she couldn't help watching it. Despite the fact that she was shivering in the deep drift, the gentle flutter of the snowflakes coming down around her was mesmerizing. Having spent her entire life in the tropics, Adele had always dreamed of seeing a driving northern snow.

This, however, was not the circumstance she had conjured for her wintry fantasy. Her outfit was white and grey, made of heavy wool, but she still felt the chill in her extremities. Her clothes were rough and tattered, similar to what the humans wore inside the city. She had to look the part of a bedraggled human to avoid raising an alarm.

Gareth stood in just a shirt and coal grey pants and boots. He was bare to the elements, and completely unaffected by the bitter cold. Once they had left camp, he had shed his Greyfriar persona. His pack of clothes and weapons was gone now, buried under the piling snow.

"Another outfit lost," she lamented, her teeth chattering until she clamped them shut.

"I'll find it," he said simply. "How close is your dragon spine?"

"It's close." She was much better at sensing them now, whereas before she tended to stumble across them. This was a relief given the possibility that her power could be triggered unexpectedly, a constant fear with Gareth around. She couldn't bear to hurt him again.

Adele wrapped a tattered scarf tighter around her nearly frozen face with fingers that were already well past that state. Her attention tracked to the west, waiting for the sounds of the battle that she knew was set to commence. Still, she jumped when the first boom sounded and black smoke billowed into the ashen sky.

The March of the Galahads had begun.

Mobs of vampires inside the city walls veered toward the attack, black spots rising framed against the white flakes falling.

"This is it," Adele said, her zeal growing, the chill in her bones forgotten. She rose, shaking the snow from her legs.

"Patience. The more that flock to Anhalt's diversion, the fewer we will have to walk past."

"It also places General Anhalt in more danger."

"He welcomes the risk to safeguard you. His effort shouldn't be in vain."

"It won't." Adele stepped away from Gareth, regarding him. "Follow the path I showed you on the map. I'll be right beside you."

She vanished before his eyes, leaving Gareth alone in the vast white field. The only thing that remained was the indentations of her feet in the snow. His eyes widened.

Her hand found his. He looked down but saw nothing.

"So you are not a ghost," he said in amazement.

Her gentle laugh was carried on the wind. "No, I'm still here. Right beside you."

Mamoru had explained it to Adele that geomancers hid from vampires in plain sight. They weren't invisible, only camouflaged by the earth, like a chameleon's skin. It was a very treacherous tactic, and Adele hadn't told Gareth or Anhalt just how easily it could go terribly wrong. Vampires could collide with her or something might break her concentration, and then she would be visible.

"Your hand is hot," Gareth said.

Adele immediately let go and saw his skin flush pink where she had touched him. Thankfully it was not burned.

His eyes narrowed to slits as he stared at the spot where he knew she was standing. "I can almost see you."

"Really?"

"Because I know you are there. There is a shimmer, a gentle outline about your size and shape. If you hadn't shown me, I would have missed you entirely. Your scent has changed too. More earthy, like wood and soil. Not like a human."

"That's fascinating. I'll have to relate that to Mamoru when I see him. I doubt he's ever gotten this kind of insight." Adele's hand brushed his one more time. "Lead on. I will follow."

Gareth started toward the city walls, and she fell into step with him. Eventually they saw a small group of vampires near the crumbling gate. They weren't soldiers, more likely citizens who were given watch duty that wouldn't place them on the front lines. One was heavy by vampire standards. Another was thin and tall, though not as tall as Gareth. The last was old with long, thin graying hair and a craggy face. He was seated between the other two. There was a dead human at their feet, obviously a recent meal.

Adele stayed motionless as Gareth strode toward the vampires. They quickly stood to challenge him. Gareth didn't even pause. He moved in a blur, leaping at them with claws extended. The first slash took out the thin vampire, the youngest and the most agile, who fell into the old vampire and together they tumbled to the ground. The heavyset one rose hissing, throwing his large frame at Gareth. The vampire prince sidestepped quickly, lightened his density and stepped up into the air. As the vampire stumbled under him, Gareth dropped heavily, taking him to the ground.

Gareth's arm drove downward toward the weakest point on the spine and snapped it. The vampire flopped once with a scream and lay immobile, though his eyes were wide open. He still had a voice and was screeching in terror until Gareth silenced him with another slash of his terrible claws. More blood stained the white ground.

Adele was distracted by Gareth's sudden violence, so she didn't see the elder vampire surging at him until it was too late. Gareth was borne to the ground in a flurry of snow. The older vampire's arm slashed downward, but Gareth blocked it. A well-aimed kick sent his opponent flying backward. Immediately and without quarter, Gareth followed and the two vampires exchanged blows, each one expertly blocked and parried.

Gareth saw an opening and slipped in, coming into close quarters, and used that position to rip out his opponent's throat. The elder vampire fell limp into Gareth's arms.

He swung the old man's legs up and carried him to where he had been sitting. Gently he laid the vampire on the ground, almost reverently, adjusting his arms over his chest. He stayed down on one knee for a moment. "He fought well. I was sorry to kill him." Then he stood, walking over to a mound of clean snow, and wiped the gore from his face.

It took a moment to find her voice, but then Adele asked, "Are you hurt?"

"None of this blood is mine." Gareth's eyes searched for her and then settled on her shimmering form. He smiled crookedly, and then turned around and strode through the gate. Adele waited a few seconds and then entered enemy-held Grenoble.

—⁓—

Sunlight glinted off the steel figures marching steadily on Grenoble. The Katangans encased in the metal frames pounded the hard icy ground of No-Man's-Land, spikes on the bottoms of their feet dug deep and gripped tight, giving them purchase. The steaming metal men formed a broad wedge aimed at the wall of the town, with the mass of the Equatorian army shuffling behind.

Anhalt rode a dappled mare in the gap between the infantry and the steel front. The horse was sure-footed even in the churned frozen ground left by the heavy Galahads, and she did not shy from the rumbling, clanking tanks. It was the rattle of Anhalt's scabbard that made her prance in frenzied excitement, anticipating battle. The general twisted in the saddle to observe his army, grunting with satisfaction. The advancing force included every man who wasn't manning the cannons or part of a skeleton crew in the trenches to guard their rear. Every scrap of armor and ammunition had been served out. If this assault failed, there would be no way to defend from the vampire counterattack. If Adele lost her mad endeavor, the campaign would end here on the frozen field outside Grenoble.

The vampires swarmed in a large black cloud over the city like an ominous storm. With every minute, more drifted in from all directions to join the flock. The more that gathered, the better for the empress, Anhalt thought.

The general was surprised that the vampires hadn't yet engaged. Perhaps the Galahads had made the creatures cautious; the new weapons, no doubt, perplexed them.

The mass of airborne vampires undulated like a single entity, causing the rank-and-file troopers to pause and tremble, but officers shouted encouragement, bolstering flagging determination, reminding them of their duty to the Empire, to their comrades, and to themselves. The men marching nearest Anhalt gripped their weapons tightly, and every once in a while he would see a man flex his fingers to keep them limber in the frigid morning air. The rumor that the empress had delivered a secret weapon did something to strengthen weak backbones and faltering hearts.

The spearhead of Galahads reached the ready point one mile from Grenoble's ancient wall. They halted with a squeal and a burst of steam.

Anhalt spurred his mount toward the front infantry. He felt the air spark with the anticipation of battle. Company commanders yelled orders, echoed by sergeants. Formations shaped up, presenting modern rifles along with tried-and-true sharpened steel, bayonets and long savage pikes, almost like musket squares of the sixteenth century.

The bagpipes of the Twenty-fifth Lost Highlanders blared to Anhalt's left. They all claimed some Scottish ancestry and therefore seemed unnaturally eager to be heading north to reclaim their mythic homeland. The sirdar cared little for restoring ancient titles or lands, but if such beliefs helped drive some of his men, he would gladly use them.

General Anhalt rode the length of the line, waving his glowing saber, his voice booming out to the front ranks. "Equatorians! Today! In this place! We begin the liberation of humanity! Grenoble will be free! And soon the entire world will be free! Because of what you do today, your children will know vampires only in ghost stories told around campfires! But you know the truth. You know these animals can die. And they will die! Today! By your hand! By the hand of Equatoria! You are human! This land is your heritage! The first strike belonged to them, but the final blow will be ours!" He stood in the stirrups, pointing his saber in the direction of the vampire city. "Kill! Them! All!"

The men bellowed as one, deafening all else, their blood burning hot with defiance and resolve. Rifles were shaken overhead and swords were struck against mail shirts, raising a raucous din.

The swarm of vampires twitched, and suddenly shifted toward the human army like a flock of birds, all wheeling as one in the sky.

"Fire!" came Anhalt's hoarse cry.

Three regiments simultaneously fired; nearly two thousand rifle muzzles flamed. The gunsmoke formed a thick barrier before the wind carried it swiftly away. The front rank of vampires were sent tumbling backward as bullets ripped into the black mass.

With a loud rumble, rockets flamed from short-barreled turrets atop the shoulders of the Galahads. They sped into the sky, exploding in the midst of the vampires, shredding them with shrapnel.

"Forward!" Anhalt screamed through the chaos.

The lead Galahad began to lumber on toward its objective. The other metal men spurted steam and ground to life. The iron forms crushed through the snow, blazing a trail toward the city as hundreds of vampires dove at them. One of the Galahads lifted its arm, and whirring gears raised multiple copper tubes from the forearm casing. With a snap and a spark, massive flames burst forth, enveloping the vampires. The creatures fell back screaming, their clothing and hair and flesh ignited. They careened into each other, and plummeted smoldering to the ground.

Four spearhead tanks let loose a salvo of rockets at the city walls. Red streaks flashed over white earth until they impacted on ancient stone unprepared for modern explosives and erupted in fire and wreckage. Through the smoke it was clear the wall was shattered. A second round of rockets obliterated it, creating a gap of nearly one hundred yards. The walking giants drove on, unstoppable objects plowing through snow and bone.

The Galahads attracted the attention of the greatest part of the defending packs. Vampires collected in the air over the metal men, diving and striking, then rising. Others scrambled on the frozen ground, like dogs attacking a bear, even climbing onto the iron frames. Many of those vampires met with steel limbs given unbelievable strength by rapidly firing pistons and ratcheting gears.

The infantry squares fought hard to keep up with the tanks, even as countless vampires dove among them. Pikes swept the air, attempting to block the drifting creatures from getting within deadly arm's length. Gunfire blasted the vampires, but killing shots were rare. The monsters took bullet after bullet, and still knocked the pike blades aside, striking soldiers from above or settling to their feet and leaping like leopards among the soldiers. Once several creatures penetrated the outer edges of the square, men panicked and fired among their own ranks, or swung swords wildly, as likely to strike their comrades as the vampires. Still, sheer firepower allowed the humans to hold off the mass of the enemy, and struggle forward amidst smoke and blood and screams.

Anhalt glimpsed the sight he was expecting but dreading. The first Galahad had just reached the smoking wreckage that had been the wall, and it stopped dead in its tracks, billowing white smoke. Its chemical fuel was spent. Vampires fell upon the motionless heap, toppling it, trying to get at the human trapped inside the heavy steel container. Then one by one, the lumbering tanks shuddered and halted on the field of battle, leaving a desolate field of frozen statues among the dead and fighting.

"With me! Make for the city!" Anhalt yelled, spurring his horse ahead of his men, leaping over one of the motionless Galahads lying on the blood-soaked ground. For a brief second, Anhalt locked gazes with the horror-struck Katangan trapped inside. Then he was past, galloping to Grenoble. Troops rallied with him, surging forward with their commander, screaming victoriously as they clambered over the rubble and entered the enemy city for the first time.

Vampires were waiting for them.

Anhalt didn't stop. His mare bowled into them. She neighed sharply in pain but obeyed her rider's commands. The general cleared a path for those coming behind. Time slowed and everything around him was as if stuck in a mire. Only he was moving. He howled a battle cry and jabbed forward, twisting and cutting at every fanged shape with his Fahrenheit saber, whose chemical coating burned. Pain actually registered in the wide eyes of the vampires who drew back. Anhalt had no idea if he was alone or surrounded by his men, but he would not stop. He only knew he had to push the line. Kill vampires.

His arm was numb with the continuous effort of driving at the creatures. He was covered in as much blood as his smoldering blade; he was slick with it, screaming a challenge like a man obsessed. He killed and went forward again. Then something struck his head and he fell back against the mare's haunches, barely keeping his stirrups and his weapon.

He tried to right himself while the horse careened into bodies. When he saw three vampires swooping at him from above, he knew he was lost. He couldn't raise the saber in time, and his pistol was long since spent. His angle was too awkward, and he was unable to do more than watch his demise approach.

A burst of rapid gunfire brushed his hair, and the vampires disintegrated in a spray of blood and bone. Anhalt twisted to see his savior, a palsied Galahad approaching with faltering steps.

With a shout, he saluted the man inside and brought his mare back under control. Then the machine gun on the tank rattled through empty chambers, its ammo at last spent; its fuel would not be far behind.

Anhalt slashed with his saber at monstrous faces all around him. Soon all ammunition would be spent. The ordnance of sinew would have to hold out until the empress made her play.

CHAPTER 6

ADELE HAD BEEN in one other vampire city in her lifetime. She tried not to think about the horrible things she had seen in London, though she knew she would see them again in Grenoble. Vampires turned every city into a cemetery.

Once-bright-red roof tiles lay in shattered rings around the buildings, torn loose by the claws of vampires perching and crawling. The windows and doorways lay bare and open to the elements with nothing but detritus inside. Adele could see the once-regal beauty of exquisite architecture still outlined in the crumbling façades. Framed against the majestic Alps the city still struggled to maintain its dignity. Balconies of stone and metal had collapsed on once-splendid buildings. In the distance she could see the points of rotund towers, so typical of the region. Beside them, Adele and Gareth strolled past pedestals that once held statues but now stood like silent soldiers.

In gruesome contrast, a tableaux of morbid humanity lay frozen on the streets, stiff from ice and death. The bodies were covered in a light dusting of snow for which Adele was grateful because the cold masked the stench and blanketed the horror of what it meant to be under the yoke of vampire persecution. All the cadavers were naked, their clothing likely put to good use by the living. Stepping over a pile of bones, her foot slipped on slick, icy stones. She reached out to catch herself, and almost struck a passing vampire before she jerked her hand away and grabbed a snapped gas lamp. To her relief, the creature sensed nothing.

A few humans gathered inside stone buildings, huddled around fires. Some glanced curiously at her, but didn't react. There were far fewer people milling around than she would have expected. As the cacophony of gunfire increased in the western quarter of the city, she suspected that the vampires had gathered their food somewhere to make sure none revolted or ran toward the Equatorian lines.

Gareth resisted glancing toward her and instead marched forward, trusting that she was near him. Adele admired his willpower. She wasn't sure she would be so resolute were their positions reversed.

The rolling waters of the Isère appeared before them, and though Gareth could have easily lifted off and floated to the other bank, he took a longer route to a footbridge. Adele had to come off the line slightly so they could cross the gurgling river. She redoubled her concentration to maintain her cover. She felt the connection strengthen again as they approached the medieval church of St. Laurent, made of typical whitish stone and red tiles. The old structure lay in less disarray than the rest of the city. Adele's route lay through the courtyard of the church and then up a steep mountain path to the Bastille, which loomed dark and misty in the drifting snow. The great walled fort on the mountain had been built over a rift, due to humanity's latent attachment to the Earth's power. It was also the home of clan leader's court.

Gareth hissed a warning and Adele started as shadows passed over the frosty stones at her feet. She glanced up and saw ten or more vampires circling overhead like a murder of crows. They had peeled off a larger group heading toward the battle when they had noticed Gareth, a stranger in a city under siege.

Adele took one more step near the church grounds, and the power beneath it swelled within her. It pushed at her barriers hungrily, and it took all her willpower to hold it in check.

"I need a moment," she whispered urgently, her voice rough with effort.

Gareth stepped closer and then away again as he could feel the discomfort of her presence. "What's wrong?"

"Too much. It's overwhelming. I can barely hold it in."

"You must!"

Gareth looked up at the vampires descending toward them, and Adele immediately knew what he was contemplating.

"No! You can't win against all of them. I can hold this. I just need time."

Gareth tensed and then stepped away from Adele, veering from the church. The vampires landed, encircling him. All of them wore the festooned wardrobe of soldiers, a mix of different styles and periods, but all military in design. Their very physique was different from the three at the gate. All muscle and attitude. They challenged Gareth in their native dialect. It always sounded so guttural and harsh to Adele's ears.

Gareth responded to their call in French. "I am Prince Gareth of Scotland, son of Dmitri of Britain, and I've come to see King Vittorio before this city falls to the humans clawing at your doors."

Gareth could play the haughty prince nearly as well as his brother, but with far less embellishment. The gathered vampires stared past Gareth's long form and Adele tensed, wondering if they could see her. Then they stated the obvious, as if it were a joke. "You are alone."

"I do not bring my packs unless I know you are worthy of aide. But they are close enough if I choose to save Grenoble. However, if you are not interested in my offer, I can leave and lend my assistance to your neighbors."

The vampires hissed their displeasure at being slighted, or compared to their neighbors, the bumpkins of St. Etienne and the pretenders of Lyon.

When one leaned to confer with another, Gareth quickly stepped menacingly to them, straightening his tall frame and stiffening with anger. It was better not to give them opportunity to ponder why he was alone and unescorted. "Soon your city will be flattened and your herds will be seized or scattered. You make the decision for your king, here and now." Gareth struck the flat of his hand against the vampire's shoulder. He waited another few heartbeats and then turned on his heel. "Very well. Send my regards to former King Vittorio."

Two vampires grabbed his arms to prevent his leaving.

"How dare you touch me!" He yanked away his arm, drawing blood as it tore from their clawed grip.

Adele broke into a sweat as more excess power surged into her looking for release. Her body burned with the effort to contain it. She felt like a crumbling dam holding back a destructive wall of water. Several of the vampires glanced around wildly, sensing the change in the energies around them. Adele dropped to one knee and closed her eyes in concentration, silently repeating over and over a calming mantra taught to her by Mamoru.

Gareth snarled. "You are wasting my precious time."

Another series of explosions shook the ground, and in the distance, dark shapes fell from the sky in pieces.

"Very well!" a vampire hissed. "Come with us."

They all lifted into the air and aimed for the Bastille high above. Gareth followed, although this time he did look back. His gaze brushed over Adele, but clearly he did not see her. He turned back to his new companions and went tò keep his appointment with the king.

Adele concentrated on maintaining her control, trusting Gareth to deal with his brethren. With time, the pressure eased inside her and the roar in her veins abated. Awareness crept back as she stood shakily and noticed a young human girl staring at her. The girl was dressed in filthy rags and her face was devoid of expression, sapped by the hopelessness of her situation. She was watching Adele with the same disassociation one would watch life pass by a windowpane.

To Adele's surprise, when she moved, the girl stepped forward to follow her. The empress knelt and smiled, lifting a finger to her lips for silence. The girl's brow furled and her head tilted to the side, the way a puppy would listen to a new sound. Ever so slowly the girl's eyes brightened and the muscles in her face lightened as her lips drew into a matching smile, and she came to Adele's side.

Adele reached out and touched the dirty cheek. This surprised the girl, whose eyes widened to twice their normal size. Adele again cautioned silence, and the girl's own finger lifted to mimic the empress.

Adele's heart swelled. This was the reason she was here. These people weren't the mindless cattle most southerners believed them to be. They deserved a new chance. In a few short hours this child's life would change. She would be free of the tyranny.

"Soon," Adele whispered. "You'll be safe soon."

A tile hit the street with a startling crash. A vampire dropped to the ground beside them. He couldn't see Adele but, with horror, she realized she had placed the child in danger. She had brought the girl to the attention of a hungry creature.

The child's eyes were full of fear, yet also penitence. She didn't cry or scream, but fell prostrate to the ground. The vampire towered over her.

No, Adele thought. She wasn't going to watch this child be killed and eaten. Adele stood over the child right in front of the vampire, still masked by the ley line's embrace. She let the energy give her focus.

The vampire hissed suddenly, and snarled. He glanced around wildly, backing away. He raised his hand to strike, assuming the child was the cause of his discomfort. She slipped off her connection to the line, almost like stepping through a curtain, and the shimmer faded from her body. The vampire reared back in surprise as he saw her dagger slashing downward. He barely had time to shout before Adele's Fahrenheit blade buried in his chest. She gripped his throat to prevent him from raising an alarm. He gasped like a fish as the heat from Adele's hand seared him, smoke rising from around her fingers, and he stumbled to the ground. The glowing dagger flashed as it was yanked out and then arced across the vampire's throat, cutting through vocal cords. Adele pressed him to the dirt with the weight of her body, knees pinning the vampire's outstretched arms.

The Fahrenheit blade plunged once more where her anatomy lessons told her that his heart should be. And then again. Adele's breath hissed through clenched teeth. Precious minutes passed before his struggles ceased, and she shoved herself away and sat panting, bringing herself under control. The rush of adrenaline coursing through her system was almost as bad as the rush of power struggling to overwhelm her.

She sought out the little girl, who was on her hands and knees gaping at her, unable to comprehend what she had just witnessed. Then the child's attention dragged up to stare into Adele's warm brown eyes. The empress offered a faint smile, again pressing a finger to her lips, wondering what the child was thinking at this moment. The girl's attention went from Adele to the dead vampire several quick times, and then she ran off.

Adele was almost disappointed. She hoped she had made a connection. Straightening, she grabbed the vampire's arms and dragged him into a secluded corner of the church. There was ample rubble to cover him. Sweeping the sky for more vampires, she moved quickly back to the ley line, and felt the warmth of its embrace.

Her pace quickened through the churchyard, risking a serious fall on the ice. Finally she reached the steep rocky footpath going up the mountainside. The way was nearly vertical. The road, if that was what it could be called, cut jarringly back and forth, going several hundred feet one way before veering back again. She had to stay in as straight a line as possible, however, to access the full power of the ley line. Scrub brush and snowdrifts were deep, but still she moved decisively, trying not to disturb the bushes. She had no idea where vampires might be. Their excellent eyesight could easily pick up movement from a great distance.

Adele's breath wheezed through her blue lips. Her gloves and shoes were wet and cold. She was in good physical condition, thanks to Mamoru's strict training regimen, but she was still a product of the languid Mediterranean, not the frigid Alps. The cold wind was growing ever more bitter, and the altitude was taking its toll.

She had to go over the curtain wall in order to enter the Bastille. Numb quivering fingers dug into the cracks in the stone, and Adele pulled herself up with aching arms. Without warning, black shadows crossed her and she froze. She craned her head to look. A vampire hovered just to her right, staring at the wall but not at her, not exactly. Something had caught his eye. The wind buffeted his nearly weightless frame farther away, but he continually returned to his original position, still staring, still hunting. Two more vampires gathered beside him, curious as to what had attracted his attention.

Adele's panic swelled. Her body shivered on the exposed stone wall. The wind cut through her as if she wore nothing. If she hung there much longer she wasn't sure she would have the strength to make it to the top.

Suddenly the three creatures dove to the earth. Adele flung herself around, one arm clinging to the wall, the other reaching for her dagger, but the vampires darted past her and fell on a small deer hiding in the undergrowth. It died in a spray of crimson.

The vampires laughed and congratulated the one who had made the kill first, as if it were a contest of speed. They left the kill; animal blood offered no nourishment to vampires. It had only been sport. They rose into the air and drifted toward the sounds of battle.

Adele sagged with ragged breaths against the frigid stones. Then she twisted and resheathed her blade. Fingers wedged deep into the gaps without feeling any pain and she hauled herself up to the top. She lay shaking, repeating her meditation technique so as not to lose her concentration on the ley line.

Each exhalation brought a wheezing mantra past her lips. It took every ounce of willpower to push herself to her feet. She conjured thoughts of General Anhalt and his army giving their lives to buy her time, of the little girl below in Grenoble waiting for liberation, of Gareth distracting the clan leader so she could make her way uncontested. Focusing on all those people, she resumed her way to the fort. Finally the gaping mouth of an arched cavern loomed before her, promising some protection from the elements.

Adele halted inside the arch to let her snow-strained eyes adjust to the inky interior. A minute dragged by before the darkness receded, only to be replaced with the blurry shape of a vampire standing no more than a foot away from her, his fanged mouth gaping slightly, but thankfully gazing past her. He was sniffing the air, as if sensing something wasn't right.

She forced her breathing to shallow. Her body, however, wouldn't stop shivering. Her jaw clamped shut against the chattering. The vampire eased its masculine frame from the wall where he was leaning and moved toward her. Adele shifted and laid her body as close against the wall as possible, trying to avoid him touching her.

The vampire followed the scent he was tracking, stepping past Adele to go outside. Only then did she remember the animal carcass down the hill. The blood was probably like a beacon to any vampire. With relief, she pushed off from the wall and proceeded deep into the Bastille.

Gareth saw the bulk of King Vittorio surrounded by his clan lords on the crumbling terrace of the Bastille. Before the Great Killing, vampires were never so fat, but now it wasn't uncommon. Snowfall cut the visibility, but the sounds of Anhalt's assault were clear, as were flashes of fire and the chatter of small arms. Scouts dropped and lifted from the terrace carrying news and ferrying orders from the king. The jowly monarch looked up with a start as Gareth and his bodyguard landed nearby. The king continued talking with messengers and his gathered nobles, but his eyes flicked to Gareth occasionally. Vittorio didn't seem shocked to see his visitor, but rather annoyed.

Gareth grew restive waiting for the king to summon him. His impatience must have shown because Vittorio smiled smugly. Valuable time passed, minutes of Adele being alone and unescorted. Gareth began to calculate what it would take to escape this situation, but he couldn't be assured of killing all these vampires, and leading a chase back to Adele was useless. He could only wait for the fat king to acknowledge him. When the last round of runners went scurrying off, Vittorio raised a finger at the soldiers around Gareth.

The cadre's commander bowed to the king. "Sire, we have found a visitor who craves your attention."

"Gareth, isn't it?" Vittorio said. "I haven't seen you in a century or more, but you look like him, only older and softer."

Gareth didn't reply that Vittorio looked like an obscenely bloated version of the last time he had seen the king of Grenoble.

Vittorio flinched from a massive blast in the valley, then said, "I know why you're here. I thought I was quite clear to your ambassador months ago that I have no interest in your Grand Coalition. As you can see, we are managing these humans quite well. I have no intention of surrendering my independence to Cesare, that upstart king of kings. Sending his brother won't change my mind."

Gareth's brow gathered in surprise just as another explosion vibrated the ground. *Cesare had courted Grenoble?*

The king smiled, mistaking the reason for Gareth's reaction. "Does battle disturb you, Prince Gareth?"

"No, Sire. I am far from danger here with you."

Vittorio bristled and shook a plump finger at the foreign prince. "Watch your mouth."

A messenger interrupted. "Your Majesty, I am sent from the war chief. The humans have completely abandoned their camp and have come in full force." Several of the nobles tensed. "But they are already flagging. Their power will soon be spent."

The king forgot Gareth's comment and glanced at his noble companions with a satisfied air. "See, gentlemen? I told you they would have to come. Humans are so predictable. They have gambled and lost, as they must." He turned to the courier. "Tell the war chief I want all packs out. Send three to fall on the humans from behind. There is no retreat for them this time. This is the moment we have waited for. We must crush them."

The messenger departed up into the flakes. Several nobles bowed to the king and also took flight, eager to be in on the glorious slaughter they assumed was coming.

Vittorio put a friendly hand on Gareth's arm. "As I told the lovely Lady Hallow, a human attack holds no dread for me. Unlike you Brits, we here in the Alps fight the humans in the south frequently. I told her we welcome an army, Equatorian or whomever. They came, and we trapped them like the foolish bugs they are. We bled them slowly until they had no choice but to attack, or lie down and die. Now we will finish them. Meanwhile, those weaklings who allied with your brother have fared much poorer. St. Etienne is gone, and Lyon may be next. I will stay safe and independent in my mountain fastness, thank you."

Gareth kept a bland face despite his surprise at the king's words. St. Etienne and Lyon allied with Cesare? His brother was clearly reaching out to clans across Europe and had created a far larger network than Gareth realized. It wasn't just Munich and Budapest. Everything he had told Adele and Anhalt about the parochialism of the clans making it easy for the humans to face them one at a time was wrong. Cesare was again innovating in horrifying ways. Gareth reminded himself, once more, to stop underestimating his brother. It wasn't just his life at stake anymore.

The king laughed, as did the remaining nobles. "Or have you come from Cesare to ask for my help? Perhaps you want my packs to save you? I know the humans continue to occupy St. Etienne despite Flay's counterattacks."

"Flay," Gareth snarled involuntarily. The vile war chief was near. He would never be rid of her. Still, Flay was not his primary concern at the moment, as he was reminded when more distant blasts from the town rumbled the terrace. He flexed his hands nervously, discomfited by his too-long absence from Adele. He sniffed the air for hints of the empress, but there were none. He had to find her, to be sure she was safely to her goal. Even if she had found it on her own, she wouldn't trigger the attack not knowing where Gareth was located.

The Scottish prince said, "Majesty, if there is nothing I can say to sway you to my brother's side, I will take my leave."

Vittorio regarded him curiously. "You haven't said anything. You may go, but there will soon be a feast. Stay if you wish."

"Thank you, no. My duties require me elsewhere. I will certainly tell Cesare of the magnificence of your packs."

The king grunted with satisfaction and patted the prince on the shoulder. "It was a pleasure to see you, Gareth. I always assumed you would succeed Dmitri, and Cesare would be your messenger." The fat monarch shrugged at the mysterious ways of the world. "Please do stop by again."

"Thank you, Sire. I hope to spend time in Grenoble once the battle is over."

Gareth lifted into the snowy air and angled hastily toward the St. Laurent side of the Bastille, dropping along the jagged path leading up the hillside where he whispered harshly, "Adele!" The wind echoed in his ears along with the far-off drumming of guns. He half crawled, half flew along the sheer stone wall, moving toward the river below. "Adele!"

He continued along the path, stopping and calling, with no response, until he arrived at the battlements immediately overlooking the church. Perhaps she had already reached the Bastille. He had been quite some time waiting for King Vittorio to speak to him. So Gareth retraced his steps back up the mountain. His limbs were numb from worry and his heart raced. He frantically searched the air for her scent. He listened for her voice, cursing the intermittent sounds of war that blotted out all sounds. The snow had increased and the wind grew stronger, so he found no trace of her on the ground either.

When he neared the Bastille, he followed the path to a doorway in the stone where an iron gate was rusted and falling aside. Snow had blown into the doorway and there, on the edge of the drift, protected from the wind, were faint tracks in the snow on the stone floor.

Adele. She was inside. Which meant she was close to her target.

Gareth scattered the white footprints to keep anyone who came after from seeing them, and plunged into the stone corridor.

———⁓⁓⁓———

Each dark turn Adele made brought another vampire standing or striding through the narrow passages. It took all of her concentration not to lose focus on the line and yet stay out of their way. One collision and she would be fair game.

Adele wished for more light, but vampires had no need of it. There were some human servants inside and they held faint candles, but they were few and far between. She kept her fingers touching the wall, and walked slowly, ever ready to step aside for a vampire who blocked her path.

Pressure built inside Adele, and she knew she was approaching the rift. Everything smelled earthy and green, full of life, even in the stone corridors of the fort. She wished she could see the lines rather than just sense them. Amazingly, in a flash of light, lines on the floor glowed white. Surges of energy flowed like blood, and much of it rushed toward her. Her mouth hung open in amazement when she saw the colors pooling around her. The sensations and smells were becoming overpowering, like overripe fruit. She was somehow drinking in the energy from the line where she stood.

There was a sharp pain, as if her skin was being stretched to its limit. Adele could barely hold the energy she contained, but she had to. There was no telling where Gareth was at this moment.

Anhalt's assault was likely well inside the city, with no hope or intention of retreat. Thousands of vampires would be swarming the Equatorians. The slaughter on both sides must be terrible. Every minute Adele delayed escalated the loss of life mounting on the streets of Grenoble.

Come on, Gareth, Adele entreated mutely. *Give me a sign.* Soon she would have no choice but to activate the rift; her body would be unable to dampen the energies piling inside. She could feel the rift beckoning her, luring her closer. She followed the pulsing line on the floor, struggling to keep her breath even and silent so as not to attract attention. The arched ceiling stretched down the corridor like a multitude of mirror images. She didn't know exactly where it led, but it was where the line was taking her, deeper into the bowels of the Bastille.

With each step, she felt as if she were wading through a wild river's cascade. The powers swirled around her legs and chest, pushing her toward the rift. It forced her to lean back or she would stumble forward with the pull of it. Only with great concentration was she able to calm the flow and make the energy slip more peacefully around her. The patterns in the earth shimmered, just as she was shimmering, in a beautiful, hypnotic rhythm.

Something jarred inside, and she knew her last step had placed her over the rift. It was like stepping over an endless expanse. Her stomach dropped. She could see nothing under her but a swirling vortex of energy. Tendrils of pulsating light reached greedily for her. Adele should have been terrified, but she only wanted to sink into the expanse and explore, to surrender herself in the grip of something warm and powerful.

Mamoru's fervent lessons shouted in her ears. The energies of the earth were terrible things. She could be lost within them.

Her mind snapped back to the present. The power bristled and crackled, sending shocks along her skin. The pain in her body swelled to a crescendo.

"Adele?"

The barely whispered word cut through the storm of sight, scent, and sensation. She opened her eyes. She was standing slumped against a wall inside a large vaulted chamber. Her head lifted, and she saw Gareth just a few feet away, his eyes scanning the corridor, his nostrils flared as he tried to follow her scent.

She pushed off the stone and her hand reached out, but then stopped as she saw the energies swirling like silver smoke around her fingers.

Gareth flinched and then, realizing what he was feeling, jerked toward her, finally focusing on a faint shimmer. "Are you there?"

"Go now!" Her voice sounded deeper, as if resonating. Other vampires in the corridor turned toward the empty space she occupied. They stiffened, sensing the discomfort of the pulsing rift.

Gareth didn't hesitate, but sprinted out into the nearest passageway, his form a distant blur in seconds. A number of the other vampires started backing away as the energy boiled inside her. Some stood their ground, sensing the danger but also sensing something else that perhaps they could attack.

Adele was counting now, giving Gareth time to get far enough away. She was also watching the approaching vampires as they stalked through the heat searching for the source, hissing and snarling.

"What is that?" one shouted.

"There's someone here," another warned.

"Where?"

Adele reached out an arm, and the tendrils coiling around her arched out and encircled the vampires. The vampires screamed an unholy sound as they burned, their flesh consumed by the searing touch of Adele's focus. The pitch-black passageway glowed as the power within her intensified, sensing release was near. Suddenly chaos reigned as vampires panicked like a swarm of bats fleeing. The grey air outside the fort no doubt darkened with them.

Adele had no choice. With a hard exhale of relief, she released the energy. To her there was no sound, just sensations of white-and-saffron light and overwhelming heat. The rift and the connecting lines flared like lit fuses racing through the Bastille and down the mountain into the city of Grenoble.

The ground beneath her opened its eye and stared at the creatures above it. In its sight, flesh melted, hair burned. Screams echoed every-where, but Adele heard none of it. Instead she heard and felt the sounds of the Earth, grinding plates, rustling wind, and the rush of heat. The world went whiter than the snow outside and blinded her. A desperate roar filled her ears. She was determined to stay upright, though she had no idea which direction that entailed.

The next thing she knew, someone was grabbing her. Her eyes snapped open as arms wrapped around her. "It's all right." The voice was gravelly and deep, unrecognizable to her ears. She struggled to sit up and turn around.

"Just rest." General Anhalt held her, his forehead bound in a bloody rag. "Gareth!"

"He's fine," Anhalt assured her. "He just can't come near you yet."

Adele sank back into Anhalt's embrace and offered him a tired smile as she reached her hand to touch his temple. Her eyes traveled up and around to plaster walls and a wooden beam ceiling. Not a dirt tunnel in the ground. Not the hard stone walls of the Bastille. "Where am I?"

"You're in a house in town." Anhalt settled the limp form of his empress onto a pillow and pulled a heavy blanket over her, immediately reminding her of how cold she had been. She melted into the soft warmth as her sirdar said, "Your Majesty, Grenoble is ours."

CHAPTER

GREYFRIAR PACED OUTSIDE the dilapidated building where Adele was recuperating. There was a distinct barrier that he could not cross. He dared step over the threshold again only to be repelled by a force of heat and pain. He retreated with a low growl.

The windows were without glass, and the Harmattan had boarded them up to protect the interior from the Alpine gales. Even so, he fancied he could still hear her heartbeat, and when the wind blew just right he caught the barest trace of her scent, a kaleidoscope of aromas, some indescribable.

Anhalt had walked inside over an hour ago, and Greyfriar found himself jealous of the man. Of course, the general had every right to sit with Adele; after all, he had been her protector for many years. But Greyfriar envied him because the general could do what he could not at this moment. The ground was still warm and he could feel it sapping his strength the longer he remained, but he didn't give in to it.

Finally, the sirdar exited the building. Anhalt glanced at Greyfriar with a tinge of sympathy. The general walked over to stand beside the agitated swordsman and remarked, "The empress is fine, just worn out, as you can imagine. She'll be as good as new in another day or so. You should get some sleep."

"I'll stay."

"You've been here for more than a day already. You look a wreck. Even someone of your constitution can't keep this up forever. You shouldn't even be near here. Go get some rest. I'll need you both at your best soon enough. When was the last time you fed?" Anhalt paused. "I mean *ate*."

Greyfriar's weary expression hardened. He didn't realize his limitations showed.

Anhalt coughed and pressed on, his voice low. "There are countless refugees about. We still haven't rounded up everyone. Surely someone will permit you . . ."

"It is too much of a risk to feed here with your troops about."

"Then go elsewhere. Adele will be here when you get back. Perhaps by then you can walk straight in instead of hovering out here like some wraith."

Greyfriar straightened with embarrassment, but then nodded. Anhalt had never laid down any ground rules on how he procured his meals, so long as it never came to the sirdar's attention, meaning feeding from someone inside the main camp. Greyfriar was always as discreet as possible.

"Our rear lines are secure for now," Anhalt said. "You must know the region well enough. You operated here, didn't you?"

"Of course. I met Adele in the Rhone Valley." Greyfriar said nothing more as memories stirred. He listened for any sign of Adele's recovery, but she blatantly refused him. He took a last step toward her only to be thrust back. Finally he turned away. Anhalt laid a reassuring hand on his shoulder before the swordsman strode into the drifting snow.

Hours later Greyfriar hovered over the deserted town of Riez. The fields lay frozen and wasted, overgrown with the remnants of weeds and thistle. The tools of the farmers lay where they had fallen months ago. Every window was unlit, and there was no smell of smoke. The town was as dead as the night he had left it nearly a year ago. He pulled the cloth from his face and removed his reflective glasses.

Greyfriar had brought Adele here to take refuge after Flay's packs had brought down the imperial flagship, *Ptolemy*. The townsfolk had trusted him, trusted the hero, and he had failed them. Failed Adele. Flay had slaughtered the entire town just to get the princess. Greyfriar had saved no one that day.

It seemed that he barely saved anyone lately. This war was made for what he had been centuries before. A monster, hungry for blood and glory. It was easy to kill. There was no finesse, no quarter given, merely violent death. The Greyfriar was not created for that. He wondered if saving a relative handful over the years justified all the effort. Maybe the costume offered hope to some, but he sensed the futility of a thin cape and simple sword when faced with the multitudes lost every day.

It was Adele who was made for modern times. There was no pretense in her. She was a true leader, capable of inspiring her people on the one hand and engaging in harsh political warfare on the other. Her nation moved as she did. She held great forces and huge populations in her hand, not simply a sword.

Gareth pushed open the broken door of the tavern where he had spent many nights with a simple farmer named Shepherd, who had been the closest thing Greyfriar had to a friend in this town. The farmer had welcomed them into Riez without fear, eager to help the fleeing couple that night. It had been his last act of kindness. Shepherd had no idea that he died helping a vampire.

Gareth slowly wound the cloth around his face to hide his features. He didn't feel right to be in Riez as Gareth. And he wasn't even sure Greyfriar deserved to be here either.

He lifted into the sterile, frozen night sky and headed back toward the camp without feeding.

———

The first thing Adele realized when she woke was that someone held her. For a split second she thought she had merely dozed off and Anhalt was still in the room only hours after the event, but then she recognized the powerful steel arms of Greyfriar. Her breath left her in a contented sigh.

"Adele," he called to her softly.

"Mmm," she said, not yet ready to stir and leave the sanctuary of his embrace. "I was dreaming."

His lips brushed the top of her head. "About what?"

"We had a cabin in the woods, and the fields outside were full of flowers. So many colors it was like an artist's palette."

"Like the hills of Corran in summer blanketed with violets. It sounds nice."

"It was."

"What were we doing?"

"We were raising mountain goats."

Greyfriar grimaced. "I hate goats."

Adele smiled against his chest, her eyes half-open as she played idly with the brass buttons on his jacket. "What do you have against goats?"

"They smell and they eat anything they find. It isn't natural."

Her humor only increased. "Do I detect some traumatic goat incident in your past? Did a goat attack you?"

"What? No. Although one of the goats belonging to Old Thomas in New Town ate my scarf once."

Her laugh was boisterous. "Do tell!"

"No. I've said too much already."

"I'm not sure I believe your whole goat story."

"That's probably wise of you."

The war intruded just then with shouts and a jarring crash. Adele tried feebly to rise, but Greyfriar tightened his hold, easily able to prevent her.

"Rest," he urged.

"How bad was the battle? How many men did we lose? Where's General Anhalt? I need to hear reports."

"We won the battle, because of you. Don't worry about reports just yet. Everyone is gone from the building. It's just the two of us. Another hour or so won't matter." His hand brushed the damp strands from her cheek. "Stay here with me."

She didn't have the strength to fight him, but it was impossible not to listen to the cries of pain and strife echoing from outside.

Greyfriar's deep voice urged her to focus on him. "Ask me any question you like. What would you like to know about me?"

Adele shook her head, and even that took too much effort. "I don't know," she whispered, finding it difficult to drown out the exterior sounds. Finally, she asked, "Tell me about your mother? What was she like?"

"Like me," Greyfriar related softly. "My hair is black like hers. She was regal and spoke her mind often. At least what I can remember of her. I was very young when she died."

"I lost my mother when I was thirteen. She died giving birth to Simon."

"I know." He smoothed her furrowed brow with light fingers. "My father often spoke to me of my mother. I know her more from his tales of bliss than from any of my own recollections. I was a very rambunctious child, always exploring. I rarely stayed at home, much to their chagrin."

"So your father and mother loved each other?" The concept of love among vampires amazed Adele. She was likely the only human who believed in it.

"My father loved her in a way I've never seen since. After she died, he took another queen who was Cesare's mother. A political arrangement. She was cold and wary of us, rightly so. Then after Cesare killed her, my father remained alone to this day. He's never again had the heart to seek solace in another."

"What was your mother's name?"

"Eleanor."

Another sound intruded from outside, the low wail of a man's sobbing. It carried past them and slowly disappeared into the distance. Adele tensed and Greyfriar quickly kneaded her aching muscles with his long fingers. She eased back against him almost against her will.

Greyfriar's voice was a bit louder. "My father said she was attracted to charismatic and tenacious warriors."

"Like himself."

"He was that without doubt."

Adele sank into the radiating relief of his touch. "What would your father think of me?"

"Well, if I brought you home, family meals might be a bit awkward, but I think he would admire you as a queen and a woman. Despite your inconvenient humanity." Greyfriar was silent a moment, looking into Adele's eyes. "I can say for certain that if you were a vampire, he would welcome you into the family with great enthusiasm."

"And then we could be king and queen of Britain." With those murmured words, Adele drifted into sleep once more, too tired to keep her eyes open.

"Yes. I suppose we could," Greyfriar replied

However, the respite could only last for the hours that she was asleep. The aftermath of the battle for Grenoble was as horrible as anything she had seen among the vampires. In the next few days, as she lay on her own bed in the secluded room, she heard the constant cries of pain and loss for hours. Whenever Greyfriar was at her side, wrapping her in his embrace, she tried to block out the horror. But soon she realized she couldn't, or more importantly, shouldn't. The thought of all the men who sacrificed everything convinced her that she needed to see them, talk to them, and thank them.

Eventually, Adele recovered enough of her strength to visit the makeshift medical ward housed in a long stone building where the battalion medical officer and his aide worked day after day to keep the wounded alive. The toll had been heavy, almost a third of the division dead or wounded, but the operation had succeeded. According to scouts and supply ships moving in from the coast, the entire valley was free of vampires.

The nervous and exhausted doctor met Adele and Greyfriar at the front door of the surgery. Captain Shirazi and the Harmattan took position outside, and after much to-do, the doctor escorted the couple to the first ward. Greyfriar held the door open for Adele as she entered, enduring a scowl from an orderly standing there to do the same. Taking a deep breath to steel herself against what she might see, she strode forward with Greyfriar behind her.

Thirty cots lined each side of the long room. Adele walked up boldly to the first wounded man, a youngster of about twenty. Then she remembered she was the same age; she felt years beyond it. No doubt so did he. With a brave smile, she greeted him. His forearm was wrapped in clean, white linen, and a bandage on his right cheek had slipped a little, revealing a deep gash, crudely stitched.

"Hello," Adele said.

"Your Majesty?" The boy's face flushed pink and he struggled to sit up, his eyes flicking to the famed Greyfriar and then back to his empress.

"Be still," she urged him. "What's your name?"

"Massud. Private Massud, ma'am."

"Well, Private Massud, I've come to thank you for your service to the Empire."

"Thank you, ma'am."

"Are you in much pain?"

"I'm feeling fine, ma'am."

"You were with the Thirty-sixth Fighting Lancers."

The young man nodded and then quickly realized his lapse in manners. "Yes, Your Majesty."

"You fought well, I'm told."

"Thank you, ma'am. We all did. What's left of us."

Adele paused. "Is there anything I can get for you?"

"No, Your Majesty."

"Perhaps a note to your family?"

He nodded, and Adele took out pen and paper from her coat pocket. "What would you like to tell them?"

"That I'm alive. No, that I'm well. Wouldn't want my mother to worry."

"Of course. And their address?" When he gave it, Adele took the note and put it in her pocket. "I will make sure this gets to her so she doesn't worry. I will tell her you fought bravely."

His eyes were glistening. "Thank you, Your Majesty."

She patted his hand gently and rose. Greyfriar fell into step next to her as they moved to the next patient. She wasn't sure if the men appreciated her gesture or not, or viewed it as artificial politics, but she only felt that it was important to do so. It was little enough and far from saintly in her mind. Again she glanced at the foot of the bed before speaking to the man with a thin mustache. Both his legs were elevated and in casts.

"Sergeant Fauntleroy."

"Your Majesty."

"That looks quite painful."

"Not at all, ma'am. I merely tripped on the hem of my dress while getting a beer."

She regarded him with astonishment before catching his wink and smile. Then she laughed. "Very hazardous duty indeed."

"You have no idea, ma'am." He offered a salute to Greyfriar, who nodded at the sergeant.

"You've done your Empire a great service," Adele said.

"If you call thunking vampires on the head service instead of pleasure, well then I suppose so."

Adele couldn't keep the grin from her face as she thanked him again. She regarded her escort. "You may talk to them if you wish. I'm sure a kind word from you would mean a great deal."

Greyfriar's head tilted as it was wont to do when he was perplexed. "There is no reason for me to say anything. They know their worth. They fought bravely. You won."

"You're a legend. It would thrill them."

"It is more important for them to hear praise from you."

"Perhaps, but you are welcome to say something if it comes to you," she urged.

He remained silent throughout, but paused at every bed as she did, and nodded to each soldier. As they continued on through the next ward, Adele noticed that none of the patients seemed severely or mortally wounded. Finally, she approached the doctor escorting them.

"These are the worst wounded here?"

"Oh. No, Your Majesty. We didn't think that ward appropriate for your eyes. These are the men who would be aware of your presence and benefit most from it."

Annoyed, Adele kept her tone even and quiet. "I intend to see as many as I can."

The doctor gulped. "My sincerest apologies, Majesty. This way."

Hours later, Adele and Greyfriar emerged from the hospital. Her heart had nearly shattered in the critical wards. There were moments she would have broken down from the despair of it all if Greyfriar had not been standing with her, giving her his strength. The endless rows of wounded were astounding. Men so ruined and savaged they were barely alive. The bloodstained blankets. The missing limbs and mangled faces. Shallow rattling breaths. The foulness of the air nearly sickened her when she entered, but by the end, she hardly noticed it. And that disturbed her even more.

She embraced the freezing dusk and drew in deep breaths in futile hopes of driving the septic stink from her nose. Instead of being invigorated by the sharp cold air, she felt weary. The day had drained her, and she slumped as her feet scuffed the snow.

Greyfriar was quick to slip an arm around her to steady her. "You are exhausted."

She shrugged, rolling her shoulders in a vain attempt to ease the ache. "I'm fine."

"You shouldn't have gone. You're not recovered." Greyfriar's tone held concern.

"Of course, I'm recovered," Adele lied, trying to put some force in her voice, but leaning against him anyway. In truth, however, she felt drained. It was as if she had expelled not only the rift's energies, but her own as well. Her bones were sore, and any activity left her winded. "Let's walk toward St. Laurent. I want to see if I can find someone."

"Who?"

"A little girl I met on the way into the city. I promised that she'd be safe. I'd like to see if I kept that promise."

Scowling but resigned against her determination, Greyfriar guided her. "Of course. Let's go."

They passed a wagon rocking its way down a narrow lane with a tarp pulled over its load, but the stench of charred flesh was unmistakable. Vampire casualties. Her gaze went immediately to Greyfriar. As always, his true expression remained hidden to her.

Adele noted her constant companions, Captain Shirazi and a squad of her Harmattan, followed discreetly a dozen paces behind, as discreetly as ten armed men could. She signaled for them to move farther back, and lowered her head to whisper, "Does it bother you?"

"Does what bother me? That you're not recovered? Yes, I'm concerned."

"No." Her head bobbed toward the departing ox cart.

Greyfriar glanced at it and then back again, his chest expanding with a deep breath. His response to the question was slow, his voice nearly too quiet to hear. "Would you think me callous if I said no?"

Adele was about to respond, but Greyfriar continued quickly.

"I've said before. I have chosen my side. I am with you. I'm sad to see my people come to this, and if I could make them see reason, I would. Would you prefer to see *us* win?"

"No. But they are your people." Adele continued to study the ragged groups around them, searching out the children with intense scrutiny. The locals stared back. Some waved and smiled, while others were confused, more suspicious of their new masters.

The snowcapped stones of St. Laurent rose up before them. Adele signaled for her guard to remain where they were. Captain Shirazi glared angrily, but she gave him an assured nod toward Greyfriar.

Adele weighed a bit more heavily on her companion's arm, although he seemed not to notice, as they walked slowly into the courtyard. She looked around, remembering the vampire she had killed here and the little girl. Adele hadn't logically expected to find the girl here, but it was still disappointing to see the empty courtyard.

Greyfriar pulled his cloak tighter around her shoulders as the frigid wind swirled. "Look at this city." He swept an arm, gesturing at the wrecked courtyard around them and the decrepit buildings visible around it. Some of the damage had been caused by Equatorian firepower, but all structures were in a state of decay, far from their original glory. "We've held this city for well over a hundred years and it's a ruin. In our hands, it would eventually fall to dust, and we wouldn't lift a finger to stop it."

Adele chewed on her inner cheek. "Maybe your kind doesn't know how to fix it."

"You always want us to be something other than what we are."

"Because I've seen you," she pointed out. "Vampires aren't just faceless monsters to me."

"I am alone."

"Are you sure? Maybe there are others and you just haven't met them. Maybe you'll find them."

"It had better be soon before you remove them all from the Earth."

"That's not what you want," she replied quietly, frightened of his desperate tone.

He reached out and swept snow off a stone window ledge, watching the powder vanish into sparkles in the sinking sunlight. "Adele, we are like the mayfly. We rise in great numbers, but rest assured, we will fall and go back to the Earth. You can be content that the time of the vampire will pass."

"You mean you'll all just die?" Her steps faltered.

Greyfriar gripped her hand tightly, holding her, their fingers entwining. "No, but regardless of what happens in this war, we will someday destroy ourselves because we chose this path of gluttony and depravity. Our end may not be in your lifetime or that of your children, but it will happen, and we will trouble you no longer."

"I fear your end may well be in my lifetime." Adele squeezed his gloved hand. "Look at your people. I am the weapon that caused this." She couldn't continue. Visions of vampire children in Grenoble and the Rwenzori Mountains tore through her mind, vampire children she had killed. They were the same creatures as Flay and Cesare, but they were just children; they were blameless. In some ways they were like the little girl she had promised to keep safe here in this church courtyard. "Do I even have the right to do this? How can I be responsible for genocide? How can you even look at me?"

"Never doubt my love for you, Adele. How could I not love you? Your mind and your heart never stop working; you never stop trying to find the right path. There is always hope in you. That's why you came here to find that girl, even knowing you would likely never see her again." Greyfriar shifted as he faced her, and his glasses caught the sun, glaring and blinding her. "You have to simply have faith that you saved her."

Adele swallowed hard, her eyes burning with unshed tears. She nodded as he drew her into his arms and his absolution washed over her, easing the weight on her chest. His cape fell over her shoulders like a shield against the world.

She drew several deep breaths. Then she sighed heavily, as she knew the moment had passed and duty once more pressed on her. "They expect me to go to St. Etienne."

"No, Adele." Greyfriar pushed her back and clutched her shoulders in strong hands. "You can't do it. You can't save the world by yourself."

"If I have this power, how do I dare send young men to die?" Adele's face was stricken, but a terrible weariness lurked behind her eyes. Even her passion for her soldiers, her people, was taxing her. She lowered herself onto a snowy ledge with a stuttering exhale and allowed herself the luxury of resting her head in her hands.

"You are completely spent. Don't forget, I can hear your heartbeat. I can sense you in so many ways. And I can tell you that you are much weaker than when you arrived. You might not survive another such event."

"You don't know that."

"I do. I may not know when, but I know it." Greyfriar knelt before her. "Listen to me, Adele. Let's say you got to St. Etienne to relieve your forces there, and grow weaker. Then you strike Lyon, and grow weaker still. Who can say how long you will last? Perhaps you then strike Geneva. And perhaps your faltering heart gives out, and you die. Forgetting the unendurable loss to your homeland and your family, and to me, your army will have no experience fighting vampires. They will know nothing but how to follow you like puppies. Those cities you have cleansed will be refilled by my kind, who will cut your people to pieces. Look at Grenoble. Without you, General Anhalt's men would likely be dead now."

"That's my point." Adele exclaimed. "As long as I'm here, I can protect them. I don't see why it can't work. You yourself said the clans wouldn't support each other. We should be able to move north while I strike one clan at a time. I can recuperate between attacks."

The swordsman replied, "Vampires aren't stupid. They learn and adapt. These clans you're encountering now don't know you, or understand what you're doing. But soon, they will. Word will spread. They will smell you and your power, and they'll flee before you can strike. They'll drift into the forests and mountains. And then they'll return when you've exhausted or killed yourself. All for nothing. For nothing."

Adele sighed in frustration. "Fine. What's our next step, then?"

"You return to Alexandria, and recuperate," Greyfriar said. "There is something I must do to the north. King Vittorio said that Cesare had already reached out to him. I knew my brother was allied with Munich and Budapest, but his politics are more dangerous than I suspected. I fear the clan map is changing, and my advice has been flawed and out-dated. Cesare is adapting faster than I. Lyon and St. Etienne are part of his alliance already. I had no idea, and my ignorance is dangerous for you and your army, since you are depending on my knowledge. I must learn Cesare's strategy."

"How do you intend to accomplish that?" Adele raised bemused eyebrows. "Ask Cesare?"

"No. That would be silly." He laid rough fingers against her cold, ruddy cheek. "I believe I'll ask Flay.

"What! Are you insane?" The empress bolted to her feet. She low-ered her voice, but not her tone. "Flay knows you're Greyfriar. She's sworn to destroy you."

Greyfriar caught Adele as she bobbled on unsteady legs. "True, that is a complication. However, there is one thing Flay desires even more than revenge."

"And what is that?" Adele asked with a trembling voice.

"Me."

CHAPTER 8

Grenoble was lost.

Flay considered this news, bestowing fearsome glares at the vampires who cowered before her. Some were still sporting burns from the Equatorian attack. General Anhalt's army was now free to move north. In response, Flay would have to divert much of her force from St. Etienne in order to protect Lyon. Damn Hallow, Flay thought. If she had provided more packs, this disaster would have been avoided.

"Tell me again," Flay demanded. "What happened at Grenoble?"

"Fire," one replied. "It seemed to come from the earth. From everywhere. So many of us died. It was shortly after the empress came."

Flay felt a knife edge on her spine. "The empress! The Equatorian empress, Adele? She was there? You saw her?"

"We didn't, but we knew she was there in the human camp. She was spied on board a ship from the south. She must have brought some new weapon." One of the refugees clasped his hands. "We beg to join with you. We will serve your pack until our deaths."

Flay grabbed one of the Grenoblois survivors. "Why should I help you now? You had your chance to join us, but your king was too proud. Where is he now?"

"Dead. Burned in the apocalypse at Grenoble."

Flay threw the vampire to the ground. "How could he let that girl into the battle? His idiocy has undone me."

"She's just one girl," came the voice from the floor.

"Shut up!" Flay pulled the vampire from the ground and lifted him into the air.

"She's just a human," the frightened Grenoblois stammered. "What happened has never been seen before. It's a new weapon."

"It was no weapon! It was the empress! It was that princess." Flay hurled the vampire against the wall. Then she seized another and cast him aside too. She could smell the faint remnant of geomancy on these miserable refugees. The scent conjured the horrible memories of nearly dying over Scotland at the hands of Adele.

"We can help you move against the humans in Grenoble. We know the cave systems. They haven't had time to dig in."

"Get out." Flay dropped into a chair, no longer interested in the opinions of rabble. "If I have to see any of you a second longer, you won't survive."

The war chief heard scraping and footsteps as the three scurried out. She was lost in thought. *Fire from the earth.* Most of the vaunted Grenoble clan killed outright. Those who escaped were injured with burns that healed slowly. Perhaps they were right and it was a new Equatorian weapon.

No. Flay shook her head. The princess was the weapon. Flay said aloud, "Adele. What is she?"

"She's your death, Flay."

———✳———

Prince Gareth stood in the doorway. Clearly Flay had been so preoccupied she hadn't noticed his scent, but she sprang to her feet with claws extended. Gareth didn't move. He was dressed in simple black trousers and white shirt. His claws were retracted. He adopted an attitude typical of a clan nobleman, as if paying a social visit, as if their past didn't exist, as if she didn't realize he was the greatest traitor their kind had ever known. It was his only option; he could only come to her out of natural-born superiority. Anything less and she would kill him where he stood. She stared speechless at him with her teeth bared and chest heaving.

Gareth waited for her to react further, and realized she wasn't going to. "I assumed your question was referring to Empress Adele."

Flay flinched when he said the girl's name. "What are you doing here? I told you back in Alexandria that I would call for you when I wanted you."

"The war has changed, Flay. Grenoble is in Equatorian hands. Along with its sizeable herds."

"So I hear. Congratulations. Another triumph for the Greyfriar. Your father would have been proud."

Gareth's face turned stern. "I know you could have gone to Cesare with the knowledge of my other identity, and whether he believed you or not, you could have used it as an excuse to strike Edinburgh. Thank you for your discretion."

"Don't thank me. I will go to Cesare when it suits me. I'll ruin you yet, Greyfriar." Flay lowered her gaze and flicked her claws in and out. "Are you here to kill me? You're welcome to try."

"I'm not here to fight."

"You smell scared."

Gareth willed his nerves to calm. He hesitated as if conflicted. "I'm here . . . to ask for your help."

"My help? Do you think I would help you do anything except die?"

"I'm going to kill Cesare."

"Is that so?"

Gareth could sense the shock that went through her as she backed a few steps farther away. Smart. She wouldn't be lulled into allowing him within reach.

However, she slit her eyes with suspicion. "I assume you've heard, then?"

"Heard what?"

"About your father." Flay studied the curiosity that flashed uncontrolled over his features as he made a quick gesture of unease. "The king is dead."

Gareth heard her words and discounted them at first. Even so, he felt his legs weaken at the thought of his father's death, and he found himself breathing steadily through his nose, studying Flay's face for signs of a lie. She smiled slowly, smelling the wash of emotion that poured out of him.

She was telling the truth. He knew it now. Dmitri was gone, his willpower to fight for life finally spent. Gareth would never see his father again.

The prince of Scotland couldn't maintain any pretense. His shoulders dropped with an exhalation of grief and he sank into a chair. "When did he die?"

"Some days ago perhaps. I only just heard myself." Flay's voice lilted with the joy she felt at causing him pain and uncertainty. She seemed heartened by his sudden vulnerability, like a hunter smelling blood. She couldn't stop herself from pushing deeper as she stared at Gareth's stricken face. "I can't help but recall the last time I saw His Majesty. Last year, I was in London and had the opportunity to speak with the king without Cesare around. It was quite odd. He had a moment of lucidity, as if he was his old self, as if he had some special purpose that allowed him to pull away from the fog that consumed him. It was quite bracing to have a little glimpse of the great Dmitri again. He recognized me, and looked directly into my eyes. And he asked for you."

Gareth looked up expectantly, eagerly. He couldn't help himself.

Flay continued in a conversational tone. "He said to me 'I wish Gareth was here with me. I want him to be my son again.' Before I could answer that of course I had no idea where you were, no one did, his mind faded again. His eyes clouded. Your father disappeared inside himself, never to emerge again."

Gareth grasped the arms of the chair, threatening to rip them from the base. His heart shuddered as she twisted the knife inside it, but his anger grew. He glared at the war chief. "Flay, you know that there was little in this world I cared for more than my father. Therefore, might I offer you the advice that you should refrain from goading me at this time."

Flay paused at his cold rage and betrayed apprehension when the prince made a slight movement, but she soon recovered her advantage.

Then she mimicked wide-eyed surprise at his threat. "I only tell you the final words I heard from your magnificent father to give you some comfort."

Gareth slowed his aching breath, willing his claws to stay sheathed. He had come to her with a purpose. He had hoped to spark Flay's once-powerful infatuation for him. His plan was minimal, it was true. Adele always accused him of being unable to think ahead; she was more correct than he liked to admit.

Now, however, Gareth realized what he needed to do. He almost smiled at the thought that his father had given him a last gift: a way to get a grip on Flay and perhaps a handle on the future. It was for Adele. After several minutes of menacing silence, he shook his head and straightened. His voice was soft, but laced with resolve. "I've made a terrible mistake, Flay."

She gave a derisive laugh at the ridiculous boyish simplicity of his statement.

He continued, "I don't know if it's possible to repair the damage I've done, but I will try."

"What are you talking about? Be plain, for once in your life."

"Very well." Gareth stood quickly, causing her to draw back. "Not only am I going to kill Cesare, but I aim to become king. And I want you to help me."

Flay's breath caught. She covered her obvious misstep with a loud laugh as she slowly leaned against the wall and crossed her ankles casually. "*Magnifique!* You are still so completely earnest that you seem incapable of falseness. That must be why you are such a credible make-believe human."

"I understand your doubts. But you know as well as I that Cesare is leading us to our destruction."

"How odd for you to say that. At least Cesare is fighting on the right side."

"Flay, I have been quite . . . mad . . . for years. I can't explain it. But I tell you, it is over. War forces one to take sides."

"You've chosen your side, *Greyfriar*."

"I thought I had. Recently I have begun to doubt myself. And now, my father's death is a sign I can't ignore. I intend to rule, and I want you as my war chief."

"Get out, Gareth."

"This is your only chance to decide. I won't come again."

Flay pursed her lips and breathed out angrily with a quavering voice, "Even if you were sincere, there is no way for you to win the clan now. Cesare is a hero. He's one step from becoming the new king of kings."

"Does Cesare have so many allies, then? I know only Munich, Budapest, and New York. And the Lyon clan apparently. Are there more?"

Flay bit her lower lip humorously and batted her eyes. "Oh yes, let me reveal all Cesare's plans so you can race south and tell your Equatorian blood nurse. It's obvious to me that you told the Equatorians about Draken and Ashkenazy. That's why they split their forces and invaded the Balkans to draw them off the Rhone Valley. If I had their packs, this war would have been over months ago."

"Yes, I told them." Gareth directed his eyes shamefully to the floor. "They trust me. I can tell the empress anything, and she believes it."

"Well, I don't trust you. You can't tell me anything that I will believe."

"Flay, listen to me for a moment." Gareth began to pace, forcing her to turn with him, keeping his lanky figure before her. "I can tell you what will happen if Cesare becomes king. He will marry Lady Hallow and make her queen. The new queen will have no use for someone as ambitious and skillful as you. So she will force Cesare to name a new war chief, one more easily controlled. Which means that you must be killed."

"A chilling tale," Flay said flatly.

"But true."

"Perhaps. What do you imagine will be your lifespan under King Cesare?"

"Hours? Minutes?" Gareth laughed bitterly. "Neither of us will survive my brother's reign for long." He paused in his pacing, glancing hesitantly at her, then turning away. "Cesare would be making a mistake in losing you. You are the greatest war chief alive. However, he is building an alliance and needs political actors like Hallow. And he needs heirs. You are a commoner."

"Do you ever shut up?" Flay snarled. "Yes, I'm a commoner. I can never be queen. I know that. You have no idea what it's like to fight your way to the pinnacle and still be prey to weak, soft creatures. Like Cesare and Hallow. And you! None of you would be where you are today without me!"

"I agree, Flay." Gareth now held her with his blue eyes. He held out his hand. "Join me. You and I. Together we can take Britain, and more perhaps."

Flay stared now at the long supple fingers extended toward her, but refused to take the offer.

Gareth looked disappointed and lowered his hand. "What can I do to convince you? Name it!"

Flay continued to watch his hands even after they dropped to his side. "Kill the princess."

Gareth expected that demand and had his plausible answer ready. "No. That's impossible. She is too powerful now. I can barely stay in the same room with her. Her touch burns. I wouldn't survive, and I'm in no mood for suicide."

Flay sneered in doubt, but gave a glimmer of both belief and disdain. "So is that why you've returned? Your princess is toxic to you now? Your new toy is tainted?"

Gareth again studied the floor pointedly. "You've felt her power. In Scotland, it was still young. It has grown to unbelievable levels."

"Her stench is always with me." The war chief almost shuddered as if with nausea. She drew a hand across her face in hopes of wiping away the dread. "Fine. If she is too much for you, the princess has a brother. Kill him."

He tried to look annoyed at her petty demands. "Flay, the imperial family is well protected, especially since the assassination of the emperor at your hands."

"But you're the Greyfriar. A wonder-worker. If your infatuation with the human is truly over, then prove it." She grinned. "The boy's life is the price of my faith. Bring me proof. And remember, I've smelled him."

Gareth ran a hand over his long black hair, searching for options while trying to feign disappointment. "Is there no other way? With my father dead, we have to act quickly if we are to stop Cesare."

"If we're so short of time," Flay retorted, "then you'd best rush back to Equatoria, hadn't you? I'm off to London tomorrow to report to Cesare on how the war is proceeding. Find me when you are ready to present me with a bloody piece of Prince Simon. And pray that I don't mention this new treachery of yours to Prince Cesare. This audience is at an end."

Gareth bowed to the war chief. "Very well. I thought you might be a bit more reasonable."

"Come now, my prince, nothing worthwhile is easy."

Flay laughed as Gareth strode like a shadow from the room. Once out of her sight, he moved quickly, lifting into the air. He struggled to calm his rapid heartbeat as he drifted south toward Adele.

CHAPTER 9

WHEN PRINCESS ADELE was a little girl she used to play in her father's Privy Council chamber. It was a spacious room with a massive table surrounded by wonderful leather chairs that were soft and comfortable. Most of the year, the private garden outside the great windows was flowering. She used to open the glass and listen to the birds, and the soldiers chatting with one another as well as with the occasional passing maid. It made Adele giggle to hear the soldiers' voices change from brusque to smooth, and back again.

The most memorable feature of the room, then and now, was a large globe in an ornate wooden stand. It was easily five feet in diameter and an antique sepia color, with national boundaries, somewhat outdated now, and even natural features. Adele had always loved to run her fingers over the bumpy mountains, trying to reach her arms around the world. The northern third of the globe was stained red, and labeled in various spots "Vampire Clans." The old geographical labels from before the Great Killing were only vaguely visible through the bloody overlay.

Now, Empress Adele's eyes drifted to that globe as she sat in her father's old place at the head of a new table with new chairs. The room had been redecorated, most noticeably with a display including the bloodstained flag that had covered her father's body after his assassination. The new empress was keen to remind everyone at all times in these early days of her reign that she was Constantine's daughter.

The Privy Council sat around the table that was layered with papers, charts, and maps. Additional dignitaries from the government and military crowded the room. Adele knew many of them well; some had been part of her father's regime, but others had been appointed by her or were newly elected to Commons in the special election required after the devastating vampire attack last summer. Everyone in the room was male, except for Adele and Ifrah Doreh, a Somali who was the new minister for foreign affairs. The men typically wore European-style suits, although often with a fez or Arab headdress. There were many heavily medaled uniforms present as well. Adele's commanders of the sea and air were in attendance. Her commander of the land, Sirdar Anhalt, was away on campaign. Of course, the ever-present Captain Shirazi, and a young blond corporal named Darby, stood like statues at her chair with hands clasped behind their backs, eyes moving about the room. Cigarette and cigar smoke hung thick despite several fans flapping overhead. Servants scurried in and out with water and tea and coffee, as well as sweets and fruit. Privy Council meetings were far less spartan under the empress than under her father.

Adele flipped the memoranda pages as she heard the end of a report. "We thank the Minister for Home Affairs. Now, Lord Aden, I have recently returned from an undisclosed tour of the western front. Our commanders impressed on me that our materiel needs are not being met." Although she could easily have given in to impatient anger in her questioning, she maintained a calm demeanor. "What measures are your industrialists taking to increase production?"

Lord Aden, Laurence Randolph, glanced up as if surprised the question was directed his way. Still, he smiled gravely, in complete agreement with her. He was trim and fit, wore a fashionable suit with a perfect cravat. His dark hair was slicked back against his head, and he ran a finger over his thin rakish moustache.

"Your Majesty," he began quietly, "production of standard ammunition for infantry has increased nearly fifty percent over the last month. Likewise, deliveries of machine guns to the quartermaster corps has increased." Aden raised a reasonable hand, flashing a diamond-crusted ring. "That in no way diminishes our failure to adequately serve. There were miscalculations in the early months of the war, and the General Staff's estimation of ammunition required for a soldier to kill a vampire was low. We took some time to retool and catch up, particularly given the loss of anticipated allied production, as well as the surprising destruction of our western air squadron in Gibraltar last year. However, none of that is an excuse. The only solution is to perform better, which I believe we are. Still, if these failures cost the life of one Equatorian soldier, it is a burden I will bear for the rest of my life."

Adele knew the handsome young industrialist craved congratulations for his tale of overcoming political missteps and miscalculations. However, his comment about the loss of American assistance, clearly referring to her refusal to marry the American Senator Clark, irked her, even though it was true. "When can we expect the first new ship to fly?"

Aden pursed his lips in disappointment at the lack of praise. "We have an air battleship and two sail frigates weeks away from a fitting-out cruise."

"What about our ironclad program? Where are we on that?"

The tycoon nodded sadly. "Progress has been slow unfortunately. The former HMS *Culloden*, now rechristened HMS *Constantine*, has experienced performance difficulties. There is a full report in your hands, Majesty. I expect the issues to be resolved soon and for our first ironclad airship to be in theater by summer."

Adele was warmed by the sound of her father's name on a new warship, but was undistracted from the delays. "The Americans have two of their steamnaughts in combat. Why are we behind?"

The jowly Admiral Romanski, chief of the Air Corps, began to speak, but Lord Aden interrupted smoothly, "The Americans use a different technology, as I'm sure you know, Majesty. Their aluminum-burst engines are simpler than our coal burners, but I hasten to add, far less powerful. *Constantine* will be nearly twice as fast as the Americans' *Bolivar* or *Hamilton*."

"I'm surprised you're able to judge its capabilities with it shackled in the shipyard," Adele said bluntly.

Aden chuckled and twisted his heavy gold signet ring. "Have no fear. *Constantine* is only the first. We are preparing to erect the frame of our second and third ironclads in my yards in Suez even as we speak. We may be slightly behind the Americans for now, but once we put our feet under us, our airships will be the finest in the world."

Admiral Romanski said with an irritable glance at Lord Aden, "The aluminum-burst engines are marvels. I saw *Hamilton* in Havana last year. Its fuel requirements are less than our coal—"

Aden interrupted again. "I agree that the American ships are impressive, for simple technology. We have studied their feasibility for our purposes, but we are committed to our route, and there is no sense in debating fancies now. We certainly have more important issues in the near future."

Adele tapped her fingernail on the table for silence. "I agree. Telegraphs. Gentlemen, where do we stand?"

Prime Minister Kemal cleared his throat and flipped pages. "Um. We have experienced difficulties with telegraph lines from both Marseilles to Valence, and to our forward posts in Grenoble or St. Etienne. Likewise there is no progress to be made from Trieste toward the Danube front. The vampires seem quite aware of the purpose of the apparatus, and have interrupted or destroyed numerous attempts to string wires. With great loss of life among our signal corps." He scanned the report for further information, which annoyed Adele. She expected her people to have command of their material.

Kemal's pause gave the opportunity for a voice in the rear of the chamber to rise. "Telegraphs are fascinating, I agree, but I have another issue to address which I feel is significant to the public support for the war."

Adele eyed the man—Murad Garang. He was the whisper-thin leader of the loyal opposition in Commons, a skillful politician from the southern Sudan. He had cobbled together a formidable political coalition during the late Lord Kelvin's premiership which had only grown stronger under the milquetoast Prime Minister Kemal. Garang was not a member of the official Privy Council; he was one of Adele's extended War Council. She valued hearing his contrary opinions, but he could grow tiresome when action was called for. His white linen suit shone against the dim interior of the chamber.

She said quietly, "I wasn't aware the public support for the war was in jeopardy, Mr. Garang."

"It isn't, Your Majesty. Yet. However, I believe the people across the Empire want a clear statement of our war aims."

"Which they haven't had?"

"With respect, no. We certainly understand the goal is to remove the vampires' control of the north, but beyond that . . . what?"

Admiral Romanski barked, "Let's accomplish that first, shall we?"

Garang glared at the admiral. "We are throwing enormous numbers of young men into Europe to die in the snow. We are spending vast amounts of money to do so. I don't believe it is unreasonable to know the ultimate goal. Liberation of the northern humans is the point, you say?" The man paused, then added, "I ask, why?"

The military professionals and many of the regime politicians broke into mocking dismissals, which were short of accusations of treason, but not by much.

The rotund Admiral Romanski shouted over the din, "My great-great-grandfather escaped the vampire holocaust with hardly a shirt on his back. My family was slaughtered by those creatures."

Garang aimed his formidable hatchet face at the heavily medaled sailor. "That was one hundred and fifty years ago. Surely you are past the insult now. Do you expect to find the family silver still in the cupboard when the army rolls into St. Petersburg?"

Romanski stood with jingling medals and slammed his hands on the table. "How dare you, sir!"

Adele rapped her ring loudly on the table. "Enough! I won't have this behavior."

The admiral jabbed a pudgy finger at Garang. "Pardon, Your Majesty, but I can't stand by and let this Sudd troublemaker demean the struggle of the human race as if he was not part of it."

"Which human race would that be?" Garang replied loudly. "The Europeans? Look around you, Admiral Romanski. How many of the people in this room, how many people on the streets of Alexandria or Khartoum or Bombay are consumed by the lust for revenge for your ancestors being driven from the north? Are we to twist the entire Empire for the ambitions of a few who have delusions of the Old Country?"

The empress said, "Mr. Garang, we are all human whether our ancestors came from the north or not. The vampires are a unique enemy, and we owe it to our brothers and sisters under their terrible yoke."

"With respect, Majesty," Garang said, "no, we do not." And over the rising outrage, he continued, "How far back must we set the clock? It has been over a century. Britain is vampire. Germany is vampire. Hungary is vampire. We have too many important issues here at home to waste money and men to free Russian herds!"

"Damn you, sir!" Admiral Romanski tugged a white dress glove from his belt and hurled it at the Sudanese politician. "I demand satisfaction from you!"

"Sit down, Admiral!" Adele shouted, and when Garang began to retort, "Shut up, Mr. Garang! The next one of you to speak will be arrested." They both opened their mouths, and Adele glared. "Test me, gentlemen."

She waited angrily for the clamor to die down and for all eyes to return to her. She huffed and tossed her pen down. "You wish to know our war aims, Mr. Garang? Let me state clearly for you what they are not. This is not a war of imperial expansion." Some politicians gasped. "Nor are we aiming to restore old ruling families to their ancient seats." Other politicians gasped.

"Will these things happen?" Adele continued. "Perhaps. Will the aftermath be neat and clean? No. We may have to administer territory for years to come. Yes, it is expensive. We are already sending enormous quantities of humanitarian aid into southern Europe. And we are accepting vast numbers of refugees into Equatoria. But that is a burden we will bear as the preeminent power in the world." She paused. "Would I prefer a reign of peace and prosperity? Yes. But the moment is here. How will history judge me? I care not. The world is on the edge of a knife and I won't have us bleed to death. Gentlemen, I would not have begun the war if I did not intend to win it, one way or the other. Humans in the north will be free and we will remove vampire power from the northern hemisphere. The day of the vampire is at an end."

"Hear hear," several gentlemen muttered, tapping the table. "Well said, indeed."

Adele stood, and all others rose in response. "Gentlemen, I will expect your notes within the day." The grandees of the Empire bowed to their empress, gathered their papers, and filed out, being careful to keep a buffer between Garang and Admiral Romanski.

When the heavy door shut, leaving her with Captain Shirazi and his young corporal, a fourth figure stirred from his spot across the room. Adele greeted King Msiri of Katanga as he stepped toward the table. He was a large man, tall and muscular, dressed in loose linen, with a regal carriage that made him unmistakably important. The Katangan sovereign pulled out a chair and dropped heavily into it with a laugh. "Excellent! You handled that admirably. It could have turned into a nasty scene. If it had been me, there likely would have been at least a fistfight, and at most a public execution."

Adele resumed her seat with a long sigh. "Mr. Garang isn't a bad man. He's a patriot, I feel certain. And he has a point. There are vast numbers of people in the Empire who've had little or nothing to do with the vampires. These old northerners hold onto their heritage like a feeble dog with a bone. I find them annoying too. And times are changing. Generations have come and gone many times since the Great Killing. The old families from the north are disappearing into the folk of the Empire."

Msiri said, "The war isn't about fighting for the lands of old northerners. You said it yourself."

Adele laughed. "I say many things. Sometimes I'm not sure what I mean by them anymore. I hear grumbling from the officer corps that I've hamstrung them because I've ordered them to minimize casualties among the northern humans. They want to adopt a policy similar to the Americans'. And frankly, it would work." She stared at the ceiling. "I worry that I'm fighting this war because it was too much trouble to stop it."

The African king leaned forward and rested his forearms on the table. "As you well know, Your Majesty, there is no point fighting a war against evil if you become evil. We know that this war will cause enormous death and devastation, but that doesn't mean you can't labor to prevent it where you can. You are not some simple politician. You are the one. You are the pivot of the world. You will end the reign of the vampires. You will save the humans of the north. I have seen it. There will be a new Golden Age when all that land in the north and all those people are brought back into useful society."

The empress sighed. "There are so many ways to view it. Unfortunately, I see all the facets. At one time, I would've sided with Mr. Garang. Now he's a bother to me."

"True, our lives would be so simple if we spoke and others acted. But, in fact, that would be a bad thing. No one person has the wisdom to make unquestioned decisions over life and death."

"I thought you said you would have executed him."

"I say many things too."

Adele reached out and took the king's hand, squeezing it in gratitude for his camaraderie. Anhalt was away. Gareth was away. Msiri, along with Mamoru, were the closest things she had to friends and confidants in Alexandria. She felt no pretense in front of the Katangan; they understood one another in a meaningful way. He had protected her last summer when she was being pursued by her own nation. He saw her powers at work against the vampires of the high Rwenzori Mountains. His own mother was a mystic in Mamoru's secret network, although he didn't seem to know that. His troops were fighting beside Adele's in Europe.

Still, even with those deep bonds, sadly, there were things Adele could not tell him. She wanted to lay out her problems and fears, but she didn't want to show weakness in front of the leader of a sovereign nation, and a potential rival. She was the empress, and she could have no true confidants.

No longer was she a child playing games in this vast room. Today she realized it had always been and would forever be a war room.

———ɷɷ———

It seemed as if the entire world was in the crystal that Adele held in her hand. Every color flitted in the infinitesimal facets. Tiny cracks emitted jets of hot or cold that she could feel as if they were fissures in the Earth. Each endless edge was the frontier where a glacier met a boundless sea.

She could see its vibrating notes, and hear the pinging colors in her head. Adele could have lost herself in the crystal's hard facets; it was complex and informative. It was so fascinating in its pure existence she almost lamented altering it.

Still, Adele took the heat of the crystal itself and spread it over one sharp edge with great care. She didn't want to ruin it. The fire softened the hard surface like paste under her finger and she pressed roughness off the crystal, creating a new angle, a new sharpness that allowed the stone to better free its nature, to express itself clearer.

She flexed her fingers and turned the crystal to engage the other side. Again, she touched it and drew its own energy to shave away the excess. The sound in her ear pitched higher. She bit her lower lip in concentration as she took two fingers and attempted to tune the stone by fashioning the interior. She had to deliver heat deep into the crystal without altering the surface. She felt herself bypassing the milky golden aura of the outer plane, dropping deep inside. Then she reached out, as if with both hands, shifting walls, opening passages to allow the heat and cold to meet and blend, balancing the interior of the crystal. The music was pleasing; all the hissing undertones were gone.

Adele sat back and stared at the saffron stone on the table. Bits of sloughed crystal lay around it. It felt right, but she couldn't be sure until Mamoru approved it. He had more experience in this than she; he had been giving her talismans for years. She was excited for him to arrive so she could show her first attempt to him.

The empress turned to a pile of books and notebooks. She ran her hand over them lovingly. They had belonged to her mother, the late Empress Pareesa, when she had studied geomancy years ago under Mamoru. Adele had only had them for a few months and most of the material was fairly mundane reports and papers, still exciting because they gave her some insight into her mother as a scientific intellect and as a poet of the Earth. However, there was one special journal bound in supple leather, with heavy linen pages covered with her mother's beautiful handwriting. As enjoyable as the geomancy notes and diagrams were, Adele was even more delighted by her mother's elegant yet fanciful doodles that covered the margins of most pages. The mysterious symbols and peculiar sketches were tantalizing and gave her mother's character even more subterranean angles to explore. Adele rubbed her tired eyes and began to read.

"Your Majesty?"

Adele opened her eyes. She had fallen asleep in her chair. Mamoru stood over her, dressed in beautiful green silk. He was no taller than she, and not particularly muscular. His expression was intense, as usual. His short hair was greying slightly, but his appearance otherwise gave no great hint of his age. He seemed a peculiar balance of samurai and priest. He adjusted the wakizashi short sword in his sash while turning his attention to the crystal on the table.

"Sorry." She yawned and stretched. "I fell asleep. The Privy Council meeting exhausted me."

"Where did you get this talisman?" The priest took the crystal and rolled it between his sensitive fingers.

Adele smiled. "I made it. I'm sure it's not up to standards, but what do you think?"

"You made it? I thought we had agreed you would wait for me before engaging in exercises." Mamoru tried to express mild annoyance, but failed because his voice was laced with excitement over the crystal. "There is little enough time to work together, particularly with your secret jaunts to the front, and your hesitance to work when Prince Gar . . . Greyfriar is about. I trust you found him well in France?"

"Yes. Thank you for asking. And since he is due back from the north soon, I thought I'd better get as much work in as possible. I started studying the crystal, and the next thing I knew, I was shaping it."

"I see." Mamoru glanced around the table. "Where are your tools?"

"They're too clumsy. I just used my hands."

"Your hands?" The Japanese man narrowed his gaze at her. He then inspected the tiny crystal slivers on the table. "This was the rough Persian stone you showed me yesterday? The one you found in your mother's possessions?"

"Yes." Adele took a disappointed breath. "Oh no. Did I ruin it? I wanted to use it since you said it was so good. I should've practiced on a different stone."

Mamoru removed a jeweler's glass from inside his robe and stepped to the window to study the crystal in full sun. He muttered to himself in Japanese. Without looking up, he said, "This is incredible. I can't conceive the control it took to cut down the outer layer without damaging the interior facets. And the interior is even more perfect than I saw before. Adele, this is one of the most beautiful talismans I've ever seen."

Adele shifted in her seat. "Well, I modified the interior too. Those aren't the natural facets."

Mamoru's head snapped around. "You altered the interior? How?"

"I just pushed until it sounded right." She held out her hands. "Why are you surprised? I melted a crystal in my hand last year. And you make those talismans all the time. Isn't this what I'm supposed to do?"

"I can cut crystals with tools to enhance natural structures. I cannot alter the interior."

"So you don't feel it? Inhabit it?"

Mamoru handed the crystal to Adele. "In a sense. My intuitive understanding is greater than most, but it is nothing compared to yours. I am banging rocks together while you are playing symphonies. No geomancer has your skills. That is why you are who you are."

"Really? Who am I?"

Mamoru smiled. "You are the one I've been seeking for decades."

"So you keep saying." Adele held the crystal, felt its comforting warmth, and heard its sound. She fancied she smelled its spice. It was so perfect and powerful, and yet so fragile, such a tiny bit of something unknowable. "I feel small and unworthy, like a child playing with a weapon."

"That's why we must train ever harder without interruptions. Your altering of crystals is laudatory and something we can explore much further later on. But crystallography isn't as significant to your progress as I once thought. You are more powerful than I suspected. And your focus now must be marshalling and directing the energies of the rifts. We must not be distracted by sideshows now."

"Mamoru, you're not listening to me. It's that very power I'm talking about. It seems unearned. I don't know if I'm using it properly. I mean no disrespect, but I have only you to tell me. And, truthfully, you seem dismayed by me at times. I have to be sure about what I'm doing.

I feel like I'm in the middle of something, but I've already forgotten the beginning. This is very important. Perhaps we should begin again so I can get a fuller grasp of what I am."

Mamoru's face froze. "There is no time for that."

Adele reached out toward her mentor. "I'm in a position where all my actions have enormous consequences. I'm the empress. I can hardly decide what to eat for dinner without changing people's lives. It's a great burden. I have to be sure of my course before I take it. Do you understand?"

"I'm afraid I do." His voice was hurt. He laid a hand on Pareesa's journal. "Do you even wish to continue with me?"

"Yes. Yes. Please, don't be offended. I believe in what you're teaching. It means everything to me. I'd be lost without you." Adele sat back into the shadows. "Still, the things I've done. All the dead spread over Grenoble. I can still see them, and smell them."

"I'm sorry. Vampires are brutal creatures. No one knows that better than you."

"Actually I mean the vampire dead. Males. Females. Children." She began to roll the talisman in her fingers. "Children. I killed them. I did it. I don't know exactly how, which is bad enough, but now I'm beginning to think I don't know exactly *why*."

"They aren't children," Mamoru said through clenched teeth. "They're monsters. What more reason could you need?"

"I need more." Adele sat quietly thinking of Gareth. She glanced up into the eyes of her mentor, hoping for some sympathy, but she saw only cold dismay, as if he could read her thoughts. "Surely there's something more to all this power I have. Something beyond just killing."

"Why can't you understand? You aren't just killing. You are saving the human race. When you see those dead vampires in your mind, try to think of all the human beings, all the men, women, and human children they have slaughtered over the centuries. Think of your father killed here in Alexandria as I think of my wife and daughter killed in Yunnan Province. You are their vengeance. That is your purpose."

"I understand. I just need time to process it all. So much is changing, so fast. It seems I am at a crossroads no matter the issue. I'm frightened, Mamoru."

"Of what?"

"Of myself. And the future."

Mamoru regarded her. "Your future is clear, Majesty."

"If only that were true." Adele exhaled and wished there were times she could banish her personal concerns. "I believe we should postpone our lesson for today."

"Majesty, on the contrary, we should press on."

"No, Mamoru. I have other issues I need to work through. I fear I couldn't concentrate."

Mamoru bowed stiffly in a posture of profound disappointment and sadness.

Adele wanted to apologize. He had given so much to her over the years. He had introduced her to ideas and concepts that no one else in the world could fathom. He had opened a fearsome door for her and then stood by her as she walked through it. Now she felt as if she was betraying him by hesitating, by asking too many questions about things he'd rather not face. But it was he who had encouraged her to be an outsider, to doubt the common wisdom of the world, and she couldn't stop that aspect of her nature, even for him.

"I'm sorry, Mamoru. I would do anything to keep from disappointing you, but I have concerns that I must face. I hope you understand."

"I do, Your Majesty." The priest did not raise his face to meet her eyes. "I fear I understand completely."

Adele watched her mentor formally withdraw from her presence and shut the door behind him, leaving her alone with her crystal and her doubts.

CHAPTER 10

T HE EMPRESS TRUSTED Mamoru without question. For more than ten years, he had been her tutor, publicly, in the sciences including geology and chemistry and botany, as well as her fencing master. Privately, he had instructed her in various arcane arts and sciences. He had come from Java at the behest of Empress Pareesa with the agreement of the emperor. Even the criticism of the hard-line court technocrats that Mamoru was a dangerous religionist, and shouldn't be on Princess Adele's staff, couldn't outweigh Empress Pareesa's will.

So influential was he that Mamoru had access to the crown's most infamous prisoner, Selkirk, the man who had attempted to assassinate Empress Adele. Little was publicly known about the assassin. The press had uncovered that he was from a poor family in Alexandria and had disappeared from school at age ten. He was unheard-of until the day he appeared as a man in his late twenties in the imperial crypt and plunged a knife into Adele's breast. It fascinated the public that he had been the tool of Lord Kelvin, the former prime minister who had been overthrown by Adele's triumphant return to Alexandria. But that tantalizing connection was made all the more mysterious because Kelvin was later killed by the empress's triumvirate of champions—the Greyfriar, General Anhalt, and Mamoru himself.

That was the story in the papers anyway.

The truth was more complicated and chilling, and raised a great many questions about the stability of the Empire, as well as the interactions between human and vampire hemispheres. Very few people knew the truth about Lord Kelvin and Selkirk, and how the attempted assassination of the empress was tied to the British vampire clan. Mamoru was one of those few, but even he didn't know the whole truth. However, he intended to.

The boy had shown promise as a geomancer, so Mamoru had taken Selkirk to Java, where he ran an intensive academy in all aspects of the earthly sciences. It was Selkirk whom Mamoru chose for the dangerous mission of mapping the dragon spines of Britain. However, something had happened to him in the north. He had left Equatoria as an inquisitive explorer, and returned as an assassin.

The clack of the key in the old lock echoed in the gloomy corridor. The heavy wooden door swung out and Mamoru looked down on a miserable wretch who lay on a simple cot. The filthy man was shackled at the ankle to a long length of chain that gave him room to move about his cell. He was cadaverously thin, clad in prison greys, with an unkempt beard and stringy matted blond hair. At the words "Good evening, Selkirk," the young prisoner shifted his look to the samurai, and then returned it to the ceiling.

Mamoru turned to the guards in the corridor. "You may go. Close the door and lock it, please."

The guards nodded. The samurai had a writ from the Court of High Justiciar giving him free rein on the prisoner, and given who he was, he could easily have produced a handwritten note from the empress. So the guards shut the door and locked it; then they all withdrew to their gloomy station at the end of the hall.

Mamoru studied the cell now that he was alone with the motionless prisoner. It was a slimy stone hovel with no window. There was a cot and a bucket, nothing more. The stench of waste assaulted his nose, and he felt a tinge of regret that his old student had come to this. Selkirk's face was a little swollen, no doubt from some careless slaps or shoves from the guards, but he wasn't brutalized. There was no blood on the floor, at least none that was recent.

"We have much in common," Mamoru said. "Your late friend, Lord Kelvin, held me in this same dungeon just down the corridor. This room is smaller even than the one I was in last summer." He stepped to the side of the cot, his sandals slipping on the greasy floor. "Do you know me?"

Selkirk again moved only his eyes, lingering on the face above him. His mouth convulsed.

"Do you know where you are, my boy?"

The prisoner blinked.

Mamoru exhaled sadly. "You are in Alexandria. Your home. But you are in a prison. Because you attempted to kill Empress Adele. Do you remember doing that?"

The ragged man moved his mouth, but stayed quiet.

"Selkirk," Mamoru said, "do you remember stabbing the empress? I mean Princess Adele? The young woman you helped in London. Do you remember?"

Silence.

The prisoner cleared his throat and made a crude attempt to speak. But then he closed his mouth again, slipping back from communication. Mamoru reached down quickly and pressed his skillful fingers into Selkirk's collarbone. The student screamed.

Mamoru said quietly but forcefully, "You will talk to me. Yes?"

Selkirk breathed hard from the unexpected pain, but still sunk inward. The samurai slid his fingers behind the man's neck, sought a pressure point, and squeezed. Selkirk screeched and flailed up, grasping his head in pain.

Mamoru pressed a hand against the man's chest. "Talk to me, son. Say something. Now. Or I will continue."

"No," Selkirk howled. "Don't hurt me!"

The teacher laid a comforting hand on the man's shoulder. "There. Excellent. Thank you. Let's begin again. Do you know who I am?"

Selkirk nodded, gasping as the pain faded.

"No," Mamoru said. "Say it. Talk."

"You're my teacher."

"That's right, lad." Mamoru sat on the edge of the cot, staring into the eyes of the prisoner. "Do you remember going to Britain?"

Selkirk looked away.

Mamoru placed his hand on the man's chest, causing him to squirm pathetically. "Do you remember going to Britain?"

"Yes, yes."

"Good. Tell me why you went to Britain."

"I . . . I was mapping dragon spines. Ley lines. For your world map."

"Yes. Good. And did you do that?"

"Yes, sir."

"Good. Excellent. Well done. Where are your charts?" When the prisoner looked away again, Mamoru tapped the man's collarbone and Selkirk flinched. "If you completed your charts, where are they?"

The prisoner shifted on the cot, trying to move out from under the samurai's hand. "The princess is dangerous."

"Where are your charts?"

Selkirk pressed his back against the wall, holding his hands out to ward off his visitor, even though Mamoru hadn't moved. "She will ruin us."

Mamoru stayed still, but watched his former student adopt a reasonable tilt of his head but with wild begging eyes. He kept his voice calm. "Where are your charts?"

"He needed them. To show me the truth about the princess. How dangerous she is."

"Who needed them, Selkirk?"

"Please don't hurt me again."

Mamoru chuckled reassuringly. "I have no intention of hurting you, my boy. As long as we are talking. Now, who needed your charts?"

"Dr. Goronwy." Selkirk stared at Mamoru like a frightened dog, expecting each change of expression to herald an attack.

"Ah. I see. Dr. Goronwy. And who is he?"

"A colleague. In London and Wales."

"A colleague?" Mamoru shifted slightly, and Selkirk pushed harder against the wall. "I know of no colleagues in London and Wales. A doctor of what exactly?"

"He is a scholar of geomancy."

The priest put a thoughtful hand to his chin. Selkirk seemed quite sure of what he was saying. The unbalanced mind often put specifics to stories to make them real. "A human doctor in the north?"

Selkirk sensed his teacher's doubts. "It's true. Believe me, Master Mamoru. He is a very important man. Very high in the court."

"The court," Mamoru repeated slowly with a chill.

"Yes. Prince Cesare hangs on Dr. Goronwy's every word. As the princess does with you."

Mamoru felt a terrifying shock rack him. He stood, but his legs were unsteady. He waited a moment until he could speak with an unbroken voice. "Prince Cesare?"

"Yes. I met him several times." Selkirk settled into a more comfortable position. "He is a man of vision, guided by Dr. Goronwy. The prince is interested in geomancy, as you are. As we all are. He was most interested to hear all about our work. Although he and Dr. Goronwy held some contrary opinions on the princess and her abilities."

Mamoru felt the cell almost spinning around him. He swallowed deliberately. What should have been mushy ravings about human geomancers in the north and meetings with Prince Cesare clicked into sharp rational slots. Mamoru had expected that Selkirk had been a tool of the British clan; after all, he had been positioned in the imperial crypt by the late prime minister, Lord Kelvin, who was a confederate of Flay. However, Mamoru assumed that they simply used Selkirk because he was easily twisted and knew Alexandria.

This was something more. Something monstrous and unbelievable. It was the second blow to Mamoru's world in six months. The first was discovering that his prize, Adele, was associated with a vampire and she couldn't understand why that was disastrous for her own kind. And now, Selkirk was telling him that he could have betrayed Mamoru's ultimate plan—to use Adele to destroy all vampires—to the leader of the enemy.

Like ley lines, the course of treachery led back to Gareth. Cesare was his brother. Lord Kelvin had been an ally. Selkirk was an informer and agent.

Mamoru covered his face with shame at his own stupidity. He had spent so many years in preparation; he had been so convinced of his unique role in the world, was so proud of his genius. He had made a critical mistake. He had ignored that his enemy could think. All he could see were the savages who slaughtered his wife and daughter as he fought to reach them. But perhaps his mistake wasn't fatal. The vampires would soon learn that a human could be as merciless as they.

Mamoru turned back to Selkirk, his face rigid. "So you discussed all you knew about the princess and the Event with Cesare?"

"More so with Dr. Goronwy."

"But he reported to Cesare?"

"Oh yes. His Highness was fascinated by our work here." Selkirk smiled. "They made an excellent case that Princess Adele is dangerous to geomancy. She could well stop the flow in the spines, which would be disastrous. Would you like me to explain it in more detail?"

"No." Mamoru's hand flicked like an adder, snapping against a spot beneath Selkirk's ear. The young man screamed and fell to the floor. He rolled on the filthy ground, clutching his head in agony. The samurai snarled, tight-lipped, "I would like you to lie there in pain until I decide it can stop."

———◦◦◦———

Nzingu the Zulu watched Mamoru as he paced restlessly and sipped Turkish coffee. The scent of burning hashish wafted thick, not surprising given they were in a back room of a posh Alexandria hash house. Her other two colleagues sat at a low brass table. Sir Godfrey Randolph considered a plate of sweets, running thoughtful fingers over his bushy white sideburns. He was an older gentleman, given over more to fat than muscle, red-faced, but with the steady hands of a surgeon, which he was. And Sanah, the Persian, wrote in a leather-bound journal with hands decorated with exquisite henna tattoos. She was short and covered head to toe in a black robe. Her face was veiled but for dark eyes. Nzingu was tall and clearly quite fit, judging from her economical movement. She was both observant and ready to react. The Zulu woman wore a fashionable gown of bright yellow silk, and a hat with a lace veil perched askew on her coiled hair.

"The news from the front is encouraging," Sir Godfrey said as he chose a sugared date. "We've occupied St. Etienne and Grenoble. In winter, at that. At this rate, we'll be in Paris by May, eh?"

Mamoru set down his porcelain cup. For the first time it rattled. "The truth from the front is not so encouraging as the news."

"Really? I attended the prime minister's speech before Commons yesterday and he seemed quite optimistic."

"Prime Minister Kemal is the empress's man. It's his job to appear optimistic."

The old gentleman worked the date's pit. "Are we losing the war, then?"

"No, no," Mamoru said. "We did take those two cities, but at great loss. Nearly ten thousand dead or wounded at St. Etienne, and almost ten more outside Grenoble. And that's to say nothing of the Hungarian expedition. That campaign is a meat grinder, and I fear the Equatorians are the filling."

Sanah said, "Listen to you, Mamoru. Politics. Economics. Military strategy. Perhaps you should be prime minister."

He laughed without humor. "I would rather die. I am a teacher, a priest, and, once, a samurai. Never an elected official. But your point is well taken, Sanah. I called you all here to discuss the empress and our plans. It has been months since I spoke to all of you at once." Mamoru poured another cup of stiff coffee. "What you may not know about the war is the reason for our glorious triumph at Grenoble. It was the empress who scattered the vampires there, allowing our army to walk in unopposed."

Nzingu stared at Mamoru, along with her colleagues. Then she laughed with a startlingly loud cackle that surprised the group nearly as much as Mamoru's announcement. "However will the steam lords of Alexandria deal with a witch queen?"

"It isn't quite so simple."

"I know that, Mamoru. We Zulu drove our vampires from the uKhahlamba with shamans leading our armies with botanicals and crystals. But then we turned on our magicians and priests. Will Equatoria have to destroy the great sorceress to preserve their comfortable worldview?"

Mamoru pursed his lips with tired bemusement. He checked his pocket watch. Sir Godfrey and Sanah kept quiet.

Nzingu flopped into an overstuffed chintz chair. "So have we reached the moment? Does the empress charge to the front and burn a swathe through the enemy? Why do we even need an army in Europe?"

"The strain on the empress in using her skill on that level is enormous. Grenoble was harmful to her. And the effect on the vampires was temporary. They could return. That's also part of the problem. If she starts rushing around Europe using her abilities like some altruistic bomb, she will wear herself out. She could well kill herself before I can make use of her. She still has much to do to prepare for the Event, and there is an additional complication."

Mamoru peered out through the bead curtain separating their plush back room from the hazy hashish parlor beyond. Assured of their relative privacy, he returned to the cabal and stood near them. In a low voice, he said, "One thing which you all must know before we go further. It is something about the Greyfriar."

Sanah sat up with alarm. "Is he dead? That will crush poor Adele."

"No. He is quite alive last I heard." Mamoru paused, considering his next words. "The man you know as Greyfriar is not a man. He is a vampire. His true name is Gareth. He is a prince of the British clan, the eldest son of King Dmitri."

Nzingu's face flushed with shock and surprise. She exchanged looks with Sir Godfrey and Sanah. They both held the same disbelief that was no doubt reflected in her eyes. What Mamoru said couldn't be true, but for him to lie so flagrantly made no sense.

"He latched onto the empress while she was a prisoner in the north, and she has fallen under his sway. I have been unable to act against him because I feared losing my contact with her."

Sir Godfrey murmured, "I had a strange feeling when I met him at the hospital after the empress was stabbed. But I dismissed it as incredible, a product of my own exhaustion at the time. How did you find out?"

Mamoru said, "I've known since I encountered him with the empress in Katanga last summer."

Nzingu asked with the incredulity cracking her voice, "Since last summer? And we're only now finding this out?"

The priest glared at her. "This is not the time for your typical difficulty, Nzingu. We have other issues to attend."

Sir Godfrey smiled weakly at his companions. "It's just that we find it hard to credit, Mamoru. How can a vampire pretend to be a human?"

"It's chilling to watch him mimic a human. It's sickening to see Adele fawn on him. He is a parasite even though Adele drapes human emotions on him the way people do with their pets. He is not a man. He is a creature. He must be dealt with."

Sir Godfrey opened his mouth, and then closed it because he didn't know what to say. He moved his eyes back and forth in confusion. "Well, he is with the army much of the time. Can't you just alert the sirdar and let him take care of the problem?"

Mamoru said, "General Anhalt will be no help to us. The sirdar would say the sun was the moon if the empress wished it. He knows everything about Greyfriar. He has the vampire under his protection and expressly forbade me to harm the thing on penalty of my own life." He continued to stalk the room. "Obviously he must be killed. However, nothing can be done in a way that might publicly embarrass the empress or reveal that she was aware of this abomination."

"This debacle just keeps getting better and better," Nzingu laughed. "It certainly won't do for the empire to learn their witch queen was consorting with a vampire. Although I would enjoy seeing that debated in Commons."

Sanah asked, "Are we sure that killing him is necessary? It doesn't appear that he has prevented her from moving forward in her practices. She struck Grenoble."

"When he is about, she suspends her studies, out of fear for his health," Mamoru retorted. "That is unacceptable. She is growing more independent and headstrong, and powerful. She is even beginning to question whether she should use her abilities against the vampires at all. I can't allow her to stop me now. I have forged her into a perfect weapon and I intend to use her."

Sanah whispered, "Surely you don't mean to sound so harsh toward your student."

"I mean all I say." The priest glowered with anger and fire in his face. "She is hardly my student any longer. I will finish what I started."

"And what of the Greyfriar?" Sir Godfrey asked. "Are you saying all those exploits of Greyfriar in the north were the work of a vampire? For what reason?"

"I have no idea," Mamoru replied. "Nor do I care."

Sir Godfrey pointed out, "Greyfriar means much to the people of the north, and south. How can we remove him?"

"There is no more need for the Greyfriar," the samurai snarled. "His day is done."

"I will kill him," Nzingu said suddenly.

All heads turned to her.

"Who else could?" she stated without pride. "It must be quiet and it must be sure. Of us four, only Mamoru or I could possibly manage it, and Mamoru is otherwise engaged training the world's suddenly reluctant savior. So I will kill this monster and save the poor empress from its loving clutches." She turned to Sanah at the sound of the Persian woman's uncomfortable sigh. "Do you object?"

Sanah replied in a hesitant voice, "No."

Mamoru nodded eagerly, rubbing his hands together. "You will serve admirably, Nzingu. It can't happen here in Alexandria near the empress. He will soon be here with us in the city. So we must wait for him to journey again to Europe and you will pursue him back to his lair in Scotland where he inevitably returns. Our network in the north will speed your travel somewhat. It won't be an easy task. He is a dangerous foe. He is skilled with weapons and has the natural cunning of his kind. We will discuss it in more detail later."

"Fine," said Nzingu, then more to herself, muttered, "No young girl should venture into womanhood untouched by the loss of her love."

This was about the future, not the past.

CHAPTER II

"LET ME UNDERSTAND this. You told Flay that you would kill Simon?"

"In so many words, yes."

Adele shook her head slowly as she selected a cutlass from a rack of weapons. She swung the sword several times, appreciating the whisper it made in the air. Greyfriar waited nearby, twirling his rapier in his fingers to practice dexterity. An early-morning wind off the Mediterranean flapped the ends of the scarf wrapping his face. Their makeshift fencing strip on the roof of Victoria Palace overlooking the sea could be quite blustery. She took up a position ten feet away from the tall swordsman.

Adele always counted on Greyfriar for comfort and relief from the pressure, and was happy he had returned to Alexandria today. While she knew it was irrational to expect him to wipe away the numerous problems that surrounded her, the memories of those days in Europe when he seemed to have every answer she needed swelled immense at times. The young princess had depended on Greyfriar utterly then, but those days were far behind the empress now. She had to stand alone and only lean on him in private, and content herself with his occasional partnership.

"Well, what's one more unsolvable problem?" Adele said with a quirky smile. Her hair was plaited into a thick braid against the wind.

"I had little choice," he offered. "She wanted me to kill you."

Adele practiced a thrust, imagining she was skewering Flay. "That is tiresome of her. I suppose we could announce Simon had died, and hold a funeral."

Greyfriar cleared his throat.

"Yes?" she asked, brandishing the cutlass. "Was there more to the bargain?"

"I have to bring a piece of him to her."

"A piece of him? A piece of my brother? How large a piece will satisfy Flay?"

"I imagine a hand will do."

"How fortunate he has two." The empress came en garde in fifth position, prompting Greyfriar to raise his weapon. She struck suddenly with three moves planned. She swung high, bringing Greyfriar's blade up for a parry, intent on overpowering his lighter sword. Metal clashed. The rapier flew off her cutlass. She dropped low for a sweep across the midsection. His sword was there fast, as she knew it would be, so she surged forward with the cutlass drawn tight against her, sharp edge toward Greyfriar, pressing his long sword flat against his chest and pushing the razor edge of the cutlass across his throat. If the cutlass had actually been sharpened, he would have suffered a vicious deep cut, likely debilitating.

As it was, Greyfriar exclaimed, "Amazing. The perfect moves. As long as you have a cutlass and your enemy is a human carrying a rapier."

Adele smirked with one eyebrow arching. "Well, you may have noticed that I do have a cutlass and my opponent is carrying a rapier."

"You're right." Greyfriar saluted with his sword. "I would have been dead if I was human."

"Even so," Adele countered, with an attempt at levity. "Such a wound could bleed out a vampire as well as a human. Just admit that I was prepared for you."

Greyfriar settled into his ready stance and waited. Adele didn't appreciate the challenge in his action. She had done what she needed to defeat him, which he recognized, but then added some pointless technicalities to lessen her accomplishment. The last person she expected nitpicking from was Greyfriar.

Adele came at him again with a precision strike. He parried and was gone, flipping over her head, putting one hand on her shoulder, and landing behind her. She was already spinning, expecting a blow to her head from the basket hilt of his sword, but he grabbed her hair and pulled her down. Her feet left the ground and his strength bore her to the hard rooftop. One of his knees pressed onto her chest and the other pinned her sword hand. Greyfriar ripped the cloth from his face and Adele saw his fangs bared. His mouth yawned open wide and his head surged toward her. There was a gentle rake of hard teeth and then soft lips against her neck.

In her ear, he whispered, "I pray you don't ever forget what my kind can do."

"I thought this was only a friendly sparring match," Adele chided.

Gareth shifted his weight off her and fingered the tendrils of her hair that had escaped the braid. Adele felt her irritation slipping away as she stared at his unmasked face and watched his gaze playing over her hair. His eyes were tight with sadness. And, he was right in his lesson. In reality, a vampire would not have a rapier and her victory against Greyfriar was only because she knew he wouldn't use his natural weapons against her. She had used that knowledge and crowed about it. There were times her overconfidence annoyed even her. *Touché*, she thought.

Adele heard a strange noise. Gareth looked around for the source. He pointed toward the sea, where a naval airship was passing off the coast, within easy sight of the palace. The crew lined the rail cheering at the empress and her consort on the roof. Adele rose to her feet with a hand from Gareth. She raised her cutlass to the ship in salute. The roar grew even louder. Gareth replaced the cloth over his face.

With a laugh she said, "You realize they thought they had caught us in an intimate moment? They only saw me reclined, and you bent over me tenderly. The stories will begin to circulate of the empress's romantic trysts on the roof of the palace. They don't know you had just pummeled me and threatened to drink my blood."

"I'm sorry," Greyfriar replied. "It was ridiculously stupid of me. I too can never forget what I am, or where I am."

She took his arm. "You can take the vampire out of the north, but you can't take the north out of the vampire. And I would have killed you with my first attack, right?"

The lines around his shrouded eyes wrinkled with a smile. "You would have incapacitated me. And you could have dispatched me with your typical bloody efficiency before I recovered."

"That's all a young woman wants to hear." Adele kissed him through the cloth. She took his rapier and tested it. "I like your sword. The balance is perfect. But why do you prefer a rapier? With your strength, a crushing weapon would make more sense."

"Crushing is almost useless against vampires. It's more efficient to penetrate. If you destroy our heart, we die."

She touched the center of his chest with the tip of the rapier.

He looked down, and then held out his arms helplessly.

Adele shook her head. Her slender hand replaced the point of his sword and she kissed the spot where it had rested.

He enfolded her in an embrace.

A singular warmth spread through her. Then she sighed. "Unfortunately, I have yet another meeting with Prime Minister Kemal, Lord Aden, and the War Materiel Committee in an hour, so we had better discuss how you intend to murder my brother without actually killing him."

"Then let us just spar. No lessons, just simple exercise. It will clear our minds."

Greyfriar crossed to the weapon rack and pulled a rapier similar to his. He then stood facing Adele and came en garde, as did she. They began to fence, their blades flashing and ringing. A few steps one way, a few back the other. Lunge, parry, riposte. Again. They fell into a pattern that matched each other so cleanly it seemed scripted.

Adele watched his long limbs whip almost as if they were an extension of the sword. His movements had both speed and a raw strength that was very different from Mamoru's purist skills. Her teacher seemed hardly to move at all; Greyfriar was a swirling mass of action. She studied what she could see of his face, wishing his eyes were uncovered so she could see the intensity and concentration in them.

"So, I'm assuming," Adele breathed hard as they fenced, "we can find a suitable hand from the morgue, and that will satisfy Flay."

"It isn't that simple. Flay knows Simon's scent."

"Then how? Besides the obvious, which is out of the question."

"I noticed when you were in the hospital, they gave you blood from bottles."

"Yes."

"I propose doing as you say and finding a suitable hand, then removing some of Simon's blood and soaking the hand in it. It should be enough to deceive Flay."

"That's gruesome."

"Will Simon object?"

"Oh no," Adele said. "He'll love it."

"We'll need a lot of blood to make her believe that he is dead. We'll take some of his clothes drenched in it too, as well as the hand. She'll assume with that much loss of blood he will have died of grievous injuries."

"It might work." Adele lunged forward with a remise, perfectly executing a number of short attacks in quick succession, not allowing any quarter, but Gareth deflected them all.

"Good. Of course we'll need to make Simon dead to the public. It must appear a vampire murdered him. Cesare and Flay have agents everywhere. If your old prime minister was in league with London, we can safely assume there are others here still passing information northward."

"I pray that's not true. We combed through Lord Kelvin's papers and, as meticulous as they were, if there were other agents in Equatoria, he would've mentioned it. Knowing Kelvin, he would have registered their pay slips. He was incapable of not keeping records of everything."

"All of Cesare's spies may not be part of the same network. Greyfriar has agents across Europe; they don't all know each other. It's safer for them that way. You must decide whom you trust, and limit the most sensitive information to that group. But there may also be information you tell no one, even me."

"I trust you." Adele began to retreat, now unable to maintain her speed of riposte before Greyfriar's tireless attack. "And General Anhalt. And Mamoru."

"Then the truth about Simon can go no further. To everyone else, he must be dead."

Adele's voice was nearly lost in ragged breathing. "King Msiri. We'll need his help too." She stumbled and fell with a grunt.

Greyfriar was on one knee beside her. "Are you all right?"

The empress could barely answer with one hand on her heaving chest. Her face was bright red, but she shook her head and forced herself to say, "I'm fine. Just tired. I'm fine."

He went and dipped a cup of water from a nearby pitcher. "You are exhausted. You shouldn't be so winded. Are you sleeping at all?"

She drank deeply, huffing for breath, and gave a wet cough. "Not much, no. There's so much to do. Dispatches from the front. Meetings. Speeches. Training with Mamoru."

He studied her intently. "Adele, you look many years older than when I first saw you."

"That's so sweet, thank you." She glared up at him wearily, shaking her head. "Let me give you a little tip. Human women don't like to be told they look old." But she had noticed it in the mirror too. There were darkening circles under her eyes and creases showing on her forehead. Even more, her lush hair seemed different, wirier and more brittle to the touch.

Adele stood as quickly as she could muster to put him at ease, but it was just pretense. She was weary, and it wasn't from fencing practice. She wiped her perspiring face with a towel. "If I look old to you now, what happens when I'm sixty, but you still look the same?"

"Nothing will happen," he replied with no hint of falseness. "I will still be here. I only said it because you seem to be suffering. Should I not tell you?"

"No. I want you to say something if you think there's a problem. You just could tell me in a nicer way."

Greyfriar responded, "I adore you, and you look very tired."

"That's better." Adele laughed and handed his rapier back.

He swept the sword back into its scabbard. "There is one more thing that I learned from Flay that will impact us."

She groaned. "Yes?"

"My father is dead."

Adele heard an unusual catch in his voice, and her heart dropped.

She took him in her arms. "Oh Gareth, I'm so sorry. I know he meant a great deal to you."

"Once, he did. But he hasn't been that person for a long time." He put his arms around her. "His death wasn't unexpected, but it complicates the immediate future. On the other hand, it gave me the perfect sparkling object to dangle in front of Flay. I told her that I intend to kill my brother and become king."

Adele pulled back with eyes full of surprise.

Greyfriar quickly held up a calming hand. "It's merely a ploy. Flay has dreamed of being my war chief for centuries. She's more likely to give me what I want if she thinks that great prize is looming on the horizon." He paused to think. "If I have the chance to kill Cesare, I will. But odds are he will be heavily guarded at all times from now on."

"Well, in any case, you're not likely to see Cesare any time soon, are you?"

"Yes, actually. He has called a coven in London to choose a new king."

"You're not going, are you?"

"I must." He pressed a finger against her lips as she began to argue. "Adele, there is no need. We both have our duties that we can't avoid. No amount of worrying will stop them. And whether I go or not, the outcome will be the same. My brother will be king, and my days of freedom in the north as Prince Gareth will be at an end. Cesare will want to have me killed, but I suspect he'd prefer to wait until he is the king so it looks like he won because he's better, not because he was the only choice."

Adele gasped. "What about everyone in Edinburgh? Morgana and the rest of your subjects? What will Cesare do to them?"

"He will obliterate them." Greyfriar took a long breath. "I need to move them out of harm's way before he is crowned. After I get what information I can from Flay, I will return to Edinburgh to help my people. Most I will send into the countryside, into the Highlands, where they will be somewhat safer at least. There are desperate times ahead."

Adele wanted to ask Gareth to stay in Alexandria, not to return to the north, not to meet with Flay again, and certainly not to go back into the domain of his brother. She knew, however, that he wouldn't listen to her, and more, she could never ask it. He was a prince, and a decent man.

He had obligations that were more important than risk to his life. She knew that all too well.

Adele almost offered to protect his subjects with her geomancy but realized she couldn't stay with them for any extended time. It would be safer for them to evacuate. At least that way they still had a fighting chance to build a life.

Instead, she said, "Don't worry. We'll think of something. I won't leave those people in Edinburgh to your brother's good graces. Shall I cancel my appointments today? Would you like to be together?"

"I've made a peace of sorts with my father's death. Don't alter your plans. Anything that pushes the war forward is important, so attend your meetings. We'll see each other later."

"We will. In fact, come to me late this afternoon. I have arranged a gift for you."

"What is it?"

"This afternoon." Adele kissed him on the cheek, holding her embrace for a long moment. Then she strode from the roof. She knew Greyfriar was watching her, so she was careful to hold her head high and not show any of the frailty she felt.

—◦◦◦—

Adele sequestered herself within her small garden located on the northern side of the palace. The meeting with the War Materiel Committee had finally come to a bickering halt, and she was relieved to have just over two hours before her next official function, this time with the Phoenix Society, an organization of Equatorian matrons of influence, at the newly erected War Memorial. Her brother, Simon, would meet her here in an hour. Until then, Adele was determined to have a quiet moment, desperate to meditate and forget momentarily about the terrifying prospect of Gareth returning to London. Kicking her shoes off with decadent abandon, she settled into a long chair beneath a lemon tree and stretched out her legs with a sigh. She lay utterly still for a few minutes, just because she could, although she half expected a knock at the gate from someone clamoring for her attention.

Adele had brought her mother's leather-bound journal. As she read she was reminded that her mother's theoretical, almost whimsical approach to geomancy was at odds with Mamoru's very strict concrete science. His red corrective marks were scattered liberally throughout the notebook. This amused Adele because Mamoru's harsh scrawls were always overwritten with Pareesa's bored doodles in the margins.

One note in particular Adele found herself reading over and over. It had to do with the concept of *pathfinding* using ley lines. Her mother's charming little sketches of spiders in their webs stretched and draped over the page. Mamoru had tapped this particular skill when he tracked Adele to the Mountains of the Moon last year, after she had set off a geomantic event equivalent to the eruption of Mt. Vesuvius. The sheer size of that event sent shockwaves through the ley lines, and Mamoru had felt the shivers in the web of the Earth as he waited passively on a rift in the Sahara.

Pareesa also strained orthodoxy with her thoughts on pathfinding, surmising that perhaps such a skill could be reversed. If one could receive information, one could also seek information. She theorized that one could use geomancy to move through the webs and seek out other spiders. Mamoru marked the section heavily with comments like "Please stay on topic!" Pareesa's ideas were definitely a different slant on geomancy compared to the teachings of Mamoru, which centered on summoning the Earth's energy through a rift and channeling it in the most destructive way possible.

The temptation of reaching out and tracking Mamoru was devilishly appealing, just to see if it was possible. However, if Adele succeeded, he'd only be angry that she had tried something so unconventional without his supervision. Still, the thought that she could sense others like herself was alluring.

Adele's mind was still swirling with the concept when she noted the time. Simon was late. The boy's head was always in the clouds, and something had most likely distracted him. Usually she wouldn't have been so vexed, but today they were honoring those who had fought and died in Operation Bengal, named for Simon, and he should be there. In a palace this large there was no telling where he was, and Simon was not the sort to tell anyone what mischief he was up to.

"Captain Shirazi!" she called out.

The soldier appeared as if by magic. "Majesty?"

"Prince Simon is tardy. Please send someone to locate him, if at all possible."

As Shirazi went to see to the duty, Adele had a wicked thought. Her brother wore a crystal talisman. Adele had given it to him last year right before her disastrous wedding. She wondered if she could find him by tracking the crystal. Her mother had thought it possible.

Adele would perform just a small test. It was no more destructive or harmful than holding a stone in her hand and determining its point of creation. A parlor trick really. It wasn't the type of activity that weakened her. In fact, the smaller exercises actually renewed her. Plus, Gareth was nowhere close by; such a small event wouldn't affect him, and would leave little residue in her for long.

She covered her own talisman with her hand. Smells and colors danced before her, singing with quiescent power. Adele felt the urge to wade into the energies, but refrained, not sensing the need to go so deep. She could find what she wanted on the surface with little guidance. Just as in Grenoble, the ley lines flared into life around her. Breathing slowly and deliberately, she began to apprehend patterns within a background cacophony of sounds and smells. She plumbed it for a familiar resonance.

The talisman Simon wore had once been hers, so she knew it well. It was from the far north, a land of ice and snow, so she searched the swirling sensations for something similar. Then she smelled it exactly as she remembered the day Mamoru had given it to her. She tasted a chill from a note of frost embellishing one of the many fibrous lines she could see around her.

Adele grasped that line. The ley shivered like a taut silken string in her hand. It stretched eastward toward the wing where Simon had his quarters.

Perhaps he wasn't going to be that hard to find after all.

Adele realized Captain Shirazi had returned and stood next to her with a look of confusion on his face so she regarded him cheerfully. "I'm off to collect my brother."

"Where is His Highness?"

"Let's find out," she replied with an almost girlish glee as they departed through the garden gate.

Adele hurried along the tiled corridors of the palace. She stopped outside the archway leading to Simon's second-floor quarters. Shirazi started to continue, but realized the empress had paused. She took a deep breath and stroked the crystal with her thumb. Again the unique taste of Simon's talisman caressed her tongue and drifted up into her nose, leading her away from such an obvious location.

"This way." Adele laughed with excitement, veering sharply to the left. Another few minutes and Adele rushed into a lesser-used area of the palace and threw open two curtained French windows. A broad terrace spread out before her. She saw men's backs, all of them craning their necks to see something. She heard the sound of wood cracking off wood. She heard the deep chuckling grunts of a man, and the lighter exclamations of a boy. She started to plunge into the crowd of men in uniforms, but Captain Shirazi placed an arm in front of her, and stepped forward.

"Make way for the empress!" he bellowed loudly enough to shatter the glass in the French windows.

Men, both Equatorian and Katangan, turned in shock. The ranks of soldiers slipped aside one by one until finally Adele beheld an unbelievable sight.

Standing on the stone balustrade of the terrace were King Msiri of Katanga and Prince Simon of Bengal. Both of them wore simple duck trousers and no shirts. They faced one another and each held a six-foot-long staff of dark wood. They moved and retreated, slamming the quarter-staffs against one another. High. Low. Low. Back. Parry. Twist. Thrust.

Msiri spun his staff high over his head with a deep laugh, slipping his hands to one end, and sent the length of wood swinging at Simon's knees. Adele nearly shouted in alarm as Simon leapt into the air and drew up his legs so Msiri's staff passed beneath harmlessly. The boy managed to slap his feet back down onto the stone rail, but he teetered off-balance. Msiri laughed and poked Simon's chest with his quarterstaff, and the prince began to topple off the side of the balcony, easily thirty feet above the ground.

Adele cried out.

Msiri turned at her in surprise, and then suddenly realized he was supposed to grab Simon before the boy fell to his likely death. The king's hand snaked out and took Simon's upper arm, pulling him back onto the balustrade.

Simon was wide-eyed, but smiled at Msiri. And the boy laughed. Then he looked at his sister with annoyance. "You threw me off-balance, Adele."

She marched forward and took her brother's wrist, yanking him onto the firm tile balcony. "What are you doing? You could kill yourself!"

"No, no. He's safe enough." Msiri leaned on his quarterstaff leisurely, with ankles crossed.

She glared up at the king. "Is there some reason you are sparring miles above the earth on a thin railing that looks as if it could crumble under your weight?"

Msiri nodded toward Simon. "He suggested it."

"Hardly miles." Simon rolled his eyes. "The bushes are soft down there anyway."

Adele took the quarterstaff from Simon's hand. "Since when am I the one in Alexandria with common sense?"

Msiri knelt, still perched on the rail, and gave a grand smile. "Your Majesty, I assure you, the young prince was quite safe. I would never allow harm to come to mighty Simon. And he's quite skilled at the quarterstaff."

Simon took a proud breath, puffing out his chest. The talisman around his neck sparkled in the sun.

Adele ignored his unspoken boast and said with great seriousness, "Simon, we are due at a ceremony at the War Memorial in an hour. That, above all else, is not a duty to be shirked."

The boy exhaled and put one hand on his head. "Oh. I forgot. I'm sorry, Adele. It won't take me long to get ready."

Msiri intoned, "I deeply apologize, Your Majesty. It is my fault for detaining the boy. Having raised five beautiful and willful daughters, I admit that I enjoy the prince's company. It is as if I've suddenly acquired a son."

Simon grinned.

Adele allowed her bluster to fade. Inclining her head, she pointed out to Msiri, "You are required at the ceremony as well, Majesty."

"I will be there, of course. I am honored to memorialize our brave soldiers."

"Excellent. Thank you." Hefting the wooden staff several times, and studying it with interest, she glanced up at Msiri. Then she slapped the weapon into the king's hand and released it. "An interesting choice of weapon."

Msiri laughed loudly. He laid both quarterstaffs behind his neck and rested his hands easily on the ends. "Curious, Your Majesty? You are reputedly skilled with many weapons. Is the quarterstaff one of them?"

Adele gave him a coquettish flutter of her eyelids. "A lady of proper upbringing does not discuss with which weapons she may kill a gentleman."

Msiri and the soldiers all broke into great peals of laughter. The obviously smitten soldiers parted again as Adele took her waiting brother's curved arm and turned to leave. Shirazi followed, trying to hide a smile.

Msiri pointed his quarterstaff at Simon. "Young prince, I await our rematch."

Simon glanced furtively at Adele. She raised an eyebrow and reached back, snatching one of the staffs from the Katangan king, which she tossed to her brother.

"Not until I can clear my schedule to attend," Adele said. "And I will look favorably on a wager that says my brother will take you."

Msiri nodded with a smile as Adele started off through the admiring troopers with her brother.

Simon's delight made him more animated than usual. He bumped her while walking and muttered, "How did you find me?"

"I'm a witch," Adele replied pleasantly. "There is nowhere you can go where I can't find you, Simon. Such is your lot in life. You'd best get accustomed to it."

"I don't think I can."

She pulled her brother close as the imperial siblings departed the crowded balcony for more important duties.

CHAPTER 12

"You honor us, Majesty." The man bowed and kissed Adele's gloved hand. "We are at your disposal."

"Thank you, Mr. Szigily," the empress replied. "I have the honor to present the Greyfriar."

"A great pleasure, sir." Greyfriar shook the man's hand and Szigily winced.

Adele took Greyfriar's arm and started toward a massive building in the Equatorian style—clean classical façade with Doric columns and eastern domes. It shone with the fading sun in great flashes of colored tile and glass, as well as overlays of gold. "Let me show you the Library of Alexandria."

She could tell Greyfriar's step faltered a bit, although no one else could have possibly noticed. He was staring with awe at the edifice before him as they climbed the stairs to the portico of the cradle of civilization.

Szigily began his practiced speech. "Alexandria was the home to the world's first great library, conceived by Alexander the Great and built by his Ptolemy successors to be a repository for man's classical and ancient knowledge. Alas, it was lost to time and savagery. Construction on this current library was begun in 1937 by Emperor Ismail. Progress was halted in the 1940s during the period of the Choir of Twelve, when religious fanatics dominated the city. However, order and reason were restored in 1952 under Emperor Alexander the Second, and this magnificent building was completed in 1963." The breeze rustled banners that hung from the porch roof two stories above. "We believe that this edifice, like the original library founded by Alexander, serves the purpose of a repository of human knowledge, preserving the greatness of the Earth's cultures in these days when much of our birthright is denied to us by the dark creatures of the north."

The imposing bronze doors were twelve feet high, with panels depicting great scenes of civilization. At eye level was a bas-relief of a crowd of people driving a stake into the heart of an animalistic vampire. Greyfriar ran his hand over the scene as he passed into the coolness of the building.

Inside the vast foyer, the gathered library staff bowed and curtsied as one when the empress entered. Adele motioned for them to rise and slipped the scarf from her head. Her trailing maid, Zarina, relieved her of the scarf as well as her sapphire blue cloak, revealing her magnificent teal gown with fur trim. She noticed that no one was admiring her fashion sense; they were all staring at Greyfriar. Empresses were, apparently, not so rare and wonderful as heroic swordsmen from the bloody north.

Smiling, Adele said, "Mr. Szigily, if you don't mind, I should like to show Greyfriar the reading room myself."

The librarian bowed with a hint of disappointment. "Of course, Majesty. You know the way."

"I do. I feel as if this is my second home. My first home, really." Even the smell of the building comforted Adele. She allowed the head librarian to kiss her hand again, and then she passed along the rank of his staff, nodding to them all, greeting a few by name.

Adele pressed Captain Shirazi's chest and nodded for him to stay where he was. The soldier glowered, but remained in place while she and Greyfriar walked together between stern bronze statues of Alexander the Great and Sultan Muhammad I, and down an intricately tiled passageway lined with paintings of notables in Equatorian history.

Greyfriar leaned down to sniff at her neck. "You've been practicing your geomancy today."

Adele gasped in alarm. "Oh! Is it hurting you? Blast, I had hoped it had dissipated by now."

Greyfriar shook his head, chuckling. "It's very faint, barely a discomfort. Nothing that will interfere with us this evening."

The anticipation in his voice quieted Adele's fears.

Greyfriar looked up at the arching corridor lost in the shadows above the reach of the flickering lamps. "You have a building this large to house your library?"

"Yes. It is the largest library in the world. Scholars come from the world over to study here." She touched his arm. "Including Scotland now."

He laughed as they reached a rich mahogany door marked *Rotunda*.

Adele said, "It's similar to the Reading Room in your British Museum."

"Ah."

"Except . . ." She threw back the door and ushered him into the sun-splashed chamber, a vast circular room with countless rows of tables radiating from a high desk in the center. Dust sparkled in the beams of light streaming in from the sweeping glass dome overhead. On every spot where the eye rested were books. On every wall were books. Thousands. Hundreds of thousands of books.

Greyfriar stood mute. He could hardly look up; he seemed oppressed by the sheer volume, the great weight of books surrounding him. He reached out and seized a desk to steady himself.

"I had no idea," he whispered. "I had no idea."

"It is impressive." Adele took his hand. "Humbling."

"More than humbling. Humiliating." He shook his head. "I just keep thinking of when I showed you my library in Edinburgh. Six books in a trunk. You must've thought I was so pathetic."

"No." Adele put an arm around his waist. "For you to have that library is more incredible and miraculous, even if this were ten times as large. We're humans. This is what we do. We preserve."

He looked down at her in awe. "And you've read all these books?"

Adele laughed loudly, and it reverberated through the hall. "Of course not. No one has read all these books. I suspect there are many here no one has read except the person who wrote it."

Greyfriar took the first book that came to hand. He opened it and stared. "Where is this?"

Adele joined him to see photographs of a busy city street full of carriages and wagons and people. "It looks like Bombay. In India."

"Have you been there?"

"Yes. Many times."

Greyfriar turned the page and studied a photo of a large palace with crowds of people surrounding it. "Where is this?"

"That is Khartoum. South of here."

"Have you been there?"

"Yes." Adele flipped to the book's cover—*Gazetteer and Atlas of Equatoria*. "You'll be hard-pressed to find a spot in this book I haven't been. I'm sure you could find something more interesting to look at."

"What could be more interesting than places where you've been, but I've never seen?"

Adele smiled. "Wait here. I've an idea." She wandered off, studying the shelf markers.

Greyfriar shouted from his spot. "What about Jerusalem? Have you been to Jerusalem?"

"Yes. I had my tenth birthday party there."

"And Constantinople, have you been—"

"Yes!"

"Oh. So have I, actually."

"Well, we have something in common, then. Perhaps we stayed in the same hotel." Adele appeared with a small leather-bound book in her hand. "Probably not. Look what I found."

"Is it a book?"

She stared at him. "No, it's a giraffe. Of course it's a book." She handed it to him and he glanced at the title—*Tramps About Europe and the British Isles*. "It's a travel book published in 1867."

Greyfriar was already deep in study, opening the brown pages carefully. He exhaled sharply in surprise. "It's London! Look, the British Museum!"

Adele shushed him habitually and slid close to his shoulder to look at the grainy photo of the rambling old pile she remembered from her British captivity. "Ah. Your home away from home."

"Do you remember teaching me about Ramses there?"

"I do." He had been so curious then about the artifacts strewn in disarray within the museum. Even though they had been enemies still at that time, she had felt compelled to answer his questions.

"Buckingham Palace." He removed his shaded glasses to see better. "It looks exactly the same."

"Well, the building anyway." Adele could picture cruel Cesare behind one of the many black square windows, and she shuddered. She had seen horrific things inside that palace. "Go to the page I marked."

Greyfriar noticed a slip of paper, and with the concentration of a surgeon, he worked the book open to that page and gave a cry of delight. "Edinburgh! Our castle!"

Adele laughed again at his excitement and squeezed his arm. She regarded the black-and-white picture of fog-shrouded Edinburgh Castle on its jagged stone pedestal looming majestically over the smokestacks of the old wood-and-brick city.

"Now," she said, "that looks the same."

"No." He draped an arm over her shoulder and drew her close. "You aren't there."

Adele leaned against his chest and began to caress one of the brass buttons on his tunic with her finger. "Show me more places you've been."

He held her gaze a moment longer, and then began to turn pages eagerly. "Inverness. I lived there as a boy. My father taught me so many things in the forests and moors around it."

Adele pressed closer to him, trying to ignore the fact that he was talking about hunting humans, and concentrating only on his lingering study of the photo that conjured memories of his beloved father.

Abruptly, he flipped pages and pointed at a map of France. "Brittany. I spent time there."

"As Greyfriar?"

"Oh. Well, yes. But before Greyfriar too." He quickly turned pages. "Ah, Paris. I lived here for many years three hundred years ago. You would have liked Paris."

"But not now?" she chided.

"Doubtful. It's declined considerably."

"Do you know the king there?"

"Yes."

Something in his voice and attitude saddened Adele. "Is the Parisian king an enemy of yours?"

"No. A friend. Or he was." His eyes were focused elsewhere in the past.

Adele touched his sleeve. "I'm sorry. You seem so solitary. I assumed you'd always been so. What's his name?"

"Lothaire."

"Is he a good king? From your point of view."

Greyfriar shook his head slowly. "I don't know. I haven't been to Paris since the Great Killing, and I haven't had any contact with him since he became king. I know Lothaire fought a long struggle with his cousins for the throne. Many of the smaller clans took advantage. So he's not nearly the king his father was." He adjusted the scarf covering his face. "But who is?"

She gently took the book from him. "Let's not think about the past. Or the present. Or anything outside this library. This is our sanctuary. Such things shouldn't intrude here. We won't allow it."

He nodded. "You're right. Show me something else."

His hand in hers, she led him around the vast chamber. "Right now, we're in the history section."

"So much." Greyfriar gazed at the towering shelves filled to the brink with human history.

She didn't linger and moved onto another area. "And these are books on science and medicine."

"Like Randolph's *Treatise on Homo Nosferatii*?"

"Yes, there's a copy here somewhere." Adele's slender fingers slid along the leather folio spines. "Here it is."

Greyfriar pulled the tome carefully from its place and said with wonder, "It is the exact book. And in much better condition than my copy in Edinburgh."

"There were many copies printed. I believe I heard Sir Godfrey boasting the book's print run was around three thousand."

The book dropped from Greyfriar's numb hands. It landed on the floor with a booming thud. "So many copies of just one book?"

"I hate to tell you, but your copy isn't a collector's item," Adele jested as she lifted the book from the floor and set it on a table. Then she answered him earnestly. "Multiple copies allow it to reach more people. A book must be read by many if it is to have its message known."

"Amazing." His eyes were afire with the possibilities and wonder about him. His finger ran along the spines, mimicking Adele's earlier action. He turned toward her suddenly. "Which books do you prefer?"

Adele mused for a moment. "Fiction. Though the court tutors would be aghast at such a thing. They'd much prefer me to relish art history and musical theory."

"Where are your favorites?"

"Here." Adele darted among the rows and he chased after her. She twirled girlishly in a large alcove, her arms gesturing around her. "These are the ones I adore. I sometimes had to sneak a book from here and read it in the chemistry section so they thought I was studying."

"So you read them in secret?"

She blushed. "Yes. Like you."

Greyfriar caught her up in a swift embrace, and together they stared at the volumes around them. "May I see one of them?"

"Of course, silly." She climbed a ladder to the top shelves. The book she chose was a very large dusty volume, so he climbed up to help her.

"What is it?" he asked.

"An illustrated book of fairy tales."

"Fairy tales," he said. "Stories of make-believe. I have a book full of them in Edinburgh."

"Yes, I remember. Tales of monsters, beasts, heroism, magic, redemption, and true love." She ran a finger along the line of his chin hidden beneath the scarf. "But fairy tales also warn of evil deeds and dark thoughts to scare you onto the path of good and pure."

"So they are lessons meant to teach?"

"Yes, cloaked in a fanciful story." Adele's tug on his cloak ended with a reverent caress.

"Do we have time to read one?" He guided her to a chair.

They didn't really. The empress had a late conference with the prime minister, but that could wait.

"Of course," she replied, taking a seat. Greyfriar perched on the arm of the leather chair and stared eagerly as she opened the book. Inside was a glorious painting of two beautiful young girls, one with raven hair and one blonde, standing face-to-face with a horrifying bear.

Adele began to spin the tale of Snow-White and Rose-Red. These two sisters helped everyone, even a miserly evil dwarf who would just as soon have sacrificed them to a terrifying bear to save his own hide.

"The evil creature pled, 'Sir Bear, I beg you, do not kill me. Rather here are two young girls, easy to catch and delicious! You should make them your meal!' The bear was not moved by the dwarf's hateful claims, and used his mighty paw to clout the evil creature on the head. The miserable little man fell to the ground dead.

"Snow-White and Rose-Red ran away through the forest, afraid that the bear would eat them. The bear chased after the two girls, but he offered them no danger. He called out: 'Snow-White and Rose-Red, please do not run from me. I would never do you harm. Listen to my words and know the truth.' The two sisters listened to him and stopped in their flight. When the bear came near, his coat of fur dropped away to reveal a beautiful young man in golden armor. 'I am the prince of this land. The evil dwarf took from me my treasure and then cursed me to walk the land as a ferocious bear. Now he is dead and the curse is lifted.'

"Snow-White fell in love with the prince and they were married. Her sister Rose-Red was wed to his brother. The vast treasure they split between them, and they brought their old mother to live with them. She dug holes for the two rose vines outside her window so that she could see the beautiful white roses and red roses when they bloomed each and every year."

"The frightening bear was really a prince," Greyfriar observed.

Adele nodded with a broad smile. "Yes."

He stared at the elaborate illustration of the bear shedding his animal skin to become a prince. "The story could be about me."

"Would that make Cesare the wicked dwarf?" They both laughed at that comical image.

Greyfriar played with an auburn curl. "It seems you read a great deal about monsters. No wonder you weren't frightened of me in Edinburgh."

"Oh I was frightened, though maybe more angry. When I found out Greyfriar was really a vampire, it was . . . devastating. Of course, I didn't truly know Gareth then. If you shed your Greyfriar guise, I would marry you, bear or not."

Greyfriar's finger froze on her forearm, and he looked down at her quickly. She swallowed the lump in her throat, but didn't regret her words. They were the truth.

He leaned in to kiss her, leaving the scarf in place, pressing against her with a layer of rough cloth between their lips. "For that alone, I love you. The skin of a bear or man makes no difference to you."

Adele deepened the kiss. "I will never stop believing there is a future for us."

"I love that too about you."

"Something you won't love is that I have to return to the real world. I'm sorry."

"Don't be. Some things cannot be denied."

Adele moved away with a lingering touch and was collecting the books to place neatly on the front desk. When she saw Sir Godfrey's anatomy book, she turned to Greyfriar, who was examining the librarian's desk. "May I ask you something?"

"Of course."

"Something personal."

His blue eyes regarded her. "Ask."

Her hand on the vampire book, she said, "What would happen if we . . . made love? Is it dangerous?"

"Dangerous? I would never hurt you."

She held up her hands, red-faced. "Oh I know. That's not what I meant at all. I'm talking about the potential for . . . pregnancy. Can vampires and humans . . ." Adele gave an embarrassed sigh.

"Ah. There have been instances of humans and vampires . . . copulating."

"Really?"

"Not out of affection, I assure you. The less said the better, but it has occurred. No children have ever been conceived to my knowledge." Greyfriar pointed at Randolph's *Treatise*. "In here, as you must know, Dr. Randolph says vampires are a different species. We could never bear children together."

"Never?" Adele frowned.

"Is that what you are afraid of? I have never asked about your hesitation with our relationship because your reasons are your own. But is that the reason?"

"Yes, partly. I remember the stories you told me about vampire babies killing their mothers by feeding off them. Like Cesare killed his mother."

"Yes, it happens. Some mothers, particularly modern ones, use human bloodnurses rather than allow their infants to feed from them. Out of fear."

"How does that happen exactly? I thought vampires couldn't feed from another vampire."

"Mothers are able to nourish their newborns. There is some change in the mother, but only for a few months. Then the child must switch to human blood." Greyfriar held out his hands to show the issue was settled. "That isn't something you need to worry about."

Adele bit her lower lip. "Pregnancy isn't my only concern. I'm afraid of what I could do to you. I'm a geomancer. There are times I don't feel in control."

"If you haven't killed me by now, I suspect I'm safe enough. But it must always be your decision."

"You do still want me?" Adele asked hesitantly, her mind filling with foolish fears.

He covered the space between them in seconds, standing over her, his cobalt eyes intensifying. "Yes, but I won't let my desire push you into something you do not want. You have enough people trying to force their will on you. I know you are not a woman easily pushed. We are both standing on a dangerous precipice, and caution is a wise watchword."

Unexpectedly, Greyfriar tore the scarf from his face, pulled her close, and kissed her.

She went limp in his arms, pressing against him. Command radiated from his body, but his grip was as delicate as if he held a glass figurine in his steady hands. She never tired of being in his sway. It was like being held by steel and silk all at the same time.

"Thank you," he whispered. "For the library."

"You're welcome," she returned softly. That he was so moved by this small gesture caught her breath in her throat. She held him in an embrace a moment longer, almost afraid to let go.

Greyfriar glanced longingly at the stack of books.

"Would you like to stay longer?" Adele asked.

"No. You no doubt have pressing matters. And we'll see each other tomorrow night for the opera." He patted the cover of the fairy tale tome. "It's just been a long time since I felt closer to Greyfriar than Gareth."

"We can come back whenever you like."

He turned from the table and took her arm. Together, they started up the aisle sweeping between long curving tables with their great stores of books. His cloak furled out behind them. Greyfriar's light steps made no sound and Adele's footsteps echoed loudly off the tile floor as they leaned on one another.

CHAPTER 13

"GRENOBLE HAS FALLEN to the humans," Lady Hallow announced to the figure that stood beside the throne. Her words echoed in the huge chamber, and settled unpleasantly to the filthy floor.

Cesare grasped the back of the empty throne and spat angrily, "On the eve of my coronation? Is our war strategy ruined now?"

Hallow drifted to one side to ensure the question struck fully on Flay, who stood in the shadows behind her. The war chief snarled in her throat.

"All was going as planned," Flay said quickly. "We of course had no control over the situation at Grenoble, as that clan had refused your advances. However, I had the Equatorians pinned down at St. Etienne, unable to advance or safely withdraw. I asked Lady Hallow for additional packs, with which I could have broken the humans' backs. Those packs did not materialize."

Lady Hallow ignored the accusations and added with a sarcastic tone, "The refugees from Grenoble say the Equatorians unleashed a weapon of unspeakable power."

"Nonsense," Cesare scoffed. "The man who builds all of Equatoria's weapons is my creature. They have nothing we don't know about."

"It was the princess," Flay said.

Hallow sighed loudly and strolled farther to the side.

Cesare stepped down from the dais, his attention riveted on Flay. "The princess? You mean Empress Adele?"

"Yes, my lord." The war chief came closer. The subject of Adele was something that she and Cesare shared; Hallow had no part in that history. "She was the weapon that killed the Grenoble clan."

Hallow said, "My lord, I don't believe such a ludicrous—"

"Stryon!" Cesare called, and his bailiff peered into the room. "Bring my witchfinder. Bring him. Now!"

Flay smiled.

Dr. Goronwy was virtually thrust into Cesare's conference chamber. The human's white hair and beard were uncharacteristically ill-kempt. He wore a long robe thrown over his ankle-length nightshirt, and had lost a slipper somewhere in the long damp trek from Bethlem on the south side of the Thames.

Members of the Pale, Cesare's personal militia, filtered into the room, having dragged the human to Buckingham Palace. Flay was relieved by their presence since she was their commander, and they tilted the atmosphere from political to military.

Goronwy blinked in the deep gloom relieved only by faint moonlight filtering through great windows. "This all seems quite urgent."

"I am told," Cesare said slowly, "that the Equatorian empress killed every vampire in Grenoble. Over ten thousand. By herself. Is that possible?"

"My, my," Goronwy muttered in his thick Welsh accent, "that is news that would startle you, isn't it? Could we possibly find a candle or something? It's so dark I can hardly think straight."

"Answer the question," Cesare snarled.

"Well, the answer is I don't know. As an academic, I'm bound to lean on facts, and not opinion. If I still had my Equatorian colleague, Dr. Selkirk, with whom to consult, I might be able to formulate a better answer."

"You had him for a month. What did you learn from him?"

"Most of it I've told you already," Goronwy began, settling into his role as professor. "Dr. Selkirk believed that the princess has some unique skills to understand certain natural phenomena . . . phenomena described by the science of geomancy. The study of the Earth. It is poorly understood, but seems linked to human proclivities to establish meaningful connections to the natural world through science or meditation or prayer. In the old days, when humans would pray, at least some humans, it created effluences that repelled your kind."

"Just answer the question!" Flay shouted.

Dr. Goronwy reared back in offense at Flay's outburst. Then he adjusted his dressing gown. "Yes. If what Dr. Selkirk believed is true. I have studied his notes, and the books you have provided to me from various Alexandrian authorities. Theoretically, it is possible. But, to me, it seems quite far-fetched that she could actually manage such energies."

Cesare growled and began to stalk the room. Hallow slid away from him. Flay watched her prince tread through streams of moonlight, muttering angrily to himself. Then, in midstride, he broke off and walked up to Goronwy, staring directly at the man.

"Witchfinder, can you do anything to stop the empress?"

"Stop her?" Goronwy asked uncomfortably. He obviously wanted to back away from Cesare, but that would prove he was being threatened rather than simply consulted. "She's merely human. You could kill her."

A clawed hand raked Goronwy and drew blood. "Don't toy with me."

The wide-eyed witchfinder pressed his palm against his bleeding cheek. "Oh! You mean her geomancy. I don't know. I suppose there might be a way to counteract her abilities."

"Find it."

"It's a very complicated scientific matter, my lord. Pure research can't simply be converted into a practical tool just like that. If I might just explain the place of research in most modern nation-states, there may be years between fundamental discoveries and practical applications, if any."

"If I might explain the place of research in my state—do it or I'll kill you." Cesare stared evenly at the Welshman. "And if you say another word besides *Yes, my lord*, I will slice you open and leave you to bleed to death on this floor while the clan feeds off you."

Goronwy glanced from Cesare to Flay. "Yes, my lord."

"Good," the vampire prince said, stepping away from the man. "You have until my coronation to understand what the Equatorian empress is doing, and give me something to stop her."

"Yes, my lord."

"Excellent." Cesare turned to Flay, who stiffened expectantly. "Flay, return to Lyon and block the humans from advancing further."

Flay bowed. "Then I should expect new packs?"

"You'll use what I give you!" Cesare yelled violently, his fists quivering in the air. "Keep the humans trapped in the Rhone Valley no matter what it takes. You will do what I tell you. I am your king! Do you understand me?"

"Yes, my lord." Flay could almost see a smug grin even on Hallow's blank face. "I will always obey my king."

The war chief watched her prince and his advisor pass her as they walked together out of the room into the corridor, joined in significant conversation, much like Flay used to do with Cesare. She stood in the empty chamber listening to the wail of wind through broken glass.

CHAPTER 14

"THE OPERA IS in Italian," Adele said over the sound of the clattering carriage. "But I can explain it to you."

"*Capisco l'italiano*," Gareth replied.

"Okay." She stared evenly at him in the dim light. "How many languages do you speak anyway?"

He thought. "I'm not sure. Twenty? It depends on what you consider a language. In the north, dialects vary greatly from region to region, even from village to village in some areas. My Italian is northern. But even usage in Savoy can be very different from Lombardy. I've never been south of Milan. Very few vampires have. Have you ever been to Rome?"

"Yes. Several times." Adele was suddenly less than satisfied with her languages—English, Persian, Arabic, Swahili, and French, as well as some familiarity in several northern tongues such as Italian and German, and snippets of a few extinct sacred languages. She was facile with languages, or so she had thought until she witnessed Gareth. He had picked up very nuanced Arabic from a single boat ride up the Nile. His absorption of human languages was remarkable, and typical of his kind. However, she did have one untold secret tongue, a singular ability to rival his own.

Gareth was in the midst of asking a question. "Does Rome . . ."

"Ask your question in your own language."

"My language?" He looked at her with suspicion. "What do you mean?"

"Your vampiric language."

He smiled slightly and nodded. "Ah. I wasn't even sure your people knew we had a language."

"Most of us don't. We tend to think you just hiss, like cats. But some of us know differently. So ask your question."

Gareth laughed and then growled deep in his throat and almost spit as he pulled and pushed sibilant air over his palate. Still, his hands gestured conversationally, as if he was chatting over dinner.

"No," Adele said. "Rome is not part of the Empire. In fact, none of the Italian states are, nor do they care to participate in the war. Yet."

Gareth's eyes widened in shock, and his mouth hung open. "You understood me."

She grinned in acknowledgment.

He asked, "How long have you understood our language?"

"Since I heard it spoken in France, when *Ptolemy* was downed. I'm never sure I'm understanding it properly, but I get a sense of what is being said. Of course, if several of you are talking at the same time or there is too much distraction, I can't follow it."

Gareth pursed his lips in thought. "I hope I never said anything untoward within earshot."

Adele laughed loudly. "No. I don't recall anything insulting. In fact, you hardly ever speak vampire." She reached out to him. "I'm sorry for keeping the secret so long."

"On the contrary, you shouldn't have told me now. We're still leaders of rival houses. Don't give away all of your secrets to me."

She grew serious, and her face clouded. "But we're together. We shouldn't keep secrets from one another."

Gareth considered her words in thoughtful silence.

"Why?" she pressed. "Do you have secrets you're keeping from me?"

"No. But you're different. You must protect yourself from any eventuality. I don't matter."

She eyed him with mock suspicion, trying to play it off as a joke, but even so, some of the hurt was real. "I'm not sure I can believe you. Perhaps you're lying to me now to cover your secrets."

"Perhaps, but I'm not." Then he blurted, "No, I do have one last secret. My true name."

"*Gareth* isn't even your name?"

"It is. But my kind are born with a name in our language. We don't use it; it's secret. We believe that knowing someone's true name gives you power over them. At least, that's the tradition; it's largely forgotten now."

Adele sat quietly watching the reflection of her diamond tiara sparkling from its place atop her rigidly ordered curls. She tapped her fan against her knee.

His brow wrinkled in question. "Shall I tell you?"

"No," she answered.

"I will happily tell you."

"No, don't."

"Why?" Shadows flashed across his angular face as light from passing streetlamps slipped through the edges of drawn shades.

"I don't ever want to know the last mystery about you," she replied softly.

"As you wish." Greyfriar smiled and laid a steady hand over her nervous fan. "At least you'll know that the power you have over me has nothing to do with my name."

The muffled din of cheering from outside increased, and the clomping of the mounted columns of White Guard around the carriage grew louder. A colored card showed on the wall, triggered by the footman riding outside to indicate they were nearing the opera house. Adele searched her small clutch for a mirror and checked her make-up. "How do I look?"

"Magnificent."

"Thank you." She smoothed the lap of her gown. "I used to hate dressing up. And I wouldn't want to do it every day, but I quite enjoy it now. Maybe because I have someone to do it for." She glanced up at him.

"It suits you. You carry yourself like an empress. And you do attract my attention, though vampires are always drawn to high fashion naturally."

His deep laugh calmed any last nerves as the carriage rocked to a stop. There was a whistle at Adele's side and she picked up a small speaking tube. The footman's voice came from outside, "Are you prepared, Your Majesty?"

"Yes, Gregor. You may proceed."

The carriage door swung wide and the blare of countless trumpets filled the air. Greyfriar stepped out to screams of excitement. He paused at the foot of the steps and turned to offer his hand to the glittering empress. The footman posed with mute annoyance as Greyfriar handed Adele down to the red-carpeted walkway, which extended across the sidewalk and up the many steps to the portico of the Grand Macedon Opera House where a line of brass horns blew an earsplitting welcome.

Adele appeared in a pale yellow gown, accented in magenta. It showed her olive complexion to wonderful effect. The skirt was voluminous, but her waist and bodice were tight, and sparkled with intricate gem work. Her strong shoulders were bare under a magenta silk stole, appropriate for single women, if daring for an empress. Long opera gloves above the elbows completed the elegant ensemble.

Adele glided up the steps with a grace that thrilled her; managing vast gowns had always been a challenge. Greyfriar followed just behind her shoulder, scanning their surroundings constantly, an all-seeing sentinel. Her White Guard stood at attention, lining her path. Captain Shirazi acknowledged her with a brief nod before returning to his duty.

On the portico, she turned with a brilliant smile to wave at the multitudes, most of whom would never set foot inside the Grand Macedon in their lifetimes. Adults held children aloft to catch a glimpse of their empress and her mysterious companion.

Adele then entered the vast building of sparkling chandeliers, bold mosaics, marbled columns, dark but intricately carved woodwork, and a veritable jungle of green plants in massive pots and cisterns. There facing her across the spacious lobby was the interminable greeting line of tuxedoes, gowns, uniforms, and veils.

With her secretary at her side to announce names, the empress passed down the line, shaking hands, acknowledging bows and curtsies, secretly delighted as all eyes locked on Greyfriar, who went with her but did not acknowledge anyone, like a guardian angel or vengeful spirit.

Adele paused to speak to the two blue-haired colossi of the Phoenix Society. Lady Tahir was accompanied by a devilishly handsome young man who did not bear a family resemblance. Mrs. General Alfred Cornwell (ret.) was with her husband, the grey-whiskered General Cornwell, whose head quavered slightly, but who was resplendent in a uniform adorned with medals of the Burmese Campaign.

"General," Adele said, "most delighted to see you. I have the frequent opportunity to greet your wife, but I believe I have yet to make your esteemed acquaintance."

"Thank you, Majesty," the old gentleman replied briefly, then stopped talking, which caused his wife to smile, but when he opened his mouth again, her eyes flew wide in alarm. "And may I say, as a military man, well done in Grenoble!"

"Thank you, General."

He carried on in a muttering baritone. "I daresay those boys gave the vampires what for when you showed up, let them know what they're fighting for, so to speak."

Mrs. General Alfred Cornwell (ret.) went ashen, horrified that her husband had just referred to the empress as some sort of barracks pinup, giving the boys at the front a bit of home. She touched the general's ribboned sleeve and tittered nervously, signaling that his time with the monarch was at an end.

"And, if I may," he persisted, pointing a knobby finger at the delicate young empress, "all the chaps at the Polo Club are bully for you. Every man jack of us wishes he'd been at Grenoble." He clenched a quivering fist and flecked his bushy mustache with emotional spittle. "If only I wasn't so blasted old! I'd join up in a second!"

Mrs. General Alfred Cornwell (ret.) was breathing raggedly from the fear that her hard-earned position in society had been undone in a few blustery words from her demented husband. Lady Tahir, who typically was so attached to the general's wife that they finished one another's sentences, subtly turned herself away in order to distance her social status from the plummeting stock of her former friend.

Adele took the old general's rough hand. "We thank you for your kind words, General. We wish you were able to be at Grenoble as well. Your service to our father is sufficient to earn you praise and rest. If the men of the army in Europe are half the men you and your comrades were in Burma, we daresay the vampires stand no chance."

General Cornwell's lip quivered until he tightened his jaw manfully. He bowed deeply to her.

Adele looked at the confused Mrs. General Alfred Cornwell (ret.). "And the women behind our men at the front are what make Equatoria the great empire it is. We thank you for your service." She then glanced at the equally confused Lady Tahir and said with an impeccable straight face, "And your ladyship, I am so glad to see you with your son."

"My . . . son? Oh yes! Quite!"

Adele moved on to receive the remainder of Alexandrian society. She tried to hurry so the opera could begin. *The Greyfriar* was reputed to be an epic of more than four hours. It had been slated originally to premiere in the autumn, but the outbreak of war made it seem temporarily frivolous. So the season was put off until the empress gave permission for social life in the capital to begin again. The delay gave the creators of the show time to add an unprecedented fifth act in which Greyfriar leads Equatoria to victory in the vampire war.

At the end of the receiving line was the director of the Imperial Opera Company, who greeted Adele, then led her and Greyfriar to the door of the royal box. Soldiers were positioned outside along with Adele's social secretary with her agenda. The door opened, and she heard an expectant hush from the house. As she entered, the crowd rose, turned toward her expectantly, and applauded. Adele went to the curved rail of the box high above the sea of people and acknowledged the uproar.

"God save Your Majesty!" came a shout above the din.

There was an audible rush of surprise at the exclamation. Adele looked for the source, but it was lost in the shadows. That outburst would be in the papers tomorrow, she thought. A public expression of faith, even at so bland an event, was cause for comment. Add to that her reputation as a religious acolyte, and it would become a topic of pointless debate across the coffeehouses and tearooms of the city, as well as the cloakrooms at Commons.

Gratefully, for the moment, the crowd was instantly distracted by the appearance of Greyfriar at her side. Opera glasses snapped up to multitudes of faces as men and women sought a closer view of the mystery man.

Adele kept her expression neutral and settled into her seat. Greyfriar joined her, and the director handed them both hardcover copies of the evening's program with an unctuous, "We fervently hope you enjoy the production."

"We're sure we will since the program is already a hit," Adele replied as Greyfriar pored over the pages of the playbill, taking great care to turn the fragile paper with his gloved hands. "Well, shall we get started?"

"Indeed. I should hate for the war to conclude before the opera." The director laughed but noticed the deadpan look on the empress's face. He sobered instantly and straightened with a look of terror at his faux pas. "We shall begin momentarily." He withdrew, bowing until the door was shut by soldiers, leaving Adele and Greyfriar alone with only several thousand of Equatoria's elite looking on.

The Grand Macedon was a lush and magnificent venue, larger than Algier's La Premiere, but considered a second to it still. Two levels of ornate private boxes along the sides and two balconies in the rear overlooked the floor that sloped toward the orchestra, where the conductor was mounting the step behind his podium. An audible hush swept the hall as the maestro tapped his baton, then raised it. Held it. And down it came with a thunderous percussion beginning the prelude. House lights began to drop. Conversations in the private boxes wound down with handshakes and waves and promises to speak later.

Adele saw Greyfriar scanning the theater, but not out of concern for security. He was clearly fascinated by the melee around him, the movement and the sound. He rose from his seat for a clearer view of the orchestra as rows of arms pistoned in unison over violins and many fingers played piccolos and oboes.

"Look at that," he said in wonder. "Look at their hands. They're all moving in harmony."

"Shh." Adele gently guided him back to his velvet chair. She took his hand and squeezed. With his other hand, he was mimicking the fretwork of the violinists. She couldn't draw her gaze away from him, caught up in his excitement and wonder.

The prelude thundered on with dramatic crescendos, achingly beautiful passages, and hints of darkness. After a few minutes, the music calmed, the footlights brightened, the grand drapes parted, and the curtain scalloped up to reveal characters spread about the stage on a stylized set resembling the deck of an airship. A rosy spotlight hit a young woman in a regal gown and cloak.

Greyfriar sat forward. "Is that you?"

"Yes," Adele replied, and then suppressed a delighted squeal as a man wearing a martinet's uniform and turban came downstage toward the beatific princess. "It's General Anhalt!"

The music rose and the actor portraying Anhalt extended his arm and sang in Italian, "Your Highness would be safer below. It's getting dark. Vampires are very unpredictable."

—◦◦◦—

Greyfriar laughed a bit too loud as Act II began with Cesare alone onstage. The villain was a massive figure, broad chested, swathed in black and, like all the vampires in the production, brandishing long yellowish claws from his fingertips. He also sported a long black beard. He said, "Looks a bit like Senator Clark."

Adele had to stifle a guffaw behind her fan.

Gareth scanned the cast list. "Where is Senator Clark? Isn't he in this show?"

"No. They never use him in plays about us. He complicates the plot."

Gareth laughed again.

The onstage Cesare began to sing in a rumbling growl, "Behold, I am Cesare. I am the death of humankind. Bring me Princess Adele."

Flay entered stage left, a tall beautiful woman with long black hair, clad in black robes. Princess Adele followed with her hands chained but her head unbowed. Other vampires, all in black, crouched or scurried around the stage, up and down the backdrop, in and out of torchlight. It was an extraordinarily disturbing effect and gave the real Adele chills to watch.

Cesare launched into an aria about vampires and their destruction of human culture in the north. It was a boastful, arrogant litany of vampire successes, not at all untrue, if a bit long. The scuttling vampires around him provided a mournful, unsettling chorus.

Greyfriar asked, "Where's Gareth? Just Cesare?"

Adele whispered, "There's no Gareth."

"I'm not important?"

"No one knows Gareth . . . yet. They know Cesare. And Flay. They're the villains. And besides, the opera is named after you. *The Greyfriar*. That's you."

"Is it?"

Adele turned toward him. "Isn't it?"

He stared at the stage.

———

Act III drove forward with Princess Adele about to be sacrificed before the gathered British vampire clan. The proud young woman stood surrounded by black-clad figures, including the smug Cesare and sinister Flay. The princess sang a sad call to Greyfriar, whom she believed dead.

"Is Greyfriar even still in this play?" Greyfriar complained impatiently. "Where have I gone?"

Adele rolled her eyes and slapped his fidgeting leg with her fan. "Did you ever think the princess could save herself? She may not need a man to do it."

"Then why call it *The Greyfriar*?" he muttered. "All these people paid money for this. I'd be upset if I had paid money for *The Greyfriar* to hear this much Cesare singing."

Suddenly the princess's aria drew to a bittersweet end. As Cesare and Flay closed in around her, a trumpet cried, a spotlight shot out onto a black-cloaked vampire who threw off his shadowy raiment to reveal he was the Greyfriar. Mayhem ensued as Greyfriar fought to reach the princess.

The real Greyfriar gripped his chair arms with excitement.

Adele said, "There, you see. He was disguised as a vampire." She paused. "How odd."

The operatic swordsman engaged Flay in a choreographed battle. They moved across the stage and back, leaping, spinning, and twirling with admirable athleticism. Although it was a fight to the death, it was an impressive ballet with two figures, man and woman, closing, touching, and drawing apart.

Adele sat back in the royal box with an annoyed huff at the almost erotic dance between two characters, but it was Greyfriar and Flay, not the princess. She watched the two colliding, pushing off, lingering together with deep emotional stares. Greyfriar's rapt attention on the duo below added to her aggravation.

Finally, onstage, Greyfriar struck down Flay and turned on Cesare. The evil prince threw his cape over his face and fled, vanishing into shadows. Swordsman and princess came together in a crescendo and began a song of love and redemption.

It was nice, but it lacked the passion and physicality of the ballet with Flay. There had been a raw emotion between the two rivals that was lacking in the traditionally proper lovers of Greyfriar and the princess. Not at all satisfying to Adele. The authors had missed the mark.

After their song, Greyfriar and the princess raced from the stage to make their escape from London. In the imperial box, Adele was ready to stand for the traditional intermission, but the music shifted into something new. A spot fell on the body of Flay, and the vampire slowly rose to her feet.

Flay began the most beautiful and horrifying aria that Adele had ever heard. It was full of passion and heartache and rage. Flay expressed her hatred for the princess, which Adele found enjoyable. Then the aria shifted again and Flay dropped to her knees, and wailed that she loved Greyfriar. They could never be together because of the fact that they were enemies. Flay knew Greyfriar was good and pure and true, something she dreamed but could never be. Flay's last wrenching note faded into tears.

The curtain dropped on the act. Adele's cheeks were wet and she realized she had crushed her fan in her fist.

—◦◦◦—

The hours passed and characters came and went across the stage. Finally, the armies of Equatoria surrounded the unassailable walls of a London castle, leaving only Cesare and his chief weapon, Flay, trapped. Greyfriar volunteered to enter the villains' lair, even though it was likely he would be killed. He couldn't bear for one more soldier to die if he could prevent it. With him standing alone, the grotesque set piece for Cesare's castle settled to the stage around him. It was physically disturbing. The lines were uneven. Doors were crooked. Floors slanted. It was disorienting to the audience.

Adele whispered, "So you're going to win the war all by yourself? Where am I?"

"Shh," he replied. "It is called *The Greyfriar.*"

She was prepared to say something disgruntled when a burst of sound from the orchestra heralded the appearance of Flay onstage, who attacked the hero. Cesare appeared up from out of a trapdoor in the black floor, delivering a nightmarish aria above the struggle.

"Typical," Greyfriar muttered. "Singing while others fight."

When the stage swordsman was pushed close to Cesare by Flay, the vampire prince struck and drove Greyfriar to the floor, and his sword went flying. Flay rose up in clawed triumph, preparing for the death blow, singing that if she could never have him, no one would. Cesare bellowed a deep resounding note that rang for a long moment, then ceased abruptly in a gunshot.

Flay clutched her heart and fell.

The young empress appeared from the wings with a smoking revolver.

Cesare exclaimed in surprise, and Greyfriar leapt to his feet, drew a dagger, and raised it over his head. He plunged it into Cesare's chest while singing, "I strike for humanity. And thus humanity triumphs!"

The real Greyfriar suddenly twisted away from the stage. Adele reached out her hand, and he gratefully grasped it.

As the stage swordsman and empress joined hands and sang their final love duet, the army of Equatoria entered and surrounded them. The cast finale was rousing and patriotic, for country, for flag, for empress.

For humanity.

The curtain dropped. Adele was watching the troubled Greyfriar when she realized the theater was in silence. She looked down confused to see all faces glowing toward her. Waiting.

She rose and began to clap. The audience responded in kind, standing as a body, with thunderous applause. Cheers rang out. Greyfriar joined her, mimicking the act of clapping his hands.

"What happened to you at the end?" she asked him. "Why did you turn away?"

"I killed my brother."

Adele turned to him. "I thought you want to kill Cesare?"

He continued to clap with his hidden eyes focused on the cast on stage. The masked swordsman below whipped off his disguise. "I don't want to. I will have to. And I won't do it as Greyfriar."

"We are scheduled to meet the cast, but we can simply go, if you'd prefer."

"No. They worked hard. They deserve to see their empress." Greyfriar's chin bobbed with a sarcastic huff. "And the great hero of their people."

CHAPTER

As THE AUDIENCE cheered at the couple in the high box seat, Empress Adele waved politely, her bright smile visible for all to see, the infamous Greyfriar stoically beside her. The ever-present mask and glasses prevented the crowd from seeing what emotion the show might have generated in the dark swordsman.

Sanah adjusted her dark plum silk burqa, the same one she had worn to the play where she'd first met Adele, and idly wondered how long the empress intended to play such a dangerous game with the vampire prince. Eventually the truth would come out. Already more people knew than should.

Sanah couldn't contemplate the idea of touching a living vampire with the intention of anything other than violence. Inwardly, she shuddered. Mamoru was convinced the Greyfriar was using Adele for some nefarious and deeper purpose. Of course that was the case. What else could it be? No vampire in the thousands of years they existed had ever looked at a human without bloodlust in its eyes. Why would this one be any different?

However, none of this was Sanah's primary concern tonight. She was here for only one purpose. When Mamoru told about Adele's doubt, it reminded Sanah of another woman who had stood in her place once. Although Mamoru guided Adele spiritually, someone was needed to assist the empress in other things, things that only another woman or even a relative could understand. Perhaps if Adele had that additional guiding hand, matters wouldn't seem so confusing to the young woman.

The packed theater emptied out into the lobby, where a receiving line formed awaiting the return of the empress and her consort. Much to her consternation, Sanah was shuffled to the end of it. But she knew the empress would make time for all. A side door opened, and the White Guard emerged and moved with precision through the crowd, forming a path along the red carpet. Finally, in the close air of the crowded lobby, Empress Adele and Greyfriar emerged from the heavy doors to the polite adulation of gathered high society. People packed in tighter, but Sanah would not be moved or shoved past. Her dark contoured eyes locked onto Adele and pierced her sharply.

Adele paused from her cursory scan of the long line with her brilliant smile and tracked back to settle on Sanah. Her brow creased as she attempted to place the familiar woman. Sanah lifted a henna-covered hand in greeting, hoping to convey a memory, and closed her eyes to show the tattooed eyelids that stared at Adele from across the room. When Sanah opened them, Adele's eyes were wide in sudden recognition.

Abruptly, Adele excused herself from her place along the greeting line and left many shocked and indignant expressions on the grandees, including Lady Tahir, as she walked to the end and stood before Sanah.

The Persian blushed behind her veil and curtsied. "Your Majesty."

"So you did make it to the premiere. As you said when we met last year."

"I wouldn't miss it," Sanah replied.

"I thought you might have recognized me that night."

"I admit, I did. I remember fondly our talk during the production of *Desire in the Dead North*.

Adele laughed out loud. "My art of disguise is awful, apparently." She stepped aside. "May I introduce the real Greyfriar. Now you can see why no imitation would do."

Sanah curtsied again and fought the urge to step back from what she knew lurked behind the cowled face. "Sir."

The tall figure nodded in a semblance of politeness, his tone almost bored. "A pleasure."

Knowing she didn't have much time with the empress's attention, Sanah grasped Adele's hand and slipped her a card. "We have much to talk about, Your Majesty. I knew your mother."

"My mother?" Adele's expression was one of surprise. "May I ask your name?"

"It is written on the card along with my address. Send for me when you do not have more pressing matters to attend and we can talk more privately about her."

"I shall. Thank you." Adele allowed herself to be directed back to the receiving line, with a lingering glance over her shoulder at the Persian woman.

Sanah watched Adele return to the far end of the lobby where the expectant crowd waited to bestow their curtsies and salaams on the empress. Suddenly Greyfriar stiffened sharply. He shoved Adele aside and went for his sword. It released from its scabbard with a hissing scrape and then sang as Greyfriar spun around. The blade moved in a precise arc and struck a man in an ill-fitting tailcoat. It drew the barest amount of blood, but the coat burst open and something from his chest fell forward, straps dangling.

"Bomb!" a White Guard shouted.

People screamed around Sanah. Greyfriar was still in motion. He grabbed the device that had been strapped to the man's chest and flung it away. Then he grabbed Adele and shoved her to the floor, covering her with his own body.

The massive blast shook the establishment, filling the air with a sound so loud it punched Sanah in the chest as she was flung backward. The buzzing of a thousand angry hornets filled the air along with a sudden fierce flash that blinded her. Then everything went silent.

Smoke filled the high ceiling hall in a rolling wave. Sanah's eyes stung and watered, making it hard to see Adele or Greyfriar. Blood and wreckage were everywhere along with the palsied motions of the wounded and dying. Glittering crystal fluttered in the air as slivers of glass from an obliterated chandelier fluttered down like snow. Any sound was buried under a high-pitched whine inside Sanah's head.

She struggled to her unsteady feet and saw the still form of Adele, covered by the bloody body of the vampire. Jagged shrapnel fragments lay imbedded in Greyfriar's back. He looked dead. Mamoru had his wish finally. However, they might have lost the empress along with him.

Sanah watched in awe as Greyfriar stirred, raising himself on arms that shook. Blood flowed from multiple wounds. He grabbed a semiconscious Adele, and for a panicked moment Sanah thought he was going to feed on her to save his miserable life. She shouted to a stunned White Guard captain who was rushing in from outside at the head of a line of troopers, but her voice was ragged and useless against the smoke.

Then, to Sanah's astonishment, the vampire called for help, cradling the dazed empress. His mask still hid most of his face, so she could not see his expression, but there was despair in his voice, so different from the cold greeting of just moments before.

"The empress!" he rasped. "Here!"

A young blond corporal from the White Guard grasped Greyfriar's arm as the captain and two other soldiers tended Adele. "You're hurt, sir."

"Forget about me! Help her!" The swordsman shoved aside the aid and attempted to stand.

"Yes, sir. But you are a priority too."

Greyfriar hunched over on one knee, trying to shake off the weakness. "There may be more bombs. We need to get her to safety."

"We will," the White Guardsman insisted, grabbing hold of the Greyfriar's arm. The soldiers already had Adele and were carrying her out of the theater. The empress twisted in the arms of the captain and turned back to the vampire, determined not to leave him behind. Greyfriar gained his feet with the assistance of the corporal, and at Adele's frantic urging, followed her outside.

Sanah stood staring after them, having a hard time comprehending the vampire's actions.

The creature had saved Adele with no thought of his own safety. From the blood trail he left, his wounds were grievous, more than capable of killing him. Sanah swayed on her feet and leaned against a wall to steady herself.

The implication was astounding. Mamoru was wrong! This creature did *love* Adele, enough to risk his life for her.

Even as Sanah tried to comfort the wounded and stunned, she couldn't shake the image of Greyfriar throwing himself on Adele.

A vampire saving a human.

A man saving the woman he loved.

This changed everything.

CHAPTER 16

THE ROOM WAS dark and quiet. Adele was hesitant to disturb the silence. Her head pounded. The powerful explosion had only been a few hours past, but the pain wasn't bad enough to stop her from what she needed to do. Despite the darkness, she moved unerringly through the room and placed a tray on a table at the far wall. A dim shape shifted on the bed next to her and a pale face turned toward her.

"I didn't mean to wake you," she said softly.

"Don't be foolish. Did you have any trouble getting what you need?"

She laid a hand on his shoulder and kissed him. "No. The good thing about being an empress is people don't ask too many questions." She turned up the lamps and winced at the sight of Gareth's back still riddled with shrapnel. She had cut away the ruin of his clothes with scissors, but more delicate surgical instruments were needed to extract the vicious shards.

Gareth raised himself up. "You know you won't hurt me. You let me feed, so I'm already stronger. The remaining ministrations are simple."

"Easy for you to say." Adele took a deep breath. "I've done it before, I can do it again. Lie flat, please."

Blood oozed slowly from some of his wounds, staining the sheet below him a dark red. If it weren't for his bravery she would be dead along with many others. How many times now had he thrown himself on the pyre to protect her? How long before his luck ran out? She didn't want to think about it and focused instead on the task ahead of her.

His back was bare and raw. After sterilizing the tweezers, she went to work on a small piece of metal shrapnel protruding from his back. She pulled hard at the shrapnel but it resisted, which meant it was wedged in deep. Her gut knotted at the thought, but she had no recourse but to take the scalpel and cut around the shrapnel. Mercifully, he never flinched. Then she leaned over and gripped the metal more firmly. "I'm sorry."

"Don't be," was his swift response. "Scars just add to the mystique."

"We both have far more than we need. My new goal is for us to go at least six months without an injury."

He laughed quietly. "That's far too optimistic."

"Three?"

"Two."

"I'd be happy even with one," she admitted softly. She moved into a better position over him and pulled, ignoring her own aches and pains as she wrestled with the jagged metal. A nasty five-inch fragment of steel came free of his muscle with a spurt of blood. Adele gasped at the size of the shrapnel as her stomach rolled.

"Easy. You did fine. It didn't hurt," he reassured her.

"I know," she panted, breathing harshly through her nose to stem the nausea. She dropped the shard into a metal tray with a loud clank. No matter how many times she mended him, it never seemed to get easier for her, even though he felt no pain. She was terrified that perhaps someday she would be as blasé about it as he was. Adele never wanted that to happen.

"Then breathe deeply, slowly."

"Just keep talking to me. How did you know that man was carrying a bomb?"

"I could smell it."

"You know about explosives?"

"My time spent on the front has burned the smell of explosives into my memory. The bomber did not expect that. But his kind are not skilled assassins."

"His kind?" Adele tweezed out another fragment, this one smaller and easier to extract.

"I suspect the man was Undead."

Shock burned through her, pausing her hand. Gareth had told her about the human cult of the north. The thought of them chilled her to the bone. Adele instead concentrated on removing more shrapnel. She had only another three dozen pieces to pull out. "Undead. In my city."

"It raises the question as to how they got here," Gareth remarked. "They need transportation. Someone had to ferry them here. And a ragged bloodman airship couldn't possibly slip through unnoticed."

"Meaning a human conspirator."

"We know they exist."

A scowl marred Adele's face. "And where there was one, there are more."

"Most likely."

"Is there any way to tell an Undead from a free human?"

"No. It was only the bomb that gave this one away. We were very lucky. If he'd had a knife like Selkirk, it might have been another story." His voice drifted away into brooding silence.

She knew where his thoughts were taking him. "I will always trust you with my life."

"I didn't stop Selkirk." His tone was harsh and angry. The anguish of that moment forever haunted him.

"You're only human," she remarked simply and kissed him, but Gareth didn't respond to her compliment.

Finally, the last piece of shrapnel was pulled from his mangled back, and Adele hung her head, utter relief spent in a long sigh. "I've gotten them all."

Gareth shifted onto his hip and reached for her, his hand cupping her flushed cheek. "I couldn't ask for a better surgeon."

Adele scoffed. Then she pressed him down again and disinfected the wounds with alcohol before stitching the deepest ones. To her amazement, the hole from the first one was already healing over.

Her blood did that. It healed him.

Her hand brushed over the muscles on his back, her fingers fluttering over the deep well-developed curves and the ragged scars. Those scars told the story of how hard they were trying to have a life together. She doubted he could even feel her light touch. But her touch didn't need to be physical. It was how she touched his heart that mattered.

Then something caught her eye. It was a dark mark at the base of his neck. His long hair had covered most of it so she had not noticed it before. It resembled the burn scars that marred his chest and the one that creased his left cheek and jaw in a thick line, the ones she herself had inflicted on him in the Mountains of the Moon.

The mark of geomancy.

"What is this?" she asked, her hand tracing the scar.

He fidgeted. "It's nothing. Just another old injury. It happens in my line of work."

"No. This wasn't from me. Where did you get it?"

"It is nothing, Adele. Merely an echo."

"An echo of what? I know of only one other geomancer who can do what I do." Her eyes focused on the middle of his back, where a small round blackish red mark blazed. It was an injury bestowed by Mamoru when the secret of Greyfriar had been revealed to him, and the man's hatred had overwhelmed him. The wounds were identical.

"Don't jump to conclusions," Gareth said.

"Am I wrong? Or is this something I did to you, and you didn't tell me?" Her expression turned to one of horror, and a small gasp escaped her lips at the thought.

Turning, he took her in his bare arms. "It wasn't you." He kissed her, wiping away her fears. But she would not relinquish the matter.

"Then it was Mamoru."

Gareth was silent.

"It was. He tried to kill you?" Rage was building inside her like a wave.

"He failed. That's all that matters."

"No, it isn't!" she exclaimed. "He lied to me."

"Adele, he will not have another opportunity. I will never turn my back on him again."

"He's a geomancer! He does not have to be near you. He has the same power that I do."

"Far from it. What you do is completely on another scale, trust me."

"What did he do?" Adele asked, almost afraid to know.

"It's in the past. Your Anhalt saved me, and he is as good as his word. Someone I trust with my life." Gareth proceeded to tell Adele what had transpired in the catacombs beneath Alexandria, the night Flay learned his secret.

Adele fumed at the conclusion of his tale. "You mean General Anhalt knew of this? What is the matter with you two? How could you keep this from me?"

"Because you care for Mamoru, and because you need him."

"Nothing is worth the risk of losing you!"

"And you never will."

"Gah, you are such a romantic! But that doesn't mean we shouldn't take precautions."

"What do you intend to do?"

"Make Mamoru realize making a promise to me is nothing to be trifled with." She gathered her strength and rose to her feet.

"I think that's unwise. You still need him, Adele."

Fury filled her face as she made for the door. "We'll see who needs whom more."

———

Adele entered the dojo with extreme civility, though that was not what consumed her thoughts. Mamoru's head lifted and he smiled at her in surprise, but when she did not return it, he sobered.

"Your Majesty? I did not expect you. What did the doctors say? I rejoice that you appear uninjured."

"Did you think I wouldn't find out?" Her voice was low and quiet, a desperate attempt to remain calm.

"Find out?"

"You tried to kill him," Adele stated harshly. "In the tombs while I lay in surgery."

Mamoru showed shock. "No, I was aiming for Flay."

"Oh please. If your geomancy is that shoddy, perhaps I need a better teacher. You knew full well what you were doing."

"Who told you that? Your pet vampire? Of course, he did." He waved aside the entire conversation. "He is paranoid."

"Being that Gareth bears the scars of your geomancy, while Flay escaped scot-free, pardon my skepticism. Gareth said that you were looking straight at him when you cast the runes. Not at Flay, who murdered my father!"

"You believe a vampire over me?" Mamoru's words were cold.

"I didn't think I needed to. I thought I could trust you both! You swore to me you wouldn't hurt him!"

"I promised loyalty to *you*."

"Don't bandy words with me. Not after all we've been through."

"All *we've* been through? You have no idea. You are naïve about that thing. It has you under its sway. You are a fool to think I would allow that creature leave to do with you as it pleases."

Mamoru's hatred of Gareth, and his disrespect of her, scalded Adele. "Nothing occurs between he and I that I do not wish."

Mamoru threw up his hands, increasingly livid at her words. "Yes! I don't need to be reminded of that! You are as mad as everyone says. You see nothing. Because of that *thing*! It's made you complacent to everything it does."

"Gareth is an anomaly. Where every other vampire is trying to kill us, he is helping us, forsaking his own kind. He is something to protect, not destroy. He could be the future of vampires."

"The future of vampires is death. There will never be peace between us so long as they drink our blood!"

"He drinks my blood, and I am fine."

"Are you?" Mamoru stepped close to her, his face ablaze with unusual anger. "You are weakened by what it does to you! You must know that!"

Adele was taken aback by his fire, and stammered, "The geomancy is what weakens me. Gareth's feedings are fitful, hardly affecting me at all."

"It hampers your control."

Adele rallied her argument, once more sure of her facts. "My control is better than yours apparently, better than most, you keep telling me."

"You don't practice when *it* is here. Precious days of training are lost because of it."

"The few days lost are inconsequential. I do it to protect him. And he is with me little enough thanks to the war."

"Yes, off it runs to the warfront with new information," Mamoru sneered. "Only with whom does it confer? Us or them?"

"You don't know him," Adele replied succinctly. "You refuse to admit there may be something in this great world that you don't already know."

"Why don't you think for a moment? What could it possibly gain by acting this way? It wants you, Adele. The empire falls without *you* and it knows it! It orchestrated the attack on Alexandria, murdered your father, ruined the American coalition, and steers us on a losing war!"

"That's rubbish!"

"It has used you from the start. You are just too blind to see it. Cesare may be devious and bloodthirsty, but your vampire is the greatest mastermind of them all. With one stroke, it has disarmed the sole weapon that would lay its kind to ruin."

"He didn't even know I was a weapon when we first met. Neither did I, for that matter."

Mamoru's eyes were wild with desperation and fury. "Can you not see how everything has fallen into place for the vampires since it found you?"

"All I see is scores of dead vampires, by my hand. I see our empire has the strength of true allies, and is not under the rule of a foreign nation. Tell me how that plays into the hands of the vampires!"

Mamoru shouted, "Adele, you are blind beyond compare! And every day its hold on you strengthens. Soon it will have you darting off into vampire territory again, from which you will not return. It will make its final play and you will be murdered, and the one chance we have will be gone."

"You are absurd! If that was his plan, then why the big charade? It's ludicrous to go to such great lengths when all they need do is kill me, which Gareth could have done at any point since we met. Trust me, a great planner, he is not."

"It will kill you, Adele. That is their nature."

"And you will kill him before he does such a thing, I suppose."

Mamoru remained silent, but his eyes told everything.

Adele's mouth settled into a hard line. She hadn't intended for this moment to occur, but there was no turning back. Terror filled her at the precipice she now stood upon. "Dear God. Then you leave me no choice. I can't trust you. You are confined to quarters until I deem fit to set you free."

The expression on Mamoru's face became one that frightened Adele. It held something dangerous. "You wouldn't."

"You've pushed me to drastic measures! Your network is far too vast for me to allow you to walk free. All I asked was to keep this one vampire safe, and you failed me. I trusted you, Mamoru."

"No. You trust *it*."

"At least I know I can." Adele turned and strode from the room. Her breath became ragged in her chest as she closed the door behind her and signaled Captain Shirazi, who stood with several White Guardsmen down the corridor. The men jogged to her side, clearly alarmed by her frantic demeanor.

"Majesty, are you well?"

She gathered herself, looking into the faces of her captain and his soldiers. With a deceptively steady voice, she said, "Master Mamoru is confined to his quarters. Station a watch at every potential door, and even at his windows. Do it quickly. He is to have no contact other than myself. No visitors. He is not to speak with anyone, including yourself and your men."

Shirazi leaned forward in surprise. "Ma'am? Master Mamoru?"

"You heard me, Captain. Post your guard." Adele strode off, head up, outwardly calm, but digging her nails into the palms of her hands. Bitter at Mamoru for his hatred. Furious at herself for letting her emotions drive her. Heartbroken at what she had done.

CHAPTER 17

THE EMPRESS, THE sirdar, and the Greyfriar walked into Iskandar Hospital. Anhalt had rushed to Alexandria after receiving word of both the bombing and Mamoru's fall from grace. The halls were lined with soldiers. Staff bowed and curtsied. She had to slow her step several times as Greyfriar lagged behind. The warmth of Alexandria was taking some small toll on his ability to heal from the damage caused in the bombing. They took the stairs to the top floor, the fourth, rather than trust an elevator. The hospital director, Dr. Turabian, met them outside a heavily guarded ward.

"Your Majesty, General . . . sir," the doctor said to each of the three, "the assassin is conscious, but has yet to speak. He's in decent-enough health. Bit anemic. I don't believe he's from Alexandria, or even Equatoria. But that's just my opinion."

"Thank you, Doctor," Adele replied. "I apologize for the disruption to your hospital. If my reign lasts much longer, you'll need to build a new wing to hold my would-be assassins."

Dr. Turabian coughed with embarrassment that she might have heard that now-common joke in the halls of his hospital.

She held up a calming hand. "You and your staff have performed heroically in the aftermath of the terrible opera bombing. We thank you." She indicated for him to lead the way into the ward.

The four pushed through the swinging doors into the gaslit chamber that had been designed for many patients, but only held one. This was the same ward where Selkirk had been confined after his attempt on Adele's life last summer. They marched across the green-and-white tiles toward a bed. A squad of soldiers came to noisy attention.

"Leave us." Anhalt saluted, and the troopers escorted the doctor from the ward.

Adele looked down at the bruised, battered face on the pillow. "Good afternoon. My name is Adele. What is yours?"

The man stared at the ceiling with lost eyes. He turned slowly to look at her with an expression of regret. "When will you kill me?"

"Soon enough," General Anhalt snapped.

The prisoner actually smiled and lay back.

The sirdar gave a snort of bemusement. "Well, that seemed to please him."

"He's Undead," Greyfriar said coldly. "I'm sure now. His voice. He's from London. He's disappointed he wasn't killed in the bombing. There is only one fate sufficient for him. He must be kept alive for a very long time. Let him die the natural death of an old man, the death of a failure. The death from which there is no escape." The prisoner glared at Greyfriar with terror in his face. The swordsman leaned over the frightened man, and said, "Or tell us what we want to know and we will kill you."

"Do you swear it?"

He repeated, "Tell us what we want to know, and we will kill you."

The man looked from him to Adele to the intense Anhalt. He nodded.

Adele asked, "Who sent you?"

The prisoner hesitated, and then said, "Prince Cesare is my master. I am General Montrose, commander of Cesare's Undead Legion."

Adele silenced Anhalt's scoff with a look before asking the prisoner, "What was your mission here, General Montrose?"

"To kill you."

"How many Undead are in Alexandria?"

Montrose replied confidently, "Many. We are everywhere. Our faith is spreading."

Greyfriar whispered in Adele's ear, "Those bombs did not come from Cesare. I've never seen anything like them in London."

Adele asked Montrose, "Where did you get the bomb?"

"From an ally. The one who brought us to Alexandria."

"His name?"

"I don't know."

"That won't do, General," Adele said tersely. "You can't earn resurrection for such feeble information."

"He didn't give his name and I couldn't see him well," Montrose asserted. "He must have been one of your Undead, now risen. He seemed very much like a vampire."

Adele glanced at her companions, eyeing Greyfriar curiously. Then she turned. "I've heard enough, General. You may rot here forever."

"No!" Montrose croaked. "You promised to kill me. I must be reborn."

The empress continued walking, followed by her two men.

"Wait!" the Undead general screamed and struggled to rise. "If I give him to you, will you kill me?"

"You said you didn't see him clearly," General Anhalt said suspiciously. "Suddenly you can identify him?"

"I didn't see his face," Montrose retorted. "He brought us here as if we were refugees from the war because he knew you were soft and would take us in. He was a man of position and wore a ring, a large golden ring with a stone."

Adele crossed her arms. "Many men wear rings. That's not helpful."

"It had a symbol on it. Give me a pencil and paper, and I'll draw it."

The empress gave her companions a glance of suppressed excitement. Anhalt shook his head, unconvinced. She slid back the panel in the door and called for pen and paper. After a few minutes, the door opened and Corporal Darby handed her several sheets of heavy rag stationery and a silver inkwell with an ornate pen.

Adele smiled. "Well, I'm not drafting a formal letter, but thank you." The door was closed again and she took the material to the eager Montrose.

He dipped the pen and starting scratching awkwardly across the paper, pausing frequently and cursing. "I long for the day I won't have to use my hands for things like this."

Adele stared at the man as he concentrated on the page. He was so focused and sincere. He was the enemy and had blindly tried to kill her, murdering nine people rather than her, and wounding scores more. He fascinated her. He was no mindless bloodman who served out of habit. Montrose believed he was part of the vampire culture. He would rise from the dead and inherit the Earth. All his suffering in this life would be repaid in the next.

Adele could tell from Greyfriar's posture and tone that he loathed the prisoner. No doubt much of it was the bombing, but there was more to it. The swordsman held an unexpected sense of disdain for this mere slave who was so gullible as to believe the slavemaster's promises. Or perhaps he felt disgust that Montrose thought he could ever be like Gareth, or wanted to.

"Here," Montrose announced. "I didn't see it clearly for long, but it looked like this."

Adele took the sheet with a flush of dread and excitement. The design on the paper was a stylized "A" with vague bordering lines. Under the letter was a shape, rudely drawn, but clear enough. It was a gear.

The empress silently held out the paper to General Anhalt. The sirdar took it and, at first, turned it several directions as if he could make nothing of this foolishness. But then he looked at it for a second and his face froze. Slowly his eyes grew dark.

He breathed, "Your Majesty, this is nonsense. It's just something he saw."

"Saw it where?" Adele replied quietly. "We both know what that is."

Anhalt folded the paper as if not to see it. "You can't possibly act on this thing's evidence. He's a lunatic at best. And we know he's an agent of Cesare."

"I'm not going to act, per se." Adele stepped to Greyfriar's side. "But I am going to investigate."

Greyfriar asked, "What is it?"

The empress took the sheet and held it up. "This is the seal of Lord Aden. And he does, in fact, wear a ring with this symbol emblazoned on it."

The swordsman said grimly, "Let's have him then."

"Wait!" Anhalt exclaimed.

"Easy, General," Adele said. "I'm not going to do something rash."

Greyfriar snarled, "I'll do something rash. If he tried to kill you, let's finish him."

"No, no," Adele cautioned. "We have a little thing called law. This sketch is hardly evidence. It is suspicious, however, and we can't ignore it."

Anhalt said, "Lord Aden is the master of our war-building program. Why would he conspire with vampires?"

"I have no idea," Adele replied.

"Coal," came a word from Montrose.

"Beg pardon?" the empress said.

"Coal," the Undead said with a conceited smile. He enjoyed parading his knowledge of the great court in London in front of these southerners. "Cesare arranged for this man to extract coal from clan territories. I've heard His Highness speak of it. In fact, Prince Cesare's arrangement with the clans on the continent for this human to take coal was one of the first elements of the Grand Coalition."

There was a long silence until Anhalt said, "Your Majesty, we must proceed cautiously with this. Lord Aden is popular with the old powers of the capital."

"Yes, yes, General. I know all that. Trust me to act in my usual thoughtful and diplomatic manner."

Anhalt took a frightened breath.

"What are you going to do?" Greyfriar asked.

Adele cleared her throat demurely and started for the door. "I'm going to take a company of soldiers and pay His Lordship a social call."

Montrose sat up with a rattle of chains, reaching for Adele. "You promised! Kill me!"

Greyfriar smashed a hand against the prisoner's chest and slammed him back into the cot. "Welcome to the human race."

—◦◦◦—

The gatekeeper at Lord Aden's mansion was no doubt surprised to hear a carriage roll to a stop on the street at three in the morning. Roused from his comfortable cot in the gatehouse and wearing a liveried cloak, he trundled into the blustery night. He was taken aback to see a soldier standing on the other side of the wrought-iron gate backed by a company of mounted lancers in their smart dark green tunics with brass buttons and white trousers with high black boots. Their lances, held straight like fence posts, sported imperial pennants whipping in the wind, and atop their heads were dress turbans. Then, amidst the shuffling hooves, he noted with shock a black brougham with an imperial crest emblazoned on the door.

"Open the gate," the soldier commanded. "Her Imperial Majesty to see Lord Aden."

The gatekeeper stared dumb for a moment, then stammered, "It's late."

"Open this gate, damn you! Or we'll take it down!"

The gatekeeper jumped with shock and yanked a ring of keys from his waistcoat. Unlocking the gate, he drew it open. The soldier leapt onto the rear of the carriage as ten lancers trooped in, two abreast on horses prancing in unison, followed by the brougham, and then another ten soldiers in red jackets and khaki helmets, all staring straight ahead. As the dour parade clattered up the macadam drive between gas lamps toward the gloomy house, the gatekeeper scampered for his booth, where he scrawled a note with an unsteady hand. He stuffed it into a cylinder and let the pneumatic tube propel it ahead of the approaching riders.

The company drew to a practiced halt before the shadowy portico of the sprawling mansion. Captain Shirazi turned from his spot on the carriage and barked orders to his mounted White Guard, who all slipped from their saddles and withdrew carbines from scabbards. They fanned out around the brougham, rifles at the ready. Shirazi jumped down and opened the carriage door. Greyfriar leapt out, with a hand on the hilt of his rapier, and preceded Empress Adele quickly up the steps to the front door.

The captain was soon at her side and insistently rapped the heavy brass knocker. Adele was calm and collected, her hair covered by a silk scarf, and dressed in a fashionably long navy skirt and heavy topcoat. Shirazi slammed the knocker again, and through the opaque glass in the door, a faint light appeared wavering inside the house. It grew brighter until finally the sound of bolts being thrown back came from the other side.

A blinking face appeared. The butler had done a creditable job of rapid preparation, but he still looked somewhat undone and confused. His thin white hair was askew, and his bleary eyes widened in astonishment at the figure of the empress a mere two feet away.

Shirazi said, "Her Imperial Majesty to call on Lord Aden. Is His Lordship at home?"

"Um." The butler straightened out of habit. "He is, ma'am." Then he bowed deeply toward Adele. "He is abed, I fear. But won't you come in and I will rouse him."

Adele swept past the butler, nodding politely. Greyfriar followed her, and then Shirazi stepped in. The servant closed the door as an older woman, the chief maid, scurried into view with a terrified look on her face. The butler glanced at her.

"Mrs. Torrialba, ready the staff, if you please. We will be serving breakfast to the empress and her guests."

"Oh no, please," Adele said to the shell-shocked servants. "We are not here for a social call. If you will simply tell His Lordship we are here, that will suffice." She turned to Shirazi. "Unless you and your men would care for breakfast, Captain?"

He remained stone-faced, refusing to acknowledge her playful comment. "No, thank you, ma'am."

The butler shooed the maid and raised an arm for everyone to follow him. "Will you wait in the salon, Majesty?"

Adele said, "Captain, please wait here." Then she and Greyfriar trailed the old servant into a richly adorned sitting room.

The butler turned up all the gas lamps before returning to take Adele's topcoat with a bow. He folded it over his arm and paused before Greyfriar. "May I take your . . . wrap, sir?"

The swordsman tilted his head.

Adele chuckled. "He will stay wrapped, thank you."

The butler paused at the door. "His Lordship will attend you presently. I will return with coffee." And he was gone.

Adele sniffed and noticed a strong, sweet smell in the room. There were many vases stuffed with extravagant flower sprays. If the scent was that strong to her, Greyfriar must've been overwhelmed. She strolled around the room, studying the books and the shelves of vases and porcelain objects and photographs of Lord Aden with various celebrities. The walls were crowded with paintings. She stopped at one street scene and gave a low whistle. "This is a Rembrandt, I think."

"And?" Greyfriar was pacing the room, parting the curtains on the French windows to peer outside into the back garden.

"It just means he's rich."

"We knew that."

"Yes. We did." Adele smiled. "When he appears, let me take the lead in conversation."

Greyfriar looked over his shoulder at her. "You're just going to talk?"

She pointed at him. "Remember, we have no idea if he's a criminal. He's not an assassin. We're just here to discuss issues of the day. It's all quite social and normal."

"Of course. Because he won't be suspicious about the empress dropping in at three in the morning."

"I want to throw him. He's far too smooth normally. I want him off-balance."

"This should do it."

The door opened and Lord Aden entered at a crisp pace, smiling and alert, fully dressed, not off-balance at all. Adele immediately noted the glint of the gold signet ring on his right hand as if it was a beacon.

"Your Majesty, what an enormous honor." The young man bowed and took her offered hand. "You look amazingly well, but knowing you, I can't say I'm surprised. I haven't had time to see you since the terrible event at the opera. Let me say, as I wrote to you, that the nation is grateful for your well-being." He nodded formally to Greyfriar. "And we are grateful to you for your aid to Her Majesty that night. May I say, welcome to my home, sir. It's a great pleasure to see you outside the palace. I'll have coffee brought in." He turned and tugged a bell pull.

"Thank you for your sentiments, Your Lordship." Adele hid her annoyance at how alert and awake he seemed. "Most fortunate that you were not at the opera that night. How odd. You rarely miss a premiere, as we recall."

Aden closed his eyes in agreement. "True. I was away on the business of increasing our war-materiel production."

"Ah. Well, we are terribly sorry to have roused you from sleep."

"Not at all. I sleep only rarely these days. The issues of the day weigh on me. Won't you sit? What may I do for you? I hope there isn't some bad news about the state? Or the war?"

"Nothing like that." Adele settled into a wingback chair with Greyfriar lurking behind her. She smoothed her navy skirt and tugged on the hem of her embroidered short-waisted jacket. She felt her heart beating with anticipation as she slowly drew out a sheet of paper and unfolded it with appropriate drama. "May I ask you to look at this?"

"Of course." Aden reached for the pince-nez in his vest and set them on his nose. His eyes widened slightly in surprise as he glanced at the paper, and then showed curiosity to Adele. "I'm confused, Your Majesty. What should I take from this?"

"Do you recognize it?"

"It appears to be a crude version of my own crest." Aden lifted his right hand, and his ring caught the gaslight. He reached into his jacket pocket and removed a pipe and a pouch of tobacco. "I fear I'm lost as to your meaning. Do you mind if I smoke?"

"Not at all." Adele paused. Then she raised her eyebrows, and said with an unruffled professionalism she didn't feel, "That drawing was made by the man who wore the bomb at the opera."

"What?" Lord Aden looked up rapidly in true alarm for a second before gathering his calm again and proceeding to tamp tobacco into his pipe. "I heard the bomber died of his wounds."

"A little misinformation," she replied. "He is alive and well, in fact." She heard Greyfriar shifting behind her in response. Aden appeared completely serene, but began to breathe loudly through his nose.

"Strange." Lord Aden laid the sheet on his desk. He struck a match and began to puff out clouds of intense aromatic smoke. "I have no information for you, I fear. I suppose it's possible he had been given my crest in hopes of targeting me for death."

The empress said, "This bomber was one of the Undead from the north. He was an agent of Prince Cesare's. And he claimed that a human confederate here in Equatoria brought him and other Undead to Alexandria. And provided him with bombs. He also claimed this Equatorian traitor wore a ring with that crest on it."

Aden's face grew stern. "With all due respect, Your Majesty, I must protest this in the strongest possible terms. On the word of some northern refugee lunatic, you are accusing me of attempted regicide?"

"We are accusing no one, Your Lordship. Nor do we care for the tone of your voice. We are merely telling you what the bomber said." Adele stood and eyed the man. "We are informing you that we are launching a complete investigation of war production, which will include detailed oversight of government contractors. But after all your sound arguments in the Privy Council, that won't be a problem for you, will it?"

Aden adjusted a porcelain vase filled with pungent paperwhites a fraction of an inch as if it were desperately important. "I need not remind Your Majesty of my family's long service to the Empire. My grandfather invented the Randolph Boiler to increase the efficiency of our limited coal resources. My father financed the expansion of Equatoria into Burma and Zululand, and built our modern fleets. I have brought vast new coalfields into production, including many on the frontier. My coal lights Alexandria. My coal fires our steamships. And my coal will drive our new ironclad air fleet. I have given everything to this Empire. And I must tell you honestly, I resent your implications."

Adele replied icily, "We make no implications, Your Lordship. And you need not cite your forebears' contributions to this nation. We are well aware of the importance of your coal, and your unique place at the center of our economy and our war effort."

"Is it truly in the court's best interest to antagonize your industrial leadership during wartime?"

"It is in the court's best interest, my lord, to have no doubts about our industrial leadership. Don't you agree?"

"I have nothing to hide." Aden buttoned his jacket.

Greyfriar said, "You're lying."

"That's rich!" Lord Aden laughed viciously and scowled at the swordsman while blowing a scented fog of smoke into the room. He paused to consider some thought, moving behind a desk in the corner, where he remained standing. "Very well. Let's spread our cards on the table, shall we, Your Majesty? I have information which, if made public, would shake the Empire to its foundations and end your reign forthwith."

Adele shifted nervously despite herself. Aden always sounded confident and capable, even now when she assumed she'd have him at a disadvantage. She did her best to give a bemused look. "Is that so?"

"Yes." Lord Aden studied his glowing pipe with a smirk at the skittish empress's attempt to seem assured. "Let's just say that if the court attempts to tie me to the bomber or interfere with my business concerns in any way, I will be forced to inform the world as to the true nature of your relationship with the Greyfriar."

Greyfriar started to move, but Adele held up a hand. "Meaning what, Your Lordship?"

He rolled his eyes. "Don't play games. I know what he is."

Immediately the door opened. Greyfriar started for his weapon and Adele reacted with alarm. The butler entered quietly, pushing a service cart. Silver pitchers and china cups rattled as the man wheeled the coffee into the room. He paused, glancing up curiously at the imminent visitors frozen in aggressive postures, staring at him. He looked from them to Lord Aden and back.

Adele's face transformed from intense to pleasant, and she slowly straightened to full height. "Ah. The coffee is here."

The butler asked, "Shall I serve, sir?"

"No, that's fine," Aden replied as if they were sharing a polite cup after dinner. "I will deal with Her Majesty." The butler bowed and withdrew. Once the door clicked shut, Aden said sarcastically, "Would you care for coffee, ma'am?"

Adele returned to her seat, trying to regain some inner calm.

Aden glanced at Greyfriar. "I assume you don't drink coffee." He laughed at his little witticism as he poured himself a cup and carefully added cream and sugar. He carried the tinkling cup and saucer back to the desk, where his pipe smoldered in an ashtray. All very domestic.

After a moment of silence broken only by the gentle clink of a stirring spoon on fine bone china, he said, "Please be aware, I have no personal interest in your situation. Your affairs are your own. I have no agenda that impacts the state, private or political. I am content that we should lose the war, or win. I will profit handsomely either way. I look forward to a closer relationship with the court. We have been too contentious, you and I." He sipped coffee. "So there we are. I think you see why you wouldn't care to have me testifying before Commons or in a court of law."

Adele looked down at her hand as her fingers toyed with a loose thread on the arm of the chair. "My lord, what makes you think you'd make it to a court of law? What makes you think you will make it out of this room?"

Aden blew on his coffee to cool it. "That would be murder, Your Majesty. Surely that is outside your vision for a proper empress."

"Are you wagering your life on that?"

"I am. I've seen you work. You badly want to rule based on law. You're not your father. It was Constantine's threat to disband Commons that was the trigger for Lord Kelvin to send Flay after him. It wasn't out of love for vampires, but out of love for Equatoria." Aden sipped coffee and looked thoughtful. "I would submit a path that perhaps you haven't considered. Why not investigate the possibility of a truce with the vampires. We both know they're not animals, and can be bargained with." He glanced briefly at Greyfriar. "Wouldn't you prefer to be the champion of world change based on economic and political evolution rather than a wasteful and destructive war?"

"That's ridiculous," Greyfriar retorted. "You can't make deals with vampires. You have nothing they want, except one thing. You must crush them. And if you think you've mastered Cesare, you are deluded. He'll kill you when you cease to benefit him."

Aden shrugged. "Well, that's hardly enlightened thinking, but it makes no difference to me. Personally, I don't care what Greyfriar is. Or what you two do. My message to you is that I just want to be left to do as I please. Human or vampire. Business is business. I think we understand one another."

Adele sneered at the man. "No, we do not. My subjects are dying in a war against vampires. You were in league with Kelvin, who ordered my father's death. And then you tried to kill me." She stood up and opened her jacket to reveal the khukri dagger at her belt. "You are a traitor."

She noticed Aden's eyes on the French window as he gave a quick nod. Greyfriar must have seen it too, because he suddenly leapt at the window. Glass shattered from Greyfriar slamming his hand out and pulling a writhing figure into the room. The figure in his grip hissed. A vampire.

Two more vampires roared into the room, smashing glass, bowling over Greyfriar as he struggled to hold the first. Adele automatically drew her dagger and moved to help him. She crushed a knee onto the back of one vampire, seizing his filthy hair to pull his head back. She drew the razor-sharp glowing khukri across his throat. His growl turned to a gurgle.

Suddenly Adele couldn't see. She took a deep breath and her lungs seared. The smell was familiar and terrifying. Shroud gas. It was an oily gas designed by the Americans to blunt the senses of vampires. Through misty breaks in the black, Adele saw Greyfriar holding one snapping vampire by the throat while another clawed for the swordsman's neck. Then her vision went out again. She instinctively lashed out but only caught the tip of her blade against a vampire's arm. The creature snarled and whirled on her. Claws came through the opaque fog, cutting her high on the forehead, tearing at her clothes. Then it screamed when it laid a hand on her. The vampire struck blindly and Adele saw his face near hers, wide-eyed, unseeing. Then his crystal blue eyes locked on the young woman, and sharp teeth came at her in wild desperation.

There was a quick glint of metal and a deafening explosion with a bright flash. The vampire fell into the darkness. Adele felt a strong shape at her side, grabbing her and shoving her back. There were several more blasts. She was already diving to where she knew Greyfriar lay. She felt his rough cloak with her hand and reached out to find the struggling vampire still in his grasp. Adele lashed out with the khukri, contacting deep and hearing a screech which ended in a dull grunt as Greyfriar snapped the thing's neck.

Adele felt herself grabbed awkwardly under the arms and lifted off the floor. Before she could attack, she heard Captain Shirazi in her ringing ear. "It's me, Majesty!"

She felt a rush of cool air on her face and quickly sucked it into her aching chest. Her vision cleared enough to see she was on a patio outside the shattered French windows. Black oily smoke boiled out of the salon, slowly dissipating in the stiff wind.

"We must help Greyfriar!" she cried, starting for the door, eluding Shirazi's grasping hand.

A looming cloaked shape intercepted her and propelled her farther onto the soft lawn. Greyfriar knelt at her side gasping for breath. She clutched his arms.

"Are you all right?" she asked.

"Yes," he croaked in reply. Then he touched her face, and his gloved fingertip came away wet. "You're injured."

"Nothing serious." With watering eyes, she looked up at Captain Shirazi, who knelt with his service revolver trained at the door. "Where's Lord Aden?"

"I don't know, ma'am," he said without moving. "I didn't see him."

"We have to search the house." Adele started to rise.

"Stay down!" the soldier snapped. "There are vampires inside."

"They're dead," Greyfriar said. "Captain, alert your men to search for Lord Aden."

Adele nodded to Shirazi, saying, "Find him. And Captain . . . shoot on sight."

—⟿—

Rome would do for now.

Lord Aden had a vast estate just outside the Eternal City, and the Romans were notably contentious in their dealings with the Empire. They wouldn't be quick to give him up should the Equatorians locate him and demand his extradition. However, if he feared that the empress had designs on his life, he could move to more isolated locations until the situation was rectified.

He stared down at the moonlight rippling on the Mediterranean far beneath his airship. The lights of Alexandria were a mere glow astern. He envisioned this as some romantic exile from which he would soon return in triumph. Surely it wouldn't take long for the empress to be driven off or even killed, once the truth about the Greyfriar was revealed. Aden would be known as the man who freed the Empire from the rule of the insane Adele. But there was nothing romantic about this exile. He was losing money every minute he wasn't attending his business, and he didn't want to think about what havoc the imperials would cause to his operations in his absence.

Flay had given him several vampires to use as he saw fit, and they had come in handy after all. He had rigged his mansion with American shroud gas in case he needed protection against those things, and it had been a simple matter to trigger the gas in order to hamper Greyfriar's vaunted skills. Then he slipped out of his mansion via a tunnel right under the noses of the empress's toy soldiers.

Imagine the nerve of that little girl to call him a traitor for dealing with vampires. With one standing right beside her. Clearly all the rumors about her had been true. Adele wasn't just unfit to rule; she was irrational.

Lord Aden stepped from the stern gallery into his vast cabin. He closed the glass door behind him and slipped off his heavy overcoat. Options raced through his mind as he stirred a gin and tonic. Equatoria deserved to lose the war, as indeed it would, if he had anything to say about it. The government was incompetent if it couldn't even stand up to an unbalanced girl like Adele. A modern state needed a firm-minded businessman at the helm, not some ancient holdover from an era of divine right. Lord Aden would see to it that things changed in the coming regime. Perhaps it was time for the royal family to be deposed totally. Let men of sense and accomplishment rule the Empire.

Aden felt a blast of wind on his back. Damn latch never held properly. He turned, and in the blowing drapes he saw the figure of a man in the moonlight. Tall. Stern. Long black hair tousled in the gale. His eyes were vampire blue.

Lord Aden took a long drink to steady his nerve. He set the sweating glass on the sideboard. "You must be Gareth."

"I am."

"Have you come to kill me?"

"I have."

"I'm very rich, and I can make you very rich. Would that appeal to you?"

"No."

Aden held up a hand. "Hear me out. I have influence in many places, some you wouldn't suspect. What if I told you I could make you a king? Would that interest you?"

"No."

"All right. Fair enough. Then tell me, what do you want?"

"To protect Adele." Gareth was a blur in the dim light that Aden could barely see. And then Aden saw nothing else.

CHAPTER 18

EMPRESS ADELE AND General Anhalt stood alone on the forefront of a reviewing stand as the men of the Twenty-fifth Suez marched past. The sergeant major shouted a command, and all heads turned toward them. The troopers flowed by, each man in lockstep with the drums, with rifles on their shoulders and bayonets shining in the early-morning sun. Their eyes were lost in the shadows of their khaki helmets. Anhalt held a salute, and Adele watched with a stern look.

Anhalt murmured to her with an offhand air, "Don't worry about Greyfriar. He will be fine."

"I'm not worried." Adele sighed.

"You seem worried," the sirdar said.

"Not about him. He can handle himself."

"Then what? If I may ask. Please speak freely. No one can hear us over this band."

Adele glanced at the sharp profile of her most trusted advisor. There was an unwavering sturdiness to him that she valued, now more than ever.

"What," she asked, "do you think of me as an empress?"

"You are excellent," Anhalt said without hesitation. "You have become a symbol that is uniting the nation, not just toward the war effort, which you see before you, but as Equatorians. You rule with passion and wisdom. You are thoughtful and just. You are everything I knew you would become."

"Thank you." Adele felt a flutter of emotion at the general's appraisal, but she had doubts that even his worshipful opinions couldn't overawe. "I'm afraid of what I'm becoming."

"I don't understand."

She clasped her hands in front of her, and then lowered them because that looked childish. "I just sent someone off to execute a man. With no trial."

"Ah." Anhalt pursed his lips in understanding as columns of cannons newly manufactured in the factories of Lord Aden rolled past accompanied by the clip-clop of horses drawing caissons. "Aden made his choices. He must now deal with the consequences. His fate isn't murder, Your Majesty. It's justice. Lord Aden is the vilest of criminals. He is in league with our enemy."

"Am I so different?"

"Completely different. Your relationship with Greyfriar isn't affecting your prosecution of the war."

"Isn't it?" she wondered aloud.

He dropped his salute as the artillery unit moved off, but remained at attention. "No, Your Majesty. I am your commander in chief, and my orders have been to kill all the vampires we encounter and liberate the humans under their sway. I must assume those will remain my orders. So far as I can tell, Greyfriar has not altered your commitment to the war."

Adele considered his statement and admitted, "I'm not sure about that. There are things about me that you don't know. You saw what I did in the Mountains of the Moon and again in Grenoble. I know you're a man who believes in the power of steam and steel, but there are powers in this world beyond those. I can marshal those powers in ways I still don't completely understand. But Mamoru says . . . said . . . that I have a unique role to play in the defeat of the vampires."

"There are things about me that you don't understand, Majesty. Yes, I believe in steam and steel. Fervently. But I am a man of strong faith as well. I don't discuss it because such beliefs are not looked on with favor, particularly in a man of position. I practice Hindu tenets, quietly. And yes, I have seen what you can do. I don't understand it in any way, but I accept it even though it frightens me. I pray you can control it."

"I pray I can too. More than you know." Adele smiled at her commander with an awareness of their shared unpopular beliefs. "I never knew you were a Hindu, dear Anhalt."

The sirdar snapped up a new salute as the Seventh Isfahan Lancers passed. The unit's five hundred pennants swept into the air accompanied by the thunder of hooves and the dancing plumes on their turbans.

Adele gave a grateful nod to the passing horsemen. "You see, Mamoru believes that Greyfriar is attempting to subvert me, and the war effort, through some long convoluted scheme to gain my trust and separate me from those who truly serve humanity's cause."

"I understand that argument."

"What?" Adele gaped at Anhalt before recovering herself and turning back to the passing parade. "You don't think that he's using me, do you?"

"I believe what you believe, Majesty."

"No. That's not good enough, General. I want to know whether you trust Greyfriar."

Anhalt held his hand rigid before the brim of his helmet, squinting in the sun. "I understand Mamoru's claims. Greyfriar has, in fact, created a grain in your mind that vampires may have some redeeming quality, that perhaps they should not be wiped from the face of the Earth."

Adele felt the pounding of the drums. Her head began to spin and her breath quickened. She was terrified by the doubts she heard from him. She raised a hand to her forehead, careful to maintain her imperial visage on the passing men going off to fight her war.

She whispered, "I can't believe this."

"If I may, Majesty," Anhalt said, holding his salute steady. "I have seen Greyfriar operate under many circumstances. I have served with him on the battlefield. There are many things he is—a swordsman, a ranger, even a figure of enormous melancholy and subtle wit. If his goal was to remove you from events, he would have killed you when he first set eyes on you. The fact that Greyfriar has troubled himself to protect you this past year means only one thing: that he means to protect you. That is his single goal in life."

Adele took a deep breath of relief. "Thank you, General."

"If you'd care to direct your eyes to the roof across the square, just to your right."

The empress looked beyond the marching troopers passing their reviewing stand, across the crowded Victoria Square where units moved in undefined order. The chaotic border of the Turkish Quarter rose up with its shuttered windows and awnings. In the jagged shadows created by the old buildings, she saw a figure moving strangely above the ground. Some flowing shape moved across the gap from one structure to another, and then it paused.

Greyfriar.

He clutched an iron balcony, leaning off into space, his cloak fluttering in the wind. Adele knew he could see her clearly given his amazing eyesight. She let out one breath of relief. He raised his arm and waved to her. It was done. For better or worse. She nodded, as if to the soldiers, but he would've known it was to him.

And then he was gone into the shadows.

—⁓—

"They'll never find Aden," Gareth said, tugging the scarf from his face. "He's at the bottom of the sea."

Adele sat quietly staring at a tray of sweets without appetite. She stroked her grey cat, Pet, a gift from Gareth and a remembrance of their time together in Edinburgh.

General Anhalt poured coffee for Adele and then himself. Gareth paced thoughtfully along the far wall. The door to her private chambers was locked against the constant parade of servants, and Captain Shirazi was posted in the corridor to ensure privacy.

Gareth asked, "What do you intend to do with Montrose? Kill him as he wishes?"

Adele laughed bitterly. "I don't know. Kill one man without trial. Leave another alive who wants to die."

Gareth said, "Don't waste your sympathy on either of them, Adele.

Aden was your enemy. Montrose is Undead. He would do anything Cesare told him."

Anhalt stared out the window at the blurry lights of distant airships in the night. "They seem completely human. Difficult to tell them from real human beings."

"They are real human beings," Adele replied with a tired smile. "That's how Aden brought them in, as part of the humanitarian refugee relocation from the front."

"Of course. I only meant . . . *civilized* human beings. It seems rather complex planning for vampires."

Gareth laughed as he slapped his gloves against his thigh. "Why do you continue to underestimate us? After Adele's kidnapping? After Gibraltar? After the attack on Marseilles? And after your own near disaster at Grenoble? Even with your superior weapons, your inability to see us for what we are could be your undoing."

"Thank you," Anhalt said frostily, "for the lecture on your kind."

Adele studied the ripples in her coffee cup and took a deep breath, loathing what was coming next. "I need to talk about Mamoru."

Gareth and Anhalt halted their pacing out of respect for her obvious dilemma.

"It is painfully clear to me," Adele began with a strong voice that still quavered beneath, "that Mamoru cannot bring himself to accept my situation. I have overlooked his lack of forthrightness over the years, but I don't have that leisure any longer."

"With due respect, Your Majesty," Anhalt said, "he's always been a shady character. I believe he has manipulated you, and the court, to pursue his private agenda. You need not labor to convince us."

"I need to convince myself. I believed in him."

Gareth's voice was cold. "There comes a time when we must face the future, no matter how dire. Youth is gone forever, and those ideals must be sacrificed, when necessary, to greater causes. Mamoru is party to every secret you have, large and small. If you no longer trust him, you must deal with him."

She looked up sharply at the unmasked face of the vampire prince. "What do you mean, *deal* with him?"

He stared at her in silence.

Adele got a chill and heard echoes of Mamoru's ravings about Gareth's sinister schemes: *It orchestrated the attack on Alexandria, murdered your father, ruined the American coalition, and steers us on a losing war!* Now Gareth was suggesting she eliminate Mamoru. "Dear God. I feel sick. He has committed no crime."

"Then why are you holding him?" Gareth asked.

"You know why."

"My point exactly. You already know what must be done."

Adele swung her feet to the floor and bent over in anguish.

General Anhalt moved to her side, but remained rigid and military. "Your Majesty, do you trust Mamoru to do your bidding?"

She took a deep, shuddering breath. "No."

"Do you believe that he will use his privileged information for his own purposes, whatever they may be?"

"Yes."

"Do you believe that if the secret of the Greyfriar ever became known, it could shatter your reign?"

"Yes."

The sirdar said, "There is your answer, Your Majesty."

The empress looked up at the general and whispered hoarsely, "He's Mamoru. I can't kill him."

"Very well, but . . ."

"But I can never let him go. Can I?"

"No," Anhalt said. "You cannot."

CHAPTER 19

ADELE HAD BEEN studying reports for hours, but not really seeing them. She was preoccupied with difficult thoughts of Lord Aden's fate and Mamoru's future. Greyfriar stood at the window of her private office, watching the dark skies outside, nearly motionless for more than an hour. He suffered no remorse for killing Aden, so he must have been contemplating his coming actions in the north. Or perhaps he was simply silent out of respect for Adele's discomfort. It was difficult to know.

Anhalt's voice penetrated the quiet. "Greyfriar is riding an elephant."

"He's what?" Adele's confused eyes rose over her tower of memoranda to confirm that Greyfriar indeed was not riding an elephant.

The general sat at a table across the room with a stack of paperwork in front of him. He looked up in surprise, seemingly shocked that he had spoken aloud. Anhalt had been flipping through a potboiler novel titled *Swords of the Jungle*. He held the open book toward Adele sheepishly, displaying artwork of a man with a trailing cloak atop an elephant. "I'm sorry, Majesty. I found this book here. It's about how Greyfriar defeated the vampires in the Mountains of the Moon."

"*He* defeated them?" Adele grunted in annoyance. "Ever since I became empress, it's become improper to use me as a character in those cheap books. So now he does everything."

"I'm very popular." Greyfriar crossed to Anhalt's desk, where he took the pulp novel and studied the picture with a satisfied hum. "Impressive. However, elephant-riding prowess aside, I do have something serious that needs discussion."

Adele set down her pen and rubbed her eyes. Here it was. This was the reason for his brooding.

General Anhalt rose from the corner desk where he was supposed to be annotating a pile of reports for the empress's attention. "I'll take my leave."

"No, General. I'll want your opinion." Greyfriar perched on the corner of Adele's desk.

The empress appeared calm and engaged, but nervous energy clenched her stomach. She pulled the scarf from Gareth's face and slipped his glasses off, as she did ever more frequently when they were alone. She saw a tense uncertainty in him that she had rarely encountered, and it frightened her.

He looked her directly in the eyes. "Adele, I've been thinking about this for a while now. I am going to kill Cesare and actually become king of Britain. It's no longer a ruse in my mind. It must happen."

Adele looked bewildered, glancing at the equally surprised Anhalt, and then back to Gareth. "I'm sorry. What did you say?"

"I intend to be king."

"When did this happen? You said that it was just a story to get Flay to play along."

"It was. I believed what I told Flay was nonsense. I was merely trying to work myself into her good graces. But she accepted it, so easily. She believed I could become king. And Flay knows as much about clan politics as anyone."

"Couldn't she be clouded by her feelings for you?"

"Perhaps. But if she thought it was a ludicrous idea, she would've said so. So I have to believe it is indeed possible."

Adele clasped her fingers together nervously. Gareth reached down and covered her fidgeting hands. When she glanced up, she now saw a passionate clarity in his face. His blue eyes were intense, purposeful, and inspiring.

"Think of it, Adele. Just as we talked about in Edinburgh. Neither of us believes the differences of our kind must be played out in blood. There must be another way, and with me ruling there and you ruling here, it's more likely that way can be found.

"I've fought against the brutality and wastefulness of my kind by pretending to be something I'm not, hiding from my own nature. Dressing as Greyfriar for another year, or a hundred years, won't make me human. I can never be human. And I don't want to be. I'm the eldest son of King Dmitri. I should be his heir."

Adele shifted in her chair and regarded him sympathetically. "Please don't take what I'm going to say the wrong way. Are you merely thinking this because you're grieving over your father's death?"

"Maybe. I began to consider it after Flay told me about my father, although I didn't realize it at the time. However, there's so much more to it. I won't have my brother soiling Dmitri's legacy." Gareth's voice grew hard. "He doesn't deserve to be mentioned in the same breath as my father. I used to think I could turn away, but I was wrong.

"The fact is Cesare doesn't even understand what my father stands for," he continued. "Humans know the name Dmitri as one of the leaders of the Great Killing, and so he was. But that wasn't his true nature. He was pressured into becoming a war king, pressured by fear. We were afraid of the humans. We believed that we had to strike when we did. To wait any longer meant we would be overwhelmed and destroyed.

"Dmitri had spent his long life preaching that vampires should tread light on the Earth. We had our place, as humans had theirs. The Great Killing was against everything he believed. But he was also committed to the survival of his kind. So he joined the growing war movement and turned us into something we never should have been. That act drove him mad." Gareth sighed sadly and leaned into Adele's hand stroking his hair. "Perhaps it drove me mad too."

"Don't say that," she said.

His gaze lifted to stare into her dark eyes. "Now Cesare has started another war, born of that same fear. Fear of the humans. But this war won't just drive us mad. It will finish us. How odd that I, of all people, should develop some messianic desire to save my father's people, my people."

"I understand." Adele paused to let him gather his emotions. She was battling her own. There was such a change in him that it was infectious. But she had to have the more sensible head. "Gareth, I'm not saying I approve of this idea, but if it were to happen, how would you do it?"

Gareth took a deep breath. "It won't be easy. A clan coven is a peculiar thing."

"How so?"

"All the clan lords gather, along with whatever foreign kings wish to participate, usually few, but I suspect Cesare will have his allies like Draken and Ashkenazy. The lords sequester themselves without outside contact for a few days while they make a decision. I would strike Cesare once the clan lords went inside. That would leave me as Dmitri's only heir. But even so, that's not sure enough, so I need to arrange for Flay to use her packs to overawe the clan into naming me the king."

Adele stood and began to pace. "Certainly I fully support the goal of killing Cesare. It creates confusion among the clan allies, and protects your people in Edinburgh. However, this whole subterfuge with Flay is too perilous. The risk of playing it through and placing you on the throne is very precarious. Why should we take that chance?"

He stepped in front of her, bringing her up short. "We both know with Cesare on the throne, the war will have a bloody and miserable end. I may be able to affect it otherwise." His fingers entwined in her hair. "This war is wearing on you, and you are paying the price every day. You need my help, and this is how I can do it. You can't save the world by yourself."

"Well played, my dear," she said with a deep breath. Then Adele suddenly froze as another thought occurred to her. "What about Flay?"

"What of her?"

"Whatever shall you do with her? You're going to use her to gain the throne, and then what? You've said yourself she's the most dangerous creature you know."

"So she is." Gareth stroked his chin. "I don't know for sure. I'll need her to consolidate my rule, as I have no packs of my own. With time, I can create my own loyalists to replace the more troublesome clan lords. But you're right, I'll have to deal with Flay eventually. And so I shall. I'll destroy her."

Anhalt noted from the side, "You said you couldn't beat Flay."

Gareth nodded. "Not in a straight fight. I'll have to think of something else."

As he was talking about the fearsome Flay lurking next to the British throne and his obligations to the clan lords, an idea swirled into shape in Adele's mind. She saw it with amazing lucidity, and even though it was surrounded by ill-defined shades of risk, it was a plan that she, and only she, could accomplish. It allowed her to play a role in safeguarding Gareth during his dangerous journey, potentially removed Flay from a formative role in the coup, and it relieved any others from taking a terrible risk, which was the sort of plan she preferred.

Gareth settled on the arm of a chair and leaned back, watching her obsessive gaze with uncertainty. "Whatever you're thinking now, I'm against it."

"I'm thinking of all the damned clan lords and all the kings of the vampire alliance trapped together under Buckingham Palace. All in one place. I'm thinking of a way that you wouldn't need Flay's packs to launch your reign."

Anhalt stood. "No, Your Majesty."

Adele didn't listen. "I can eliminate them all. Every bloody one of them. They will never see it coming."

Gareth rose also and took her by the shoulders. "Now you're talking madness."

"Was it madness in Grenoble?" she argued.

"Yes, it was. But it happened to work."

"I could kill Cesare and every significant enemy leader. And just them."

"It isn't your place to kill Cesare," Gareth said stiffly. "It's mine."

"But don't you see? I can end the war with one stroke. I have that power!"

"At Grenoble, you had the support of an army. You're talking about London far to the north."

"I've been there before and survived, you may recall."

"Adele, I pray you listen to me. If you use your . . . ability, your power, again on that level, it could kill you."

"Oh, you don't know that!" she dismissed. "You're just trying to protect me. How can you be such a mother hen toward me when you're going up to face your entire clan alone? And you expect me to wait here for a telegram that you're just fine?"

"I am trying to protect you, from yourself. I've tasted your blood, and I know how drained you are. I have never felt you so weak."

"Nonsense! I feel fine. Grenoble was weeks past. I'm completely recovered."

Anhalt came closer. "What is he talking about?"

"Nothing." She flashed Gareth an annoyed glance.

Gareth didn't relent. "The power she wields is slowly killing her."

The general fixed her with a panicked stare. "Is this true?"

"Of course not. I feel fine." She glared at Gareth. "Don't bring General Anhalt into this."

The general said, "You didn't tell me about any risk to your health, beyond the normal danger of war. You inserted yourself into my tactics without informing me of this existing threat to your life? That is unacceptable, Your Majesty."

Gareth towered over the young empress. "Believe me, Adele. You are frail on a level that you cannot conceive. I know you in ways you can't."

Adele was annoyed that he tried to overwhelm her with his height. "None of that matters. I can do it. How can I stand here in Alexandria and watch the bodies of our dead soldiers be shipped back to their wives and children for years to come when I can prevent it?"

"If I may," General Anhalt said loudly, parting the glowering empress and the vampire prince with his sharp tone. "There is another way to accomplish the same objective without risking your life, Majesty."

Adele started to argue that perhaps she *wanted* to risk her life, but silenced herself and motioned for the general to continue.

The sirdar said in a measured tone. "If we could determine the date of this coven—"

"We can," Gareth said eagerly. "It can't begin until I arrive in London, and I control my own progress."

Anhalt nodded. "Excellent. We could certainly arrange a traditional solution."

"What do you mean *traditional* solution?" Adele asked.

"A fleet of bombers to kill the clan lords as they gather."

"But again, General, why should I put those airmen at risk?" Adele replied fervently.

"I won't lose you for something so unnecessary," Gareth shouted.

Anhalt replied after him, "Your Majesty, there's not a soldier, sailor, or airman who would not give his life in battle for you."

Adele clenched her fists in exasperation. "Why won't you see the simple fact that I'm a geomancer and more than capable of succeeding?"

Gareth took her fists in his hands. "You are a geomancer, true, but there is so much more to you. You are the guide for your nation. And you are the woman I love. You must relent, Adele. In this case, you must allow us to be what we are: loyal soldiers. That is all we do. That is all we are."

With gentle fingers, Adele brushed his temple and gazed into the crystal blue of his eyes. "My darling, I would've swooned for that speech last year. But I'm older now. Do you actually think for one second that I would allow you to be in London under the bombs of my own navy? Do you think I'm deranged?" She kissed him on the cheek. "The answer is no."

"But I won't be under the bombs." Adele began to object, but Gareth continued, "Let me finish. Once the coven commences, I will kill Cesare. Then I will fly up to the approaching ships with the signal to attack. There will be no significant resistance because it's customary for all the clan packs to be sent away during the coven. When the bombs fall on Buckingham Palace, I will be with General Anhalt aboard an Equatorian airship. And then, I can even remain in London and take charge of the clan during its hour of crisis." He pulled her close. "Adele, I have steered your army wrong with my mistakes. Cesare has made me look like a fool, and caused me to endanger your people on the battle-field. I must pay him back. I must pay you back."

Adele saw the flame deep in Gareth's eyes. He sensed the potential of this bold action, and it created a confidence and hope in him that was intoxicating. Even General Anhalt tensed like a racehorse straining for the gate to open. She felt a sense of relief and comfort that two such extraordinary men were at her side. And, perhaps, they were right. She couldn't deny she was still fatigued weeks past Grenoble.

"Very well, gentlemen, draw up a plan." She took a shuddering, nervous breath. "Oh, I wish you hadn't said anything at all now."

Gareth said with fervor, "It's brilliant. History will mark you as a great ruler."

"I don't care about that." Adele kissed the palm of his hand. "I would still rather lose me than you."

He replied softly, "You can't feel that way, Adele. It's selfish. You are the empress, but I'm just the Greyfriar, popular elephant-riding hero."

"No. You're the future King Gareth of Britain." Adele felt his arms around her, strong and full of purpose and rectitude.

———✶———

"Simon! Stop touching that!" Adele slapped her brother's wrist as he reached to grasp the dead hand that lay on the unrolled oilcoth.

"But technically it's mine," Simon argued with typical disregard for reality, staring at the grey-fingered thing with boyish wonder. The thirteen-year-old was dressed in his usual Bedouinesque robe with linen trousers and soft desert boots. His face was flushed redder than normal under his close-cropped red hair. The boy rebelled against his sister's grasp and began to inch toward the hand again.

General Anhalt laid a deep metal tray on the table along with a canvas bag that tinkled of glass. They were in Adele's private conference room. He pulled a jar of blood from the satchel and wordlessly began to pour the liquid into the tray.

Simon blurted, "Can I put the dead hand in my blood?"

"*May* I put the dead hand in my blood," Adele corrected. "Yes, go ahead."

"Outstanding!" The boy giggled and gasped at the same time as he lifted the rubbery hand. He took one of the fingers and wiggled it, making a cute playful noise. He thrust the dead limb toward Pet, who sat on the table, ears pricked forward with interest. The cat sniffed the thing and tightened his face in disgust.

"Just do it!" Adele shouted. "What is wrong with you? Show some respect."

Simon scowled and dropped the hand into the tray, raising red splashes that elicited a groan of annoyance from his sister. The empress ignored the scarlet spots on the boy's robe and her own golden gown, and asked Greyfriar, "How long must the thing soak?"

The swordsman leaned over and looked at the lifeless appendage, now partially covered in blood. "I have no idea. Between the hand and the clothes, we should fool Flay."

Adele turned to General Anhalt. "How many people know anything about this blood or the hand? Other than the people in this room?"

"None, Your Majesty." The general cleared his throat uncomfortably. "There is, I fear, no shortage of dead boys in the military hospital. And I drew the blood of Prince Simon myself. Unfortunately, I have some experience with battlefield surgery."

Simon was studying the glass jar, watching the remnants of red liquid dribble in the bottom. "So this will make the vampires think that hand is mine?"

"Yes," Adele answered.

"Vampires are stupid," the boy said, causing Greyfriar to chuckle.

King Msiri approached the table. He wore loose cotton clothing with sandals, and a leopard skin band around his head, a crown of sorts. Msiri glanced at the hand too with a sour shake of his head.

"How you Equatorians manage your affairs is your own business," he muttered, "but this is bad. I'm not a superstitious man, but the bodies of the dead are sacred. And this was a child."

Adele replied, "There was no other way, Your Majesty. But I thank you for helping us."

"Of course," the Katangan said earnestly. "There's nothing I wouldn't do for you after how you served me." He pointed at the hand. "And if this abomination is your wish, so be it."

The empress shook her head. "I find it distasteful too, but necessary.

Are you prepared with a cruiser to take Simon to Katanga? With complete secrecy?"

"Yes! I was mistaken before. This fellow is not my son. He is my brother!" Msiri put a rough arm around Simon's shoulder. The boy laughed. "I will pack him in a box so no one knows he is aboard ship. Except for me, of course."

Simon asked, "What if you forget and I starve to death locked inside a box?"

"I shall write myself a note," Msiri offered.

The boy seemed satisfied with that glib response.

"Good," Adele said. "Keep him hidden and quiet, if that's at all possible."

Simon asked, "Why do I have to stay hidden? Vampires won't know what's happening here." The boy pointed at Greyfriar. "Oh! I can wear a mask. I can be Whitefriar or Blackfriar! I can go with you and fight vampires in the north."

Greyfriar began to speak, but Adele interrupted, "You are not going to wear a mask and fight vampires, Simon!"

"Why not? You get to go everywhere. You get to run around. And you're the empress! Why can't I do anything?"

Greyfriar said, "It's very dangerous, Simon."

"I'm not afraid!"

"No one said you were afraid," Adele countered. "You clearly aren't afraid of anything, unfortunately. It's just that you aren't prepared. And you already have an important mission—"

"Well, I won't do it, then. I won't pretend to be dead."

Msiri stood before Simon, grabbing his shoulders tightly. "Young prince, listen to me. What I have planned for you in Katanga will test you more than fighting vampires in the north. I am taking you to a place from which you may never return. In my country, there is a secret river valley in the most foreboding forests in the world. You cannot see the sky for the trees. It is a mysterious place where few men have set foot—and lived. The houses there are built of bone. It is the realm of strange, monstrous races. Men with no heads and five arms and tails like crocodiles. There are vicious beasts that kill and eat full-grown men as if they were small birds." The king stared deep into Simon's wide eyes. "Young prince, if you can survive there, vampires will be like gnats to you then. You will be the mightiest of men."

Simon stared up at Msiri with mouth agape and trembling slightly.

"But fear not," Msiri continued loudly, "I am beside you. I will train you in the fighting arts of Katanga. You will become a warrior unmatched around the world. You will strike terror in the hearts of your enemies with gun or blade. You will be terrible to behold!"

"*Deus vult,*" Simon breathed with excitement.

Greyfriar added, "I asked Msiri to train me, but he said I wasn't ready." The swordsman pulled his rapier from the scabbard and handed it to Simon. "But even if I can't be there, will you do me the honor of using a blade of mine? And when you become the weapon that Msiri has said, I hope I may join you in fighting vampires."

The boy took the sword with an awed grin.

General Anhalt scowled at Greyfriar. "That trumps the dagger I gave him in Marseilles."

"Next time, you can give him an airship," Greyfriar whispered.

Simon looked up at Msiri. "When do we leave?"

Adele breathed out and replied, "Soon. I will announce your death—" Her voice caught with unexpected emotion. She dropped to one knee, as she usually did, but then realized suddenly that Simon now was at least a foot taller. Biting her lip, she gathered Simon in an ironclad hug as she stood back up. The boy didn't fight back, but did roll his eyes. "I will announce your death in a few days. But I want you out of Alexandria before that."

"I can't even attend my own funeral?"

"No! Don't be morbid."

"How am I going to die?"

"Vampires kill you."

"How many? A hundred?"

Adele laughed softly. "As prodigious as you are, a hundred seems a trifle much. It will be only one."

"One?" Simon snapped angrily. "I could kill one."

Adele took an exhausted breath, so Greyfriar stepped in. "It isn't any vampire who kills you, Simon. They send Prince Gareth of Scotland."

The boy shoved his hands in his pockets and kicked at the floor. "Well, he's okay, I suppose. But he's no Flay."

Greyfriar made a disturbed sound. "That's true enough, but he is a fearsome warrior. Known far and wide as the deadliest hunter his kind has yet produced. In fact, Gareth is credited with the killing of—"

Adele touched his sleeve as her lips quirked upward. "Um, yes. We get the point. Prince Gareth is a god among vampires."

The swordsman lowered his head with a rebuked cough. "Well, he is known to be quite impressive is my only point."

"Fine." Adele waved her hand to stop that discussion. "So, yes, Prince Gareth of Scotland will be your assassin."

Simon asked, "But won't the real Prince Gareth know he didn't do it? Why won't he just tell people, and your whole story will fall apart?"

Greyfriar turned expectantly toward Adele with a bemused tilt of his head. "An excellent question."

She rolled her eyes again. "Please. Simon, we've gotten it all worked out. Don't worry about it. There is no way it can fail."

The boy began, "But I don't think—"

"Enough, Simon!" Adele shouted, and immediately leaned heavily on the table. Greyfriar, Simon, and King Msiri all moved to her side, but she waved them off with a weary shake of her head. "Please, trust me."

Greyfriar said, "Adele has planned this intricately. There is no chance of failure, Your Highness."

Simon nodded begrudging agreement. "What about my body? What are you going to bury? Oh! Can I design my monument?"

General Anhalt spoke, "There will be no body, Your Highness. It seems that you, being an impetuous boy, sneak out of the palace tomorrow night. A foolish practice, but consistent with this royal family."

Adele gave an expression of mock offense at the sirdar.

He continued the tale. "Being the most loyal of retainers, I note your absence and set out to find you. Your intention is to attend a public performance of questionable taste, but you are set upon by Prince Gareth. I intervene to defend you, but the vampire lifts you into the air and laboriously carries you over the Mediterranean, where you are dropped and lost in the embrace of the sea."

"You can't save me, General Anhalt?" Simon asked, a bit hurt.

"I fear not." The general's face was stern. "But take some solace that this is a work of fiction. If it were real, you would be safe."

Adele moved toward the sirdar. "General, if this part disturbs you, we can concoct another story."

"No, Majesty. It's only temporary, until it is revealed to the world that Prince Simon is alive and well, and living with bloodthirsty creatures in the wilds of Katanga."

"We have no idea how long the ruse will last."

"So be it. We must all sacrifice in time of war. My reputation is little to ask."

"Wait!" Simon shouted, throwing his arms up. "I don't want to die sneaking off to some show. How about I'm protecting Adele."

She said, "That's nice, but it has to happen somewhere private. No one can see you die except one of us here in this room."

"Oh wait!" the boy announced. "What about this story? We're up on the roof, practicing fencing. Me, Adele, and Greyfriar. I am teaching Greyfriar a few of my moves, when Prince Gareth swoops out of the dark and attacks." Simon swept up Pet under the front legs and acted as if the cat had pounced on him. The boy dropped to the floor, thrashing from side to side, pretending to be struggling in combat with the semiconscious cat. "While Greyfriar tries to get Adele to safety, I fight Gareth off. Screeching. Clawing. Moving like lightning. But he's no match for me!" Simon jumped to his feet and leapt around the room, swinging the rapier, causing everyone to duck or shrink back against a wall. "But finally, no matter how hard I fight, no matter how many times I strike him, he will not die. Finally, even I can fight no longer." The boy dropped dramatically to one knee as if struck. He took Pet, who was beginning to grow annoyed, and held him up to his face. "Aagh! He hovers over me with his claws and teeth dripping with my blood. But I must hold him off a bit longer. He tries to break away to reach Adele, but I slide in front of him. He curses at me: 'Stand aside! I am Gareth of Scotland!' And I reply with a smile, 'And I am Simon, prince of Bengal. I would like you to meet my dagger!' With my last breath . . . one . . . last . . . blow! We slam together. Claw and blade!" He slid the flat of the blade harmlessly along the cat's abdomen. Pet finally growled and sprang free from the boy's hands, but he only went a few steps and collapsed contentedly to the floor. "Prince Gareth cannot long withstand my savage strikes, and so he seizes me and flies high into the air." Simon gurgled and jabbed the sword into the empty air before collapsing next to the cat. "Adele is safe, but I am mortally wounded. And due to the cruelty of bloody Prince Gareth, I die."

The empress put her hand to her tight mouth, struggling to fight tears. But it was futile. She felt the drops slipping down her face as she stared at the little body on the carpet, his chest heaving from exertion. The men in the room watched him with smiles of admiration, which brought her emotions out even stronger.

Greyfriar pointed at the sprawled boy. "That's a good story. I like it much better than the first one."

"Fine." Adele turned away briefly to wipe her eyes. Then she knelt next to her brother, who was still supine on the floor. "Simon, would you like to take Pet to Katanga? Look at the lazy beast. He's growing bored and fat, and needs adventure."

The prince laid a hand on the cat, who rolled on his back inviting a belly rub. The boy pressed his face against the cat's fuzzy midsection and shook his head back and forth with a laugh. Then he lifted the languid feline, kissed him on top of the head, and handed him to Adele.

"I'll be too busy becoming a killing machine to take care of him," Simon said with his gaze locked on his sister. "And with everyone away, you'll need him."

She squeezed the purring cat and cupped her brother's cheek with her other hand. He had grown up without her even noticing. He stood over her in a protective posture. Adele took a deep breath and sat cross-legged on the floor, facing her inner circle. "Gentlemen, shall we proceed?"

Greyfriar and Msiri grasped Simon's shoulders while General Anhalt stood by proudly with hands clasped behind his back. The boy looked at each with admiration. The young prince had lost his father months before at the hands of Flay, but he had new fathers now who would die before they failed him.

Adele studied her brother's face out of fear that it could be a very long time before she saw him again.

CHAPTER 20

GARETH WATCHED ADELE as she stared out of the window toward the open sea. A day that was bright and clear had ended, and now darkness stretched before them. Her mouth was a grim line, and her hands clenched the sill as if she dangled from it for dear life.

In the span of bare weeks, her life had been shaken to the core. The fall of her beloved Mamoru had come without warning. The exposure of Lord Aden had revealed that the peril of betrayal still existed. Simon was already on an airship on his way to Katanga for an unknown period of time. Tomorrow she would make the public announcement of her brother's "murder." And Gareth's own imminent departure for the north weighed heavily on her. Where once their days had been bright with promise, even if false, now they seemed forever mired in politics, deceit, and death.

He stepped behind her and placed his arms around her. She did not react or lean back into him, as if afraid to allow herself to enjoy the moment.

"Everything will turn out fine, you'll see," Gareth told her.

"I can't sense him."

"Sense who?"

"Simon. He's too far away. I lost him a few hours ago." A shuddering sigh escaped Adele, and she turned to Gareth. "He's out there alone. He's just a little boy."

"He isn't alone, and he isn't a little boy. Simon is a young man, if you haven't noticed. And he has King Msiri to help him. Please don't worry. He'll return."

"What about you? You're off to the arms of Flay and Cesare. This could be the last time—" Her throat convulsed, unable to voice her dismal thought.

"Shhh." He stared into her eyes, sparkling like part coal and part diamonds. "I would enjoy having a meal together before I leave."

"It's not like you can eat it."

"I enjoy chewing as much as the next man. Flavor is overrated."

His jest didn't sway her bitterness. "I'm not hungry."

"You have to eat."

"I'm not in the mood to talk pleasantries to anyone," she insisted.

That Gareth understood, after all he was a consummate brooder. He kissed her throat. Her skin was cold. His warm breath made her shiver. He picked up his scarf where it lay with his gear and lightly wound it around her neck. "Here. Keep this. It will keep you warm while I am away."

Her hands reached for it at first annoyed, but then relishing it. The lonely nights without him frightened her. Her fingers crushed the cloth. She didn't trust her voice, so she said nothing. But her chest shuddered with the swell of emotion within her. He stood with her for a long time, both of them staring out into the black.

Finally, he said, "I'll leave you alone. I have something to take care of, but then I'll come back."

Adele started to remove his scarf, but he held up a hand. Gareth pulled one of her long red Persian scarves from the back of the door and wrapped it around his face.

"I'll wear one of yours," he said. "This gives me a bit of color, yes?"

Adele forced a wan smile, but clearly her heart was not in it. He drew in her scent from the scarf as he padded out of the suite into the hallway, where he found Zarina pacing back and forth.

"Is the empress all right?" the maid asked, eyeing the colorful cloth around his face.

Greyfriar nodded. "She has much on her mind."

Zarina wrung her hands. "She has barely eaten in two days. Almost three. She cannot go on like this."

"She will come around." He turned to go.

Zarina clutched at his cloak. "Please, sir. Do whatever you can do to make her take a meal."

Greyfriar could smell the fear in her. The servant had always been hesitant around him; his masked face did not affect all humans positively. That she was asking this favor showed just how distraught she was over Adele. He reached out to her to reassure her, but she jerked back her hand. "I will do what I can. Don't worry."

"Thank you, sir." She curtsied before him.

Greyfriar headed toward the bowels of the palace and the kitchen. It was well past dinnertime, and the staff had concluded their work and had headed for their quarters, intending a good evening's rest before starting all over again tomorrow. The kitchen was quiet, and Greyfriar liked it. However, he had no idea where anything was. A plaintive cry at his feet attracted his attention. Pet was curling between his legs, apparently hungry, as he usually was. Most likely the cat was a regular in the kitchens, looking for scraps from a softhearted cook.

The cat gave another meow and then sat staring in front of a cupboard. Greyfriar took it as a sign. Reaching down to scrub the cat between the ears, he opened the cupboard. There were dishes inside, including one that had Pet's scent on it. He pulled it out and the cat grew more excited, only he didn't know what to put it in. He figured the cat would tell him eventually. He had more pressing issues, and he started opening more of the various panels looking for what he needed. Then he spied something familiar.

A teapot. His mind cast back to the memory of Adele making tea on the floor of the British Museum when she had been a prisoner of the dreaded prince of Scotland. It brought a quick smile about his lips. She had used a helmet to boil water then, but the teapot was ideal. He had seen many of his subjects use them. His mind made up, he proceeded to explore the rest of the kitchen with a curious Pet trailing along behind him.

He found drying herbs hanging from nails in a rafter, long bundles tied together with thin string. It wasn't long before he found an herb that was reminiscent of the one Adele used so long ago. The smell of mint was unmistakable. Their brittle leaves crumbled under his thick fingers, coating the tabletop in a rough dust. Grumbling under his breath, he painstakingly labored to separate a few whole leaves from the stalks and place them in the teapot. Soon the sharp scent filled the kitchen.

Finally he had enough to brew a decent pot of tea for Adele, and he had only to find water to boil. There was a spigot over a ceramic sink, and he filled the teapot nearly to the brim. He brought it over to a massive stove along one wall. Thankfully the stove was still warm. It was a large squat contraption made of cast iron adorned with elaborate nickel filigree work at the corners. He had a similar one in Edinburgh, though he had never had to deal with it. Morgana kept it running when needed. Pet flopped in front of it, stretching out on his back and basking in the warmth.

Stepping over the sprawled cat, he put the sloshing teapot on the stove and sat and watched. Half an hour later, with Pet languishing in his lap, he was still watching. The water was warmer, but not hot. Annoyed, he stood and lifted a circular lid from the top of the stove to peer in. The coals beneath were mostly grey ash with just the hint of a glow at the center. Growling, he seized an iron rod and jabbed them. The glow intensified, but it didn't get much hotter. He stalked about the kitchen until he found the coal bin. He grabbed as much coal as his hands could carry and dumped it into the hole. Gripping the iron poker tightly, he stirred the coals again, waiting for them to catch fire. When none did, he went back to the coal chute. As carefully as he could he added more coal, but the black soot was getting everywhere. Using the sleeve of his jacket he tried to wipe down the stovetop with little result. Pet sneezed violently as coal dust settled over him. He jumped up on the counter to get out of the way and yowled in displeasure.

To Greyfriar's delight, the heat was building and the coals were starting to glow. He put the iron lid back on the stove with his bare hand and then shoved the container of water directly over it.

"Ha," he declared triumphantly to the dubious cat.

He remembered Morgana throwing eggs in boiling water to make a meal. He could take care of both things at one time. A basket of eggs sat meekly upon a shelf. He grabbed a couple of them, but immediately they crushed in his hand. Surprised by how delicate they were, he cleaned his hands as best he could, leaving a runny sooty mess in the sink, and everywhere else. This time, ever so carefully, his fingers plucked four eggs, as they seemed rather small, and gingerly carried them to the pot of water, which was just steaming on the stove top. He placed them into the teapot, and two eggs immediately cracked and exuded filmy whites.

Scowling, he left them to boil and located a loaf of crusty bread. Greyfriar used his own dagger to cut a hunk of it off. At least this action was familiar. He offered a piece to the cat, who sniffed and walked away. Apparently, Pet did not eat bread. Greyfriar was still pleased with his work, and he brought the nicely sliced bread back to the stove. To his annoyance the water still wasn't boiling, just steaming. He sat down to wait. Soon he had to remove his jacket, as the air was getting warm.

Standing by his empty dish, Pet was growing impatient and griped to Greyfriar.

"You've been here longer," the vampire said. "You should know where things are."

Pet just stared, emerald eyes boring into him. Morgana used to feed the cats milk when they stared like that. Wearily, Greyfriar went in search of milk, but found none. But he did come across a large haunch of lamb hung up high. He threw that on the cat's dish. Pet jumped about three feet in the air when the meat landed with a thud, then rushed back in sheer joy at his prosperous meal. Pet gripped the hairy thing with his claws and started to eat, growling and grunting at the effort.

Greyfriar went back to the stove and stared at the murky boiling water now swirling with mint leaves and bobbing eggs with greenish whites hanging out.

"Finally," he murmured, gathering his jacket and gloves.

He had no idea how long to let them cook so he sat down to rest; the sweltering kitchen, along with the growing heat of early spring in Alexandria, was starting to impact his energy. He let the eggs bounce around for another few minutes before he proceeded to grab a tray and load it with what he had wrought.

The preparation had only taken two hours.

Pet lay on the floor next to his meal with an extended gut and meowed in stuporous satisfaction.

"I'm heading back to Adele. Are you coming?"

Pet rose lazily to his feet and stretched, but was unable to move more than a few steps. Greyfriar grabbed the engorged cat and placed him on his shoulder, where the feline settled immediately with sharp claws clutching his jacket and scarf. Greyfriar then went back upstairs, tray in hand, leaving a war-torn kitchen behind.

—⁓—

Adele tried to still the dread thoughts in her head and the anguish gripping her heart. Everything had spiraled so quickly out of control. She had been forced to make decisions that weighed upon her like a mountain of stone.

The worst of it was that she was wasting her last night with Gareth. She was tired of letting logic dictate their future. Always the fear of their differences stopped them from going further. Yes, they were wildly different, but there was much about them that was similar. Despite the dangers and uncertainty of a physical act, Adele now longed to let go.

A horrifying unease invaded her being every time she thought of him leaving. If she waited too long the chance could be gone forever. She bit her lip. That thought jarred her. Enough with lamenting things that couldn't change. They would have a quiet night together and dream of days without war and strife in the sanctuary of her room. She refused to let her heart stumble over things she couldn't know.

Gareth had said he'd return soon, but that was hours ago. He most likely assumed she wanted to contemplate in solitude. Cursing her own stupid selfish behavior, she shoved herself away from the window ready to go hunt him. There was a knock at the door and Adele assumed it was Zarina with another attempt at a meal. She strode over and opened the door, ready to protest and bid her maid to go.

Instead, there stood the man himself, with Pet perched contentedly on his shoulder. Adele's gaze lowered and caught sight of the tray in his hands.

"I thought you might reconsider an evening meal," he told her. "I cooked it myself."

"You cooked?" Abruptly, Adele's throat caught. She bit her lower lip before it trembled. "Gareth—"

"It's my first attempt. It may be appalling."

A smile broke over Adele's face as she tugged him into the room. He set the tray on the table on the balcony. Stars had appeared in the night sky, and filtered light from the city of Alexandria cast a warm blush over the Mediterranean shoreline.

She joined him on the settee and watched in amazement as he poured her tea with careful precision. There were even porcelain teacups, which he gingerly handled. "How on earth did you manage this?"

"Pet was no help at all, but it is rewarding just to see you smile."

"You made tea," she stated incredulously. "And eggs!"

"I had no idea how fragile they were."

"How many did you break?" she asked, laughing.

"I'm not answering."

"Two-minute eggs are my favorite."

"Two minutes?" he said nervously.

Adele proceeded to grab one and crack it open. The yolk was hard and very firm. The whites were discolored and like rubber. "Well, five-minute eggs are good too. They smell a bit . . . minty."

"That's the tea," he said.

Her mind brought up that same day in the British Museum. "You remembered."

"Yes."

Adele lifted her teacup and took a sip. Immediately the musky flavor of eggs mixed with mint and something like coal hit her tongue. She made a great effort not to grimace. She closed her eyes and swallowed, and then smiled at him. "It's wonderful."

She set the teacup to the side and turned to him. She wanted to live only in this moment and in the warm touch of his hand. Tonight of all nights, she didn't care about policy or species. She only wanted to lie with him forever. She removed his glasses and slowly unwound the scarf from his face. His hand lifted to hold the nape of her neck as she kissed him. Resting against him she wrapped her arms around his chest, clinging to him. Her eyes closed. Another captured moment frozen in time. She had learned to relish them more than any other. They were fleeting, as was his time with her.

"I don't know how to let you go," she whispered with a voice broken by soft despair.

Pulling back, he brushed her lower lip with a callused thumb, barely touching her, and then kissed her once more. It was like being scalded with an open flame one second and then soothed with ice in the next. Adele closed her eyes and felt his gentle fingers move to her cheek and temple, ear and neck.

He pulled her closer to him so that their bodies crushed together. Adele's skin was flushed, and his hands were cool and reviving. She heard his scarcely constrained breathing as it drew in and out in a poor imitation of a normal function. Where his fingers were coarse, his lips were soft and firm. The contrast made her sway in his arms. He bit back a moan and pulled away from her again, but she wouldn't let him. There was no hesitation now. She ran a tongue lightly over his lips as if searching out one last taste of him.

He froze and then asked, "Are you sure?"

"Yes." She repeated, "Yes."

"We will never be parted," he assured her. "Never." His voice was soothing, full of a future life that they could only dream about.

Her consciousness fragmented into a dozen separate sensations. She felt as if she were in freefall, her arms wrapped around Gareth's neck as they stepped off the precipice. The soft rolls of the cushion beneath them; the scent of mint on the evening ocean breeze; the cool timber of the settee against her bare thigh; his firm hands across her ribs. Sensations swirled and coalesced behind her eyelids, fading and then surging again.

She would never stop loving him no matter where their paths led them. Never would she have regrets.

CHAPTER 21

ALEXANDRIA WAS SWADDLED in black. Windows, doors, shop fronts, and lampposts were festooned with somber drapery blowing in the wet Mediterranean wind. It was the day of Prince Simon's funeral. Men went about with black armbands, and women wore widow's weeds, or mourning robes and scarves.

The city was heartbroken, but there was also a sense of bottled rage waiting to surge north. *Avenge Simon* was the watchword of the day. Broadsheets were plastered on the grand avenues and narrow lanes, as well as the back alleys, demanding the manhood of Equatoria rise up and show their mettle.

In the days since the palace had announced the terrible news that shocked the city, volunteers to the army had increased by thousands. Men from all walks of life crowded recruiting stations in Alexandria, but also in Cairo and Mombasa and Ulundi and Damascus and Shiraz and Bombay and Mandalay and in countless towns and villages across the Empire and associated states. They raised their hands, took the oath of loyalty to the empress and the sirdar, and demanded to be armed and dispatched across the Mediterranean to kill vampires.

The front page of *The Times* brought citizens to tears with a photo of General Anhalt greeting the empress dressed in black. The sirdar was well known to have been a favorite of Simon's, a natural father to both imperial siblings. And there, in a stark candid photograph, was the stern officer and the sister caught in a moment of shared sorrow. Those who had been present at the touching meeting noted how particularly stricken the empress appeared when the crowd began to chant "Death to Gareth."

The Greyfriar was not in Alexandria. In fact, he had not been seen since the murder of Prince Simon. His disappearance saddened many who were sorry that he was not present to comfort his empress. The overwhelming belief, however, was that the swordsman was in hot pursuit of the murderer Gareth. Only the legendary Greyfriar could track the prince of Scotland to his lair, and kill him.

At the funeral, Empress Adele defied protocol yet again by walking in the funeral cortege. As a woman, she should have ridden in a carriage behind the casket. However, she insisted on walking alone behind Simon's coffin carried on a black ammunition caisson drawn by six massive black horses whose hooves clopped loudly in the dense silence as black feathers bobbed with each horse's steps. Behind her trod General Anhalt, leading an Arabian stallion with a black cloth draped over its riderless saddle. A drum beat slowly in time to the shuffling feet moving out the main gate of Victoria Palace.

The wagon carrying the casket clattered into the narrow streets of Old Town, where onlookers hung out windows and overhanging second stories. Following the sirdar came the Privy Council and General Staff. All members of Commons who were physically capable walked slowly behind, headed by Prime Minister Kemal. More than two hundred official mourners flowed south to the main city, where they reached the great crossroads at Karnak Square. Under watchful but tearful eyes, the parade circled the roundabout and went back toward the palace via a different route.

Prince Simon had been the nation's little brother, and they all needed to see the funeral since he would be interred under Victoria Palace, away from access to the general population. To most, the only pretense in the ceremony was that the prince's body was present in the black-and-silver casket. Simon had been lost at sea after being carried away by Prince Gareth before the eyes of his horrified sister. The thought of that brave boy struggling to stay afloat, sinking exhausted into the water, dying frightened and alone, only added to the rage toward the callous vampire assassin.

The procession wended its way back into Victoria Square, passing the mighty equestrian bronze of Emperor Simon I. Those in the crowd bowed their heads, removed hats, and saluted in honor. The empress placed a hand on the back of the casket as she followed her brother through the mob. Tears flowed from everyone.

The horses and caisson passed through the gate and entered a phalanx of White Guardsmen at attention. The cortege halted before the front portico. The empress stepped back to Sirdar Anhalt's side. She watched, idly stroking the empty horse, as a single drum beat out mournful time. Members of her Harmattan led by Captain Shirazi approached the small coffin with slow, measured paces. They reached up and took hold of the silver handles with white-gloved hands. Then, with each beat, they drew the casket back, taking the burden onto their shoulders. When the weight was fully on the soldiers, they wheeled and marched up the steps, again led by the drummer. Empress Adele fell in behind, followed by Anhalt and the rest of the court mourners. Slowly, the recessional disappeared into Victoria Palace. The great entry doors closed. Soldiers moved into place across the portico.

The remainder of the ceremony in the crypt below the palace would be away from prying eyes. Funerals of the imperial family were always private, and the fear of attacks after the opera bombing meant everyone understood the increased need for security.

The crowd began to drift away, their thoughts turning to their own families and the threat from the north. If the vampires could reach out and seize the royal family, there was no one they couldn't grasp. The growing fear and anger over the enemy to the north was tempered by the one figure so notably absent in the funeral procession.

Everyone expected and fervently hoped that when Greyfriar returned home, Prince Gareth would be no more.

—✺—

Lyon seemed more crowded than the last time Gareth had passed through. There was a frenetic war sensibility, packs moving about, herds being brought in from the countryside and left to wander the city. The stink of close-packed humanity had risen.

Gareth drifted to the Hotel de Ville, and the Lyonnaise watched the stranger with suspicion, another sign of a city at war. Two vampires confronted him as he started inside.

"Name yourself," one demanded. "What's your business here?"

Gareth drew up haughtily. "I am Gareth of Scotland. I'm here to see Flay."

Both guards stepped aside with sneers. "Fine."

Gareth strode past them, ignoring their curious glances at the canvas bag he carried. He passed through corridors clotted with recently spilled blood until he found Flay in conference with another vampire whom Gareth took for the Lyonnaise war chief. Their tone was not collegial, and the anger was palpable.

As soon as he entered, Flay rose with her eyes locked on the bag. The Lyonnaise continued debating tactics, arguing for an attack on Grenoble to liberate it from the humans. When he noticed that Flay was no longer listening, nor even pretending, he glared at Gareth.

Flay moved toward the prince, nostrils flaring. "So, you have it."

Gareth tossed the bundle on a nearby table and slouched in a chair with unconcern.

The Lyonnaise war chief raised his arms sarcastically. "Are we finished, then? Is our discussion concluded?"

"Yes, Murrd," Flay said without looking at him. "I'll send for you when I require more from you."

"Oh. Well, fine. I'll just go then?"

"Yes. Go."

Murrd huffed from the room, muttering about how this was Lyon, not London.

Flay lifted the bag and smelled it. The canvas was stained with an enormous amount of dried blood. She then dropped it.

Gareth asked, "Don't you want to look at it?"

"It's a hand, I'm sure. You did it. You actually killed the boy." She smiled broadly as she perched on the edge of the table with an open posture she hadn't shown to Gareth in very many years.

Gareth posed with a cavalier finger to his cheek, but his gut twisted with bile at the war chief.

"I imagine the poor princess is quite distraught with grief." Flay laughed and lay back on the table, her long arms stretched out languidly and her night black hair swirling around her pale face. The long coat from her blue-and-buff military uniform fell open, and her high leather boots squeaked as she twisted her feet together.

Gareth could kill her in this moment. He desperately wanted to do it and wipe Adele's name from the war chief's lips. He might never get such a chance again. Her bare chest and sternum lay open as she exulted in her moment of triumph. He sat up and flexed his fingers. However, killing Flay now wouldn't serve the long-range goals he and Adele had. He needed the war chief if he was to become king.

She glanced at him from her place supine atop the table. "Nothing to say, my lord? You're not concerned about the princess's discomfort, are you?"

"No, Flay. I'm only thinking of the future."

"The future? What's next for the Greyfriar?"

"Nothing. The Greyfriar is dead. He'll be seen no more."

Flay looked strangely saddened. "That's too bad. I wanted to kill him."

"You have, Flay. In your own way." Gareth grew stern.

"Fine." The war chief sat up, almost disappointed that a grim Gareth had truncated her excitement. Still, there was a sense of relief about her, a calmness that he rarely saw. She picked up the bag with the boy's hand, swinging it idly. "You are summoned to London for his coven and coronation."

Gareth laughed bitterly.

Flay said, "Cesare wants you to witness his triumph. He won't be crowned without you there."

"Or dead."

Flay shrugged. "That's not his preference. Yet."

He said, "Then it will benefit me to take my time traveling to London."

"That won't please Cesare. He's already missed one full moon." Flay tossed the canvas bag into a corner. "What is your plan?"

Gareth leaned forward. "Can you still turn the Pale against Cesare?"

She scowled. "My control over them isn't what it once was. Many of the old members died in Edinburgh at the hands of the butcher Clark.

The newer recruits are more loyal to Cesare than to me. I have specific fighters I can call on, but many of the packs were reorganized by Hallow and Cesare during my exile."

"It's obvious that Cesare fears you. Tell me more about Cesare's allies. Perhaps there's a weakness there."

Without hesitation, Flay laid out what she knew of Cesare's politics. Gareth already knew about his brother's so-called Grand Coalition of the North—consisting of London, Munich, Budapest, and New York—but there was more to learn. She explained the ties with St. Etienne and Lyon, and the failure to draw Grenoble into the group. Already it was annoyingly complicated with deals on provisions of herds for the packs of allied forces. And Cesare was providing promises to allow his human, Lord Aden, to mine coal in clan lands. Gareth smirked, but didn't interrupt. Flay was grateful she had little to do with the politics, even though she had to suffer constant bickering from Lyon about receiving compensation for feeding the British packs who came to fight. Fearing an imminent human push from the south, the packs of Draken of Munich were breaking off from the Hungarian front to reinforce Lyon.

Flay concluded, "The key to the future is Paris. The northern French clans will come into the war, but only if Paris does. King Lothaire will only treat with a king. Hence Cesare's rush to the throne."

Gareth nodded thoughtfully, considering with silent alarm the wide swathe Cesare was planning. This would be the greatest clan alliance since the Great Killing. It would be a federation of packs likely sufficient to roll back the struggling human offensive. And it would make Cesare king of kings in all but name. However, Paris was an interesting twist.

"King Lothaire," Gareth said, "was a friend of mine."

"Was?"

"Well, I haven't exactly maintained my companionships among our kind for a century or more. But we were quite close once. I lived with him in Paris for many years." He pointed at Flay. "I think we should pay him a visit on the way to London."

"We?"

"Of course. We have to coordinate our action against my brother. Is there some problem with you leaving Lyon?"

Flay said eagerly, "No. I'm the alliance war chief. If I have reason to travel, so be it. When should I meet you in Paris?"

"A few days. Keep a low profile, if possible. We dare not let Cesare know that you and I are together. We'll sound out Lothaire's support for our coup."

Gareth grinned at the war chief's toothy smile and quickening breath. Flay would be a most fearful opponent on the battlefield; he doubted he could best her in even combat. But she had been alone so long it was a simple task to twist her and bind her with tiny little words like *we* and *our*.

CHAPTER 22

"SIGNAL FROM *BOLIVAR*, sir. They are ready to commence bombardment."

Senator Clark saluted the ensign. The massive USS *Bolivar* cruised alongside the senator's relatively small frigate, *Ranger*. Unlike the frigate, *Bolivar* was a "steamnaught." It was a dirigible-shaped steel colossus with its buoyancy elements enclosed inside armor and one hundred guns bristling from six rows of gun ports along both flanks, as well as heavy turrets on the dorsal and ventral. This airship was the pinnacle of American military engineering, a new era in air firepower.

Senator Clark was the master of this grand armada. He was a tall man, muscular and powerful. His weathered face sported a heavy black beard, and his eyes shone with nearly manic clarity of purpose. He wore a blue officer's tunic with brass buttons and gold piping. He adjusted the heavy Fahrenheit saber dangling from his leather gun belt. White gaiters glowed stark against the dark uniform. His usual white Stetson hat was missing, and his collar-length wavy black hair tousled in the wind.

He put a brass spyglass to his eye to scan the ragged little city below him. Wilmington. It sat beside the Cape Fear River, close to the Atlantic. Not perfect, but the best harbor between Charleston and the Chesapeake. And he intended to have it as his rear base for the campaign against Richmond.

He saw vampires swirling low over the city.

He sensed someone at his shoulder: Major Stoddard, his ever-present adjutant. "It's a beautiful sight, isn't it, Major?"

"Wilmington?"

"*Bolivar*. The steamnaught may lack the charm of sail, but there's a brutal loveliness in that steel hulk."

The major nodded. He was thin and not quite so tall as the senator. His dark face was still and observant. His eyes moved frequently, but his expression rarely changed. Stoddard's thoughtful stillness was the corollary to the boisterous flamboyance that the senator invested in his every move.

Stoddard found no great delight in the massive battleship that blotted out the sky on *Ranger*'s port beam. Its aluminum-burst engines boiled rancid smoke from multiple stacks. She wasn't maneuverable and took ages to bring her boilers up to top speed, but she packed more firepower than the entire sailing airship fleet that darted around her.

Clark must have taken Stoddard's silence for dissension rather than thoughtful consideration. He said with a pointed guffaw, "Ah. You've become argumentative on this campaign, Major. You're old-fashioned. If I had a fleet of steamnaughts, I'd conquer the Earth. After we take care of these monsters, we'll have a go at South America, eh? Fancy a house in Buenos Aires?"

Stoddard thought it best to give a brief chuckle, then asked, "You think they'll come when we open up?"

Clark swiveled his telescope back to the black specks flitting over Wilmington. "Oh, they'll come. Surprised they're not here already. They know we took Savannah and Charleston. Hell, half these things came from there. They'll fight."

"Not so sure, Senator. Southern clans tend to be itinerant. Move with the season. They're smaller and don't have much love of territory."

"No. This is the place. They'll try to hold Cape Fear. From here north is real vampire territory." Clark growled with anticipation, then shouted over his shoulder to the quarterdeck, "Captain, you may signal the fleet to commence operations!"

"Aye, sir!" Within seconds, colored flags ran out along the yards on *Ranger*. The frigate and the other escorting airships peeled away from the battleship's mighty flanks to clear the gun ports. *Ranger* surged forward and below the goliath, like a slim shark guiding a whale. *Bolivar* shifted its course slightly.

"*Bolivar* may fire when ready!" Clark laughed. New signal flags ran out, and the frigate fired two loud deck guns, but they seemed loud only for a second.

Bolivar opened fire. Massive deep booms vibrated the air. Stoddard felt them roll over him as if they would crush his chest, and they drew a great rush of adrenaline from him. Smoke blasted out of *Bolivar* as the cannons on the port side roared. Nearly fifty steel monsters belched volcanic smoke in concert. The belly turrets fore and aft opened up too, throwing tongues of fire into the sky. The sound and power were unbelievable. The ship was an awesome sight.

Stoddard and Clark turned as one from the thundering *Bolivar* to the unsuspecting little town below. The whistling shells ended in explosions of flame. In addition to fire, oily green smoke puffed up around the city, and emerald clouds slowly rose and spread.

Small black shapes lifted into the air above the green haze. They rode the wind toward the fleet cruising over the jagged coastline. Soldiers on board *Ranger* crowded the side with rifles ready. Men stood at heavy machine guns mounted on the rails and in the tops.

Stoddard's pulse throbbed in his head as he watched the drifting horde close. The vampires shifted in the air like summer insects, making it nearly impossible to draw a bead on them. Most of the creatures made for *Bolivar* until the escort ships peppered the sky with small-arms fire and shrapnel shells from their cannons. Stoddard felt the deck vibrate as *Ranger*'s guns opened up. The weapons fire drew the attention of the vampires.

Soon the air around *Ranger* and her sister ships was thick with vampires. Machine guns chattered. Bullets cut through the creatures tumbling in the air, who then maneuvered and righted themselves. It never failed to surprise humans to see vampires absorb massive damage and keep coming as if nothing had happened. It was easy for humans to panic and break if they were unfamiliar with it. The creatures seemed supernatural and undefeatable.

"Keep firing!" Clark shouted. "Keep at 'em!"

Stoddard pulled his long-barreled Colt Army revolver and shot into the masts, where vampires landed and crawled among the sails and spars like horrible lizards. The faces of the creatures were horrific. The vampires came ever closer, seizing the railings, crawling down the masts, and over the surface of the metal cage enclosing the dirigible.

"Shriekers!" Stoddard yelled, unsure if he could be heard over the thick gunfire. "Shriekers!"

He swung his glowing Fahrenheit saber at a creature as it tried to push through the line of troopers who were already being pressed back from the rail by savage claws and teeth. Some soldiers drew short swords and pistols for bloody close action. Others fired their rifles up into the yards to keep the creatures from dropping behind them.

"Keep them back!" the senator commanded with amazing composure. If the vampires broke the line and got to the center of the deck, they would create a terrible melee and throw the humans into chaos.

A high-pitched scream started across the length of the ship. Stoddard saw an airman standing at a pedestal, turning a handle attached to a simple brass box contraption with an amplifier horn on one side. The shrieker's terrible whine felt like a knife in Stoddard's head, and the vampires, whose hearing was far more sensitive, staggered and even drew back. The soldiers pressed the advantage with guns and blades, hacking and shooting the creatures, gaining back precious feet of deck space.

The victory was short-lived. Two vampires dropped onto the sailor at the shrieker and bore him to the deck. In seconds, they eviscerated him and then tried to damage the metal gears of the shrieker.

Stoddard leapt to them, firing his pistol and delivering a solid saber blow to one vampire's neck. The thing jerked and fell. Stoddard fired again, and then the hammer fell on an empty cylinder. A bloody smile appeared before him.

The grinning vampire's face exploded. Senator Clark kicked the flailing thing to the deck and shot it several more times. Dripping with gore, Stoddard reloaded his revolver and, without comment, stepped onto the shrieker's platform. He tugged the handle slowly at first, but then it caught and the noise began to rise, cutting through his head. Clark turned away to rejoin the smoke and blood around them.

Creatures moved overhead like monkeys in a tropical forest. Stoddard shot upward when he could see a target, and ducked wildly when he couldn't. The wail of the shrieker became a dull thud in his head. He could no longer hear the sounds of gunfire or soldiers screaming. It seemed like hours that he stood turning that handle while pale arms reached for him. Razor blades raked his head and face. Warm blood drizzled down and fell onto his hands and the wooden planks. Soldiers protecting him fell bloody at his feet. Vampires dropped twitching, heads smashed by rifle butts, chests opened by swords and axes.

Stoddard saw Senator Clark draw a hand across his throat in a signal to stop. The major released the shrieker handle and let it wind down on its own. Only when he let go did he realize he was too weak to stand and stumbled to the deck on top of bodies, both human and vampire. Hands grabbed him and he saw faces mouthing words he couldn't hear. They pressed him back against the shrieker pedestal and he stared at the underside of the dirigible, watching the tattered lines and flapping sails.

Fabric rustled overhead, backlit by the sun. Sails.

Stoddard had to report to Senator Clark. He struggled to stand, but his feet were trapped by cloth. Perhaps one of the yardarms had fallen on the deck. Oddly enough, his boots were gone. He was barefooted. He reached down to pull himself free of the entanglement. The deck was strangely soft and spongy; it was difficult to stand. Still he pushed up until something gave way and he tumbled hard to the ground.

Voices shouted. Fingers seized his arms, pulling him to his feet. He tried to shove them away. He had to find the senator. He recognized the face of Dr. Lo, the ship's surgeon on *Ranger*. The doctor stared at him and spoke softly with unintelligible words. Stoddard was pushed down onto a cot. He felt the edge of the makeshift bed, the hard wooden slats and the rough canvas.

This wasn't the deck of *Ranger*. He turned to each side and saw rows of cots filled with men. They were all injured. The canvas around him wasn't a sail. It was a tent.

He was in a camp hospital. He wondered why.

"Can you hear me, Major?"

Stoddard looked at Dr. Lo, who smiled with obvious relief.

"Excellent," the doctor said in an oddly muffled voice.

"Where is Senator Clark?" Stoddard asked slowly.

Dr. Lo laughed. "Don't worry about him. He's fine. Not a scratch, as usual. You, on the other hand, took a beating. They say you stood at the shrieker while vampires clawed you to pieces. And since I put every one of five hundred stitches in you, I'd say they're right." He took Stoddard's wrist and felt his forehead. "You can hear, at least. Pulse is strong enough. No fever that I can tell. Lucky your wounds haven't gone septic. Vampires are filthy things."

"Where am I?"

"Wilmington."

"We took the city?"

"Yes. The vampires fled."

"How long has it been?"

The doctor thought. "Four days? Something like that. I've lost track of time with all the casualties."

"Four days." Stoddard started to rise. "I've got to get back to duty."

"You're not going anywhere, Major. Just lie still."

Stoddard grimaced and fell back, exhausted. His head was splitting, and there was a sharp buzzing in his ears. He smelled a nauseating stench.

Apparently he made a face at the stink because Dr. Lo said, "We tried to move the hospital far enough out, but you can still smell it."

"What is it?"

"They're burning the herds. Or burying them as fast as we can. Thank goodness it's still cold or I'd be a lot more worried about cholera. I don't look forward to spring and summer assaults."

Stoddard asked groggily, "How many did we kill?"

"Oh, I couldn't tell you. The vampires fought for a few hours, then took off to the north."

"No. How many humans?"

"Last figure I saw, across the fleet, we lost six hundred and fifty killed in battle. Over five thousand wounded, and nearly twenty-five hundred seriously. And a thousand of those will die soon enough from infection."

"How many of the locals? The local humans. How many did we kill?"

"All of them. All of them in Wilmington anyway. Thousands? Who knows? Who counts? They just stood there and died like animals in the gas."

Stoddard tried to block out the smell of burnt flesh by covering his nose with the crook of his elbow before rolling to retch over the side of the cot.

———

Major Stoddard left the medical tent the next day. The makeshift hospital was a collection of large tents set amidst a vast forest of tall straight pine trees. The medical camp was surrounded by a barbed wire fence and machine-gun emplacements, and it was patrolled by soldiers with pikes. Troopers saluted the major as he limped toward a gate, or gap in the wire enclosure. A crude wagon waited with a single thin horse. The private on the buckboard gave Stoddard a hand up.

"Where'd this wagon come from?" the major asked.

"Here in town. Found the horse not far away from some herds who lived outside town." The soldier laughed. "Pretending to be real people. Funny, huh?"

Stoddard didn't reply as the wagon lurched forward. They rolled between countless crackling cadaver bonfires that sent black greasy plumes into the sky. More wagons lumbered the rutted path. They were loaded with twisted limbs of the dead.

As they rolled out of the pine forest, Wilmington appeared squat and brick. It was dwarfed by the bulk of *Bolivar* floating above it, its shadow like a pall over the city. The smell of burning mixed with the faint sweetness of poison gas. The poison lost its potency after twenty-four hours or so, but enough of the green residue clung to surfaces to give the town a sugary stench. The wagon jostled over cobblestones, aggravating Stoddard's injuries, but he refused to show it.

Gangs of soldiers moved through town, carrying tools rather than weapons—shovels, axes, and crowbars. They wore gas masks or kerchiefs over their faces. Stoddard saw them lugging bodies out of buildings. Then he noticed a group squatting and lounging on a long porch of what had once been a fine home surrounded by great oaks now just beginning to show budding leaves. The windows of the house were boarded up, so one trooper was busy hacking at the front door with an axe.

"Hold up," Stoddard said, and as the wagon slowed, he stumbled to the ground. He approached the house, and all the soldiers stood and straightened themselves. They saluted and greeted him; everyone knew Senator Clark's right hand. He addressed the private with the axe. "What are you doing, trooper?"

"Checking the house for bodies, sir," the private said in a monotone. There were dark circles under his eyes.

"How long have you been at it?"

"Our squad? Two days, sir. Pretty much since we came in on the *Juarez*.

"Are you finding people inside these homes?"

"Yes, sir. Pretty much every time." Several of the other men nodded or gave exhausted moans in agreement.

"Carry on. I want to see inside."

The private returned to chopping at the door. Fortunately the wood was old and nearly rotten. It splintered easily, opening large gaps. The soldier began to kick it with his boot. Others joined in and pulled wood away with their hands. Finally, when the door was largely gone, the private stood aside. "You want to go first, Major?"

"Yes, I would. Thank you."

"Just a second, sir." The trooper pulled a cloth from his pocket and soaked it with liquid from a small flask. He handed it to Stoddard and pulled a kerchief up around his own face. "I'd wear that, if I was you, sir. It stinks something awful sometimes."

Stoddard tied the cloth around his head and positioned it over his nose. It smelled of citrus. Lemonade. He pulled his sidearm and stepped into the entryway.

The house was orderly, if simple. There was no furniture to be seen, but it was not a wreck. The soldiers entered behind him, rather casually. They didn't seem to expect any resistance.

"Shouldn't you boys be armed?" Stoddard asked.

"Haven't found anyone capable of causing trouble yet, Major."

The rooms on the ground floor were empty, but for a few simple chairs. In the rear of the house was a kitchen of sorts with a table and chairs. And at one end of the table was a handmade highchair. Along the countertop was a row of crockery. Stoddard opened the tops and saw dried beans and peas, as well as potatoes. In a side cabinet, there were strips of dried meat and fresh sausages. The downstairs yielded nothing more, so they started up the staircase, each step emitting loud creaks that echoed through the house. At the top of the stairs there was a hallway with several doors, all closed.

One of the soldiers muttered, "It's like a creepy dollhouse. It's almost as if the vampires wanted us to think the damn herds lived better than I do in Valladolid."

"Spread out and search these rooms." Stoddard noticed several soldiers rolling their eyes at his unnecessary command as he went to the door at the far end of the hall.

There had been a doorknob at one time, but it was long gone. The door was cracked, and any paint it may have had was flaked away. Stoddard pushed it open.

It swung back, and flies rose in a swarm from the middle of the room. He saw five corpses. A man and a woman, around his age, huddled together. An older man lay off to one side with a boy around fifteen years old. Stoddard stepped closer, noting their simple homespun clothing. Everything in the room, including the bodies, was coated with a light dusting of green.

On the wooden floor between the man and woman, he saw another shape. The couple was crouched, trying to cover it, to shield it, to protect it. A child that was perhaps two years old. It was a girl. Her hair was tied with a bow of red ribbon. And in her little fingers was clutched a doll made of straw. She was huddled over the doll, like her parents, trying to protect it in turn.

One of the soldiers dropped into a crouch and covered his face with a groan.

"She has a toy," Stoddard breathed to himself. "My God. What have we done?"

CHAPTER 23

"**M**AJOR STODDARD, GLAD to see you up and about."

Senator Clark was bent over a table studying maps, so he couldn't see the major as he entered the room. The vast upper bedroom of a spacious waterfront house was now the senator's command center. The window faced the wharves, and the sounds of men and machines and animals wafted in. None of the carnage was visible from Clark's high window, but the blue sky over the Cape Fear River was crowded with airships, helping to fortify this northernmost outpost of the American Republic. The walls of the room were papered with poor maps of the east coast of the old United States.

"Thank you, sir." Stoddard stepped to the table and glanced down at the map that now had Clark's handwritten notes for the coming assault on Richmond.

"Wilmington was no trouble, eh?" Clark puffed a gigantic black cigar. "Hardly any resistance at all."

Stoddard felt his wounds burning. In his hand, he clutched a small ragged doll.

Oh!" The senator reached into his jacket and pulled out a folded piece of paper. "Good news. This ought to interest you some."

Stoddard could see from the broken wax seals on the paper it had been issued from both the Office of the Senate War Committee as well as the Office of President Somoza. The highest possible level of communiqué. He opened the paper and read: "Ambassador Hull, Alexandria, reports the death of His Imperial Highness, Simon, prince of Bengal, brother of Her Imperial Majesty Adele I. Killed by vampires. Details to follow."

Stoddard read the line again. His face flushed with shock. "Oh my God." He looked at Senator Clark for confirmation of both the news and his dismay.

The senator was tapping his fingers on the map, consumed by strategy. "That's something, eh? Vampires finally got the kid. Too bad, I suppose. The boy was annoying as hell, but he had grit."

"How is this in any way good news?"

"Think about it, Major." Clark turned a conspiratorial eye on his adjutant. Cigar smoke rose in front of his face. "With the boy dead, Adele has no backup. She can't breed a proper heir with that commoner. There are no clear successors. If something were to happen to her, Equatoria would be looking at civil war."

"And so?"

"So, this is my opportunity. I've already received thousands of cables from Equatoria begging me to come back."

"Thousands of cables?"

"Give or take."

"Did any of them come from the empress?"

Clark snarled, removed his cigar, and spit on the wood floor. "She's got nothing to do with it. See, times have changed, for everybody. People with power want me back. And I don't give a damn anymore what that girl does with her private life. But she's got to have someone who can assume control if she dies. And she's got to have an heir. And damn soon. I think the marriage could be back in play." He chuckled. "I think I'll move the capital a little bit south, though. Alexandria seems pretty friendly to vampires these days. Maybe Cairo. I'd like to have a pyramid."

Stoddard ignored his commander's dreams of glory as he thought about the brave boy he had met in Equatoria. Simon had escaped death at the hands of vampires twice; once in France and again in Alexandria. Stoddard had fought with Senator Clark, as well as Adele's teacher Mamoru and his mysterious African companion, to repel the creatures from Simon's door after the monsters had killed Emperor Constantine.

He studied the senator who showed no remorse for the loss of the child, or the loss of the children of Wilmington. The death of Simon was nothing to the senator but an opportunity for tactical advantage. Stoddard's grip on the toy trembled.

Clark said, "Got a little more news too. Seems the Equatorians finally advanced on the vampires. They took Grenoble."

"Really?" Stoddard nodded approval. "Excellent."

The senator eyed him. "Excellent? Incredible is more like it. With your friend Colonel Anhalt in command, I am surprised they managed to find their way out of Marseilles."

"I have great confidence in General Anhalt," the major retorted curtly.

"Do you now? Well, apparently it had nothing to do with the general. Reports from the front say that the Equatorians have some unknown weapon."

"They do? What is it?"

"I have no idea, but I intend to find out." Clark offered a lush Cuban cigar to the major, who declined with a sharp shake of his head. "I want you to cable your friend Anhalt and see what you can find out."

"He won't tell me anything confidential."

"Do it anyway. I want to know what they have that we don't."

Stoddard said, "Very well. Maybe it will allow us to suspend our bombardments."

"What do you mean? The attack on Wilmington was a total success. Our casualties were minimal, and the vampires withdrew. And haven't returned. These damn vampires are worthless. There's no fight in them once we show them we mean business." Clark ran his hand over the map of the Atlantic coast. "What I see here is a successful strategy. We have Savannah, Charleston, and now Wilmington. We can start bringing in materiel for the strike west to link up with the Gulf Army. We'll bombard Richmond next. Hell, by April we'll be in Washington, DC."

Stoddard said hesitantly, "We took Savannah and Charleston without using gas. We could have tried that in Wilmington too, sir. As I suggested."

The senator waved his hand at Stoddard's comment. "If you have something to say, Major, spit it out."

The images of burning civilians, of a small doll clutched in little dead hands, filled Stoddard's head. Families huddled together in terror, not of vampires, but of human weapons.

He said, "Sir, have you seen any of the civilians here?"

"Civilians? There aren't any civilians."

The major replied forcefully, "The herds, sir. It's not that simple. I was in one of their houses. There was a family. They had preserved food. The child had a toy." He set the doll onto the map.

Senator Clark drew on his cigar with a cold stare. "Major, I know you took some hard shots during the assault. Do you need more time to recover? I can send you back to St. Augustine to rest for a week or two. We aren't moving on Richmond for a month or more."

"I'm fine. I'm just saying . . ." Stoddard paused, knowing he was preparing to enter dangerous ground. This was the subject that smashed the senator's marriage to Empress Adele. Well, this and a complete discontinuity of personalities.

Clark added with quiet prescience, "You need to think hard about your next words, Major."

"Sir, with all due respect, I know common wisdom has always been that the Cape Fear signaled the end of the frontier, and the beginning of vampire territory. But these people here are not animals. They may have been poor and oppressed, peasants really, but they are humans."

"I never expected this." The senator's hands tightened into fists, and Stoddard actually thought his commander would strike him. "I raised you up from nothing. Put you one step from the center of power in the American Republic. And this is how you repay me?"

"Senator, I'm not trying to defy you, but it is my job to advise you. I would be doing you a disservice if I didn't speak my mind."

"When has it ever been your job to advise me? Your entire job consists of doing what I say. And I say there are no humans here!"

The major tightened his mouth in an angry slash. "I disagree, sir. I feel I must tell you that, in my opinion, we have caused the deaths of many thousands of human beings here in Wilmington."

Clark breathed out harshly. "And if we did, what of it? This is a war, Major. You expect me to take this continent away from those monsters without killing a few people? Please, advise me about that." Before Stoddard could respond, the senator swept the doll off the table. "Maybe you need to join up with the Equatorians and take orders from that girl. She intends to win a war without killing anybody. Perhaps you would enjoy a life of tea parties in Alexandria and endless chitchat. I'm not sure there's a place for you in my army."

"It isn't *your* army, Senator. It is the American army, and I'm an American. My constitutional oath requires that I speak."

"Don't you dare cite the Constitution to me! My father helped rewrite the Constitution!"

Stoddard felt himself separating from his rank. He was losing any sense of concern for the future; he no longer saw himself as the adjutant to Senator Clark. He was just a soldier who had played a role in killing a little girl who died clutching a doll.

"Senator," he announced in a clear voice, "I intend to write a memorandum to the War Committee detailing my observations here and expressing my opinion about the human population in the old United States. I will state in unequivocal language that I feel our current tactic of deploying poison gas to destroy the vampires' food supply is tantamount to genocide, and beneath the morality of a civilized nation."

Clark studied the glowing tip of his cigar with apparent disregard for Stoddard's warning. "Are you really going to destroy your career over what you saw in one house? Major, I'm ordering you to take a few days in St. Augustine, or even Havana if you wish." He laid an awkwardly kind hand on the major's shoulder. "I can't let you make a mistake like this. Take some time. Get your head right. Then we'll fly to Equatoria to get everything back on track. I need you there, Major. Your connection with their commanding officer will be invaluable. And don't worry, this conversation stays in this room."

"It isn't just one house, sir. We have to rethink our opinions about the north. We believe there are free humans in Charleston, but not here? It doesn't make sense. I read Empress Adele's reports of her time in the north—"

"Dammit!" Clark slammed his hand on the table. "Listen to me! This is a direct order. You will not write any memo to the War Committee. I've been getting notes from Panama City talking about politicians trying to outlaw the use of gas on the herds. There are even protests against the way I'm fighting the war. Against me! So I'm telling you that you will keep your damned mouth shut! You will take a week in Havana. And then we will discuss your future on my staff."

"I resign from your staff, sir."

Clark's mouth opened in the first look of surprise that Stoddard had ever seen from him. The senator seemed torn by whether he was unsure he had heard the major's words correctly, or if such words even existed. It was disconcerting to Stoddard to see the great man in a state of confusion. It even angered him that the senator could show such feeble emotions. Fortunately, the faltering of the bearded Achilles didn't last long.

"I'll break you," the senator growled. "You'll be lucky to muck stalls for the Seventh Cavalry in Tampico when I'm done with you."

"I would welcome that, sir."

"I should kill you here, you insufferable traitor. I knew those Equatorians had ruined you. Now you're no better an officer than your friend, Colonel Anhalt."

"High praise."

"Get out." Clark turned away from him. "If I ever see you again, I'll kill you."

Stoddard spun on his heel and strode away. He felt sad, not frightened or wary of the future. He was content with his choices; his steps were lightened and his wounds no longer burned so hot. No matter what happened, he had taken the right path.

The major stopped at the door and turned to face Clark's back. He saluted, unseen, to the promise the man had shown and now, he feared, wasted.

CHAPTER 24

"Y ou've brought this on yourself," General Anhalt said over the din of the rattling elevator cage.

Mamoru didn't respond, staring straight ahead. He and Anhalt and four White Guardsmen stood facing the door. The wrought-iron elevator rose fitfully past an endless brick wall as it churned up the center of the great tower of Pharos One.

Anhalt didn't turn his head. "Her Majesty regrets that she is unable to see you off. Despite all that has happened, she wishes me to convey her best wishes and sincere gratitude for all you did for her and her family."

The samurai was apparently unmoved. His crimson robe fluttered in the wind pouring down the shaft.

The sirdar produced a heavy envelope with imperial seals. "This is an official edict of *persona non grata*. As well as a secret proclamation signed by Empress Adele the First confining you to imprisonment for the remainder of your life. You are to be taken to Jahannam Prison, a facility reserved for imperial enemies of the highest order. You shall be its only current inhabitant, but your accommodations will be hospitable, even luxurious by some standards." Mamoru's hands were chained behind his back, so Anhalt replaced the letters into his own tunic. "Your fate will be tucked into your luggage."

The general clasped his hands behind his back, content to see the rest of this duty done in silence. He took no pleasure in it. He'd never had much contact with Mamoru over the years, and had never completely trusted him. However, the teacher had fed an intellectual curiosity in the empress that no one else could. She needed challenges to be happy, and the samurai priest had always provided that. This betrayal by her beloved Mamoru could've been a crushing blow, but Adele's all-encompassing duty as empress kept her aloft.

Still, Anhalt feared for Adele. He was typically far away at the front, Greyfriar was frequently gone, and now Mamoru was banished. He would stay in Alexandria until the spring offensive began, but the days when he could remain by her side were over. There was no one to block the fierce winds that were sweeping around her.

The elevator cage jerked to a rough stop and Anhalt yanked back the gate. He stepped out into near gale-force winds that blasted the mooring platform atop Pharos One, the highest airship tower in Alexandria.

Beyond saluting soldiers, across the hundred yards of concrete, looming above the busy mooring crew, was an Equatorian frigate lashed close to the tower. The hull of the ship was a dull brown and grey, but the aluminum cage around the dirigible sparkled with the sun of a painfully blue sky. Mobs of teamsters lugged cargo over multiple gangplanks. A spiderweb of hoses hung from the ship's dirigible as buoyancy gases were pumped in. Anhalt strode toward the airship with Mamoru and the White Guard behind. A parade of reports met him as he passed.

"The prisoner's quarters are ready, Sirdar."

"*Khyber* is scheduled to make way in two hours, Sirdar."

"The prisoner's baggage is stowed, Sirdar."

Anhalt acknowledged each announcement until he reached a gangplank where a naval lieutenant waited. They exchanged salutes, and the young naval officer looked past Anhalt to study Mamoru. The sirdar produced multiple envelopes that flapped in the wind, threatening to escape into space.

"These are your orders, Lieutenant," Anhalt said loudly, "regarding the disposition of the prisoner."

The officer in his dress blue uniform with gold piping took the papers delicately in white-gloved hands, noting the highest imperial seal on the heavy paper. His nasal voice was not suited to the occasion. "I relieve you of your prisoner, sir."

"I stand relieved." Anhalt turned for a final word with his one-time ally. "This is good-bye then. We shall never meet again."

"No, we shan't." Mamoru kicked back and struck one of the White Guard in the face and, in a single motion, slammed his foot into another man's head. There was a hard snap. Then he leapt into air, striking out with both legs, spinning in the air, smashing two soldiers aside. He was so fast he could barely be seen, and he didn't stop moving.

Anhalt's saber was barely clear of the scabbard when the samurai cracked a foot into the general's knee. As Anhalt staggered, Mamoru jumped and brought his chained hands under the soles of his feet. He had hardly touched the concrete again before he pulled a soldier's sword free. With foot planted, he brought the saber against the sirdar's chest. Anhalt reared back violently, off-balance, trying to gain distance from the deadly blade. He felt pressure pass along the front of his uniform jacket, and then a strong hand fell across his neck with a foot against his shin, tumbling him to the ground. He rolled off his right hip, trying for his revolver. A flash of red robe passed and slammed into the lieutenant, who had barely time to blink since the attack began. The young man toppled helplessly over the rail of the gangplank and off the tower.

"Mamoru! Stop!" Anhalt shouted, tasting his own blood in his mouth. He struggled onto one knee, fumbling with his holster flap.

The samurai raced along the gangplank onto *Khyber*. Sailors looked in surprise or scattered wildly as the saber blade came at them. Mamoru hurdled a pile of cargo waiting to be stowed in the forecastle. When he landed, he kept going at a full run. He leapt, one foot touching the rail, and then catapulted over the far side. His crimson robes were beautiful against the blue sky for a second, and then he was gone.

Anhalt's boot steps thudded on the wooden gangplank. He bowled onto the ship, shoving stunned airmen aside as he stumbled across the deck, shouting, "Make way! Make way!" He reached the spot where Mamoru had jumped and leaned over the rail, revolver in hand.

He saw nothing below but the dark waters of the Mediterranean with white edges of foam where it merged with the shore.

"He jumped from Pharos One?" Adele could barely form the question because it was so incredible, so unspeakable. Her hands crunched the paperwork she had been reading in the Privy Council chamber.

"I fear so, Your Majesty." General Anhalt stood at rigid attention. Beads of sweat rolled down his brow, and a thin line of blood stained his new tunic. "He killed two men and wounded four more."

The empress put a hand to her face. "I can't believe it. My God."

Anhalt said, "There are those who suggest it was ritual suicide."

Adele waved dismissively. "Could he have survived the fall?"

The general replied in a strained voice, "Normally I'd say it was impossible. However, Mamoru is not normal. We searched the shoreline and the harbor, and found nothing."

Adele rose from her private desk and took Anhalt by the arm with a loving rebuke. "Sit down, General, please. You're wounded."

"Not at all, Your Majesty." But he allowed himself to be guided to her chair. "I regret my failure to—"

"Stop it," Adele barked. "I should have had him wrapped in chains and locked in a trunk. Oh, even that probably wouldn't have been enough. Mamoru is one of the most skilled fighters I've ever seen. A regiment couldn't have stopped him. You're lucky to be alive."

"What of you, Your Majesty? What if he is alive? We must bolster your security."

Nearby, Captain Shirazi shifted slightly on his feet with a creak of leather boots.

The empress went to the window, the train of her gown hissing over the floor. She looked out on the garden where she and Mamoru used to study together. She watched the white blurs that were flowers tossing in the twilight breeze.

"General," she said, "I've been kidnapped, stabbed, and blown up. And that's just in the last calendar year. There's only so much security can do. If Mamoru's alive and he wants to find me, he will. He could be watching me even as we speak. He knows the palace inside and out." If

Mamoru was alive, she feared more for Gareth's welfare than hers. Fortunately, Gareth was far away in the relative safety of Europe.

Adele ached for Gareth. She valued his steady judgment and brilliant counterpoints in this crisis. But more, she wanted to sense the steel shadow of his presence beside her. She wanted the touch of his hand.

Anhalt pushed to his feet and moved to her side with a hand on his pistol. "Does Mamoru have any confederates here? Where would he go to hide?"

The empress said, "Sir Godfrey Randolph."

"The surgeon who operated on you?"

"Yes. He and Mamoru are close friends. Direct the Home Secretary to dispatch police to watch Sir Godfrey's home in Giza. Follow him, should he venture out. Give it several days. Then, if nothing happens, have him brought here so I may talk to him."

"Yes, Your Majesty. What of that woman who was with Mamoru when Flay attacked the palace last year?"

"I don't know who she is. Mamoru has a vast network, but I learned no more about it than my father did. Perhaps Sir Godfrey will know something, although I doubt he'd tell. We'll handle the situation here. You have other concerns. Do you have your ship?"

Anhalt slipped a surreptitious eye toward Captain Shirazi, who stood at attention. Eventually, the general replied, "There are difficulties, Majesty. The Undead attack on Gibraltar last year nearly halved our fleet. Recent action has taken several of the best candidates. I wanted HMS *Mysore*, but she went down near Graz last week. Others are damaged. And any ship I remove from action will cost air support for men who need it. An operational ironclad would be best, but that is out of the question. But don't worry, I'll find a suitable candidate for the mission."

"Time grows short, General." Her fear for Gareth being left unsupported in the north made the comment more biting than she intended.

The general merely said, "I understand, Your Majesty."

There was a knock at the door, and she called out to enter. Her secretary appeared in the door looking officious, with an army officer in the corridor behind. "Your Majesty, there is an urgent message for the sirdar."

Adele motioned the young soldier in. He tried to march ahead with military aloofness, but his eyes were wide. He stared at the empress and at her sanctum. General Anhalt appeared in front of him like a statue stained with blood.

Anhalt slipped a finger under the flap of the envelope and drew out the single sheet of close typing. As he read, his shoulders dropped and his eyes closed.

Adele came to him with concern. "What is it, General?"

"Rotherford's position at St. Etienne has been overrun. His corps is in full retreat with massive casualties reported."

"Dear God. How?" Adele's thoughts went from worry about Gareth beyond the bloody frontier to the endless train of young men slogging through the mud, huddling in the endless night, terrified of death.

"Fresh packs. Apparently, a huge reinforcement of vampires kept up an attack for three days without pause." Anhalt rubbed his brow and retrieved his khaki helmet with its scarab badge. "Barely a month from Greyfriar's deadline, the new moon after the equinox. This dispatch is a week old at best."

"Did Field Marshal Rotherford survive?"

The general scanned the sheet again and nodded. "Unfortunately, yes."

Adele touched his sleeve. "You must go." It took a great deal of effort to phrase it as a statement and not a plaintive question.

"Yes. I must return to the continent immediately to salvage the situation or we could lose untold ground."

"I understand." She placed a gentle kiss on his cheek. "Stay safe."

He took her hand in his and reverently kissed it. Then he stepped back and saluted. "With your blessing, Your Majesty."

Adele nodded and then watched her general, her confidant, and her friend march from the room, leaving it quiet and still. Anhalt was gone.

Simon was gone.

Mamoru was gone.

Gareth was gone.

One by one she was losing all those she trusted, and the one she loved. There were so few people whose counsel she relied on, and that circle was growing smaller every day. Soon she would be alone and the only advice she could depend on was her own.

Adele's hand brushed the huge wooden globe. She imagined her father standing here. His large hand covered twice the land her slender hand could. She wondered if he would be proud of her. Every day as she grew lonelier, she felt closer to him and understood what he must have felt, separate and distant from his friends, family, and subjects, each one slipping further and further away with every decision made. The burden of sovereignty was heavier than she had realized.

And now Gareth walked the same path.

CHAPTER 25

"WHAT SHALL WE do?" Sanah asked from her place on the leather sofa.

"I believe I shall have another gin and tonic." Sir Godfrey gave a heroic attempt at a laugh and winked sadly at his companion.

The library of his Giza town home seemed terribly dark, even frightening. Just the two of them now. Nzingu gone north and out of touch. Mamoru missing and likely dead. Both Sanah and Sir Godfrey were lonely and disconnected without the force driving their cabal. They had no idea what to do next. Or even if anything could be done.

Sir Godfrey fixed a haphazard drink with very little tonic in his gin, and drank half of it in one swallow. He stared at his bookshelves and shook his head. "I simply can't believe it."

Sanah didn't reply, knowing he would continue.

And he did, tapping the thick gin bottle with a fingernail. "Even with all our preparation, we weren't ready. We still underestimated them. We had one chance, one bullet if you will, and they took it away from us. But not by killing her, don't you see. That's the damnable thing. Gareth. He took her mind. He broke her will. He cut the human out of her like a surgeon. So cunning. Who would have thought them capable?" He drained the glass and poured another without benefit of tonic.

Sanah understood Sir Godfrey's comment, but she knew the truth. When she saw Gareth save Adele's life, she had witnessed something she could never have imagined. A vampire that was not a monster. Much of the blame for the break with Adele had to lie with Mamoru himself, but there was no point in saying that. Sir Godfrey would not hear it; there was no reason to alienate him now.

He fell grunting into an overstuffed armchair, gin spilling on his jacket. He stared angrily at the glass, then shouted into the air, "Laudanum! Majid, laudanum, do you hear!" When his manservant didn't appear in seconds, he struggled back to his feet.

Sanah went to intercept the besotted old gentleman. She reached for the glass, but he pulled it back, drained it, and then allowed her to take it.

He looked blearily into her black eyes and wavered on his feet. "Would you care for opium, Sanah?"

"You should lie down, Sir Godfrey."

There was a knock at the library door and he shouted, "Come in! Why do you knock, damn you! I asked for laudanum hours ago."

There was another knock, prompting Sir Godfrey to stagger toward the door, which was open, and peer out. "Where are you?"

Sanah heard the knock from another direction, from inside the library. When it came a third time, she moved deeper into the room, her senses leading her to a grand Old Kingdom sarcophagus against the wall.

"Here," Sanah said as she laid a hand on the gold, bejeweled surface.

"Here what?" Sir Godfrey stomped back into the library, staring at Sanah until a louder rap sounded again from inside the ancient coffin. The old man huffed with annoyance and pushed his age-spotted hand against the jewels. "What's all this? No one was in the pyramid."

"Allow me." Sanah gently pushed his hand aside, and her fingers brushed over a series of gemstones in succession. There was a click.

The lid swung out, and a short, stocky figure in tradesman twill stepped into the library accompanied by a blast of stiff hot air from the passageway that ran to the Great Pyramid. He pulled off his cap and looked up to reveal a bruised, swollen face.

"Mamoru!" Sanah exclaimed, and grabbed him before he fell.

The samurai leaned heavily against the Persian woman as if losing his strength now that he was safe. He still nodded toward the window. "Lower your voice and the shades, if you please. Shut the door as well. The house is being watched by every policeman in Giza." As Sir Godfrey hurried to comply, Mamoru weaved, with Sanah's shoulder for support, to the sofa, where he collapsed.

The old man leaned out to scan the hallway for eavesdroppers, and then shut the door and turned back with a great, inebriated grin. "Well, well, it's lovely to see you, old boy. We thought you were quite dead and the whole game was up, and the vampires had won the day."

"I am alive. The game has reached its final move, and it will end with *every* vampire dead," Mamoru whispered in a rasping voice, his eyes beginning to droop with long-denied sleep.

———

Long ago Mamoru sat on the edge of a wooden veranda in the courtyard of the largest house in Lincang, a small village in Yunnan Province, China. Above the crumbling edge of the second-story roof, he could see the stars beginning to be blotted out by large whitish grey clouds. Through an overgrown archway on the far side of the courtyard, he saw his soldiers passing. There were no townspeople about, which was just as well. The inhabitants of Lincang had seemed properly cowed by the arrival of the dragon airship yesterday followed by the Japanese troopers marching into their town square and erecting the rising-sun flag.

He adjusted his gun belt and noted a rip in his khaki uniform trousers. He would have his adjutant mend that; he couldn't afford to look unkempt in front of new subjects of the Japanese Empire. He shoved back a metal mess kit with the remains of tonight's mediocre meal. The food would get better once his chef settled in and imported quality ingredients. It would be interesting to try local produce, but he would miss the fish so plentiful in Singapore. Such was the price of duty. Mamoru laid a hand on his father's katana, which rested beside him. He heard the sound of soft footfalls and sat expectantly until a small hand fell on his shoulder.

246

"It's cold," said a woman's voice. "Would you like your overcoat?"

"No, thank you." Mamoru removed his officer's cap and turned to look up at the woman. He touched his light cotton tunic. "It's warm enough."

Tomiko was small, just over five feet tall, but she was sturdy and moved with a delightful economy. Her face was flawless, soft and round, framed by cascading jet black hair. Her eyes were comforting and challenging at the same time. Her lithe figure was swathed in a heavy white fur coat. Her breath was visible hanging in the cold air.

Mamoru stood and took the baby from the crook of his wife's elbow. He hummed with pleasure and touched the tiny wet chin with his oversized finger, and his daughter cooed. Her wriggling sent a shock of affection through him. He plunged his face inches away from her, eliciting giggles from both of them.

He bounced the infant while grunting lightly. He stared at the baby, but said to his wife, "We'll have a wonderful nursery for Kiyo when I have a proper governor's palace built."

Tomiko watched her husband and daughter. "I'm worried about the rats and bugs."

"You should stay on the ship."

She smiled. "There are rats and bugs there too."

"Yunnan Province isn't Singapore. I'll have some of the locals clean tomorrow."

Tomiko brushed strands of ebony hair from the baby's face. "You have more important duties. I'm sorry I complained."

He kissed his daughter's chubby cheek. "I have no more important duties than caring for my wife and daughter."

The woman beamed with pride and used her foot to tap a thick oilcloth packet of papers with the seal of the Serene Court in Singapore. "The emperor expects results from his youngest prefect. A few rats and bugs won't matter in the long run."

"He'll get results, as he always has. Within a month, I intend to have coal and iron-ore sites surveyed. And I will need estimates on agricultural output. And I can manage to provide a clean home for my family." Mamoru handed the baby back to his wife.

"Well, it is pretty here. The mountains are beautiful, and I saw lovely fields outside town."

He pointed at her sternly. "Don't be fooled. The forests are full of headhunters and cannibals."

"And vampires?"

Mamoru shrugged. "They cannot be ruled out, but I don't worry about them here in Yunnan. We are at the southern edge of their frontier. For my peace of mind, however, you are not to be outside this palace without an armed guard."

"Of course." She gave a plaintive look around the crumbling courtyard at the boundaries of her new world.

"Would you rather return home? You are free to. You said you wanted to be with me."

"I do." Tomiko reached out. "I want to be beside you and watch you as you create this place. And I want you to be with your daughter."

"I couldn't do it without you." Mamoru took her wrist and kissed it. "I wouldn't want to."

Tomiko sat on the wooden veranda bouncing the baby as Mamoru began to pace the dirt. He grew animated as he explained how he intended to tame the wild fringes of the civilized world. The mines would expand. The farms would spread. The towns would rise. He would create a prosperous and powerful province on the northern frontier, a source of wealth for imperial growth as well as a brake on Equatorian expansion.

As Mamoru planned their future out loud, Tomiko took several crystals from her coat pocket and rolled them between her fingers. She tossed them on the wooden planks and stared at them. Her gasp caused him to pause in his speech, and she quickly snatched the crystals up again.

Mamoru asked with an indulgent smile, "What does your geomancy say about our path? Great things?"

"Nothing." She wouldn't meet his eyes.

"No?" He took the crystals from his wife's unwilling fingers and studied them. His mind filled with images of lush green mountains and particular scents that he recognized. "These are from Java, aren't they? One day, I would like to learn more about this science."

Tomiko seemed flustered and nervous. "It's a mere game not worth your time. You should focus on the real world. Build your political career."

"I have. But in a few years, once I have made Yunnan into the richest province in the Empire, we will return to Singapore, where I will receive a high position at court. There will be little more I can accomplish in the realm of the known world, since I can't become emperor." Mamoru laughed. "I will need some new field to conquer. You said once I had great promise as a geomancer."

She merely shook her head. "No."

Mamoru bent over her worried face with a look of false alarm, and put a hand on her trembling shoulder. "Did your cast predict something dire? Am I doomed?"

Tomiko stood and struck the crystals from his hand. "Stop! Don't mock it!"

The prefect stood with open mouth. He took his resistant wife by the arm. "I'm sorry."

She reached inside the collar of his shirt and pulled out a thin chain with a small crystal in intricate silver filigree. She exhaled in relief when she saw it.

"What?" Mamoru looked at her with curiosity. "Are you surprised to see it? That's the talisman you gave me last year. The perfect match to yours. I always wear it."

"I just wanted to know you had it." Tomiko squeezed her eyes tight and placed the palm of one hand on the side of his face. "Promise me you will never ask me about geomancy. I don't want you to study it. Ever. I don't want you to be that man."

"I don't understand. You said that I had great skills—"

"Promise me!"

Mamoru took the back of her head, feeling her silken hair. "Tomiko, please calm down. You are overwrought. It's all the travel and new surroundings."

In the night air came the sound of gunshots.

Mamoru immediately reached for his pistol. Soldiers posted by the archway jumped in alarm, gripping their rifles, hands reaching for cartridge pouches on their belts. Shouts and screams began in the distance.

Mamoru pushed Tomiko toward a door and grabbed up his katana. "Run. Get Kiyo inside."

"What is it?"

"Run, I said!"

Tomiko started for the door when several figures dropped into the courtyard and fell on top of her. She screamed and the baby shrieked.

Mamoru was turning to her when sharp hands seized him and thrust him to the ground. Claws. Teeth. Humanlike shapes surged around him. The feral creatures where like men, but naked and hairy. They circled him on all fours.

He began to rise, hearing his wife's gurgling cries amidst the hissing and growling. He saw one of the vampires tear his infant daughter from Tomiko's desperate grip. With a scream of fury, from one knee, Mamoru brought his katana around in an arc, feeling it bite the chest of one creature. He drew it back, stepped, spun, and thrust into another vampire. Twist. Pull. Spin and cut through a throat. In an instant, three vampires lay bleeding around him.

His wife struggled against one of the things as it brought its jaws down on her throat. To his stunned surprise, the creature screamed and reared back, Tomiko's own amulet tangled in its yellow teeth amid a wash of blood and smoke. With a clear path to his wife, the prefect started to bound onto the veranda. Then a hand seized his ankle and yanked him back onto his stomach in the dirt. The creatures that should have been dead all rose around him.

Mamoru rolled quickly onto his back, trying to keep the sword up as protection. The monster holding him gibbered and spit, and leapt up onto his abdomen, ignoring the blade slicing cleanly along its rib cage. A gnarled hand with long yellow claws streaked down at him, digging into his chest. The vampire screeched and fell back off him. It rolled in the dirt, clutching its smoking hand, before scurrying away. Its two companions followed like pack animals, and all three streaked across the courtyard and vanished into the darkness.

Mamoru felt warm blood spreading across his shredded tunic. Still, he struggled desperately to his knees and crawled up onto the veranda, shouting his wife's name. Another vampire hunched over Tomiko looked at him, seemed almost to smile with bloody teeth even though its eyes were nothing more than a savage beast. It didn't flex and leap upward, but in a surreal scene, it just lifted slowly off the ground, still in a crouching position. Its brethren with the talisman in its blackened teeth writhed on the ground and finally lay still.

Mamoru dragged himself to the figure of his crumpled wife. Her coat and robe were shredded and the flesh nearly flayed from her bare chest. The wound at her throat was raw and horrific. He pulled her up from a pool of sticky blood and clutched her tight against his grief. Her round perfect face was stained bright red.

"Kiyo," she gurgled, trying to reach.

Mamoru saw the shape of his poor little daughter lying not far away, completely still. He could tell there was nothing to be done for her, and his heart shattered. He pressed Tomiko's face to his chest, silently clinging to his anguish.

"Kiyo," she repeated, struggling weakly.

"Kiyo is fine," Mamoru said, shielding his wife from the horror burning his own eyes. The sight of his daughter lying unprotected left him feeling as if his bones were frozen and broken. But he deserved the torture; he couldn't tear his eyes away from the little figure. "Don't fight, Tomiko. I will get a doctor for you."

"Kiyo is safe?"

"She is here next to us."

Tomiko sank against him with relief. "Do you still have the talisman I gave you?"

"Yes." His voice cracked with anguish. He touched the stone resting against his bloody chest and realized with a shock that it had repelled the creature. But his wife had not been so lucky. His tears dropped onto her face, creating spatters in the blood.

"I'm so tired," she whispered.

All he wanted to shout was *No, no, no! Stay awake! Don't leave me alone!* But instead he said quietly, "Rest then."

"Yes, I will. Kiss Kiyo for me. I'm too tired."

"I will see you both in the morning."

A small red hand tried to grip his arm. "Be a great man."

"If you say it, I will." He couldn't finish the sentence because his breath was gone.

Tomiko died there along with his daughter, leaving Mamoru with his unrelenting grief.

—◈—

Mamoru jerked awake from his nightmare, startling Sir Godfrey, who fussed nearby with Sanah. His face ashen, he reached for the watered-down wine beside him.

"You need to eat," Sanah remarked, gesturing to a plate of food beside the wine.

"I'm not hungry," the samurai muttered, throwing the cashmere blanket aside. "You shouldn't have let me sleep."

"You're dead on your feet, my friend." Godfrey stepped closer.

"I can't risk one of your servants seeing me and talking to the wrong person. You two must stay free to coordinate my needs."

Sir Godfrey harrumphed. "They wouldn't arrest me. Would they? I am a man of some position. And I did save the empress's life on the operating table."

Mamoru gulped more of the wine, washing the bitterness of despair aside, letting his anger once more rise. "I no longer know what Adele will do. If she fears for that beast of hers, she may be capable of anything."

Sanah flinched at his harsh tone, and he noticed because he glanced disapprovingly at her. His frown showed he would brook no dissension now.

"Is there a problem, Sanah?"

"No. I'm simply worried about you."

"I'll need you to gather crystals. I don't have access to my personal collection." He took a pencil and paper, and began to scribble notes. He handed the sheet to Sanah. "And mark you, they must be perfect."

Sir Godfrey set a bowl of rice and vegetables in front of Mamoru. It was only grudgingly that he began to eat, more for nourishment than for hunger.

"There is no more time for pleasantries and schooling. I have lost control of the empress. Clearly the beast has her in his thrall." He pointed his fork at Sir Godfrey. "I'll want an airship standing by. A fast one. Do you have the ready resources?"

"Yes, indeed. I'll make arrangements for a yacht. Do you intend to escape the Empire?"

"It isn't for me. It's for Adele. I need a ship to take her to the rift on Malta, if possible. But there are other sites that may suit me. Bring me the maps."

Sir Godfrey went to a painting of a Turkish seraglio on the wall and slid it up to reveal a safe. A few twirls of the dial and he opened the heavy door, and retrieved leather-bound folios that he carried to the table next to Mamoru. The samurai shoved the fine bone china roughly aside and shuffled through the books until he found what he wanted. He opened the folio to reveal detailed maps of the Mediterranean and the north coast of Africa. The maps were marked with dots of various colors all connected by a network of lines. Rifts and the ligaments of their ley lines or dragon spines. They had been all painstakingly charted by Mamoru's legion of geomancers over the last decades.

He touched the island of Malta, where a nearly infinite number of spines converged on a large rift. There were several rifts on the African littoral too, but none hosted nearly the number of lines.

"I much prefer Malta," Mamoru muttered. "Nabta Playa could serve."

"What about the Soma here in Alexandria?" Sir Godfrey suggested.

"If necessary. But not optimal. And I would much rather have her away from the capital and all her soldiers. I will need time to prepare her, and that would be difficult with her precious army knocking down every door in Alexandria."

Sanah pretended to study the map, but she felt chilled fingernails scraping across her chest. "How will you convince her to do this? You said she had grown hesitant."

"My days of convincing Adele are at an end. There is no reasoning with her. Her mind has been irrevocably corrupted. I will force her to initiate the final event."

"You can force her?"

"I can. It isn't my preference, but it will serve."

Sanah turned to face him, her dark eyes glaring out from the veil. "She can trigger the rifts even against her will?"

Mamoru froze in place as he leaned over the maps. His muscles tensed. "Yes, Sanah."

"And would you truly do such a thing? To her?"

"Yes, Sanah."

The room seemed to darken with silence. Sir Godfrey rubbed his muttonchop whiskers. Mamoru continued to stare at the maps, but his breath hissed through his nose.

Sanah struggled to keep her voice steady. "But how will you live with yourself after the act?"

"I don't care about anything after the act."

"I know you won't hear it, Mamoru, but I've come to believe that she loves this Gareth. And he loves her. The potential in that relationship could change the world too. Don't we owe it to ourselves to explore that?" Sanah laid a henna-painted hand on Mamoru's bruised knuckles.

"No. We owe it to the human race to destroy them all."

"You loved Adele too, once. I can't believe you would wish this future on her. It is an act of violation. If you don't care about your own good, then what about that girl? How will she live with herself knowing what she has done?"

Mamoru turned his head and met Sanah's gaze with blank eyes. "She won't have to live with it. She will not survive."

Sanah tightened her grip on his hand. "What? You're going to kill her?"

"Not I. The energies of the Event will destroy her. If she were conscious, she might survive. But she surrendered that right when she surrendered her humanity."

The Persian woman stepped back and pounded her fist on the table, rattling the dishes, and shouted, "It's you who has surrendered your humanity! You are like that girl's father. How can you even conceive of this?"

Mamoru turned back to the maps and began to run his fingers along the lines.

Sanah screamed, "Answer me!"

254

The samurai tore the North African map out of the book and folded it. "Sir Godfrey, I'll trouble you for antiseptic and bandages before I go. I injured my ankle in the fall from the airship."

The old gentleman looked from Mamoru to Sanah with alarm, slowly moving to the door. With a nervous nod, he darted out.

Sanah seized the samurai by the sleeve. "You must listen to me."

Mamoru replied quietly, "I will find the crystals elsewhere. Don't worry yourself over it."

"Mamoru." She pulled him around to face her. "Taking Adele's life won't bring back your wife and daughter."

He slipped the map page into his shirt.

Sanah stared at him. There was no life behind his eyes, no reason at all. She released him. He moved like a terrible, unhurried automaton. Every motion drove the story toward an irrevocable conclusion, a heavy curtain dropping over the last act of a play.

The door opened and Sir Godfrey returned carrying a glass bottle and several rolls of gauze. "Shall I attend your wound?"

"No." Mamoru took the medical supplies and went to the sarcophagus. "I will contact you when I need you."

Sanah began, "Mamoru, I beg you—"

He triggered the secret door and vanished into the shadowy passageway, pulling the lid closed behind him. Sanah sank into a chair with a long ragged exhalation.

The old surgeon started to touch her shoulder, then drew back his hand. "Sanah, we've trusted Mamoru for years. We can't change horses now, so to speak. It will all be fine. He has given his life to this. We all have. There's nothing to be gained by doubting it all now. Is there?"

Sanah closed her eyes, revealing the tattooed eyes on her lids. She clasped her hands together, seeking a moment of purity to cut through the confusion. She needed a sign, guidance, peace. She wished for a message of comfort and support from her beloved sister, Pareesa.

She opened her eyes suddenly. She needed to talk to the empress.

CHAPTER 26

PARIS STRADDLED THE moon-flecked Seine River. The countryside, once threatened by urban expansion, was once again cloaked in gloom, and only the center of the old town was spotted with the lights of its human inhabitants.

Floating shapes rose above the city, while others clutched onto miles of broken chimney pots and once-magnificent colonnaded palaces. Flocks of vampires settled to the wide boulevards in their own sinister version of an evening promenade. People hurried about their business through narrow lanes while shuffling herds of humans also wandered in the wild green spaces.

Gareth had lived in Paris centuries before, but many of the old venous streets and crowded warrens he knew were gone, replaced by long straight avenues and uniform buildings. Lucky the city hadn't been that way in his day because old Paris was a fertile hunting ground of shadows and corners. So much of this new city had been altered as an open display of human ego just a few decades before the Great Killing.

Now humans were no longer so proud.

No one confronted Gareth as he drifted toward the shambling old pile of the Tuileries Palace north of the river. Only when he reached the vast palace, and lit on the front façade, did several figures separate from the masonry and advance on him. Before they could speak, he said, "I am Prince Gareth of Scotland. I'm here to see King Lothaire."

One of the vampires, an older fellow, smiled broadly. "Gareth! I know you. We fought together in Brittany."

Gareth studied the creased face, and managed to recall it younger and covered in blood, but always smiling. "I remember. Fanon?"

The vampire laughed with joy at being remembered by a prince of the British clan. "That's right, sir! I haven't seen you in a long time. What's it been, a decade?"

"One hundred and fifty years."

"Almost like yesterday." Fanon backhanded one of his companions on the chest. "Prince Gareth here killed more humans than any other I know. Such a sight to see."

The Scottish prince nodded in uncomfortable modesty.

"He was incredible," the vampire continued. "He moved so fast, I could barely see him. Killing. Just killing." He pointed at Gareth. "Do you remember when we struck those ships trying to escape Brest? Why, when Gareth was through, there were thousands dead on those vessels. So much blood flowing off the decks that—"

"Thank you, Fanon," Gareth interrupted. "I'm honored you remember, but I've forgotten much of that time. Is the king at home?"

"He is," came a bellow from above, and a figure dropped to the ground. He was a young male, likely under one hundred years old, and he wore a uniform jacket with epaulettes along with striped trousers. He looked a great deal like Lothaire when Gareth had known him; shorter, but more muscular, with a full face and flowing flaxen hair.

"Honore?" Gareth bowed. "I see your father in you."

"I am the Dauphin," the boy said without any welcome, using the old term for the French royal heir, another seizure of human traits by vampires. "So you're Gareth? I've heard about you, but have never seen you in all my years."

Fanon gave Honore a hard look of reproach, but it found no purchase on the lad's demeanor.

"You wish to see my father?" the Dauphin said with a pompous breath. "Come with me."

Gareth and Fanon followed Honore inside, and the trampled glories of the Tuileries enveloped them. Portraits were torn and crystal shattered. Windows were cracked and jagged. Tattered fabric hung mildewed, and rugs decayed underfoot. They went up a once-grand staircase now crusted in dried blood and bits of hair and bone. The hallways were crowded with clan lords and retainers hurrying about their great business. Some faces latched onto Gareth with recognition, but none spoke, preferring to stop and stare and whisper about why the Scottish prince was in Paris.

Gareth and Fanon walked, but Honore leapt and floated everywhere, vaulting up stairs by bouncing from wall to wall, grasping columns and spinning. It wasn't exuberance; it was aggression, directed at Gareth. Honore was a young male, spending energy in pointless display, and since energy wasn't needed any longer for hunting, it was free to waste. Fanon seemed annoyed by the rudeness, but Gareth was amused by the boy showing his power in front of his father's old friend.

No doubt, Gareth reflected, he and Lothaire had been the same in those times together. Both young, ambitious, strong, and violent. Gareth, like most young males in those days, spent much of his early life wandering. He found Lothaire to be an agreeable companion, so they hunted Paris and environs together for decades. Then during the Great Killing, Gareth had returned to join Lothaire in battle to cement the alliance between Dmitri and Lothaire's father. The battles they won and the bloodshed they caused were legendary. The sheer destruction of human life was enormous. Shamefully, Gareth could still recall the screams, the feeling of claws tearing flesh, and the smell of fear everywhere, the pure stench of terror that fed the vampire hordes nearly as much as the oceans of blood.

Honore settled onto a massive door lintel, crouching impatiently above Gareth and Fanon, who approached on foot. "I'll leave you here."

"Thank you, Dauphin. I hope to see you again."

After the lad lanced up into the darkness, the embarrassed Fanon exhaled. "My apologies, sir. Prince Honore is . . . young. Please forgive him."

Gareth shook his head and laid a hand on the old fellow's shoulder.

"Don't worry. We were all like him once. I certainly won't mention it to His Majesty, if that's your concern."

"Thank you. The boy is good at heart. A bit impulsive." Fanon shouldered open the door onto a horrific chamber of noise and motion. It was a room full of children of all ages. Toddlers. Young males and females. Even a baby who crawled on the floor. Shouting. Screaming. Frantic motions and bodies flying from one place to another. The children looked openly at Gareth as he shuffled uncomfortably into the room. A small female stopped at his feet and stared up at him. Gareth nodded to her, but she continued to glare at him like a snake. An adult female vampire standing quietly near the baby lifted her head briefly, and then turned her attention back to a child beside her.

With one eye on the girl with the reptile stare, Gareth asked with an uncertain stammer, "Fanon, is this the clan nursery?"

"Of a sort," was the answer. "These are the princes and princesses. Some of them."

"These are all Lothaire's children? There must be ten here."

"Yes. But these are not all of his children. Honore is the oldest, but there are . . ." Fanon rolled his eyes up in thought. "Four others beyond these you see here."

Two children roared up to Gareth, using him as a barrier, as they clawed at each other, screaming and hissing. He tried to step aside, but the boys grabbed his legs, leaping from one side to the other. He reached down to urge one farther away, but when he covered the male's face with his hand, the wide-eyed female jumped the boy and smashed him to the floor.

Gareth was about to ask if they could wait somewhere else a bit less like the center of Hell when a distant door opened and a man who resembled an older, fatter Lothaire entered. Several children shouted and ran to him. He smiled and reached out, grasping or touching each one. He lifted a young female into his arms, and as he was swinging her around, his gaze fell on Gareth. Lothaire halted comically with his mouth open. He pushed his head forward as if that would clear his vision.

"Gareth?" he muttered in confusion.

"Your Majesty." Gareth bowed.

The French king staggered forward with several children attached. He stopped a few paces from the Scottish prince and stared while a grin slowly broke over his face. "I don't believe it. Why are you in Paris? No, never mind." He impetuously embraced Gareth, pressing the wriggling little girl between them.

Gareth inhaled the familiar scent of his friend and his youth. Lothaire's frame was softer, with less muscle and anger, but he was still much the same.

The king set the complaining girl down and grasped Gareth by the shoulders. "It is so good to see you, I can't tell you. I can't believe you're here." Then Lothaire's face fell into suspicious disappointment. "Oh no. Are you here from your brother? You're not bearing messages from Cesare, are you?"

Gareth smiled to comfort his companion. "While this isn't entirely a social call, you may believe me, I am not here on Cesare's behalf."

"Good!" Lothaire scooped up a different child out of habit. "I've heard entirely too much from your brother recently. Why didn't you tell me you were coming?"

"I had no way. I don't have packs of retainers to do my bidding."

Lothaire pursed his lips reproachfully. "So I've heard. How's Baudoin?"

"He's well. Thank you."

Lothaire began to jiggle the boy in his arms to placate his cries for attention. "Gareth, I heard about your father. My condolences. Dmitri was a remarkable king."

"He was indeed."

"All the more remarkable to have avoided killing both you and Cesare at some point."

Gareth laughed and indicated the menagerie of children. "Is that the voice of a father?"

The king rolled his eyes. "Sometimes. I'd introduce you, but they're young and they don't care who you are. My eldest is about. He'll want to meet you."

"The Dauphin. We intersected briefly. He seems quite . . . vigorous."

"If he was disrespectful, I apologize. The younger generation is uncontrollable. They've had everything too easy. Not like when we were boys." Lothaire brushed at the soft hair of the child in his arms, and smiled to himself. "Gareth, you have no children?"

"No."

"So you never found anyone . . ."

Gareth hesitated and then, to save complications, he said, "No."

"What about Hallow?" Lothaire asked, falsely casual. "What became of her?"

Gareth let silence stretch out, pretending to be amused by the stampeding offspring all around him. Then he replied politely, "That ended. Badly."

"Ah. Well." Now the king found some distraction to pull his attention away.

Gareth felt no discomfort, but was amused by Lothaire's. So he decided to ask a question that might bring embarrassment on him. "So, how is . . . your queen?"

Lothaire guffawed. "My queen is well. And she is still Katerina. She will want to see you, of course."

"Katerina bore you all these children?" Gareth shook his head and nodded toward the female across the room. "I thought perhaps she was the new queen. She seems exhausted enough."

"No. She's a nanny." Lothaire noticed the infant on the floor was screeching, red faced. He caught the nanny's attention. "He's hungry."

Without a change of expression, she went out another door and quickly came back with a human woman walking behind her. They waded through the children to the spot where the infant bawled. The human sat on the floor, and the nanny used a clawed finger to slice her across the throat. Dark red blood oozed out immediately. The baby stirred toward the woman, crawling onto her lap and staring at the dripping neck, crying out, reaching up.

"Help him," Lothaire said.

The human woman reached down with a blank stare and caught the baby under his pudgy arms. She lifted the snarling infant to her throat. The little thing latched itself onto the woman with frantic arms and legs, burying his face in the bloody neck. The sucking sound brought the attention of all the children, who gathered in a circle around the feeding.

After a few moments, the king called out, "Enough."

The vampire nanny pulled the infant off the human, who then pulled a cloth from her pocket and pressed it against her throat. The woman stood unsteadily and walked out of the room, seemingly unperturbed by the hungry glances of the royal brood.

Lothaire turned to Gareth with a cheerful smile. "Shall we adjourn to more comfortable quarters?"

"Yes." Gareth studied his friend with new eyes. "Why did you allow that woman to live?"

The king bristled as if at a common criticism. "Why are you, of all people, asking me that? You are Dmitri's son. Surely you believe in moderation and preservation?"

"I do," Gareth replied quickly. "I'm not criticizing you. I applaud it. It's just an unusual attitude for our people."

Lothaire set his little son on his feet with a comforting pat on the backside. "I have many mouths to feed, and I am merely a poor king. I have to use human bloodnurses, of course, but I see no reason to kill humans just to feed."

"I knew I was right to come to Paris." Gareth smiled and placed his arm over his friend's shoulder, feeling a sense of comradeship with one of his own that he hadn't felt in over a century. The French king latched a companionable arm around Gareth's waist as they left the room just like they were still old hunting partners out for a night of adventure.

The two vampires slipped from a window in the Tuileries and lifted over the city, silently agreeing on the direction. They floated over the Seine, looking down on the jumbled structures and tight lanes of the Rive Gauche, still like the killing grounds of old. Gareth felt a disturbing sense of comfort. Life had been simpler in those days; well, perhaps not simpler but more direct. Feeding and staying hidden were never easy tasks, but they were at least clear.

He followed Lothaire to the very familiar terrain of old Montparnasse. They settled by an old stone wall with a gate now rusted and fallen aside. They padded down stone steps into murky passageways where they were surrounded by bones. Every wall was stacked with skeletons. One wall boasted long leg bones and another skulls. Many of the macabre collections were still in artful displays with skeletal faces peering out over crossed long bones. The floors were littered with more recent skeletons left from vampire feedings. Even so, there were humans inhabiting the catacombs. Gareth heard them moving about, and not far away. They seemed to have little fear.

"Remember this place?" Lothaire asked as Gareth looked around in confusion.

"Of course. We lived here centuries ago." Gareth waved at the macabre walls. "But it wasn't full of bones back then."

"No. Not too long before the Great Killing, humans decided to use this place for their dead," Lothaire replied. "And they organized their refuse in clever designs. For some reason. Humans are strange. Or used to be. They're fairly predictable now."

"Paris seems quite active with humans. Quite different than London."

The king shrugged. "In general, I leave them be as long as they don't cause trouble. Day-to-day things have to be done, and they work better if some of them aren't fearful for their lives at every turn. Herds can sustain themselves nicely so long as you don't cull them to the breaking point. And I try to impress on the clan lords outside Paris to keep slaughter to a minimum."

"Have you had much success impressing that on them?"

"Not much, I fear. But things change slowly with us." Lothaire sighed, and then said with a sarcastic tone, "I hear rumors that you treat your Scottish herds like they're your family."

"Oh, I treat them much better than that." Gareth laughed and hummed thoughtfully as he ran his hands over the knobby ends of countless femurs. He stuck his fingers into the eyeholes of a skull and pulled it from the wall, tossing it toward his friend. Lothaire reacted quickly, but fumbled the white object that clattered to the stones at his feet.

He looked up quizzically. "Why are you throwing garbage at me?"

"Just to see if you could catch it."

"Why?"

"No reason. I assume you haven't lived in these catacombs for a while."

"No. I live at the Tuileries Palace. Although I do come here frequently. I like it here. Gareth, I hope you'll stay in Paris for a little while. Or are you hurrying away?"

"No. Where would I go?"

"London?" Lothaire looked surprised. "Hasn't Cesare summoned you for your coven?"

"Oh yes. I believe I heard something about that. I'll find my way there at some point."

The French king's laugh echoed through the macabre chambers. "I can just imagine Cesare's face when he hears you are lingering here in Paris."

"Are you going to tell him?"

"No, but I won't have to. Your Lady Hallow has spies all around me." Lothaire growled. "Your brother wants my packs for his war, so he's virtually colonized my court."

"So you've committed to him already?"

Lothaire kicked a rib cage, sending it skittering across the floor. "Gareth, I believe your brother has stirred up this war just to force a clan alliance that he will control."

Gareth tilted his head in mute agreement.

The French king pursed his lips in concern. "But what if I'm wrong? Cesare claims that humans have weapons much more powerful than during the Great Killing. And they don't fear us as they once did."

"Do you believe him?"

"I don't know. Many do. My cousin, the king of Orleans, wants to join Cesare because he's afraid of the humans. I hear they smashed Grenoble. And if Lyon falls, the Equatorians will pour out into central France, which is full of weak, bickering clans. Bordeaux was obliterated just last year by a handful of airships." Lothaire prodded the skull with the dusty toe of his shoe. "If only Cesare wasn't going to become the king of kings. I don't trust him. But, frankly, I don't see an option but to join him."

"I can give you an option."

The king raised an eyebrow. "Yes?"

"What if I were king of Britain?"

Lothaire stood against a wall of bones, looking at his old friend. "When I told Lady Hallow that I would only ally myself with a king, not a prince, she assured me that you had abdicated your claim to the throne, and that Cesare was the unquestioned heir. Is Lady Hallow a liar?"

"She is, and a prodigious one. Though she was correct at that time."

"And now?"

"Things change, Lothaire. At my advancing age, my brow grows chilly and needs a crown to warm it."

"Damn." The French king breathed in conspiratorial delight. "What will Cesare do?"

"I'm afraid he will die."

Lothaire looked askance. "What of your brother's terrible claws? What of the lovely Flay?"

Gareth smiled with evil relish. "Flay is no concern."

The king laughed and blinked with wide eyes. "Truly? You're going to do it, aren't you? Finally. You're going to kill your brother. Are you prepared to be king?"

Gareth's smile vanished. He suddenly noticed the smell of the chill air unfiltered by Greyfriar's scarf. He felt the absence of a heavy gun belt or dangling sword on his hips. He looked deep into the warm eyes of his friend as if seeking some comfort. "There is nothing else I can do now."

"You were born to be king and you have my support, Your Majesty. I'll fight the Equatorians at the side of King Gareth with gusto." Lothaire picked up the skull and lofted it across the chamber.

Gareth reached out and snatched the dead thing from the air with great and unusual facility, much to the surprise of his friend.

CHAPTER 27

I T WAS A balmy evening heralding spring would soon be on them. Gareth stepped between two smashed French windows onto a veranda outside the Tuileries. The week spent among Lothaire's family had been hectic. Cesare would be foaming at the mouth to have the coronation done, and if Lothaire was right about spies in the court, surely his brother knew Gareth was delaying here. He was about to lift into the air when a voice behind him softly called out his name. He turned. Lothaire's wife approached, tall and regal, in a simple but elegant dress that swept the floor behind her.

"Katerina," he replied, coming toward her.

"I finally have a quiet moment with most of the brood asleep, and I thought we might chat without the din." Her smile was genuine. "Lothaire has been regaling me of your exploits as the lonely prince."

Gareth stifled a groan, wishing he had left a minute earlier. He was in no mood to be nagged by married friends about being the consummate bachelor. Katerina didn't let him escape.

"You must quite love Scotland," she continued.

"Scotland is quiet."

Katerina took his hands and guided him to a chaise. "Well, Baudoin is known for his profound silence, but surely you don't spend all your time in that damp castle."

"No, I get out of the city from time to time. The countryside is good for one's health, I hear. Sometimes I sleep in tombs and caves for old time's sake."

Katerina's laugh was sweet. "I have missed your wit. And you must be missing the peace and quiet of your beloved Scotland right about now."

Gareth shrugged politely. "It is good to see you both. It's been too long." He noted the diminutive bite marks on her neck. Most were healed, but there were fresh ones as well. Even with the help of bloodnurses, she still had allowed her nearly innumerable children to feed from her. "I've never seen you look so happy, even teetering on exhaustion."

"The lure of motherhood is strong." Katerina's smile broadened, and a dangerous twinkle filled her eye. "So Gareth, Lothaire tells me you haven't found anyone to share your damp castle. But I think you look different."

Gareth leaned back slightly, cautious, then remarked, "I merely found my backbone. That changes the stature of a man."

She scrutinized him through blue eyes. "I fear you're lying to me. You have found someone."

He hesitated, taken aback by her intuition. Then he conceded to her open persuasive face, smiling at the admission, "Yes, you are frighteningly perceptive. It's true."

"Won't you tell me about her?"

"It's . . . complicated."

She leaned forward and laid a kind hand on his knee. "It always is. You need not say anything if you don't wish it. I won't pry, although I'd like to."

"Thank you. That means a great deal to me. Katerina, you and Lothaire have been together for as long as I've known you. Your love has crossed centuries. I've watched you the past few days. You're so comfortable with each other. No matter the noise or the chaos of your children or matters of state, you two treat each other with kindness. I ache to have what you two have."

"If she's the right one for you, you will have centuries together still."

Gareth almost shook his head. Adele's life could be counted in decades. "All I know is that I have something better than anything I have ever known."

Katerina embraced him warmly. "Gareth, I'm so happy for you. Whoever she is, she has brought you back to the joy of living. I long to meet her and thank her for such a gift. Cherish it. Embrace it with all your heart."

"I will."

Katerina rose. "I am off to get some sleep. I can barely keep my eyes open."

"Quickly then, before one of them wakes," Gareth jested.

She brushed the back of her hand across his cheek affectionately. "I'm glad you're here. Lothaire hasn't been this animated in a century. Please make your stay an extended one, for his sake. And for mine. You're welcome here as long as you can stand to be away from the one you love." She glided to the door.

Gareth called after her, "Katerina, how could tell that I was different?"

She stared over her shoulder with a sly grin. "You seem content at last."

—◦◦◦—

Gareth relished the solitude in the near silence of the city air above the Parisian suburb of Montmartre. He smiled as he touched the cobblestones at the top of a long flight of cascading steps, feeling hopeful. Lights glimmered in the buildings along both sides of the stairway. He leaned against the iron rail and scanned the area. He smelled humans everywhere, and only a few vampires.

He had been to this spot on the two nights previous, and had noticed Prince Honore in the distance both times. The lad likely thought himself hidden, but his skills were no match for the vampire who was the Greyfriar. Gareth had talked in court about hunting in the Montmartre district to cover these excursions. He lied about how he loved stalking the area around the hilltop because it reminded him of the closes of Edinburgh. There was no sense alarming anyone with reports of his wandering the northern city for no apparent reason. And he hoped Prince Honore would tire of following if there were a mundane motive behind his sojourns. Apparently that was the case, because tonight there was no sign of prying eyes.

Warm breezes ruffled Gareth's shirt and reminded him of comfortable evenings atop the palace roof in Alexandria. He wondered what Adele was doing at this moment.

"Gareth."

He turned quickly to see a shadow move in the darkness. Flay. Extraordinary, and frightening. He hadn't detected her at all.

He said, "I think we're alone tonight."

"We are. Your little shade isn't about." She stepped into the starlight wearing a long swallowtail coat of navy blue, with riding pants, high leather boots, and nothing else. Her expression showed she was satisfied that she had remained hidden from him.

"Lothaire tells me his court is full of Cesare's spies."

Flay huffed. "No doubt. Cesare has spies everywhere."

"Even in Equatoria?"

"Of course. You knew one, Lord Kelvin."

Gareth nodded and started down the steps with Flay at his side. He tried to sound only vaguely interested in what she was saying. "Kelvin is dead now, thanks to you. And so is Lord Aden. Thanks to me."

"He is?" Flay glanced at him with surprise. "Why would you kill him? He could have been useful to you."

"I don't like traitors who are loyal to Cesare. How could I have ever trusted him?"

"*C'est la vie.* The only excuse for betrayal is to be on the winning side." She risked a hard glance at Gareth. "Isn't that why you've given up your mask, Greyfriar?"

Gareth froze and slid his eyes slowly to her. She flinched, fearful she had overplayed her hand. Then he laughed and nodded at her brutal sagacity. "Speaking of my alter ego, have you told anyone other than Lord Aden about the Greyfriar?"

Flay smiled seductively with renewed confidence. "No, my lord. I told you in the crypt underneath Alexandria that I would use that particular piece of delicious intelligence for my own gain. I shouldn't have told that human, but I was angry. And I was only going to tell Cesare when I was ready to destroy you."

"How fortunate you didn't, Flay. Now we both have a brighter future."

Flay leaned toward the prince, as if expecting him to touch her. However, he kept his attention straight ahead and continued a slow stroll down the broad steps. The war chief snarled, "This place stinks like humans."

Gareth shrugged and waved his arm. People moved around them, even though it was well past dusk.

Flay sneered. "Perhaps if Lothaire wasn't so consumed with making little French vampires, he could clean out this rat hole."

"His Majesty is in agreement with our plot. He will support Cesare's demise, and my coronation."

The war chief didn't seem overjoyed.

"Don't fret." Gareth allowed his voice to drip entitlement. "I'm Dmitri's eldest son."

"You have been away a long time. Whom can you count on? You were once popular with Lord Ghast, but he's dead. Princess Adele killed him."

"Yes, I remember." Gareth pretended to eye Flay, angry at her doubt and complications as he tapped his finger on his chin. "What about Lord Raglan? He still has York, doesn't he?"

"Fine, there's one."

"Well, how about . . . no, he's dead. Perhaps Lady—mm, no. Not her."

Flay worked her jaw side to side with impatience. "Perhaps we should name lords who hate Cesare rather than those who like you."

"A longer list, I'd guess."

"Much."

"Even so, should we reach out to them now? We can't afford for Cesare to suspect we're polling the clan before the coven."

"You're right." She stopped and turned toward him. "This won't be a simple matter."

"You're here to make it simple, Flay," Gareth replied sharply. "Politics is a matter of killing the right people at the right time."

She eyed him hungrily. "Yes, but we must tread carefully. There is always the threat of civil war. The clan could shatter. Remember, King Dmitri had brothers, and they have children. Newcastle. Cambridge. Even the lord of Bruges is married to a cousin of yours. Any of these opportunists could proclaim you a usurper."

"Unlikely."

Flay shrugged. "Yes, but not impossible. I will sound out the clan and find several allies who will support you. And there are a few die-hard Cesare loyalists whom I can target for elimination. With proper preparation, we should be able to make you king with only the desired amount of bloodshed. You must prepare for everything. You must think on a wider scale than ever before."

Gareth stifled a laugh, remembering the similar advice he'd given Adele during their fencing match. It gave him a chill to think he and Flay had mirror worldviews.

He saw a glint to his left and began to spin as a knife slid into his upper rib cage. He grasped the wrist of his attacker. There was no fear in the human's eyes, only determination. Another flash forced him to duck, and an axe swept past his head. He heard pops from above and something punched him in the shoulder, chest, and back. Gunfire came from the roofs above on both sides of the stairs.

Flay leapt into the air and rose toward the flashes from the rooftops. Bullets struck her too, and her weightless form went spinning.

Gareth reached for his rapier, but grasped empty space as the axe slammed deep into his shoulder, missing his neck by a few inches. He pulled the man with the dagger along with him as he backed against the wall to seek cover. Bullets ticked off the wall.

He gouged the face of the knife wielder and sent him airborne screaming down the stairs. Then he yanked the axe free of his collarbone and stepped out, swinging the weapon into another determined man nearby. The point of a sword immediately protruded from Gareth's stomach. With an angry snarl, he lashed back with the axe, and the heavy blade caromed off a man's skull.

Instantly, he dropped the axe and began to climb, weaving up the stones as shells tore through newly leafed branches, clicked off bricks, and shattered windows. He heard screams from above and assumed Flay had found her quarry. When he reached the roof, he caught a brief glimpse of her slaughtering a man before pushing off and vaulting over the stairs toward the opposite rooftop.

He sailed across the space as rifle muzzles flashed, and he felt several tugs on his clothes and limbs. Then he was on the roof, in the center of four men with rifles. They tried awkwardly to spin and aim at him. He growled and slashed faces and throats, ripped weapons from hands, and smashed heads with a heavy rifle.

Soon he was the only one standing. He had been slow. So much time in the relative warmth of Equatoria, and infrequent feedings left him less than his best. He needed to sharpen himself before going to London.

Flay appeared over the edge of the roof, her face red and raven hair glistening wet. She crouched with claws out, her head pivoting in search of prey. Satisfied they were alone, she turned her attention to Gareth.

She laughed. "You didn't kill them all below, but I finished it for you."

"I was distracted," Gareth replied.

Flay took the rifle from his hand and tossed it aside. Then she gently removed a dagger from his ribs and pulled the sword out of his back. Her earlier looks of dismay were replaced by fierce admiration as she took in the carnage. "Please restrain yourself from using weapons where you might be seen."

Gareth studied the frozen faces of the assassins. Their postures and expressions had been different from normal humans. These men had confidence; they held no fear. There had been a flame in their eyes that Gareth rarely saw, even among Greyfriar's network of supporters in vampire Europe. Even more disturbing, this was no random attack. This was a staged ambush. These would-be killers had shown a methodical skill to their attacks; they were trained.

Flay kicked one of the rifles. "This gun is new. I've seen the very ones at St. Etienne in the hands of Equatorians. How did Parisian herds get them?"

Gareth recognized the weapons too, the latest bolt-action rifle off the line in Alexandria. He knelt by one of the attackers and drank from him. He sensed fading emotions in the cooling blood. The taste sparked his hunger, so he drew in more to feed his fire and calm his throbbing wounds.

"Damn it," Gareth said, wiping his bloody mouth with a bloody sleeve. "These aren't herds or southerners. These are Cesare's Undead."

—◦◦◦—

King Lothaire rushed to his friend's side when Gareth staggered into the throne room in the Tuileries. "Gareth! What happened to you?"

"Nothing." Gareth's voice was strained, speaking through clenched teeth.

The king took Gareth by his arm and led him to a seat. Several children stopped their usual writhing and slapping to watch the amazing bloody spectacle. Lothaire's eyes went wide as he inspected Gareth. "These are bullet holes. Humans attacked you? Here in Paris? Are we under attack?"

"No, my brother—"

Lothaire stiffened and cut a glance, which along with the sound of a familiar voice from nearby, silenced Gareth and sent his attention to a doorway far to his left.

Prince Cesare appeared in casual conversation with Prince Honore, but halted abruptly at the sight of his wounded brother. A flicker of angry disappointment washed over Cesare's face before he managed a semblance of concern. Just behind him, Honore peered in with open shock.

"Gareth, whatever has happened to you?" Cesare asked with false worry. "Were you mauled by your cats?"

The prince of Scotland laughed wetly in his throat. "No. They would've done worse." He rose, smoothing his blood-crusted shirt with a red hand, and smiled as best he could. "I'm shocked to see you in Paris, Cesare. Don't you have a party to plan?"

Cesare grunted in open annoyance. His grey suit with knee-length frock coat was immaculate. His black shoes were polished to a gleam, and even his cravat had been expertly tied by a human slave. Prince

Honore wore a similar suit, almost a disturbing reflection of Cesare. But now the Dauphin sought to distance himself from the British lord, slipping back against the wall, his gaze trading off between the rival brothers.

"It's prepared," Cesare replied stiffly. "But I can't proceed without you. I heard you were here and came to offer my personal invitation, if that's what it takes. Since I've found you, will you return to London with me now?"

Gareth crossed the spacious room toward his brother until he towered over the prospective king. "Alas, no, Cesare. I have more pressing matters at present."

Cesare hissed, "There is nothing more pressing in this world. Our father is dead."

"Yes." Gareth paused, then breathed out with suppressed rage. "You were obviously a magnificent caretaker."

The younger brother smiled with extraordinary boldness. "Well, the poor old thing had been ill long enough. He's better off. As are we."

"You are miserable and disgusting, Cesare. I can't believe you are a son of Dmitri."

"Yet I am. You were his favorite, there's no doubt. More the pity then. Perhaps if you had not abandoned him, he might still be alive."

Gareth slashed out with ferocious instinct, but he was too slow. Cesare blocked the attack and another. A third blow shredded the younger prince's coat before he slipped out of arm's reach to the side of Honore, who shouted, "Stop! You are in my father's court!"

Gareth halted, already winded from the exertion.

Cesare inspected his ripped clothes bitterly, and said, "Have some decorum, for a change, Gareth. We can discuss family matters when we return to London. Prepare yourself and we will depart."

"I said no."

"You must." Cesare glared at him. "I have declared it. It is the law."

"Technically, there is no king. You must convene a clan council to summon me."

"You insolent worm. I am to be king."

"So you shall. But I must accomplish several things first."

"Damn you!" Cesare stepped forward, and his claws darted out, seizing Gareth's throat. "You will do as I say."

Gareth didn't struggle; he merely reached up and grasped his brother's wrist. He squeezed slowly, grinding bone against bone, staring straight into Cesare's eyes. His strength was failing, but he focused on one thing only—crushing his brother's arm. Every fragment of his consciousness went to that single task. The younger prince narrowed his gaze with alarm and tried to push his claws deeper into Gareth's flesh.

"Retract your claws," Gareth hissed, "or I'll snap off your hand."

Cesare felt his wrist begin to crack. His claws pulled out, and after a second, Gareth let off the pressure. Both brothers lowered their hands together.

Gareth leaned closer. "Don't ever send your deluded fanatics against me again."

Cesare started to act innocent, but gave it up. He wasn't frightened or concerned; he simply saw no reason to deny it. He whispered, "You swore you would not stand in my way, Gareth, and you may not believe this, but I took you at your word. I won't stand by and watch you have second thoughts about the throne now. Don't you think I know why you're here with your old friend Lothaire? There's nothing that occurs that I don't know. I'll kill you before I'll let you ruin my coronation."

Gareth said, "I will come to London for a coven at the new moon. You have my word."

"The new moon? That is too far away. We are at war and the weather is warming."

"My schedule without a fight. Or yours, and I will contest you. Choose."

Gareth knew his brother wasn't fond of being dictated to, but by offering his own surrender, even an incomplete one, he would entice Cesare to play for the long gain. Even though the younger prince fumed at the situation, he would accept it, and plan his revenge later on his own terms.

Cesare's scowl subsided and he raised his voice. "Very well. Was that so difficult? That's all I asked, for you to honor your vow. I will see you at Buckingham Palace. Try to clean yourself up a bit. Maybe you can borrow more suitable attire from your host." He turned to Lothaire. "Your Majesty, thank you for your promises of hospitality, but I fear I must hurry back to London. Lady Hallow will prepare a conference to discuss folding the French packs into the coalition forces. I will send Flay to consult with your war chief, Prince Honore."

King Lothaire nodded. "We are bereaved that you must leave us so soon, Prince Cesare."

Cesare spun back to Gareth. "Three weeks. Don't do anything that might make me nervous. And don't make me find you again because the first place I'll look is inside the rib cages of every man, woman, and child in Edinburgh."

Gareth remained coldly silent as his brother bowed and departed with Prince Honore at his heels. Then he slumped exhausted into a creaking chair. "Lothaire, I regret to tell you that your son seems to have fallen in with a bad crowd."

"Family." The French king shrugged hopelessly.

CHAPTER 28

SANAH STOOD IN the center of a room in Victoria Palace that was opulent to the point of gaudy. Adele and Captain Shirazi observed her unseen through a one-way mirror.

"She has been thoroughly searched," Shirazi informed the empress.

Adele looked at the calling card the woman had given her at the opera. In the subsequent events, she had forgotten about the woman until Shirazi announced she had appeared at the palace gates demanding to speak to the empress on a matter of life or death. The Persian woman had been searched and questioned. After several hours, Shirazi was informed of her presence and he came to see her, but she refused to give her message to anyone but Adele. She begged Shirazi to remind the empress about the woman at the opera, and to tell Adele to make special note of a mark written on the calling card.

Despite his misgivings, the captain passed the information on to the empress, who retrieved the card and, with great shock, noticed a symbol that was repeated in her mother's geomancy journals many times. Adele ordered the woman to be brought to her despite the captain's stern reservations.

Adele folded her arms across her chest. "What more can we do to make sure she isn't the enemy? At some point I will have to talk to her."

"Not necessarily."

"Well, I want to talk to her."

Captain Shirazi strode before her, an unstoppable force, tall and foreboding in his crisp scarlet uniform. Before he opened the door, Adele stopped him with a hand. "Let's not scare her, shall we?"

Shirazi planted a hand on the door, his annoyance plain and unyielding. "Your Majesty, it is my duty to protect you. General Anhalt tasked me with that mission when he gave me command of the White Guard. And I have no intention of failing him."

"I'm most grateful." Adele smiled warmly at the echo of her beloved General Anhalt's undying loyalty in the young captain's stern words. "I'm not saying you can't come in with me, but you won't be the first one stomping in all grim and imposing. I intend to be polite."

"Why would you trust her, of all people?"

"I don't know. There's something about her."

Adele and Shirazi stared at each other like two bulls, neither giving ground. Her eyebrow rose with one last challenge, and Shirazi straightened, resuming parade rest.

"As you will, Majesty. We will treat her with respect until she proves otherwise."

"Thank you. Let's try not to be an angry mob in there. Smile." She knocked politely before entering the room.

Sanah stood expectantly, her expression immediately warming at Adele's presence until she saw the soldier behind her.

"Don't mind him," Adele assured her. "After the opera, my security is tenfold. I doubt I'll be alone well into my nineties at this rate."

Adele's nonchalant response appeared to do the trick, as Sanah bowed to the empress. "Of course, Your Majesty. A wise precaution."

"Please, sit." Adele gestured to one of the plush couches in the room. She sat near Sanah, but not so close as to be within striking range should something go awry, much to Shirazi's relief she was sure. She didn't want to give the young soldier grey hair yet. That would come in due time. "I realize this atmosphere isn't conducive to a normal conversation, but I hope we can start a friendship despite the circumstances."

"If I may be blunt, Your Majesty, pleasantries must wait," Sanah said. "You recently received several notebooks that belonged to your mother."

"Yes, that's correct," Adele answered slowly. "How did you know?'"

"I am your mother's sister."

Adele's breath caught and she leaned forward. "What?"

"I have been away for a long time. I have wanted to reconnect with you, especially after the death of your father." She looked at the captain briefly and then returned to Adele. "And the loss of your mentor."

"That is not common knowledge." Adele felt a tinge of alarm, and Shirazi stepped forward protectively.

Sanah sat stone still. "No, it is not."

Adele realized there was only one way to know such a thing. "You are part of Mamoru's network."

She nodded. "I am one of his cabal. Though currently, it is not something I am proud of."

Adele was still trying to process everything. "He never mentioned you. In fact, no one has ever mentioned you. My mother didn't have a sister named Sanah."

"That isn't my true name. Many of us change our names for various reasons. You may recall the mention of Sayeh."

That name did resonate with Adele. Her mother had in fact talked about a sister named Sayeh, a devout and curious wanderer. But that wasn't a secret; it didn't prove anything. "So where have you been all these years, Sanah? Where were you when your sister died?" Adele's voice was hard when she asked the last question.

The Persian woman closed her eyes, revealing the tattoo on her lids. "I was far away at the time. I only learned of Pareesa's death years after the fact. I would have done anything to see her again, but my life took a different path. I have spent my life traveling, studying, and watching." She opened her eyes to stare at Adele.

"Watching me?" The empress's shock continued to escalate.

"Yes, from afar. Your studies have mirrored Pareesa's. You are both very much alike. Have you been able to decipher any of your mother's notes in her journal?"

"Of course; they aren't terribly complex. I'm beyond her studies now. I learned the fundamentals of geomancy months ago."

"No, I refer to her private notes."

"Private notes?"

Sanah nodded, and Adele wished the burqa wasn't in place so she could read the woman's features. As it was she had only the woman's mysterious eyes to guide her.

"The scribblings she placed all over the pages are your mother's secret language." The eyes glistened. "It was our game, you see, when we were younger. We would pass small notes back and forth. As we grew older, and secrets became more precious, we used it extensively to communicate in utmost privacy."

"Are you are a geomancer?"

"Nothing so grand. I am a poet, and a seer. Pareesa and I both entered Mamoru's school on Java at a young age. Your mother was far more adept, her studies more in-depth. Mamoru groomed her for many years until he had to admit that she was not the one. I was never a skilled geomancer, but I had other value to Mamoru, including loyalty, and he brought me up to be one of his closest advisors after Pareesa died. I was completely entranced by his message and his mission. He *was* a great man." She shrugged. "Now, we have lost our focus."

"Where is Mamoru?" Adele demanded.

"He was here in Alexandria for a time, but I don't know where he is now. I caution you that he is no longer the man I once knew. His convictions are much less clear. That is the reason I have come forward to you now. You are in danger. He believes you are no longer in your right mind. He believes that your relationship with the Greyfriar has destroyed your humanity."

Adele gasped softly at the woman's words and quickly turned. "Captain Shirazi, leave us."

"Your Majesty, I must remain for your safety."

Her voice lowered to a whisper. "Please don't make me order you."

He stiffened. "I'm afraid that is your only option."

She scowled, although she couldn't fault the man. "Captain Shirazi, I order you to wait outside, and I absolve you of any conscience."

"If something were to happen to you under my watch, my conscience would be inconsolable regardless." He lifted his pistol from his holster and handed it to her.

Warming, she nodded. "I will endeavor to make sure that will never be a concern."

"As you command, Your Majesty." His scowl was an obvious sign of his displeasure on this matter, but with a sharp turn of his heel he departed.

When the door had closed, the empress stared hard at the Persian woman. "You will keep your voice down from this point forward. Do you understand me?"

"I do, Your Majesty."

"Tell me why I should believe a word you've said?"

Sanah took a deep breath. "I can only pray you will. You may confine me here, if you wish. But you must hear what I have to tell you. Your future depends on it."

Adele studied the woman, wanting to see falsehood in her. However, her intuition whispered something different. "So talk."

"Of course. The leaders of the cabal all know the secret of Greyfriar. Mamoru told us about your dark master." Sanah's voice softened. "However, I saw your lover at the opera. He saved you regardless of his own life. That was an act of love, not politics. I don't think you are under his sway. Instead, I see he is under yours."

Adele's chest tightened at the thought of a kindred spirit, but then she again gripped tight her rampaging hopes. "Thank you. It's nice to know you believe me. Mamoru doesn't."

"Those who blindly trust cannot be enlightened. Mamoru's actions of late have led me to question his agenda."

"In what way? He hates Greyfriar. I already know that."

"There are things you do not know."

Adele's eyes narrowed. "Then enlighten me."

"Mamoru has sent an assassin to remove Greyfriar from your side permanently."

Adele rose to her feet.

"Your Majesty, please! There is much more to tell you. You must hear the rest. It pertains to your life as well."

Slowly, Adele resumed her seat, her face a mask of desperation. "Tell me quickly."

"Mamoru had such grand plans. When he realized your mother was not the one, he began to hope that her child would be. And that came to pass. Pareesa's daughter was the one he needed."

"Needed for what exactly?"

"As you surely know, most geomancy uses the earth's energy like drinking from a fountain, like taking a cursory token. You, however, do not steal bits of energy here and there as most geomancers today do. You step boldly into the water of energy flowing along the spines of the Earth and swirling in the rifts. No person in living memory has those abilities. You are like the great mystics or saints. You can touch some level of the divine." Sanah reached out toward Adele's face, but the young woman pulled away. The Persian's eyes saddened. "You look tired."

"Running an empire doesn't leave much room for sleeping and spa treatments. Please get to the point."

Sanah said, "The whole of the Earth wants to move within you, Adele. However, your body is but flesh and therefore a weak vessel for containing it."

"Mamoru said I would master it eventually."

"Perhaps in time. But he no longer has that luxury. He intends for you to cleanse the world of vampires now."

"I told him that I wouldn't be a tool of genocide. I refused to do his bidding."

"Yes, I know. However, he doesn't need your cooperation. He has the power to force you."

Adele's breath left her. "How is that possible?"

"Do you remember the operating room incident at Sir Godfrey's home? The crystals Mamoru had you hold? He used them to initiate your reaction. It was a test of his control over you."

"You were there?" Adele's anger was growing. Once more, she had been merely a pawn.

Sanah nodded.

"Even if he could do that, does he think he can drag me to every rift on Earth, assuming we could reach every corner of the globe? Even Mamoru can't be that blind."

"No, Adele. You are the one Mamoru has been seeking because you are the key to unlocking every ley line across the Earth at a single stroke, from one rift. When he forces you to initiate the final Event, your fire will spread over the world. No vampire will be able to hide from the Earth's wrath. All of them, gone in a second. But in the process, you will be consumed."

Adele felt sick and had to put a hand against her clammy forehead. "I . . . I don't believe you. He would really do such a thing?"

"He can and he will."

"I won't kill Gareth." Adele's face grew hard with fury, her voice lowering.

"If Mamoru has his way you will have no choice. His grief has made him mad. He thought only to save the world."

"Why your sudden change of heart? You've been part of Mamoru's cabal. You've followed him all these years, as my mother did. As I have. You don't think freeing the world from vampires is worth one life?"

"Not against your will. I will not be party to murder."

Adele sat quietly.

"There is no guarantee that Mamoru's plans will work. It is all theory, but there is no doubt that in the process of testing this theory, you will be killed."

"And so what are you suggesting?"

"I'm afraid I have little influence with Mamoru now. But I'm hoping you may draw some knowledge from Pareesa's notebooks."

"The scribblings, you mean?"

"Yes. Answers may lie there. She and Mamoru often clashed. She had many unique ideas about geomancy that he found fanciful and distracting to his goals."

Adele said, "I can't read her code."

"I can help you. Mamoru once showed me the notebooks shortly before he passed them on to you. I recognized the marks as Pareesa's secret writing, but thought nothing of it. Until recently, when I received a vision that your mother may have left a message for you." Sanah squeezed her hands together painfully. "What I saw of the notes, I understood only parts of. Perhaps it is because I am not a geomancer. I will teach you what I know of the code and perhaps you can understand Pareesa's secrets. Maybe it will help save you should the worst happen."

"And save Gareth."

Sanah hesitated. "He may be long dead before that is an issue."

Adele stood, her hand holding the pistol resolutely. "That will not happen either."

"I understand. However, Mamoru has sent his assassin to Edinburgh, hoping the prince will come home to roost. Then she will strike. Nzingu is a most capable geomancer. Even I fear her."

"I don't."

Sanah's gaze softened. "Then you must go swiftly. She is most likely already waiting at the lair of your lover."

CHAPTER 29

NEVER A MAN of protocol, Captain Hariri offered Empress Adele a jaunty salute as she came up onto the quarterdeck of the airship *Edinburgh*. She returned it in a similar fashion, despite the anxiety she had felt inside since they left Alexandria three days ago.

"Your Majesty," he shouted to her over the wind. "We're across the Mediterranean and are over the French coast. Heading is north, as you commanded."

"Take her up as high as she'll go, Captain."

Hariri raised surprised eyebrows. "Very well, but bid farewell to fair skies and forgiving winds. The gales up there could shake us apart or blow us to Russia. The cold will freeze my men to the lines and turn the sails into sheets of ice. The air is so thin we'll be gasping for breath."

"So you're afraid?"

"Afraid?" Without hesitation, Hariri barked the command to his first mate before returning his attention to her. "I just want you to know that it's going to be a bit uncomfortable for the next few days."

"I appreciate the rigors your men will be facing on this voyage, Captain. But we have to fly high to avoid vampires and for speed. I haven't time to take the long route out into the Atlantic and up. Senator Clark made this same run to London last year."

"Then so shall we," the pirate said seriously. "I won't have that American doing something I can't."

"Good. I've laid in plenty of extra clothing for the crew to ward off the extreme cold. See to it that it's distributed."

"I assume this isn't a social call. There's a regiment's arsenal below as well. Are we off to save General Anhalt again?" He winked with a grin.

"Not this time."

She tightened the soft folds of Greyfriar's scarf around her frigid cheeks and neck, relishing in the warmth and the trace of his scent. In return for this token, the night he left Alexandria, she had slipped a cheap penny dreadful of fairy tales in his pack for him to read and discard as needed. Hopefully it would distract him during his journey. She thought about him reading in the dark at the base of a tree in the wilds, and it satisfied her.

White clouds drifted lazily below them. It always seemed so peaceful when they were in the sky. The brig seemed to be moving so slowly even though every inch of sail was unfurled. Mamoru's assassin was weeks ahead of her, and the passage of time ate a hole in Adele's belly.

Edinburgh lifted in a marked surge, and Adele's hand gripped the rail as she bent her knees with the upward motion. The sharp hiss of gas could be heard above as the vessel's massive dirigible filled. The rush of clouds streamed past her while thick vapors left her face wet. Ice crystals formed on her cheeks as she stared into the sodium sky. Someone handed her a heavy coat and she took it gratefully. She glanced over.

"Captain Shirazi."

The tall soldier bowed and then resumed his attentive position. His silence was deafening. Each frosty breath blatantly demonstrated his concern. She expected a rebuke, a snide comment, something. Instead, the captain's mouth was merely a stern line, and then finally came a polite request.

"Would Your Majesty care to relate her intentions for this mission?"

Adele swallowed. "I doubt you'd like the answer."

"Yes, I'm sure I wouldn't." He stared hard at her. "But regardless, I need to hear it."

"Greyfriar is in danger."

"Is that not a mission more logical to be in the hands of the Harmattan? We would defend Greyfriar with our lives, as we defend you."

"Yes, I know," Adele responded. She was taking a major gamble, and she had to tread carefully. General Anhalt had always been her confidant; she trusted him implicitly. However, she didn't truly know this man beside her, and she had too many secrets to share them openly. "When we have reached maximum safe altitude and are sailing north, come to me in my cabin. I will explain our mission then. It involves more than just a simple rescue. Bring Captain Hariri."

She retreated to her cabin to figure out how to orchestrate the next few weeks and keep Gareth safe, not only from the assassin, but from her own men as well. The bed creaked as she sat down heavily.

Adele's head whirled with all the things that could go wrong. It would take only one slip to collapse the house of cards her world had become. Her gut twisted when she realized that every move or decision she made could shatter everything. She was balancing love and duty. She was playing with the impossible. The weight of that sunk onto her shoulders again. Her fingers pressed deep into her eyes as she rubbed them. "Just once, I wish something wouldn't be so dire."

Her leather satchel was at the foot of the bed, and she dragged it over to retrieve her mother's journal. There hadn't been time to work on deciphering her mother's notes before her hurried departure from Alexandria, but she had been working on it since. Even on a fast ship traveling dangerously high, there would be many days of inactivity on a journey this long. Adele opened the book carefully and immediately felt a rush of old memories. Her mother's distinctive cursive writing stared back at her. In the margins were the strange scribbles and doodles that Sanah had said were a form of writing that could be translated into Persian. Adele again took out a sheet that her *aunt* had hastily prepared with a simple key to the code.

The young woman wondered about Sanah. Her *aunt*. The long-lost sister of her mother. Could it be true? Adele felt a kinship with the woman, even back when they met at the play last summer. She had talked too much to her that night. Perhaps that was the natural connection of women in the same family exerting itself. Adele hoped there was a future where she might share some time with this new aunt, but the future was as clear as the grey clouds outside *Edinburgh*.

She was fully aware this voyage could be a trap. Sanah had admitted to being part of Mamoru's cabal. This entire thing—the journal, a fortuitous new aunt, and a mysterious assassin—could be an elaborate ruse to lure her away from Alexandria. Even knowing that, Adele had to go. If there was even the slightest chance the story was true that Gareth was in danger, and that she could protect him, there was no question. If this was indeed a plot by Mamoru, Adele pitied him once she finished with him.

The empress forced her attention to her mother's marks. She compared them to Sanah's key, laboring to make sense of it all. The same symbol could mean words or letters or thoughts, depending on how it was used. And Sanah's notes were not always clear on the differences.

Adele noted one set of symbols that appeared frequently, and on one page were written in deep dark ink, nearly etched into the paper, next to several of Mamoru's critical red comments. Clearly Pareesa was bearing down on those symbols. Adele used Sanah's code and realized with a bolt of excitement that the symbols represented the word *Mamoru*.

It worked. Mamoru was the Rosetta stone.

Adele laughed and began to translate the next set of symbols. It started to make sense, and her mother spoke to her from the past. Fortunately, most of the scribblings were simple observations of the Earth and its relationship with geomancy. Many of them, however, were specific responses to Mamoru's critiques, so Adele was aided in her reading by Pareesa repeating some of her teacher's comments, usually with the scorn of a scolded student. It was logical she wouldn't have wanted Mamoru to read them.

Then, on the pages regarding *pathfinding*, covered with her mother's sketches of spiders and webs, Pareesa's commentary grew even more scathing. She implied that Mamoru was narrow-minded, as much as the technocrats who ruled the Empire. She described her ideas that he had dismissed as pointless flights of fancy.

It wasn't sufficient, Pareesa claimed, for the geomancer to steal upon the web of the Earth and merely rest there, feeling the vibrations, and even taking pieces of the web for their own use. She believed ley lines were not rigid, but shifted over time. The geomancer's ultimate goal had to be to engage the web, maintain it, and even repair it when necessary. She poetically claimed that the geomancer had to weave new webs.

Of course, she mourned that Mamoru refused to entertain such thoughts. In his mind, the geomancer could only understand the web of the Earth to a certain level, and use its power for his own purposes. The web was a creation beyond human comprehension. To engage it on its own terms was disaster. It would crush any human vain enough to believe she could stand up to the titanic vision of the Earth.

Adele's eyes were burning and her head pounded. She prepared to put the journal aside. There would be more days ahead to work on the complex notes from her mother. She flipped to the last page and noted a single line of symbols on the inside of the back cover. It was scratched into the leather with a pen's point, not written in ink. She touched the rough symbols and read over them, slowly moving her lips.

She sat up with a jolt. Her fingers tingled. She stared at the strange symbols and repeated the translation in a low whisper, hearing the sound of her mother's voice as she did so:

Adele is the spider.

Something brushed Adele's leg and she jerked, nearly screaming. Her heart was already pounding as she caught a glance of a small furry form darting under the desk.

"Great, a rat."

Adele took a deep breath, glanced at the symbols again, and then set the journal aside. She welcomed a more pedestrian activity at the moment. Vermin were not unusual on board a ship, but of course it had to be scuttling in her cabin. Good thing she hadn't screamed, otherwise Shirazi would have come barreling in. Only now it was left to her to kill the thing. Calling for someone else to do it seemed petty, especially for someone who killed vampires so effectively. Being squeamish over a rat didn't cry empress at all.

Adele noticed that the airship was shaking much more violently than normal. Hariri hadn't been joking about the stress of flying high. The deck jarred under her feet as *Edinburgh* slipped from side to side and dipped wildly.

Adele drew her Fahrenheit khukri dagger, consoling herself that at least a little activity would ward off the bitter cold seeping into her limbs and take her mind off the shuddering airship. Bracing herself, she sunk to her knees and peered under the desk.

"Please don't be a big one."

The glow from her blade illuminated the deep shadows and showed her two glowing eyes in the cramped space beneath her desk. Then she saw the size of the beast, poised to strike, tail swishing.

"Pet!" Adele yanked back the blade and immediately the cat came prancing forward. "You rat!"

Pet stretched, yawning lazily before brushing up against her. Adele scooped him up. "How did you get here, you little stowaway? Did you know we were heading back to Edinburgh?" He went limp in her arms and purred contentedly, staring at her with half-closed emerald eyes. They settled into a chair, and immediately the cat snuggled into her thick fur-lined coat. She wrapped it around both of them.

"What am I going to do with you? Don't you know how dangerous it is where we are going? There's a war on. This is no time to visit with your extended family."

As was her habit, Adele's fingers brushed along the inside of the cat's collar. She felt something tiny protruding and she stopped, her heart quickening. She fumbled with the leather band and pulled it from the sleepy cat. There, tucked into the seam of the collar, was a small slip of paper.

Adele knew instantly what it was. She kissed the cat's head. "You're a messenger again, little one."

The thin paper was delicate, and she labored not to tear it as she unraveled it. Gareth's handwriting stared back at her, more practiced and precise than it had been the year before when he wrote his first note to her.

Never doubt my love for you. I miss you even now. The warmth of your hand. The taste of your lips. I will see you soon.

G

Her eyes closed and she drew the paper to her lips. Memories spilled over her. The way he had so carefully made love to her, with all the focus of turning the page of a book. The thought of him holding her, flesh against flesh, made her shiver with wondrous memory. Her hand went to her chest, already feeling the wild flutter of her heart. She had never experienced anything like it. For someone who struggled to maintain control, she had been satisfyingly out of control.

She missed Gareth more so now. She missed the way his blue eyes stared at her when she woke up, the way his breathing seemed to match hers. She missed being able to talk to him. He was always so calm.

In a way, she hated that she always felt stronger with trusted friends at her side, because now she had to stand by her own decisions, good or bad. How many times had Anhalt or Gareth stared aghast at her when she announced an idea? Adele smiled at the memories of their stunned faces. Then she sighed.

Pet paid no mind, content to settle down for an overdue nap. Adele conceded that maybe he had the right idea about the future. Each bridge had to be crossed, and what would happen would happen regardless of her worrying.

There was a knock on the door. "Enter."

The door blew open, and a wave of frigid air accompanied two men. Adele straightened in her seat. Pet mewed in annoyance at the sudden cold and dug deeper into the folds of her coat. Hariri blew on his reddened fingers and stamped his feet to restore some circulation while Shirazi stood motionless. She didn't waste their time.

"Gentlemen, you no doubt are wondering what we are about. As with our last excursion to Grenoble, your utmost discretion is required."

Shirazi inclined his head, while Hariri replied with gusto, "You have it, Your Majesty."

"Thank you. First, Mamoru, my former tutor, has sent an assassin to eliminate Greyfriar. He feared Greyfriar's influence over me."

Hariri snorted. "Paranoid."

Adele said, "Regardless, we must stop her."

"A woman assassin?" The pirate's fingers caressed his curled beard. "She must be something."

"She is highly skilled, and worse, Greyfriar won't see her coming." Adele didn't elaborate on the reason why.

"I doubt that," he countered. "Greyfriar is the finest swordsman I've ever seen. He could easily handle any attack. And he's not one to be wooed by some female, not with as fine a catch as yourself in his sights."

Hariri always amused Adele. And he was partly right. Against a sword or any other physical weapon, she had faith Gareth could handle himself, but not against geomancy.

"What do we know of this assassin?" asked Captain Shirazi.

"She is a Zulu originally from the Cape."

"Do we know where Greyfriar is or where this assassin intends to strike?"

"Perhaps. Mamoru knew that Greyfriar was bound for Scotland. My sources indicate that the assassin will go there and wait." The ship dropped, causing Adele to pause until it gathered way again. "Provided we hold together."

Hariri smiled and shrugged.

Shirazi looked at her doubtfully. "You do realize that Scotland is enemy territory, and very expansive, Your Majesty?"

Adele scowled. "Of course, Captain. You do realize that I've been there?"

Pet chose that moment to complain about having his nap interrupted and stretched to find a more comfortable position.

Shirazi gave an exasperated huff. "Is it wise to have brought your cat along on this mission?"

"I did not bring him. I found him here in my cabin."

Hariri chuckled and pointed at the animal. "Ah yes. The imperial cat often comes on board while we are in dock. I suspect we are on his daily route. I don't mind. He is a consummate rat catcher. Apparently he must have dillydallied a bit too long. Or realized that you were on board as soon as your luggage arrived."

"It doesn't matter now. He's here."

"Is that all, Your Majesty?" asked Shirazi.

"No, it isn't. This mission is twofold. We have a rare opportunity to put into play another plan." Both men exchanged glances. Adele smiled in advance of her news, and hoped she would still be smiling after she explained the entire mission. "First, it is with great joy that I inform you that my brother, Simon, the prince of Bengal, is alive and well."

"Praise Allah!" Hariri clapped his hands and did a small dance in a circle. Shirazi's reaction was more subdued, but Adele could see the relief in his eyes as he touched his heart, lips, and forehead in a reverent gesture.

"The report that Prince Gareth of Edinburgh attacked him was manufactured."

"Why?" Shirazi asked.

"Word reached me that my brother was to be a target for assassination. I wanted him removed from any possible threat."

"Where did this information come from, Your Majesty?" Shirazi's questions were steady and quick, even a bit annoyed. All this had been done without his knowledge or cooperation. He seemed galled by it.

"From Prince Gareth himself, our inside man in the heart of the vampire empire." A ripple of shock went through both men. Adele stroked Pet's silky coat in an attempt to still her trembling hand, and she hurriedly continued. "It was crucial for us to lend credibility to him, making him the assassin of Prince Simon, in order to bolster his position inside his own clan. I know this is a great deal of information to take in, frankly strange information. And I realize you feel as if you haven't been kept apprised, Captain." She looked with understanding toward the two men, particularly the silent Shirazi.

He shifted to appear unconcerned, but confirmed the statement with a grunt.

Adele continued, "Trust is at a premium in Alexandria. There are traitors and plots everywhere. You gentlemen may be shocked to learn that both Lord Kelvin and Lord Aden were pawns of Prince Cesare."

The two men now looked incredulous, unable to speak.

"Quite," Adele agreed with their horrified furrowed brows. "Men at the highest pinnacle of Equatorian society. So I've had to be most careful with information about our own spy at the top of the vampire world."

"That's understandable," Hariri remarked for both men, although Shirazi was rigid in disbelief.

"So Greyfriar was sent north to rendezvous with Gareth in Edinburgh, and make certain arrangements. However, I learned of Mamoru's assassin, and therefore we are heading for Edinburgh too."

Finally, Shirazi asked, "What is this vampire's angle? What does he want?"

"Simply his brother, Cesare, dead. We will assist him in that because it serves our purposes as well. Cesare is the architect of the vampire alliance. His death will weaken the clan armies considerably."

"And this Gareth is fine with that?"

"Yes." Adele sat up and leveled a stern look at her guard commander. She was the vampire expert; she could tell these men truths, half-truths, or lies and they would have to believe her. "Vampires are naturally tribal and belligerent. Cesare is the one holding them together. He's something of a visionary. Gareth, however, is a more traditional vampire." She suppressed a smile. "He doesn't think beyond his own desires. He doesn't care what happens to vampires in France or Germany or America, as long as his brother is dead."

Shirazi muttered, "Sounds like a fool."

Adele felt herself redden and tamped down her immediate retort. She cleared her throat. "He has his own motivations. But no matter, he gets what he wants, and so do we."

"Cunning," Hariri said with a guffaw.

Shirazi remarked, "Perhaps we should have brought more than just the Harmattan if we are flying into vampire territory. We are putting these soldiers in a very difficult situation."

"If all goes well, your men won't even see action."

"So you trust all vampires in Scotland as much as Prince Gareth?"

"Actually, yes. There are only two vampires there. Gareth and his aging chamberlain, who is far too old to threaten us. I have met them both. I trust them as you trust me."

Shirazi and Hariri exchanged glances again. The pirate looked amused at the scowl on the soldier's stern face.

Adele sat forward. She could only hope she had made the two vampires appear as nonthreatening as possible. "You do trust me, don't you?"

"Indeed, Your Majesty," Hariri replied effusively. "We've seen the miracles you've wrought. We don't understand them, but we have seen them."

She turned to the silent captain. "And you?"

"I will obey you until the end. There is no doubt." He clasped his hands behind his back and regarded her. "However, I wish we had a better sense of the endgame."

"I know the endgame, Captain." Adele leaned back and steepled her fingers with a knowing smile. "I intend to place a vampire of my choosing on the throne of Britain."

CHAPTER 30

GENERAL ANHALT RETURNED to Alexandria barely two weeks after he had departed to repair the disaster wrought by the loss of St. Etienne. Sleepless days and nights in Marseilles and Valence were spent rattling dispatches to all command units to shore up defenses across the Rhone Valley. However, to his great relief, the vampire packs only probed southward with some hesitation. There was no full-scale counteroffensive, perhaps due to the warming spring weather, perhaps due to some other unknowable reason deep within the arcane alleys of the vampire command structure.

Now, Anhalt landed back at Pharos One, where a waiting staff officer named Major Naroyan fell into step and briefed him on the newest crisis, news of which had come to him on the continent by cable—Senator Clark was in Alexandria again.

"You made extraordinary time across the Mediterranean, Sirdar," the major said.

Anhalt accepted a leather pouch of dispatches. "Has Her Majesty seen the senator yet?"

"The empress is not in residence, sir."

"She's not?" The general looked up in alarm with visions of Mamoru's desperate revenge. He snapped, "Where is she?"

Major Naroyan gave a surprised look. "I assumed you knew, sir. There is a private message in the pouch. A copy was sent to you in Europe over a week ago."

The general's breath quickened, although he worked to appear calm. He found a heavy sheet of Adele's stationery, sealed. The copy must have passed him in transit. He stopped walking and worked through the wax seal with his thumb, then eagerly read the message:

My Dear Anhalt, I am departing Alexandria. Again, I know. Don't fear. I am well. I have immediate business and, when concluded, I shall return. Your man, Capt. Shirazi, is at my side with my ever-faithful Harmattan. Officially, I am in Persia mourning Simon. Unofficially, trust that I can handle myself. Yours, Adele.

He folded the sheet several times and gave a relieved sigh. No matter what dire circumstance Adele was likely thrusting herself into, at least it was of her own doing. She was not the victim of disturbed Mamoru or vile Cesare. And perhaps she was safer out of Alexandria for now.

Anhalt asked, "Where is Senator Clark?"

"I believe he said he would be stretching his legs, sir."

———◦∕∖∕◦———

Toward the western tip of the Ras el-Tin peninsula was the Cape Polo Grounds. Polo was a popular sport across much of Equatoria, and this was only one of many fields in Alexandria where league play thrived. The Cape was a grand field where officers and soldiers often drilled and played. The imperial stables were on the same grounds, and parades of prime horseflesh were always to be seen.

As Anhalt stepped down from the creaking brougham and walked to the edge of the grass, he noted a lone figure galloping on a large white stallion. The man wore a blue tunic and pants with a red stripe. His white wide-brimmed hat shaded his face, but the figure of Senator Clark was instantly recognizable to any who had once gazed upon him. And Anhalt had to admit begrudgingly that the man sat a horse well.

A collection of American Rangers lounged nearby under a tent, drinking bottles of beer from iced buckets. The general scanned the crowd under the shade of the wind-rippled tent, searching for his particular friend, Major Stoddard, but didn't see him. He strode toward the Americans, who came to easy attention with casual salutes. Anhalt recognized a few of the faces from the senator's troopers who came to Equatoria last year for the ill-fated wedding.

One of the familiar faces smiled. "Good afternoon, Colonel Anhalt. Oh, pardon me, General Anhalt. We met briefly when we were here last year."

"I recall. Good afternoon, Captain Madura. Welcome back to Equatoria."

The young officer was obviously pleased to be remembered by the Equatorian supreme commander. "Thank you, sir. We're surprised to be back." There was a round of good-natured laughter.

Anhalt grinned. The senator aside, he had liked the American soldiers. They were unpretentious and pleasant. "Where is Major Stoddard?"

Captain Madura's face fell. "I'm sorry, sir. He is not with us."

"Is he well? Has something happened to him?"

"Oh, he's alive and well. Transferred out, sir."

Anhalt was shocked. Stoddard had been Senator Clark's staunchest supporter. The grim disappointment on the soldiers' faces indicated that he should take it up with the senator if he had questions.

He felt thunder vibrating in his feet and up through his legs, and the pounding of horse muscles exploded behind him. He felt dirt clods carom off his back, and there was sudden silence except for the snorting of a horse which he felt on his neck. The general slowly turned to look over his shoulder and put a pleasant finger to the brim of his khaki helmet.

"Senator," he said calmly. "It's pleasant to see you again."

Senator Clark stared down from his shuddering, sweating throne of horseflesh. His black beard was shaved now, and he looked younger with his luxurious waxed mustache and white teeth. He smiled mischievously, as if pleased that his sudden arrival had discomforted Anhalt.

"Sirdar!" he announced, swatting the horse's shoulder. "Finally, a familiar face in Alexandria. I was beginning to think all my old friends were dead or gone."

"Not at all. You have the same number of friends here you always had."

Clark sneered, "Good one. Listen, where's Adele? I can't get a straight answer. They keep telling me she's in Persia somewhere."

"She's in Persia somewhere."

"Well, when's she getting back?"

"I couldn't tell you, Senator."

Clark said, "I wanted to express my condolences personally to Adele over the death of her brother."

"I'm sure she'd find that comforting. I must say, I'm surprised you could find the time. Don't you have a war to manage?"

"I do, and it's being managed brilliantly too. I'm so far ahead of schedule, I could afford to fly over here while my supply lines catch up to my combat units." He laughed and his men joined him. "But don't worry, I'll be in Washington and then New York by the end of summer. The North American clans are living on borrowed time. How's your war going, Sirdar?"

"Not quite so swimmingly, I fear. Issues with weather."

"Yes. Weather. Shame when a nasty frost ruins a well-planned offensive." The senator wheeled his stallion. "My mount is cooling down. Do you ride, Sirdar?"

"I do."

Clark grinned. "I have an idea, then. My boys here were drilling with some equipment your people provided." He pulled his saber to reveal a blunt edge and rounded tip. "What do you say we show them some close order work?"

The very idea of the supreme commanders of their respective armies slapping at one another with stiff rods of steel for no reason other than pride or arrogance or boorishness irritated Anhalt. He was about to dismiss it, until Clark said, "We have time, after all. Knowing Adele, she won't have the fortitude to get back to her duty for several years."

General Anhalt stretched out his hand for a saber belt and called, "Fetch a mount! Bring Jambiya."

Word of the match spread quickly as soldiers and stable hands began sprinting around the facility. Adults and children alike appeared. Blacksmiths backed their fires and came out of the barns, donning hats against the sun as they streamed toward the field. Boys with buckets raced from their work. On the far side of the field, the terrace of the Polo Club started to fill with men in uniform and suits, women in gowns and veils, and serving staff in aprons. In all corners of the polo grounds, wagering began.

As Clark loped lazily to keep his mount limber, Anhalt watched groomsmen jog toward him with a familiar horse, a grey Arabian gelding named Jambiya. The horse was at least two hands shorter than Clark's stallion, but he was thick chested and sturdy. Anhalt knew him well, and greeted him with gentle words and a firm stroke along the slim jaw.

Anhalt called out, "Senator! Will you wear a helmet?"

Clark waved his white hat. "Feel free, if you need it!"

The sirdar inspected the cinches and bit, and swung into the saddle. He then doffed his khaki helmet and handed it to Major Naroyan. "I'll be back shortly."

The major saluted as his commander wheeled the horse with his knees and loped to the field. Naroyan walked to a group of Equatorian soldiers wagering with the American Rangers, waving money at one another.

"Players on the field," Naroyan said officiously. "I must call time, gentlemen. What do we have?"

"They gave us three to one," an Equatorian captain said, handing over a large handful of American and Equatorian cash, in addition to slips of paper, no doubt IOUs from cash-poor Rangers. Naroyan expertly counted the take and nodded respectfully at the small fortune.

"Well done, lads," he said to the Americans. "It shows commendable respect for your man."

Captain Madura stroked his thin mustache with a smile. "We had to give odds to get you boys to even bet. Has General Anhalt ever been on a horse?"

Naroyan thrust the money into Anhalt's helmet. "A bit, yes. He was captain of the All-Imperial Polo squad for six years."

The Americans exchanged glances of concern, but Madura laughed. "Polo? How grand."

Naroyan said deadpan, "They invented the game in India, where the general is from. Those fellows take it quite seriously. Two hundred people are killed there every year playing polo."

"You're pulling our legs."

The major raised an eyebrow. "The sirdar went into the army because they outlawed him in South India league play. For maiming too many other chaps."

They all turned to see General Anhalt at one endline swiping his sword through the air. He sat straight like a centaur. His mount pranced eagerly. Three hundred yards away from him, Senator Clark wiped his forearm sleeve across his brow.

Anhalt could see that Clark was slightly stooped with fatigue and his mount was glistening. The senator rode well, but he was no horseman or he would've called for a new mount. However, maybe that would've seemed like weakness to him. While the general knew he had speed and maneuverability, Clark was all about strength. A big man on a big horse. A solid shot from the American's saber, blunt or no, could unhorse or even kill. This entire exercise was complete nonsense, boyish idiocy. It was something Adele would do.

Anhalt smiled and kicked his horse into a gallop.

Senator Clark whooped and surged forward, sword held aloft in classic position. The riders charged over the green field. Anhalt leaned in, saber poised. The thudding of the hooves vibrated his body. His focus narrowed. He felt the flanks of his mount with his knees. He felt the worn sword pommel in his hand. He saw the charging shape and glinting sword above it. The two horses drew closer, throwing a barrage of divots behind. Clark was ramrod straight in the saddle. Anhalt subtly slowed his horse, knowing that the senator's arm was a spring ready to fire. When the mounts were nose by nose, the American let fly. Anhalt fell back against Jambiya's rump and the saber flashed over him. He sprang up and swung back toward his opponent who, amazingly, had already turned at the waist to parry the blow.

Jambiya responded to pressure and began to wheel while Clark's stallion still thundered on. Anhalt made a tight half-circle, trying to come over onto the enemy's left, but Clark was already drifting to cut him off and pulling up hard on his reins, driving his horse into a skidding stop. The American yanked left, nearly pulling his horse over, and brought his sword to bear on a surprised Anhalt. He swung once, barely parried by the Equatorian, and then actually slammed the powerful hindquarters of his stallion into Jambiya's shoulder. The smaller horse stumbled, but the Gurkha rode it out, coaxing him up.

Clark laughed and barked, "Finesse is no good here!"

Anhalt blocked a wild blow toward his neck, alarmed that the senator was more skilled than he expected. They fenced with the two horses slamming side by side, spinning in a circle. Clark reared back to avoid a swipe, but delivered a glancing blow to Anhalt's right arm. The general felt pins and needles down to his fingertips, and the American capitalized with another blade smash, sending Anhalt's saber from his numb grasp.

Clark howled with laughter. "Too easy, Sirdar!"

"I'm still mounted. I do not yield." Anhalt kicked the gelding into a run for the far goal.

He heard Clark's monstrous mount take up the chase. A risked glance over his hunched shoulder showed the senator grinning, hat trailing in the wind, his saber eager for another blow on the disarmed enemy. He almost felt Clark's breath. He could sense the sword about to fall.

Anhalt locked his knees against Jambiya's shoulders, and the little mount stiffened his forelegs into a skid. The Gurkha ducked as a giant mass roared past, sword whistling through the air. Jambiya spun and took up the gallop again without argument.

The gelding roared along the torn-up grass. Anhalt slipped his left foot from the stirrup and took a handful of Jambiya's mane. He dropped his other foot free and slid down the right side of the horse's chest with one leg curled under the belly and the left calf on the saddle. Jambiya's churning legs pounded so close. The ground roared past, only inches away. A stumble by the gelding would send Anhalt crashing headfirst to the hard field with little chance he wouldn't break a shoulder at least, or neck at most. Without fear, he reached forward with his right hand, feeling the tips of the grass skimming along.

Something hard hit his fingers. He clasped. And he rose up, fighting to regain the saddle with only one arm for leverage. Jambiya leaned from the pressure and missed a step. Anhalt tightened his left boot against some flange on the saddle, and a hard thump nearly threw him.

He managed to twist his right foot and gain a toehold in the stirrup. Push up. He came straight in the saddle, seeking the left stirrup, just as he caught a glimpse of a blue shape alongside.

Anhalt raised his recovered saber and parried a thunderous blow before pulling Jambiya to a halt. Clark reined in and turned to meet him. They fenced again. The senator was in a rage. His moves were wilder, but fueled by enormous muscle. Anhalt's arm was still rubbery.

The general drove Jambiya hard against Clark's mount. Then he kicked back deep inside the gelding's flank. Jambiya snorted angrily and lashed out at the nearest victim—the hindquarters of Clark's stallion. The gelding sank his teeth deep into the white horse's flesh.

The startled stallion shrieked and reared. Clark yelled too, trying to keep his balance. Anhalt drew his boot up and slammed it into the senator's brass-buttoned chest. The American's face went through his typical range of emotions in an instant from disbelief to anger to fury and back to disbelief. And then the mighty Senator Clark tumbled from the saddle, crashing to the ground. Hat and saber sailed through the air, and the white stallion galloped away from his downed rider.

Anhalt wheeled Jambiya and pointed his sword down at the American. Clark glared up in pain and embarrassment. His breath tore from between his clenched teeth.

But then Clark started laughing. He pounded his hands against the ground and lay back, guffawing. Anhalt watched suspiciously, half expecting the man to pull a pocket pistol or leap up with a knife. Clark looked at the sirdar and fell into another paroxysm of breathless laughter. The senator climbed to his feet, dusted himself off, and retrieved his hat. He regarded the Gurkha with a posture Anhalt had never seen from the American, one of a comfortable friendliness.

Clark adjusted his hat. "You're a damned fine horseman, Sirdar. You picked that mount on purpose, didn't you?"

"I did."

"He's damn nimble."

"And a biter." Anhalt swung from the saddle with a nod of respect to the American's skills. He took Jambiya's reins, and he and Clark started back. The senator threw an arm over the sirdar's shoulder, causing Anhalt to flinch. Clark laughed again, shaking the Gurkha. By the time they passed the celebrating Equatorians and disgruntled Americans on the sidelines, the sirdar was almost convinced the senator was not going to try to strangle him.

———

Senator Clark asked over the top of a glass of beer, "So you're telling me that Adele really is in Persia?"

Anhalt stared him straight in the eye. "As she says."

"Well, damn it." Clark stretched out his long legs, nearly tripping a passing waiter. The Polo Club's private dining room swarmed with servants and well-heeled guests, all of whom whispered and stared surreptitiously at the table shared by the sirdar and the empress's jilted fiancé.

The senator snatched a lobster tail and began to crush the meat out of it. "Who the hell's in charge around here? I haven't seen Lord Aden at all. Nobody seems to know where he is. That little snob used to scurry around like he ran the whole show."

"We do have an entire government that is capable of functioning in Her Majesty's absence."

"Really? I'd have thought she would've gutted anybody with any manhood." Clark immediately rolled an apologetic hand at Anhalt. "Sorry. I didn't mean to speak ill of her, in front of you. I still have a few grudges of my own."

The sirdar didn't excuse him, but understood. Adele had humiliated Clark, not only in casting him aside, for good reason, but quite literally running from the wedding on Greyfriar's arm. Such an event would have turned any man bitter, particularly a man used to having his own way in all things.

The senator signaled for two more beers. "Simon's death must've been hard on Adele. She worshipped that boy."

"Yes. It was a terrible blow."

"And it was that Gareth character who did it?"

"Yes. Greyfriar is in pursuit of the Scottish prince."

Clark glowered at the mention of the swordsman, but then looked regretful. "Same vampire who had her when I found her in Edinburgh. Used her as a shield. If only I'd killed the thing then."

Anhalt nodded and remained silent to drive home the fact that even the great Clark failed occasionally. Then he asked, "If you don't mind, Senator, may I ask why you are in Alexandria now? Surely you didn't fly the Atlantic just to express your condolences over Prince Simon."

Clark guffawed and leaned forward. "True enough. All right, back to politics. My reason for the visit is to see Adele and try to get the American-Equatorian coalition back on track."

"By *coalition*, do you mean alliance? Or marriage?"

"Both. Sirdar, your operations in Europe are stalled. I fully appreciate the differences you face in population and climate, and I know you're hamstrung by political considerations. So I'm not trying to be critical, but it's a fact."

Anhalt remained calm. It was a fact.

Clark continued with a remarkably reasonable tone, "And now Prince Simon is gone. There's no backup for the throne. And if anything should happen to Adele—" The sirdar began to interrupt, but Clark said, "Please, hear me out and try to see the situation with fresh eyes. Look at the number of times that girl has been close to death. And she's barely twenty years old. She's unpredictable. She's likely to take off on a lark, putting herself in danger. In that way, she's a terrible monarch. Of course, in other ways, she's magnificent. Even I can see that. But there's a question which side of her will prevail."

This was a new demeanor, Anhalt mused silently, but the same old tactic. "What do you hope to bring to the situation?"

"Stability. And the chance of an heir."

Anhalt cleared his throat uncomfortably. "Keep your voice down, if you please."

Clark smiled, but nodded. "Sure. She needs a child, a son if possible. There is no clear-cut successor. If something happens to her, this Empire would shake itself apart."

"Her Majesty has made her choice of companion rather apparent."

"Oh yes. I was there when she did it." The senator crunched through another lobster tail. "I'm not talking about love or any of that foolishness. I'm not interested in anything beyond a political arrangement. Marriage. Alliance. And a future for your Empire. It doesn't do me any good if I clear all the vampires out of North America, but they're still infesting Europe."

General Anhalt finished off his beer. "Step onto the terrace with me, if you would."

Clark tiredly held out his hands. "If I've insulted you or the princess somehow, I'd rather apologize than fight a duel."

Anhalt shook his head. "Strictly business, Senator. But it requires privacy."

The two men rose and crossed between tables through the lush dining room with many eyes on them. Major Naroyan opened the French windows to the terrace and closed them again after the duo, placing himself firmly against the door.

On the broad, tiled terrace, a soft evening breeze and long shadows were taming the heat of the day. The two men leaned against the stone balustrade, and Senator Clark pulled two cigars from his inner pocket. With quick work, he snipped off the ends and handed one to Anhalt. He flicked a wooden match with his thumbnail and lit both. The sirdar blew smoke into the air and regarded the cigar appreciatively.

"Cuban," Clark said. "I'll send you a case."

"Thank you." Anhalt placed his helmet on his head, felt something odd, and removed it. He reached in and pulled out a one hundred pound note. He shrugged, pocketing the cash. "I have something of utmost importance and secrecy to tell you. The Greyfriar has given us detailed information about vampire society and strategy, and recently he has informed us of the death of King Dmitri of Britain."

"Old Dmitri, dead?" Senator Clark looked up with interest from his glower at the mention of Greyfriar's name. "That is interesting. Any chance of a succession struggle that will throw the clan off its game?"

"Of a sort. According to Greyfriar, the clan will go into a meeting he calls a coven to select the next king. He assures us that the preferred candidate is Cesare."

Clark spat. "The animal that slaughtered all of Ireland."

"Exactly, and the primary author of the vampire alliance whom we are both fighting. But there is something more." Anhalt proceeded to lay out what he knew of vampire succession ritual as well as the fact that all the British clan lords and visiting royalty would be isolated inside Buckingham Palace until a king was chosen, usually by tradition, a process taking several days.

The American asked sharply, "How could he possibly know this? What is he, a vampire?"

Anhalt adjusted his helmet and coughed. "If Greyfriar says it's so, it's so."

Clark stared eagerly at the sirdar. "Well, all right then. The question is, what do you intend to do with this information?"

"I'm glad you asked, Senator." Anhalt stared at the glowing tip of his cigar. "If I can make use of your steamnaught, I say we fly to London on the equinox and firebomb Buckingham Palace into a crater."

Senator Clark stared curiously at the general. Then his mouth split into a wide white grin. "To be honest, Mehmet, I never thought much of you before. But damn it, you're growing on me."

"Thank you, Senator. We'll need to be under way very soon. We have a tight schedule."

CHAPTER 31

Adele held fast to *Edinburgh*'s rail as the ship descended with terrifying swiftness to her namesake below.

We're not crashing, she repeated to herself. Hariri was thoroughly enjoying flexing his remarkable mariner skills, which ought to have calmed her, but didn't. He barked orders, his robe flapping wildly in the winds. Her own heavy coat thumped hard against her calves, but she was trying to keep her stomach in place and the scream in her throat.

If Greyfriar were here, he'd be laughing and enjoying the wild ride. The thought of seeing him again banished some of Adele's fear, and she clung to that thought as the clouds parted and the ground could be seen rushing toward them.

Hariri shouted something that was whipped away by the wind, but the men around him heard and the ship's plummet slowed markedly. Timbers creaked and sails billowed, and soon they were skimming the treetops. Scattered leaves found their way onto the deck, and the air smelled faintly of heather.

As the clouds thinned, Adele saw the grey city of Edinburgh with its winding Old Town and gridlike northern suburbs. And above it all, the sprawling castle perched on its volcanic peak. Adele was overwhelmed by memories of cold rain and warm fires. She recalled the effort

Gareth expended to make her welcome here despite her best efforts to remain bitter and infuriated. It was in those days she had begun to see the man she now loved with the amazing revelation of his secret library and watching his struggle to write. She remembered the plain simplicity of the wonderful friendship of Morgana, a servant in the castle, who didn't know or care if Adele was an empress or a scrubwoman. And, of course, it was here she had first encountered Pet. The biting wet wind splashed her face and made her happy.

The ship slowed its descent, and airmen took in sail as the vessel spiraled down to the castle. Lookouts maintained a watch in case vampires should appear, despite Adele's assurances that there were only two here. When the brig drifted across the edge of the battlements, heavy mooring anchors went over the side and scraped into the stone. The ship lurched to a halt. Men vaulted the rails to fix grapples so crew at the capstans could winch the wooden hull down to touch the castle's edge.

The gangway slammed down and the Harmattan rushed ashore, clutching their rifles, eyes wary under their helmets. Adele followed leisurely, carrying her bag and her cat. She stopped at the battlements to look over the city. Plumes of lovely wood smoke curled into the air. She could see people stopped in the street, staring up at the airship moored to the castle. Crowds were beginning to grow all around the base of Castle Hill with every second.

Captain Shirazi stood at her shoulder. "Look at that mob forming all around us. We'll need to disperse them before they can cause trouble."

She laid a hand on his arm and shook her head. "Easy, Captain. There is no threat from them. The people here are harmless, I assure you."

"They could be Undead," was his reply.

He was right, of course, she realized with a shock. Cesare could have infiltrated Gareth's home with his cultists. However, they would be aimed at Gareth. They would have no contingency for the arrival of this strange group of humans, and it would take too long for anyone to make it back to London for new orders. As brilliant as Cesare could be, he would never assume Adele would come back to Scotland. And the fear of Undead couldn't distract her from her primary mission: saving Gareth.

He still had not appeared despite the arrival of the airship and soldiers. Adele grew more anxious that she was too late, suddenly envisioning Gareth lying dead on the floor by Nzingu's knife. Pressing through the shoulders of the men ahead of her, she rushed into a courtyard of grey stone buildings, aiming for one in particular. Adele shoved open a heavy door, and the entrance yawned into darkness.

"Is anyone home?" she shouted.

"Adele?" A solitary figure appeared at the distant end of the hall. His kilt flapped in the harsh wind that had followed the open door. He bobbed his head in confusion. "So that is your airship. I thought we were under attack."

"Baudoin," she exhaled in relief. "It's a pleasure to see you again." She hoped her men mistook her familiar greeting as diplomacy rather than the truth. His presence made everything seem normal. She had to fight the impulse to hug him. "These men are mine. They mean you no harm."

The castle's chamberlain didn't reciprocate her greeting. She was sure the last thing he expected or wanted was her arrival.

"Is this the frail aged retainer you mentioned?" Shirazi sneered.

Baudoin moved slowly forward and spared the captain not even a glance, keeping his attention on Adele.

"Is your lord in residence?" she asked.

"He is not."

She took a deep, anxious breath.

"Is there some danger?" Baudoin's glare settled on the soldiers around her.

Adele gave a subtle nod and bit her lip. "I have come to offer a proposition to Prince Gareth. I assume we are welcome to wait." She tried to remain a politician but still convey to Baudoin that they needed to talk privately.

The servant remained stoic. He merely turned on his heel and proceeded back down the dark passageway toward the main hall. There soon came a familiar rustling amongst the shadows, and the Harmattan stiffened in alarm.

Adele spoke loudly as Pet began to struggle in her arms for the first time. "You are in for a rare treat, gentlemen. Don't be afraid and consider this a warm welcome from the true residents of Edinburgh Castle."

Feline shapes swarmed forward from every nook and cranny.

"Cats!" exclaimed Shirazi.

Adele knelt and released the eager Pet into a mob of his old cohorts. She greeted as many as she could within her reach. The Harmattan stood staring, though Adele was pleased when the youthful Corporal Darby bent down and scratched one of the many heads pleading for attention.

Shirazi leaned close to her and asked, "Does he eat them?"

Adele laughed. "I thought the same thing once. But no. They are just companions. The castle is an empty and lonely place."

Shirazi said, "I'm beginning to doubt your choice for the next king of the vampires."

Baudoin had disappeared, but Adele knew her way through the gloomy passages. Luckily they had brought lanterns from the ship and their way was illuminated slightly. The glow preceded them into the great hall where once she had dined on a magnificent feast. It looked dim and vacant now with no one there. Even with Baudoin's departure the Harmattan did not relax, and if anything, drew tighter around her, facing out toward the shadows. She couldn't laugh at their fears. They were too reminiscent of her own once upon a time.

"Put yourself at ease, Captain."

"Not likely, Your Majesty, given where we are and what we just met."

"Baudoin may seem mysterious and stoic, but he's not a threat. Or did you mean the cats?"

With a scowl in place he replied, "He may be old but he's still a vampire."

To her relief, Baudoin soon returned. He entered through another door on the far side. Adele saw him first and sidled away across the room to stand near the mantel of the dead fireplace, well away from her men but not so far as to cause concern.

"When do you expect Prince Gareth to return?" she asked as Baudoin approached her. The Harmattan caught by surprise made to close in around them, but Adele held them at bay with a hand.

"He will return when he wishes."

"It's imperative that I talk to him."

"I'm sure. Life is a long series of imperatives with you."

"Is there a way to send word to him?"

Baudoin regarded the soldiers, contemplating how much to relate in front of them. He looked long-suffering. "Has there ever been? What do you want with my prince now?"

Adele lowered her voice. "An assassin is in Edinburgh. A woman. She is here to kill Gareth."

"A human?" There was the barest sense of derision in his voice.

"A geomancer." Then not knowing if he understood the term, added, "Someone like me."

That brought a rise out of him, but it showed only in the widening of his eyes. Baudoin cursed quietly in vampire. "You bring this danger to our doorstep."

"I am here to make sure she doesn't have the chance. Where vampires may not see her, I can. I will stop her."

Baudoin scowled and repeated with an air of resentment, "Frail old retainer?"

Adele offered a half shrug along with a wry grin. "I had to make you appear less threatening to my men."

"So long as they don't attack me, they're safe."

"They won't disobey me, but remember they are far from home and frightened. I would ask you to show restraint. If some incident does occur, don't kill them, as I know you are fully capable of doing."

Baudoin tried not to look impressed. "Such words. You are quite adept at using them. Is that how you mesmerized Gareth?"

"He knows exactly what he's doing."

The servant closed his eyes briefly in dismay. Then he turned to depart, shoulders slumped. "You will be the end of him."

CHAPTER 32

ADELE BUSTLED AROUND her old room. It hadn't changed, still pristine as if it had been waiting for her all this time. The early spring sun couldn't penetrate the dense stones of the castle, leaving the room damp and cold, but a fire crackled in the fireplace.

There was a knock on the door and Captain Shirazi's voice called out. "Your Majesty, you have a visitor."

Adele's heart raced at the thought that Gareth had arrived, and she said swiftly, "Enter."

The heavy door opened and Morgana flew into the room, her face an expression of utter joy and excitement, shouting Adele's name.

"Morgana!" Adele returned, rushing to her friend and embracing her in a fervent hug. "Oh, how I've missed you! I've thought about you so often."

"I never dreamed in a hundred years you would return!"

"I only had to become empress to do it," Adele replied jokingly.

"Our lord will be happy to see you. He broods so when he is here alone."

"As I do when he is away from me," she assured the woman, readjusting the blond hair that she had displaced on her friend's head. "You've let your hair grow longer."

Morgana blushed. "So did you."

Adele's hand touched her long curls and remembered the shearing

Gareth had once given her long ago. To dispel her returning worries, she grabbed Morgana's hands and drew her to the chairs by the fireplace. "Tell me everything I've missed! How have you been?"

"I've been well, miss. Life here isn't near as exciting as yours, I'm sure. Baudoin drove off three vagabond vampires, bless his soul. Thomas tore his best net, and we lost Ol' Mary only a month ago." Morgana's eyes glistened at the last.

Adele couldn't help but feel the same. Mary was the second human she'd met in Edinburgh after Morgana. Adele's hands were chafed for days after helping Mary at the washtubs. "She went peacefully?"

"Aye, she did. She lived a good long life thanks to the prince."

"I'll miss her. She showed me such kindness." Adele squeezed Morgana's hand. "All of you did."

"Of course we did. You were lost. We wanted to make you feel at home here. The prince included, though you didn't know it at first. Now tell me, miss, what brings you back? Baudoin told me there is some danger."

Quickly, she told Morgana about Nzingu. The handmaiden had not seen anyone matching the Zulu's description. If Nzingu was here, she was covering her tracks well. That made Adele even more anxious.

"I'll make sure to spread the word," Morgana assured her.

Someone must have seen Nzingu if she dared enter the city, and the more people looking for her, the better the chance of discovery. In addition, Adele explained about the potential for Undead here. She asked Morgana to alert the city to be aware of recent arrivals, particularly those who seemed distant or odd. And if any of them should suddenly disappear, Adele needed to know. All she could do was be mindful and pray time was on her side.

For now, however, Adele sat quietly with her friend, content to pass a few moments woman to woman without fear of the outside world.

—◈—

The dark shape silhouetted against the grey sky made Adele's heart jump. Any human with any sense would be terrified at the sight of a vampire hunting. Instead, Adele immediately started briskly from the jumbled courtyard toward the familiar shadow. Her Harmattan moved into place around her without question. She paused. "Captain, remain here."

"He's a vampire."

"I can handle him."

"I'll be one minute behind."

"Five."

With that, she moved with measured and resolute steps toward the western quadrant of the castle where *Edinburgh* was still moored. As soon as she was out of sight of her men, she broke into a sprint, waving her arm. Gazing upward for a glimpse of him, she stumbled.

Suddenly a shadow passed over her and landed directly in her path.

"Gareth!" She ran the last few steps into his crushing arms. He smelled of wind and rain and grass. His clothes were damp from a passing storm. She should have been cautious of someone seeing them, but in this moment she didn't care. She only knew she needed to feel his touch.

"What are you doing here?" he demanded with unexpected ire.

"Saving you!"

Anger made his frame more rigid. He gripped her arms and held her out from him. "This foolishness must stop. I'm perfectly capable of fighting my own battles. I've only come here briefly to begin moving people into the countryside. What am I to do with you here?"

"I can help you with that."

"Adele, you can't be so impulsive. We've talked about that before."

"I'm not being impulsive. You don't understand. Mamoru put an assassin in play before we arrested him. She is on her way here to kill you. I came to warn you, and to help you. She is a powerful geomancer."

Gareth sighed and surrendered his anger. He brushed his lips over her flushed cheek. "You worry too much."

"Someone has to." Adele embraced him again. Everything would be okay now. Together, they could deal with any obstacle.

The stomping of heavy boots on cobblestone and the rattle of weapons heralded the approach of her Harmattan.

"Do your men know everything?" he asked quietly.

"They don't know you are Greyfriar, but they know there is an assassin about. And they know I intend to put you on the throne."

He cocked a sarcastic eyebrow. "You are *putting* me on the throne?"

"In this scenario I am."

"Well, thank you for that," he said playfully.

"You're very welcome."

Adele and Gareth pulled apart as Shirazi rounded the corner with his men.

"Your Majesty." The captain's greeting may have been to his empress, but his stern visage did not stray from Gareth.

Adele waited nervously for Shirazi to recognize the vampire as Greyfriar. She saw the similarities so plainly now, she couldn't believe anyone could be fooled. However, Gareth's alteration of voice and posture was subtle but effective, and the soldiers showed no recognition.

The prince bowed. "A pleasure to meet you, Captain."

Shirazi responded with practiced courtesy. "Prince Gareth, I presume."

"At your service."

"And I, apparently, am at yours." Shirazi stared coldly, and his men looked murderous behind him.

"I bid you welcome." Gareth's hand gestured around at his castle. A rain shower arrived suddenly, forming a grey shrouding mist. "Let us go inside and discuss our new friendship."

Gareth led the way, greeting the cats as they rushed him. He picked up a wiry young white cat and placed it on his shoulders. The animal perched there proudly.

"Is she new? She's adorable." Adele reached up to scratch the cat's head, but it shrank back and slapped a quick paw at her, thankfully with the claws retracted.

"She was a gift. I call her Adele."

"Oh really. She seems very antisocial."

"Some consider it strong willed." Gareth's eyes crinkled at the corners.

Adele longed to reach out impulsively and squeeze Gareth to let him know how much she loved his small gesture, but watchful eyes were everywhere.

"Has Baudoin seen to your quarters?" Gareth spoke to the entire group. "If they are not to your liking, please feel free to choose any room. There are many, and few are used."

"I chose my old room," Adele told him. "It suited me then and it will serve me well now." A gentle smile played about her lips, though she attempted to keep it hidden from Shirazi.

"It is the best room in the castle," he replied. "Morgana keeps it pristine. I'm sure she's delighted to see you again."

Adele's smile grew wider. At least she didn't have to be shy about her feelings for her good friend. "And I her!" She regarded him suddenly as she asked, "Do you think it's possible to empty the city in so short a time?"

He nodded. "With your ship here things may move quicker."

"It's at your disposal," she said.

"Why remove them at all?" Shirazi countered, obviously not liking the fact that she had just offered up their sole means of escape.

Gareth replied, "It's better the people be removed in case things don't go well in London and my brother retaliates."

"I didn't realize there was so much love lost between vampires," Shirazi said. "What do you have to fight over?"

Gareth said stiffly, "Power and food, much like humans."

"Not quite like us," Shirazi replied. "We don't fight you over food. We are your food. You eat us."

"Captain," Adele admonished. "You forget your place."

Gareth smiled graciously, but turned a cold glare on the impertinent man. "It's true. We do eat you. You make it sound so dastardly, but it's really just nature. We feed off you. You kill us."

"Yes," Shirazi said in a low voice. "Things balance out."

Gareth smirked, unimpressed by the soldier's attempt at menace. The windows behind him spattered with heavy raindrops. "Every creature has its day. Vampire or human."

Adele felt a growing ache in her heart. She remembered a distant conversation with Gareth about the fleeting mayfly and the end of the vampires. The thought of a world without Gareth ate at her soul. She stood quietly, unable to reach out to him.

CHAPTER 33

THE NIGHT ENVELOPED Edinburgh. For the first time in many days, the clouds blanketing the sky parted to allow the thin moonlight to hold the worst shadows at bay, keeping them from wandering too far into the streets.

The castle ramparts were lit as if there were a hundred lanterns shining down upon them. Gareth gazed out over his city with a sense of sadness that it would soon be abandoned. Even though it was for the best, he wondered how his people would endure. In time, they could return to Edinburgh.

When he was king.

That sounded strange. He had never wanted his father's throne, but now he didn't want Cesare to have it either. He was jealous that his brother had spent the last days with their father while he was off playing Greyfriar.

The masked hero was unnecessary in this new world he and Adele were shaping. Perhaps he would become like Adele and use a disguise as a means of escape from the oppressive duty to the throne.

Soft footfalls below made him smile. His heart beat faster. Seconds later an auburn head appeared through the wooden hatch set in the roof. The scent of Adele was plain on the breeze. Gareth stepped forward and offered his hand. Adele grasped it so he could lift her one-handed off the ladder and onto the roof beside him.

"You're so strong," she said. "Like a bear."

"I was a bear once."

She leaned forward and kissed him. The excitement lingering on her lips spread to match his own. He picked her up, lifting her onto the edge of the ramparts. She had his worn scarf tied neatly around her head and neck.

"You still have it." Gareth tucked the fluttering scarf tighter around her face.

"Of course. It's my prized possession."

"I still have the book you gave me. I've added it to my expansive library." He caressed her cheek lit by the starlight. His hand nearly glowed white like some macabre specter against her deep olive skin. Her lips pressed against his palm. He barely felt it, but his every other sense filled with her. "Alone with you. It's been too long."

It was several minutes before they parted. She glistened in the night, and the salty taste of her lingered.

Adele took a deep breath of the cool night air, indulging in his embrace, her only refuge. "This is where I'm happiest. High up, under the open sky in your arms."

"Rooftops seem to be safest for our trysts."

She laid her cheek against him. "I like that. It fits us."

"I was wondering what happened to you. I thought Morgana forgot."

"She startled me when she appeared from behind the curtain. Imagine my surprise when she showed me the passage in the wall of my room. Did you ever use it when I lived here?"

Gareth's blood fanned warmly at her use of the word *lived*. That she considered Edinburgh even a temporary home pleased him. He shook his head. "No. Though it was tempting. I was content to spy on you from the rooftops. The cats tend to use the passageways the most. Lots of food in there."

She held up a hand. "I don't want to know. Though I always wondered how Pet got in that first night. Speaking of which, where is he? I haven't seen him today."

"Baudoin saw him a few hours ago in the kitchen. He'll find you tonight I'm sure."

"So long as you do as well." Her hand stroked his long fingers as they rested on her thigh.

Gareth's head dipped to her shoulder, drawing the cloth away to reveal the curve of her neck, kissing her there. She shivered with anticipation in his arms, her breath a quivering exhale. It thrilled him that she was unafraid, so unlike most humans around vampires.

The sliver of a moon moved behind trailing clouds, darkening the rampart. Gareth could still see clearly, but she couldn't. Instead she used her hands to feel for him. Gentle fingers fluttered over his face, tracing his cheekbones and brow. She slowly kissed each part of him she touched.

Adele shivered again, though this time from the blustery Scottish wind as the perspiration dried on her skin. He wrapped his coat around her. She sighed pleasantly, drawing deeper into its decadent soft wool folds. He only wore one in case she needed it.

"I went to Paris," Gareth said, "to see Lothaire. To see whose side he would take if given a choice. Cesare or myself."

"He was your old friend, right? Is he still?"

"Yes, more so than ever."

"I'm glad," Adele said. "Tell me about him."

And Gareth did, his voice filled with excitement and hope. "The humans in Paris are left largely to do as they please. There were times in Paris I almost felt it was back before the Great Killing. Most extraordinary."

"That's amazing. Then you're not alone!"

"He's just one vampire," Gareth pointed out.

"Who's teaching his family new values. I knew you couldn't possibly be the only vampire with some compassion." She impulsively hugged him.

"I wouldn't make too much of it. Paris is a far cry from Edinburgh, and far from mutual understanding between our two species."

"Still, it's incredible. And it offers some hope for the future."

"Lothaire is a friend, but he's still a vampire. His treatment of his herds doesn't mean he likes humans. He just understands their usefulness and is practicing conservation in hard times. He isn't creating anything new."

A revelation suddenly occurred to Adele, and she gave a slight gasp. "I've just had a thought that I can't believe never occurred to me before."

Gareth pulled back to regard her as she straightened slightly in his arms. "What?"

She gazed full into his eyes. "Despite what you've always told me about vampires never creating anything, I know one who has."

"Oh really?" He crossed his arms with humorous expectation. "Who is that?"

"You. You created Greyfriar. You made him with your mind and your heart and your hands. He is a piece of our history now. Just like all the kings and pharaohs in the British Museum."

Gareth stared at her, contemplating the concept. A smile played over his lips. "It's not the same thing as creation. Just like when I was trying to write. You said I was only copying."

"No, it's not like that at all. Greyfriar is a unique creation that didn't exist before you made him. You, a vampire, created something lasting and important."

He laughed. "How simple you make it."

"It should be that simple. I want Greyfriar in my life always."

"Greyfriar. Not Gareth."

"Don't," she warned. "You know I didn't mean it that way."

"I know." For the first time since Adele had known Gareth, his eyes seemed to glisten. He blinked and nodded in acceptance. "Thank you, Adele. That's a very kind thought."

"It's a very exciting one, don't you think?" Adele crushed him in her arms. "It shows that our people may have more in common. There may be a way we can coexist."

"No, my love." Gareth kissed the top of her head. "There's nothing in Greyfriar's existence that will lead any human to accept a vampire. Not fully."

"Don't talk that way. General Anhalt has accepted you!"

"By your command," Gareth pointed out. "And he is only one man."

"We'll change their thinking one person at a time if we have to."

"It will take centuries."

"So? It takes as long as it takes."

Gareth took comfort in her steadfast determination. Once she made up her mind, there was no shaking her from her course. And it was what he loved best about humanity; she thought far into the future even though she would never see it. He might live to see such change, but she would not. His heart ached at the thought that her life was so short in comparison to his.

In four hundred years he had never loved anyone like he loved her. There was no logic, no rational explanation save who she was. He would never find her equal again, and he knew it. He would live and die beside her. Whatever happened in the future, his calendar now matched hers, no matter what.

———※———

At the break of dawn, Gareth entered the great hall alone to find Baudoin waiting for him. The servant was seated at the table with two cats curled upon his kilt. The vampire paid the sleeping cats no heed, but he did gently nudge them off to rise to his feet.

"The din around here is deafening," was his sour comment to his liege.

"It is less than a dozen people. You'll get used to it. Like you did the cats." In his arms, Gareth carried his Greyfriar clothes and swords.

"Cats seem remarkably reserved in comparison." Baudoin reached for the bundle. "I shall clean your wardrobe. It will be ready for your next excursion."

Gareth dropped the woolen garments and steel on the table. "I won't need it again, my friend. I will wear this no more."

"I don't understand."

Gareth took the rapier and swung it through the air with a sad whisper. "Soon I will go to London."

Baudoin took the clothing into his arms. "And then what?"

"I think you know."

"I want you to tell me."

"I'm going to kill my brother," Gareth said. "And then I will be king."

Baudoin stared agape. "You will be what?"

"King. It's time I give up my romantic notions and return to the real world."

"What are you talking about, Gareth?" The servant panted as if gasping for breath. "When did you decide this? You've never wanted to be king. Have you gone mad?"

Gareth laughed and pointed at the bundle Baudoin carried. "I thought you would be happy that I'm following in my father's footsteps instead of . . ." He touched the cloak. "Instead of this."

Baudoin stared at his prince. "I love you, Gareth, as if you had been my own son. You are loyal and brave and strong. But, my boy, you are no match for Cesare in London. Clan politics are his battlefield. I raised both of you. I know." He pointed a silencing finger when Gareth began to object. "I don't know why, but I know you are doing this for Adele. Now, she's a match for Cesare. I'm telling you, Gareth, that human will destroy you. She's already destroying Greyfriar."

"No, Baudoin. You don't understand her. I'm the one who is killing Greyfriar. It's time. I can't live inside storybooks any longer. My father is dead. I have to take his place. I owe that to him." He studied his old friend keenly. "I'm surprised. You most of all had no love of this . . . game I played."

Baudoin straightened and stared into Gareth's gaze. "It was no game, my lord. I have watched you over the many centuries. After your father faded, you lost heart. If this"—he touched the wool reverently—"gave you solace, then who am I to deny you? I want only for you to be content in this world."

Gareth clasped his friend by the forearm. "I am content with the people at my side. Loyal friends, trustworthy souls. You and Adele have been that. You more than make up for my brother's and my people's perfidy."

"Then you truly love the human woman?"

"Yes."

Baudoin nodded, as if he had known it all along. He drew in a deep breath before asking his next question. "Once you are king of Britain, won't that make you a target for the Equatorians?"

"Not so long as Adele remains ruler. We will try to stop the war before it claims one species over the other."

"How can there be any other solution?"

"I have faith." Gareth became grim. "In North America, Senator Clark is striking the clans by destroying their herds. Killing humans in order to starve us to death. He would have done the same here if Adele had allowed the union between Equatoria and the Americans to go forward."

Baudoin's face grew angry and then slack with stunned understanding. "Adele refused to marry him?"

"Yes, she wouldn't sanction genocide, even if it had been the best solution for her people."

"But against humans, not vampires." Baudoin's voice was harsh.

"Both. She knows, like I, that genocide is not the solution." He still believed that despite the fact that he remembered the taste of her blood and the promise of death he had found there.

Baudoin bowed his head. "Perhaps I have misjudged the woman."

"Most do. It's her greatest asset."

Baudoin smiled. "Adele will always be welcome in this house."

CHAPTER 34

A FIRE ROARED in the hearth of the great hall in Edinburgh Castle, and lanterns hung down from the hammer-beam roof timbers. Gareth was relaxed, despite the heat, as he sat at the head of the table and listened to Adele discussing details for the immediate future of the people of Edinburgh. She was excellent at details. Two of the Harmattan stood outside the door, the only members of her guard who were not out with Captain Shirazi combing the city for the elusive assassin.

Gareth had begun the difficult process of evacuating Edinburgh. Over the last week, he had announced several times to his people that they should move out of the city. He had to hurriedly explain to their worried faces and shouted questions that it was only temporary, and they would all soon be home again. Ultimately, a majority of the townsfolk had been willing to leave. Already some had packed up and departed, dispersing into the countryside, journeying to relatives' farms or abandoned villages in the Highlands. Still, many remained stubbornly behind. Gareth and Adele had just returned to the castle after hours of meeting with some of the city's elders to entreat them to push for further evacuations.

Morgana entered the great hall carrying a tray of food, followed by a smiling Captain Hariri. They chatted amiably with the pirate slathering great doses of compliments on the lovely serving woman. She accepted his attention, but maintained a studious distance.

Hariri seized a hunk of warm bread and announced, "We will be taking another journey north with more of the sick and elderly later today. I believe it may be our last before His Highness leaves for London."

Adele chuckled at the couple. "Morgana, are you taking that flight out of the city?"

Morgana laid the tray on the table and wiped her hands officiously on her apron. "Oh, I won't be leaving. There's no need for me to go."

"There's as much need as anyone," Adele replied. "We want everyone out of Edinburgh."

Hariri leaned on his elbows. "There's plenty of room, Miss Morgana. I'd welcome your delightful company."

The woman smiled. "My place is here."

"No," Adele said. "I want you to go."

Morgana looked a bit more disturbed. "But why? Nothing will happen, miss. It's just a precaution, but there'll be no problems surely. So why go?"

The empress looked at Gareth for support, then back to Morgana. "We don't believe anything will happen, you're right. But we must prepare for every possibility."

The servant shook her head vigorously. "No. It will be fine. I'll stay."

Gareth propped his chin on his hand. "There is no way to know what may happen in London. If Cesare's packs fall on Edinburgh, I don't want anyone in danger. In all likelihood, all will be well, and soon you will be able to return to your duties here."

The young woman tightened her mouth, as if fighting back tears. "But I don't want to go."

Gareth said, "Morgana, take the airship today and go. Please."

She nodded quickly and left the room. Hariri took a deep breath in sympathy and followed.

"It will work out." Adele pulled the inquisitive Pet off the table for the third time. "We can't get everyone out, no doubt. But most of them have left."

"Are you leaving?"

"Of course not. I'm not afraid of Cesare and every vampire in Britain. I'll stay here and wait for word from you." She walked over to Gareth and dumped the disgruntled cat in his lap. "Here, you wrestle with this beast a while. He's like a lion. What have you been feeding him? He's gained ten pounds already!"

"Everyone in town was glad to see him apparently. They all fed him."

Adele rolled a sore shoulder. "Well, if he's on board we're going to have to dump more ballast just to get the ship into the air at this rate."

Gareth laughed and stroked the cat's silky fur. "I could tie a note to him pleading for folks not to feed the monster."

"Don't tempt me." Her voice dropped to a breathy sigh. "Though if you wrote the note, I'd probably steal it for myself to keep under my pillow." Her lips brushed his.

"I'd write you a thousand notes if it meant staying near you."

Her breath caught every time he bared his soul like that to her. She leaned in close and whispered seductively in his ear, "My darling, do you want to come with me to arrange for horses and oxen?"

The corner of his mouth quirked upward. "As enticing as that sounds, I must decline."

Adele laughed and kissed him gently. Their fingers trailed apart as she reluctantly left to see to her duties.

—⁓—

Gareth walked to his library. Though it was nothing like Alexandria's vast collection, he still felt excitement and pride in his own meager offerings. After all, it was the only one of its kind in Britain. And it had brought Adele and him closer together after being torn asunder.

He pushed through the half-opened door into his private sanctum. It was a dark and quiet place, and one that he had not visited in some time. The sparse windows, tall thin things dotted with color, still allowed for a smidgen of light. A part of him was eager to open his books again and delicately flip through the thin pages, an exercise in warm memories as well as subtle dexterity. He wished he had been able to teach Baudoin to appreciate the wonderful nature of books, but that his friend carefully cleaned the Greyfriar uniforms and honed his weapons to a sharp edge demonstrated just how far even Baudoin had come in using his hands to accomplish simple tasks. Perhaps there was some shred of hope for his people after all.

Gareth spied the trunk on the floor. The sound of his boots thudded on the stones. There were odd shadows cast about the floor, and he paused to study them a moment, lost in the artistry of the designs.

The door slammed shut behind him. Gareth spun around, but saw no one. The room was empty. Only when his skin suddenly flushed hot, he knew he was not alone. Agony seared his flesh and he staggered forward. The shaded designs under his feet flared to life in a white brilliance. Gareth immediately recognized the runic symbols of geomancy. Every space on the walls and floor was covered with geometric drawings. The closed door completed the pattern, sealing him inside a death trap.

The assassin had found him.

In his ears came a hum like taut steel spinning and he dove to the side. A steel barb attached to a thin wire sliced the air above him. It would have taken his head.

The humming began again. Gareth tried to move, but he wasn't fast enough. He didn't even register the bite of the barb until it wrapped around his arm, slicing into his flesh straight to the bone. The wire snapped taut and jerked him off his feet. A second wire whistled, and something sharp stabbed into the small of his back, striking a nerve. His legs went numb. He struggled to rise to his unsteady feet, grasping the silvery wire to pull himself up.

Now Gareth saw the assassin he was fighting: a tall African woman. She wore numerous talismans on chains and attached to her clothing. He could smell her power surging. Her eyes were dark with determination and hatred. They reminded him of Mamoru's. This was someone whose life had been irrevocably changed by his kind. There would be no reasoning with her. Instead of pulling back, he rushed toward her, closing the gap between them.

Nzingu was prepared for his attack, however, her lithe body moving in a macabre dance as her razor wire held him fast like a fish on a hook. Her free arm gestured wide and then back, and the second wire wrapped around Gareth's leg, throwing him off-balance.

He swiped his claws at the wire holding his leg. He couldn't cut through it, but it did loosen slightly. He squirmed out of its grasp. The wire around his right forearm was lodged into the bone. It was the same arm Flay had broken months before, and it wouldn't take much force to snap it again, letting the wire sever his arm.

He staggered to his rubbery legs once more and rushed her, claws extended. He ran up along the wall and back down, attempting to circle behind her, making her readjust her aim. Her weapon, though its reach was long, required space and positioning. Gareth intended to deny her both. Her feet shifted as she tracked him, her arm swinging the silvery razor wire above her head, the hum of death filling the room with its reverberating cry.

Gareth darted in. His claws raked her arm with a spurt of blood as she spiraled aside, her whip still spinning. It lashed out again, cutting into his ribs, stabbing deep. She jerked back and the barb ripped free. Red blood splattered the pristine white of his tattered shirt. He cried out, not sure if it was pain or frustration. He came forward again, following her, his blood dripping far too fast onto the ground.

He saw her lips moving. A quick glance down showed that he stood within a circle of crystals on the floor. He tried to leap out, but a tug of her wire pulled him off-balance. The rune circle flared, and again he burned. The heat was concentrated and precise. His howl echoed through the hallowed room. He jerked, palsied in his throes of agony, and pulled Nzingu off-balance, breaking her concentration. The heat ceased. He crawled out of the circle, panting, with warm spittle running over his lips.

The woman made no sound. No cry of victory, no snide comment of derision. Her only focus was his demise. And she was going to succeed.

He rose a third time in a lurching shuffle, willing himself to continue fighting. He wasn't going to leave Adele. His mouth opened and he let loose a high-pitched scream that no human could hear, but hopefully it would carry to Baudoin somewhere in the castle.

The Zulu darted in from behind with the speed of a lioness and looped her long steel thread around his throat. He managed to bring his right arm up to block it, letting his forearm bone stop the wire from cutting off his head. Even so, the wire dug deep into his skin, silencing his cry for help while blood poured forth from his neck and arm. He felt searing heat wherever the woman touched him.

Nzingu easily manhandled him toward another set of runes on the floor. He knew he wouldn't survive another blast, and he twisted in her grip. His free arm stretched behind him and his claws found burning purchase, ripping cloth and soft tissue. She screamed in his ear and wrenched away. He collapsed onto his knees, his hand bearing the remainder of his weight against the wall. His fingertips brushed a carefully drawn rune.

Nzingu's foot smashed into his back, slamming him against the wall. His face pressed against the symbols. Her lips began the incantation. The pattern flared, and the heat rose.

Gareth prepared for death.

The heat abruptly died. His skin stopped burning. It was such a relief that he slumped to the ground. Baudoin must have heard him. He turned weakly on his side.

It was not Baudoin. Adele stood in the open door with a member of her Harmattan behind. Her face held shock, swiftly replaced by fury.

She drew her Fahrenheit blade. Gareth fought to rise, but shadows began to creep over his sight, and the last thing he saw of Adele was her auburn hair flaring in the green glow of her dagger. Then the darkness took him.

———ဢ———

To Adele's horror, Gareth was not moving. His injuries looked ghastly. Beneath her feet a ley line coursed. She attempted to quiet her anger so that she could still the undulating energy and bring it under her control. It meant taking her concentration off Nzingu.

Thankfully, Corporal Darby pulled his revolver, and in one fluid motion, aimed and fired. The bullet struck Nzingu in the arm, holding the ensnared Gareth. The impact spun the Zulu to the side, but didn't bring her down.

Adele had the attention of the energies, and she was slowly pulling them back. Corporal Darby fired again, but Nzingu was already moving. Gareth was forgotten as she addressed the new threat.

The Zulu avoided three shots, and closed the gap to the door, reaching over her shoulder and pulling an assegai, a short stabbing spear with a long wicked blade. Adele forgot about the geomancy and rushed to block Nzingu's attack. The impact of the two blades made Adele's shoulder ache.

She shouted at the young Harmattan. "Destroy the markings on the wall!"

Corporal Darby hesitated, but then jumped to obey his empress. His sword cut through the drawings on the wood panels. His foot kicked aside the crystals set in a pattern on the floor. Adele felt the power ease further.

Nzingu snarled and slashed furiously at Adele, pushing her back. In the brief breathing room she garnered, the Zulu rushed the corporal. He turned at the last second and her blade buried deep into his abdomen. Grunting with rage, Nzingu yanked up the blade, ripping his belly open. The young man screamed.

"No!" Adele shouted. Nzingu turned quickly, yanking out her blade to meet Adele's frenzied rush. The assegai came in a swift arc wet with fresh blood, and Adele leaned back at the last moment. The tip of the blade slashed her across the face high on her cheekbone. Another inch and it would have taken her eye. Adele continued to run forward till she was inside the spear's reach. She let her anger focus her attack. She swiped her blade viciously in front, but Nzingu crouched and dove at Adele's knees.

Nzingu's other hand flashed with a small dagger, and Adele barely blocked it. She needed room to maneuver. Nzingu slammed an elbow into Adele's face. The empress tasted blood. Kicking out with her knee, she connected with Nzingu's abdomen. The Zulu grunted and her grip loosened. Adele twisted away, rolling several feet until she knocked into Corporal Darby's body. There was blood everywhere. His eyes were open and he gaped like a fish at her, still dying slowly and terrified. He weakly shoved his saber toward her.

Bless him!

Adele rolled to her feet with the saber in one hand and her khukri in the other, and she came en garde. Nzingu rushed her and the blades flashed in a wild storm of feints and parries. Hot metal sparks flew from them. The Fahrenheit blade sliced deep across Nzingu's chest. Hot blood sprayed up and out, coating both of them. The Zulu warrior cried out as the chemicals entered her flesh and started burning. It was a deep cut, enough to give her pause, but not deep enough to end the fight.

Nzingu renewed her attack, her jaw gritted tightly closed. She had stamina beyond belief and was stronger than Adele. The force of her blows rained down. Perspiration dripped down Adele's face, and pins and needles surged through her arms.

The combatants circled the room, passing the bodies of Gareth and the corporal twice. Adele saw the rapid shallow rise of the soldier's chest. He was dying a slow painful death, and there was nothing she could do to stop it. Beside him, Gareth was sickeningly still and smeared with blood, with his skin burnt black as night in spots. Her sword stiffened in her hand, and she refused to give any more ground.

Her arm lifted, and in a blur she attacked. Nzingu barely avoided two thrusts, bounding away. With a swift lunge, she drew blood from Adele's right thigh, but the empress did not relent in her attack. It gave her the drive to press forward. Her blade parried three strikes and then in the space of mere seconds, she saw an opening and thrust forward, stabbing the Zulu on her right side.

Nzingu retreated and attempted to shift toward where Gareth lay, perhaps hoping to deliver a final blow. Adele cut her off time and time again, keeping her well away from him.

But she hadn't expected to step on one of the strewn crystals on the floor. It shifted under her right foot, and she staggered to one knee, connecting solidly with the floor so hard her jaw snapped shut and the wound on her thigh seared with white-hot pain.

Nzingu saw the opening and stabbed straight, her blade aiming toward Adele's heart. Adele couldn't bring her weapon up fast enough.

Suddenly a clawed hand struck out from her left, knocking the assegai away.

"Gareth!"

The vampire prince was on his feet. He glanced at Adele. Fresh blood smeared the lower half of his face like war paint. He had fed.

For the first time fear settled across Nzingu's face as she saw the rage swell in Gareth. She jumped back, but wasn't able to avoid the swipe of Gareth's other hand. It ripped across her throat and chest, eliciting a scream of pain from both of them. Gareth's hand burned bright, but the talisman around Nzingu's throat was torn aside. Then he slumped to his knees.

Adele bounded back to her feet and pressed the advantage Gareth had given her. With one hand, the Zulu attempted to stem her gushing blood and, with the other, hold off the enraged empress. Adele knew the fight was ending. None of them could keep this up much longer. All of them were wounded, but she just needed to outlast the Zulu. Bright, fresh blood continued to well between Nzingu's fingers.

"My lord!"

Baudoin had arrived. Adele risked a glance behind her and saw the vampire halt in his tracks at the threshold to the room. His face was marred with pain. He had never experienced geomancy. Even at its mildest, the effect was excruciating. A desperate Nzingu tried again to activate the energies of some of the small traps that still lay intact on the floor. Baudoin crashed through the doorway, snarling as he felt the heat, desperate to reach Gareth's side.

Adele quickly slammed a hand on the ground and wrested the crackling energy from Nzingu, whose eyes went wide as the power fell away from her and the ley lines went cold.

Baudoin took up a position in front of Gareth also, protecting him.

More footsteps pounded out in the hall. Adele's Harmattan.

Nzingu dropped a hemp bag on the floor into one of the rune circles. It exploded in a flash of sound and a crackling of energy. Baudoin threw himself over Gareth while Adele dove to the side.

A crash of glass told Adele that Nzingu had made her escape out a window. She turned to the Harmattan crowding in the doorway.

"She's outside! Stop her!"

Shirazi made fast hand signals to his men before he and three soldiers ran for the broken window and leapt through in pursuit of the assassin without heed of danger. The rest of the Harmattan spun on their heels and raced off down the corridor.

Adele crawled over to Gareth and her chest constricted. There was so much blood, and the cruel gash across his throat was like a grisly smile. When she touched him, he winced. She cursed herself; she was imbued with energy. She dare not come near him.

"I'm sorry," he whispered, his voice barely above a hoarse hiss, trying to rise.

"For what?" Adele signaled Baudoin to help Gareth as she had to force herself to move back. Gareth's eyes darted to the body of Corporal Darby.

She pulled herself to her feet. "You saved me. You both did."

Baudoin cradled Gareth's head. "He needs blood."

"I can't. My blood will kill him now." Adele shook her head in anguish. "Go. Tell the people what has happened. I'll stay here to protect him."

Baudoin slowly relinquished his place, lowering Gareth onto the floor wet with his blood. Then he rose and ran from the room at a speed Adele couldn't follow.

Immediately Gareth's head turned toward her. "You're hurt too."

"I'll manage. The wound isn't deep. It hit the muscle. I'll be sore, but mobile."

"Can you help me stand? I have to get out of this room."

"No." Adele let out a shuddering anxious breath. "I can't touch you. We must wait until help comes."

Gareth seemed satisfied by that. He held her with his eyes as they remained apart for what seemed like hours. Finally, Adele gratefully heard the sound of approaching feet.

Captain Shirazi returned, wheezing from exertion. The report on his lips faded when he saw the state of the empress, and he started moving toward her. Then he stopped short over the mutilated body of Corporal Darby, staring down. His pistol cleared its holster, and he pointed it at Gareth.

"Captain, put your weapon aside," Adele commanded.

Shirazi knelt over the dead soldier. His hand touched the bare shoulder where two puncture marks could be seen. "It fed from him!"

"To save me!" Adele shouted. "Corporal Darby was already dying. If Gareth hadn't gotten to me in time, I would be dead now too."

"He was a brave man," Gareth said quietly. "He tried his best to stop the assassin. He did not fear death. I made sure he felt no pain."

Shirazi's face remained hard, but his eyes drifted back to the still body of his chosen man. His mouth worked free of its grimace, and his gun lowered.

"Please help me with Prince Gareth," Adele said. "We need to get him to a room, but I can't carry him."

The captain hesitated with a look of disgust.

Adele demanded, "Pick him up, Captain. Please!"

Shirazi now obeyed his empress. Gareth was a terrible sight to behold; he stank of burning flesh and his wounds were horrific. The captain knelt and easily gathered the prince into his arms. Adele led them upstairs.

As Shirazi settled Gareth into a bed, Adele asked, "What of the assassin?"

"Gone," Shirazi informed her. "We followed the blood trail down to the Grassmarket and then lost it. My men are sweeping the area. From the amount of blood, I expect they will find her body soon."

Baudoin appeared in the door with Morgana behind him. The serving girl's face was terrified when she saw the state of the prince.

"He'll recover from this," Adele assured Morgana, embracing her.

Morgana gulped, but then noticed Adele limping. She saw the bloody leg. "You're injured too!"

"You help him." She gestured toward Gareth lying pale on the bed. "My men will help me. All right?"

Morgana wiped her tears away. "Aye, miss. We'll help him. Don't you worry."

Shirazi stepped over to Adele and dipped a shoulder under hers. They walked out of the room, where they found a line of townspeople that stretched down the corridor. The captain looked at the people in surprise.

"They're here of their own free will," Adele told him. "These people care for him as you do for me. Gareth isn't a monster, Captain."

"I wouldn't have believed it if I hadn't seen it with my own eyes." Shirazi stared in mute wonder as they passed the anxious people.

—◦◦◦—

A silent shadow shifted outside the window of the library. Flay was only just recovering from the shock, and willing her rage under control. Gareth and that human together, fighting side by side, as he had promised to do with Flay. All Gareth's talk. Lies! And she had believed him.

Flay pressed her hand against the glass, claws slowly extending from her fingertips, scratching the surface. She was going to slaughter every living thing in the castle, starting with the empress. Let Gareth profess his love to her then.

But her own flesh prickled with the heat emanating from the room, and the familiar, horrible stench of Adele washed over her. She could smell nothing else. Flay drew back snarling. Her fury demanded to be let loose, but she had nowhere to go. Once Adele had nearly killed her. Now the human had humiliated and shamed her. Like Gareth had. Flay would see to it he was humiliated.

Gareth would pay for his betrayal.

CHAPTER 35

ADELE STOOD IN a shadowed corner of Gareth's room, her anguish welling up out of the darkness. The townspeople had long since departed, and the room was steeped in silence. Gareth lay unmoving on the bed, his body struggling to heal the damage wrought by the geomancy.

She felt safe in the shadows away from prying eyes. She didn't want anyone to see her despair as she hovered over him, watching the rise and fall of his chest as he slept, as she had for a day now since the fight in the library. She wondered what life would be like without him. It terrified her to think that way, but their lives were so chaotic that it was an all-too-real possibility.

Damn Mamoru.

Why couldn't he have understood that Gareth wasn't any harm? Was it so hard to trust her?

Damn Nzingu and her ruthless cunning.

His library. The place held dear by both of them, and the assassin had modified it into a killing floor. Gareth had no defense against such cruelty. If he had been human he would have been dead from his wounds. Bandages stained with blood obscured the right side of his chest and arm. The burns were still dark red welts on his skin. It always frightened her to see him like this, so much like the myths of old when vampires lay still as the dead in tombs. It was more than just a deep sleep.

Adele wiped her hands down her clean skirt as if there were still some residue of blood there even after the scrubbing she had given them. Stepping quietly from the shadows, she walked over to the bed and sat beside him, her hand searching for his and taking it gently. To her relief she didn't seem to cause him any additional injury.

She couldn't bear the thought of saying good-bye to him another time. The odds of his returning were growing insurmountable. Adele's fears swirled inside her, and she couldn't quiet them. His hand flinched, and the creases deepened at the corner of his eyes. He was in pain. Geomancy created the only true pain vampires felt. Yet he said nothing. If it had been her she would be demanding some sort of relief. And he had hours to go yet before the burns faded. Frustrated, she chewed her lower lip and held his hand tightly. Over the next hour, his grip was intermittent. Sometimes gentle and sometimes strong when the pain grew worse.

He was going to be fine, she tried to convince herself. They had far too much to do together. Incredibly, it had been only a year since they met. That was too short. She couldn't lose him now. It didn't matter what the future held. It was just enough to know they had one. She hoped.

Adele rubbed her face and finally let her tears flow down her cheeks. She leaned over and ever so gently kissed his lips. She hummed an aria from the opera softly, letting it drift over him, the only thing to find its way through his haze of pain. His breathing deepened, and slowly he opened his eyes, still bright as an azure sea. His gaze swiftly found her.

"Oh, it's you," he said. "I thought I was at the opera again." His hand reached up and cradled her cheek. He saw the wetness on it. "We're all right now."

Praying that it was so, she clung to his hand. His breathing eased, and he visibly relaxed. "I could keep you here with but a word."

"Don't." Gareth put a finger against her lips. "I'd be powerless against such a command."

The air felt thick in her lungs as she drew in a deep breath. "It feels like I heal you only to send you back out into battle again. How horrible I am."

"Nonsense. This is just the way it has to be."

"No! There is a better life out there for us somewhere. I know it. We should have looked harder for it."

"We are where we are supposed to be, protecting what we love. Our people. Our own desires come second."

"It's hard, too hard. How do you handle it so calmly?"

"It's about offering everything you have in order to protect someone you care about. The trick is never hold back. Never doubt yourself or what you have to give."

"I'm going to have to let you go again, aren't I?" she whispered.

"Yes. As I will let you go when the need arises. We have a day at most before I will need to depart."

His arms lifted to collect her and hold her against him. She slid carefully onto the bed and wrapped her arms about him, just holding him, feeling his heart beat at her breast, her mouth never leaving his. It wasn't a forceful kiss but a gentle, comforting one that allowed them the reassurance of the other's life and love.

London was calm. The flocks of vampires crowding the evening skies were thinner than normal, and less hectic than a typical clan gathering. Still, there was electricity in the air for the coming coronation and the celebration that would follow. For now, it was somber. The clan lords from across Britain were here, but their packs were left at home. Likely kings and queens of other clans had come too, but they brought only token retinues. Cesare would nearly empty London for the coven. During an interregnum, vampires tried to ensure squabbles were kept to a minimum. Too many had died in internecine struggles over the centuries.

Gareth drifted in from the north watching the green countryside turn grey. His gaze strayed to the pile that was Buckingham Palace. It was no longer his father's home. Gareth had no idea what had been done with his father's cadaver. Once it wouldn't have mattered to him, but humans seemed concerned about how their dead were treated. He had taken so many human traits, this interest in the dead was but one more.

There was the British Museum, his home in London. As he

descended, he saw the grounds in front of the building strewn with wreckage. Large chunks of stone and concrete, and scattered detritus spread outward from the front of the edifice. Gareth touched down with clenched fists, looking with alarm at the massive hole smashed in the front wall. The bronze doors were flat on the portico and the stonework around the doorway had been widened rudely, leaving a gaping wound in his home. There were deep gouges in the ground as if something heavy had been dragged from the building.

Humans were the only ones who could have wrought this damage, and they would not have done so without Cesare's express orders. Perhaps it had been an act of spite in compensation for Gareth's tardiness to London. Perhaps it was simply Cesare's way of speeding his brother's official presence from the scene.

Gareth leapt into the air and angled for the palace. He contemplated a furious meeting with Cesare, and had to remind himself to maintain control. This was not the time to strike his brother. As he closed in on the palace courtyard, he saw an incredible sight. It was the colossal statue of Ramses the Great that had been inside the museum.

Gareth halted in midair and stared down at the object in its strange new space.

"Impressive, no?" came a voice.

He spun to find Cesare hovering above him. His brother smiled. "Welcome to London. Did I startle you?"

"What is this?" Gareth pointed down at Ramses. "Is this your doing? That statue belongs to me."

Cesare settled to the earth, followed by Gareth. "I had it done. I wasn't aware that you claimed the objects in the museum."

"You destroyed my home."

"Oh, don't go on so. The doorway had to be widened a bit. There are still countless pieces of stone and metal inside for you to stroke. There's still a roof to keep the rain off your head."

"Why is it here?" Gareth touched the colossus and felt sick that it had been defiled. Adele had explained the statue to him when she was his guest in the museum. It had been their first meaningful conversation. Ramses was from Adele's homeland; he was her ancestor.

"It's Dmitri," crowed Cesare.

"What?"

"It's a monument to our father." Cesare patted the pharaoh's stone trunk.

"You simpleton. This statue is someone. This is a real man. His name is Ramses. You can't just grab an object and say it's someone else."

"No? I believe I just did."

"But . . ." Gareth struggled for words. "Why are you even putting up a monument to our father?"

"He was a great king."

The elder brother shook his head in confusion.

Cesare continued as if it was all quite clear. "This monument will show everyone how magnificent he was; then they will know that I am greater still when I surpass him."

"But this statue isn't Dmitri," Gareth repeated.

"It is now."

Gareth wanted to tear the smug grin from Cesare's face. His vision swam red, and his claws extended involuntarily. Then suddenly a strange thought occurred to him. Cesare was staring up at the huge statue with pride, and Gareth started to laugh.

"Something funny?" Cesare asked with a surprised snarl.

"Yes. Very funny. Perhaps the funniest thing ever." Gareth clapped a hand on Cesare's shoulder, causing his brother to pull away angrily. The Scottish prince doubled over in laughter so loud it attracted the attention of vampires who were passing.

"You're making a ridiculous scene," Cesare snapped. "Shut up!"

"I don't think I can."

"Gareth, you ass. I hope you do enjoy Edinburgh, because you will never set foot outside it once I'm king."

Gareth laughed even harder, slipping to the ground with his back pressed against Ramses. He bent low to the earth, his body racked by guffaws he couldn't control. The gathering vampire crowd began to laugh too, slowly at first, but then louder with fits of hilarity. The sight of the royal brothers laughing—well, one of them—was a great omen.

Cesare leaned toward Gareth. "I don't even care what you are laughing about. I have business. When the sun sets, I sequester the coven. You will be there."

"Oh I'll be there," Gareth struggled to say. He took a deep breath to recover his stern visage. Then he looked up at Cesare's grim face, and a smile slowly crept back across his lips. He broke into laughter again. The mob followed with renewed delight.

Cesare said, "If you're going to do this in front of the clan lords, the vote shouldn't take long." He indicated the gathered crowd of giggling vampires. "You're a joke to everyone."

Gareth rubbed his face with a deep, satisfied sigh. "And you are a human."

"What?"

"You've become a human, Cesare. We all have." Gareth stretched out his legs. "Look at us. Look at your clothes. Look at me and my herds. Look at Ramses here. You put up a statue, Cesare. A statue!"

The younger prince glanced from his brother to the colossus and back. His brow furrowed in anger and fear.

Gareth shook his head. "We're humans now. We're just not very good ones."

"You're mad." Cesare nimbly lifted from the ground with his attention lingering curiously on his brother. Finally he turned away and flung himself toward the palace, slipping into the black sliver of a window as if he'd vanished through a wall.

The crowd milled about Gareth, unsure of what had happened, or what was going to happen. They began to drift silently into the sky too, one by one, leaving Gareth sitting alone in the dirt with the colossus of Dmitri.

—⁕—

The two brothers stood on either side of their father's throne. The gathered clan lords waited. Many of them were the greybeards who had fought in the Great Killing, but there were a few youngsters, male and female, who had come to power since. This was Cesare's event, but since Gareth was the eldest son, and technical heir, he was the official host. Even so, it was Cesare who nodded to Gareth to prompt him to speak.

"My lords," Gareth said, "it has been centuries since our clan was called for this purpose. Would that this day had been more years in coming, but death finds us all. The time has come, and you have a duty to perform. Our clan needs a king, and our tradition holds that you noble lords are the voice of the clan. You will go into isolation, and you will not emerge until you have decided. Recall, there are no candidates. Any member of the clan may be king. There are no packs about, so it is wisdom alone that influences you."

Cesare raised a hand to silence Gareth. "In addition to you lords of our clan, since we are all one people around the world, it is permissible for rulers of other clans to join this coven. Their voices hold no more weight than yours, but they are welcome." He signaled his chamberlain, Stryon, to open the door at the rear of the room.

Several males and females entered, boldly attired to give silent notice of their elevated positions.

"Noble lords," Cesare announced, "welcome among you Ashkenazy of Budapest, Draken of Munich, Natalia of St. Petersburg, and Leopold of Brussels."

Gareth was relieved that Lothaire was not among the dignitaries. He had warned his friend to stay well away from the coven, but stand ready to move to Gareth's support when needed.

There was some grumbling among the British lords when the foreign rulers entered, but tradition, even recent tradition, was powerful. And these rulers were all Cesare's allies, so there were no wildcards. The coven would end as expected, they believed.

Cesare regarded Gareth, likely mistaking his strained expression for a sudden realization that his days were truly numbered. "Gareth, if you will."

The elder brother cleared his throat. "Yes. Now that we are all here, it is my duty to send you into isolation. You are required to spend at least three nights in contemplation and discussion, more if needed, but no fewer. Go now, with the chamberlain, and do not emerge again . . . until you have chosen the new king."

The lords turned and moved out through the open doors. Soon the room was empty but for the two brothers with their father's throne between them.

Cesare said, "That went well. Don't you think, Greyfriar?"

"Yes," Gareth muttered. Then Cesare's words struck him like a polearm. He slowly turned to look at his brother and saw a mask of hate and triumph.

"Don't pretend, please," Cesare hissed. "Even you are past that. I didn't believe it at first, and I hate you more than anyone. Yet once I considered it, I realized it was true. It made sense given your insanity. I'm only glad our father didn't live to see this."

"How long have you known?" Gareth asked, trying to sound casual, moving a bit closer to his brother.

"Very recently."

Gareth heard a shuffling at the door, and he saw Flay and a mob of her beloved Pale. Her face was like steel and her glare impaled him. She had turned on him. He didn't know why, and it didn't matter. Not now.

Cesare asked, "Are you prepared to surrender?"

"Not likely."

"I suspected as much."

Along one wall of the throne room, high windows shattered; glass sprayed ahead of vampires who swarmed in. Flay raced for the throne dais with a red-coated stream of soldiers at her heels. Gareth leapt into the air, spinning over several figures that grasped for him. Claws ripped his long frock coat. He stepped on shoulders like stones in a stream, feeling the fresh wind on his face. A quick glance showed every window filled with Pale blocking escape routes.

He raced across the chamber, slamming into vampires, pushing off cracked chandeliers. The mob around him tried to respond, tried to correct for his speed, but they collided with one another. He caught a quick glimpse of a furious Flay as her own stumbling men blocked her.

The empty hallway loomed beyond the open door.

A wave of heat smashed Gareth. In a second, he wondered if Adele was there, but the scent was wrong. A figure appeared blocking the doorway. He was a human with white hair and a long beard. In his hands, he held large crystals clasped together. A silvery fire wafted from the stones and caused Gareth to falter with a cry of pain.

Then he was falling back. He saw the rotting ceiling and Flay's impassive face. Gareth tried to twist, raising one arm to cover his throat. His legs were clamped together, and he felt his wrists seized. Faces and arms and torsos crowded around him, grabbing him, locking him into position.

"Hold him!" came the shouts. "Careful! He's dangerous!"

Gareth struck out with his teeth, ripping the muscles from someone's arm. New arms replaced it. He was borne to the ground, barraged with fists and knees.

He saw the human kneeling over him. The man looped an object around Gareth's neck, and Gareth screamed as if a hole was burning through his chest. Faces blurred in the agony as the vampires holding him yelled in pain and drew away. Cesare smiled and gave orders. Flay sneered down at her former conspirator, but her bravado faded and she shook her head sadly, looking lost.

Gareth was chained in a dark cell under the palace. Perhaps the room was once used for storage or wine, but now it suited the great traitor. Rough stone walls with no windows and a heavy door defined his new world. Gareth heard or smelled little because of the searing pain lancing through his body from the crystal talisman hanging around his neck. The burning was too terrible for Gareth to appreciate the irony of his brother's choice of weapon to lash him.

A bolt shifted and the massive door swung in. The human geomancer peered in with intense curiosity before Flay shoved past him. The war chief stared at Gareth's writhing form chained by the wrists from heavy brackets in the ceiling. His wounds from the fight still ran red because he could not heal. Flay's expression was pure bitterness, more than rage.

"It hurts, doesn't it?" she said. "I hope you feel just a little of what I did when your human pet tried to kill me in Scotland."

Gareth met her icy glare, trying to put the agony aside. His jaw opened and closed.

"Don't try to speak." Flay sneered at him. "You won't be able to."

The human geomancer said smugly, "As you can see, Gareth is in exquisite pain."

"Don't speak his name!" the war chief roared, and backhanded the man into the wall.

"Flay," Gareth whispered hoarsely.

Her flickering expression betrayed surprise at his stamina, and perhaps even concern at his condition.

"Please," he gasped. "We can still succeed."

"There is no we!" she shrieked. "There never was. I meant to betray you from the beginning."

"No." Gareth grimaced as he spoke. He panted with effort. "It isn't too late."

Flay went wide-eyed with dismay. "Do you even know when you're lying?"

"You must free me."

"Beg your princess to save you. Perhaps if you scream, she'll hear you in Edinburgh. I saw her there. Do you think I'm a fool? Do you think I'm an idiot? I should kill you here, you bastard. You deserve it."

Gareth dropped his chin to his chest at Flay's scorn. It couldn't end from jealousy. Such a small emotion to tilt the world.

"Touching," came another voice from the door. Cesare strolled in, grimacing uncomfortably at the aura wafting off the talisman. He glanced at the war chief. "Why are you here, Flay?"

She retracted her claws with obvious effort. "I wanted to see the Greyfriar alive one last time."

Cesare looked at Goronwy, who studied Gareth as if he were inside a test tube. "So your trinket works, Witchfinder."

"I told you they would, my lord. You are the master of humans and vampires now."

"Yes. Just as it should be." The young king-to-be laughed. He crossed his arms and regarded Gareth. "I admired you when I was young. You were going to be a great king; my only future was to be your councilor. Then the bottom dropped out of you. When Dmitri needed you after the Great Killing, you weren't there. But I was. And in an odd way, I was angry with you. You were such a colossal disappointment to everyone. Even to me." Cesare leaned against the wall, lost in his own memories. "I almost wish I didn't have to kill you, but I can't allow anyone to know that my brother was the Greyfriar. It reflects badly on the entire family, you know." Cesare reached out and clamped his hand around the back of Flay's neck, half playfully, but with clear threat. "Your days are done, Gareth. There is no one here to help you."

Flay said in a restrained voice, "What of his princess?"

"Ah yes." Cesare raised a curious eyebrow. "The Death Bringer. Empress Adele."

With sudden alarm, Gareth said through bloodstained teeth, "You don't think she's stupid enough to come here to save me, do you? She won't fall into your trap."

"This isn't a trap," Cesare replied cavalierly. "I don't want her in London. She's far too dangerous. I've brought my packs back into the city in case she was to wander in here. But I'm leaving for Edinburgh in a moment to kill her. And to kill everyone who lives there. Alone. Personally."

Gareth laughed. "You don't stand a chance. She'll render you into a pile of ashes."

"Normally, I might agree with you," Cesare replied as he fumbled awkwardly in his coat pocket. He drew out a chain with an odd bluish crystal hanging from it. "But, you see, I am far more intelligent than you. I had the forethought to prepare a weapon against the empress."

The human geomancer chuckled with self-satisfaction and nodded. "My lord, don't bring that talisman too close to this one or it may fracture the facets."

Gareth had felt a slight weakening of the fire burning on his chest when Cesare revealed the blue stone. Cesare noticed the concern on his brother's face and clutched the cold talisman in triumph.

"This little thing," Cesare said, "will counteract Adele's abilities long enough for me to slaughter her. Correct, Witchfinder?"

"That is so," Goronwy responded. "It is a triumph of research."

Cesare grinned at Gareth and repeated, "Yes. A triumph of research. Your fearsome empress will be nothing more than a helpless girl."

Gareth surged forward, straining against the chains, snarling. Cesare nodded to Goronwy, who pressed the talisman hard into Gareth's chest. The Scottish prince screamed as fire lanced his veins, and the world went black.

When Gareth's eyes opened again, he made out blurred images of Flay and the human witchfinder. He muttered, "Cesare."

"Gone," Flay announced. "An hour past. Bound for Edinburgh."

Gareth tried to move, willed his weak limbs to fight his bonds. He couldn't hear the chains make the slightest jangling. Even so, he gasped for breath from the effort. He looked up. "Flay, I'll give you anything you want. I'll make you queen. I beg you. I have to stop him."

The war chief glanced swiftly to Goronwy for an instant, as if there was the briefest chance of believing again. Gareth held his breath until her eyes dropped to the floor. Then she quickly turned away and walked out the door.

Gareth summoned up the last of his pitiful strength to scream, "Flay! Please!"

There was no reply.

CHAPTER 36

USS *BOLIVAR* SMELLED horrible.

It had been a week of being trapped in close quarters, in narrow corridors, and tight cabins with a crew of two hundred, plus companies of marines. The airship never dropped into temperate atmosphere to air itself out. The aluminum-burst engines filled every crevice with a nauseating metallic tinge that infected every bite of food, every swallow of water, and every breath taken.

General Anhalt climbed the companionway ladder to the bridge. The metal vibrated under his hands and boots, as it always did. He longed for the open decks of sailing airships. He welcomed the freezing temperatures any day versus the damp heat of the steamnaught. He prayed Equatorian engineers paid more attention to ventilation as they built their own ironclads. With any luck, these giant air beasts would be proven inefficient and fall into the scrap heap of history.

Anhalt pulled himself through the open hatch onto the crowded command deck. The noise of the bridge was like a club to the brain. The riveted bulkheads were packed with hissing pressure gauges and rows of wheels and valves. The network of pneumo tubes clanked and whistled. Voices shouted from every corner to make themselves heard over the din of the vessel itself.

Framed in the glass of the vast sweep of bow windows, Senator Clark waved a hand at Anhalt from his place near the great wheel, and shouted something unintelligible. The sirdar had tired of making a sign of cupping his hand at his ear, so he trudged through the sweating crewmen to lean into the senator's bellow. The airship's captain, Sandino, stood next to the wheel with the young helmsman and gave Anhalt a polite nod.

Clark shouted, "We can't wait any longer. My weather boys say conditions are prime."

Anhalt consulted his pocket watch and twisted several dials to read the brass wheels. Gareth should have come yesterday. The sirdar took a painful breath at the thought of his friend's possible fate. The empress had been so worried for Gareth to go alone to London. Perhaps she had been right to be concerned.

The American yelled again, "You said the coven started the day before yesterday. It will be over tomorrow and the clan chiefs might disperse. We have to go now."

Anhalt snapped his watch shut. "Very well. I concur. Commence the operation."

"Captain Sandino," Clark roared, "take us up and make for London."

"Aye, sir!"

After a few minutes of frantic activity with signals dispatched and received via pneumos, *Bolivar* rose through the grey mist. The windows spattered with rain. Then suddenly the bridge was flooded with sunlight as the airship breached the cloud layer and sat atop an endless sea of orange-and-white cotton. The ship plowed across the surface of the rippling clouds, driving north toward her target.

Senator Clark drew deep on a black Cuban cigar. "So, how do you like it, Sirdar?"

"Like what, Senator?"

"The feeling of saving the human race? We'll be legends when this is over. Of course, I'm already a legend, but you'll be joining me." He laughed and blew smoke into the rancid air.

"I'm grateful you made room on the pantheon for me." Anhalt offered a begrudging smile. "I just hope this works."

"It'll work. Everything I do works. You should see the Atlantic coast of the old United States now. Not a vampire in sight."

"Nor anyone else, I'd wager," the general murmured bitterly and consulted his watch again. "So, London within the hour?"

"I'd say so."

"I'll observe the operation from the bomb deck, if that's acceptable with you." Anhalt saluted and climbed down from the bridge. He couldn't bear the senator's crowing company for long, despite the fact that the man's confidence and enthusiasm were terribly contagious.

He worked his way down ladders and catwalks until the roar of the aluminum bursts were overhead. He entered the bomb deck in the belly of the airship. The bombardier chief consulted with his crew, all in heavy leather jackets with fur trim. They waited by a row of pneumo-tube out-spouts studying charts of London tacked to the bulkhead with magnets. A small company of bluejacket marines stood nearby.

Anhalt paused. "Chief, do you mind if I watch the operation from here?"

The sturdy American betrayed brief annoyance. "That'd be fine, General. I'll tell you, though, it gets pretty noisy and pretty cold down here. These bomb bays kick up an awful draft."

"I'll trouble you for a coat, then."

A thick leather flight jacket was produced for Anhalt, and he was immediately sweltering in it. He and the chief went to the rail that sur-rounded a vast open rectangle in the center of the bomb deck where the steel flooring stopped. Down in the open pit was the concave outer sur-face of the airship. A red light blinked over the pneumos, and a crewman pulled out a green tube. He immediately smashed his fist against a metal pad on the bulkhead. A klaxon started screaming. Men began moving into position, fastening their coats, and tugging on heavy caps. A whine filled the air, and sunlight shot in from underneath as the four bomb bay hatches slowly opened. The deck became a hurricane.

The bombardier chief grasped the rail. "I'd hold on as long as you're standing here. We've had boys sucked out before. Also watch your step; it gets wet." Water quickly condensed and dripped from every surface.

Through the gaping rectangles in the belly of the airship, white clouds began to part and slivers of green and brown became rolling forests and broken edges of a city. Anhalt judged they were one thousand feet up and still dropping. He searched the clearing landscape and saw a curving river that looked like the Thames near Limehouse. Anhalt watched the decrepit metropolis pass below him as slowing *Bolivar* tracked west until Buckingham Palace was visible. Sure enough, there were large swathes of green, the old parks, surrounding much of the palace. Very few figures were visible through the trees. The ship descended to a mere seven hundred feet and steadied herself with maneuvering motors and held steady over the palace.

The chief glanced at the pneumo clerk, who read a new message and gave a thumbs-up. The chief shouted to Anhalt, "Spotters confirm we're on target. The senator said that you are the superior officer on board, so it's your honor, sir. The bridge is waiting for you to give the signal to burn it down."

Anhalt wondered again what had happened to Gareth. Perhaps he wasn't even in London. There was no way of knowing. He prayed Adele would forgive him if he was wrong, but they couldn't delay any longer. "Proceed, Chief."

The bombardier grinned and pumped an upraised fist to his crew. "Bombs away!"

Crewmen wrestled to turn large wheels on the bulkhead. Overhead, the four assembly-line chains started clanking. Hooks on the chains snagged bombs from their storage racks and carried them toward the open bays and dropped them into the sky like pendulous ripe fruit.

Turning to watch the bombs falling, Anhalt spied movement far below among the freshly green trees and crumbling buildings. Black shapes seemed to appear and cover the ground. Anhalt grabbed his trusty spyglass and peered down.

Vampires. Hundreds of them.

"Chief!" he shouted. "Signal the bridge we are under attack."

The American looked confused until he too glanced over the rail and swore. He ran to the pneumo tubes, scribbled a note, and sent it flying. In moments, red lights began flashing and an earsplitting horn sounded.

Nearly buried beneath the warning klaxon came the rhythmic

thumping of the ship's belly turrets opening up. Explosive shells flowered amidst the thickening flock of rising creatures. It seemed that many of the approaching vampires were buffeted aside by the blasts, but few were stopped from coming.

A marine sergeant appeared at Anhalt's shoulder. Short and broad-chested, he leaned on the rail and studied the darkening sky below the ship with calmly raised eyebrows. He scrubbed casually at his tight red beard. "Senator's compliments, sir, but I am requested to escort you back to the bridge."

"Thank you, Sergeant." The sirdar pulled his pistol and drew his glowing Fahrenheit saber. "I believe I will stay with these men."

The sergeant said, "It's likely to get a tad bloody."

"I've seen *a tad bloody* before."

"So I hear, sir." His sharp salute revealed his admiration.

Anhalt watched the sky below *Bolivar* turn black with vampires. It was hard to make out individuals in the writhing morass of limbs and pale faces. Then the ship filled with creatures exploding up through the bomb bay hatches like starlings erupting from a smokestack. The marines opened fire into the storm squall of bodies. Figures twisted and spun, slashing with claws, falling on marines and airmen with teeth bared. Vampires scuttled everywhere, clutching onto crossbeams and dangling bombs.

Anhalt and the marine sergeant fell back to the pneumo bank with the chief bombardier and his men. The Equatorian fired his revolver and slashed at dark figures that feinted in and flitted back. Marines fought bravely, but men were swarmed under vicious mobs.

The sergeant yelled, "Sirdar, you need to withdraw, sir. The bridge is the safest place on the ship. My boys have got this well in hand." A vampire swooped past him and clawed him to the ground. Anhalt stabbed the vampire through. The sergeant shook his bleeding head and pulled himself to his feet. "See? I'm fine. We'd prefer you not die down here. Your people need you."

Anhalt felt like a coward, but he nodded consent. One man more would not make the difference here. The sergeant grabbed two privates. "Make a lane for General Anhalt to the hatch. We're taking him to the bridge."

The Equatorian shouted, "Good luck to you!" to all he was leaving behind.

The chief bombardier waved cheerfully, ducking the scrabbling claws overhead. "Be careful on those ladders."

Anhalt and the three marines scurried to the door, crouching low with men stabbing up with bayonets. The sergeant pulled open the hatchway and stepped out to cover, waving the others through quickly, and slammed the hatch closed again.

They muscled their way through the crowds of men in the corridors. Screams rang in the distance. Many of the gun decks were overrun or deep in blood. The vampires were working their way in from the hull. The engine room was lost, one man shouted. The engine room was the only safe place, another screamed.

They reached the airship's core where the great multichambered dirigible loomed in front them. They mounted a ladder that stretched up to the catwalk webs around the gas works. The general stopped and pointed out three motionless vampires clutching the sloped side of the dirigible. The creatures seemed overwhelmed by the noise and smell. One marine raised his rifle.

"No!" Anhalt hissed. "They haven't noticed us. Climb."

The men climbed with their rifles hanging off their arms by the straps, watching the vampires and waiting for the telltale twitch when the things would streak to the attack. They had reached the halfway point of the long ascent when a squad of airmen came out onto the catwalk some fifty yards below. Tools hanging from their belts clanged against the iron railing. The vampires dropped from their perch, swooping toward the airmen.

"Take them!" Anhalt shouted.

The marines awkwardly brought their rifles to bear, with elbows locked around the ladder rungs, and shots cracked. Aim was near impossible. Several of the creatures were hit and tumbled in the air. They righted themselves and focused on the marines above them as the airmen ran for safety. One vampire rose through the air, while the other two scrambled up the ladder toward the soldiers.

One of the spidery things below leapt, taking shots into his chest. He slammed against the bottom marine, ripping him off the ladder and leaving him to scream as he fell. The vampire surged forward, clutching the next marine and catching a bayonet in the face. The creature hissed and grasped the rifle barrel. The marine pulled the trigger with the muzzle nearly buried in the thing's cheek, and the vampire's head exploded.

Anhalt saw a vampire facing him twenty yards above, but on the opposite side of the ladder. The private below yelled, "Behind us!" A quick glance back showed the third creature scrambling up toward the group.

The marine private pulled a long dagger from his belt. "Go! Get the sirdar away!" Without hesitation, he slid down the ladder into outstretched claws. The vampire wrapped him up, and the marine shouted as he jammed the dagger into the thing's back, then pushed off into the air, wrenching the vampire from the ladder. Both figures plunged to the bottom.

The final vampire slithered down. The sergeant moved to the reverse side of the ladder, fumbling a long jagged knife from a belt sheath, almost losing his footing. The creature surged at him and seized the soldier by the head.

Anhalt drew back and shoved his Fahrenheit saber between the rungs into the vampire's midsection. He twisted the blade and the thing screamed. The sergeant slipped his dagger across the vampire's throat and grunted with effort as he dug the knife deep. Blood poured from the gash, mixing with the soldier's own. He gritted his teeth for one final push, and the thing's head lolled loosely to the side. The creature released its hold on the ladder and Anhalt kicked it. It fluttered away like a macabre old balloon.

The sergeant started to waver, drifting backward. Anhalt quickly snatched the man's bloody wrist through the ladder.

"Sergeant!" he shouted.

The man blinked and grabbed iron. "Thank you, sir. Up you go."

Both men climbed fifty feet, where they staggered onto a catwalk. As they made their way, Anhalt reloaded his revolver and handed it to the marine. The sound of the engines faded as they trudged forward; faint screams and gunshots still echoed.

Finally, they saw the base of the companionway to the bridge ahead.

Then they heard hissing. Behind them, two vampires started loping up the corridor. One raced along the deck while the other lifted onto the bulkheads and clawed forward like a charging leopard.

"Run!" Anhalt yelled.

He and the sergeant pounded down the steel corridor, their footfalls loud but unable to drown out the sound of the closing creatures. When they reached the companionway, the sergeant dragged himself up the steps to pound on the hatch.

"Open up! They're almost on us!"

Anhalt saw a speaking tube and shouted into it, "Open the hatch! Now! This is General Anhalt!"

He heard the scraping of a latch and turned to see the grinning vampires sweeping toward them. Hands reached down from the hatch, grabbing the sergeant and bringing him in. Anhalt started up as snarling faces and claws came at him, following him gracefully up the rungs. He stabbed down with his saber and kicked. Sharp pain lashed along his leg. Hands snatched his shoulders, and he was being lifted past the edge of the hatchway. He was tossed to the deck of the bridge.

Two airmen tried to shut the hatch, but a vampire shoved its way up, arms grasping for purchase on the deck. Growling and snapping. The marine sergeant rolled back to the hatchway and pointed Anhalt's revolver at the flailing vampire. He fired multiple shots into it. Anhalt slashed his saber against the thing's neck, and the head rolled loose onto the deck. The general kicked the twitching torso back through the hatch, and the heavy steel lid slammed shut.

"Well done, sir." The marine extended the pistol by the barrel toward Anhalt. "And thanks for the use of your sidearm."

"Quite welcome, Sergeant." Anhalt slid his steaming saber into its scabbard.

"Good God!" Senator Clark exclaimed at the sight of the torn, bloody Anhalt. "You need to see the surgeon, but he's already dead. If this is light resistance, I'd hate to think what Greyfriar considers a full-on attack," Clark snarled as he tugged on his spotless tunic. "We've already lost contact with the bomb deck and the engine room. We're dead in the air."

Anhalt went to the fore windows. The sky was full of vampires, and many were crawling across the outside of the glass. The general gazed past them to the ground, which was growing nearer. There were no bombs falling now. Buckingham Palace stood largely unfazed.

He asked, "Any idea of casualties?"

Clark said, "What contact we've had with other decks report a slaughter. The dirigibles are damaged. I'm about to signal abandon ship. All hands will take to lifeboats."

Anhalt turned over his shoulder. "They'll be cut to pieces in that melee out there."

"Our lifeboats have some protection." Clark threw up his hands. "What choice do we have? We're going down in enemy territory. Even if we managed to survive a crash, vampires don't take prisoners."

Anhalt asked, "Can we maneuver at all?"

The young helmsman reported, "Slightly, sir. We have docking bursters. Limited fuel, good for a mile or two at most. So we can crash here, or we can crash a few miles south of London. Neither one sounds good."

The sirdar stepped to the wheel. "I won't need much more than that."

Clark paused from rolling up official papers in an oilskin bundle. "What are you talking about?"

"I came here on a mission," Anhalt said, "and I intend to carry it out. I'm going to crash this ship into Buckingham Palace. Between the armed ordnance and the buoyancy gases and the engines, we should constitute a formidable bomb."

"Are you insane?" The senator glared at the Equatorian. "You're talking about suicide."

"Sacrifice, Senator. I believe this operation is our best chance to turn the war in our favor, to shorten it, and save the lives of many brave young men."

The senator snapped, "You don't win wars by killing yourself."

"Senator, sound abandon ship. Let everyone who can get off, do so." Anhalt commanded calmly. His decision was made; his goal was something that could be accomplished. And if there was a chance that this action would mean safety for the empress, it was a small price to pay. "I'd like to borrow your ship, if I may."

Captain Sandino stepped forward. "I'll stay with you, General, to fly the ship. If anyone is going to use *Bolivar* to kill vampires, it should be me. The rest of you, I want in the lifeboats. At least you'll have a chance to get home."

"I'd like to stay with you, sir," the young helmsman said in a clear voice.

"Count me in too," the marine sergeant said from his bloody place propped against the bulkhead. "You'll need spotters so we can drop this thing right on top of them. And I won't survive a long trip in a lifeboat."

Clark stared at Anhalt and shook his head. "I should've done this alone. You reek of failure. Always have."

With a grim look on his face, the senator snatched open a small compartment on the wall and turned a handle inside. There was a slight hiss of steam, and a two-note alarm began to echo through the ship. The senator tucked the package of documents under his arm and climbed a short ladder to a hatch in the ceiling. "Anyone who would prefer to live to see victory, come with me."

No one moved. Every officer, airman, and marine continued to study readouts, charts, and controls.

Clark snorted with sarcasm and lazily saluted Anhalt. "Sirdar, I'll give your regards to the empress. I'll tell her how you died needlessly. It's too bad you won't see my ultimate victory over the vampires."

Anhalt replied icily. "I would sooner sacrifice myself here with these brave Americans than serve beside you for a single moment longer."

"Damn you, sir." With that, Clark disappeared up through the hatchway, which was soon closed and locked from above.

After a few minutes, lifeboats appeared in the sky around *Bolivar*. They were capsules, some fifty feet long, like miniature zeppelins. Their onboard motors pushed them at a pace that was too slow to outdistance the surrounding vampires, who began to congregate around the little ships, clambering over them, spinning them out of control. The helpless crafts began to fall one by one.

A larger lifeboat swept into view, emblazoned with a family crest. Senator Clark. His lumbering craft began to make its turn away from the giant airship when a horde of vampires swarmed it too, crawling over its exterior, clawing and pounding the portholes. The senator's lifeboat was turned and tilted by the weight of the creatures. It rocked, and smoke boiled from its motors. It fought to keep its head, to maintain its way to freedom. But there was no hope for it. Just like all the other crafts in the air around it, the boat suddenly upended and plummeted. The vampires launched themselves safely into the air as the lifeboat spiraled sickeningly out of control, smashing into the distant Earth with a fiery bloom.

Anhalt stifled a sigh of despair. He could hear the distraught murmurs of the crew around him, stunned that their mythic commander had been brought down like a mere mortal. If he could die here, there was surely no hope for any of them.

The sirdar turned to the crew with the chaotic sky behind him. "Gentlemen, I want to thank you for your service to your nation as well as to humanity. What you do here today will leave the world better for your children. You will not be forgotten. It is my great honor to serve with you. Now, let's rain hell down on them."

The captain and the young helmsman calmly returned to their duties and steered the crippled airship using short spurts from burster motors. Several men perched by the windows and directed the ship in its attempt to stay over Buckingham Palace and keep the wind from pushing them off target. The helm brought the ship tail-down to maximize the impact of the bombs along the belly, and lift the bridge as high above the blast as possible.

The sound of monsters slamming the underside of the entry hatch grew louder. The metal suddenly bent inward. Clawed fingers probed in through the gap between hatch and metal frame as the pounding continued. The metal buckled more with each strike.

Anhalt laid a hand on the hilt of his saber. "How long will that hatch hold, do you think?"

Captain Sandino shrugged. "No idea. Won't matter much in a few minutes."

The airship vibrated madly, rattling as if bolts and rivets would pop across the bridge, or the bulkheads would crumple like paper. The helmsman had both arms locked around the spokes of the wheel, and Captain Sandino braced himself against the wheel too, legs straining, teeth grinding, holding the ship on course against the numbing vibrations. They both recited the old Lord's Prayer. The marines and airmen at the window interlocked their elbows and clenched their eyes shut.

The hatch smashed open and rang off the bulkhead. Vampires crawled in, smiling and bloody. They stopped when they saw Anhalt standing with feet wide apart on the tilting deck, glowing saber in hand, staring at them.

One vampire said in English, "Welcome to London."

"Empress Adele sends her regards," General Anhalt replied evenly. Then he charged the creatures.

CHAPTER 37

WHAT WOULD GREYFRIAR do?

Gareth had read all those penny dreadfuls. Greyfriar had been captured by the evil Cesare countless times and always escaped. Just when everything looked bleak and hopeless, when humanity was down to its last gasp, Greyfriar always triumphed. There was always some vampire weakness, some steam-powered gimmick, some experimental weapon. There had to be a way out. There had to be some last-minute heroics. Greyfriar always escaped and saved the day.

Always.

Gareth had nothing. No secret knowledge. No tricks. No rocket-powered bombs. He might not save the day. But he couldn't fail. Adele couldn't die. Gareth tried to struggle, but his body was a mass of excruciating pain. Cesare might be nearing Edinburgh by now. Adele wouldn't be expecting an attack. If Cesare managed to take her unaware, he could kill her. Gareth cried out and strained against his bonds again. The clank of chains mixed with the grating of the door bolt. Gareth looked up expectantly.

"Flay?" he breathed.

Baudoin appeared in the doorway with a confused smile, but eyes that showed horror at his master's plight. "Flay? I should hope not."

Gareth breathed out through the agony. "Baudoin!"

The servant took several eager steps, then stopped, reeling from the power of the talisman hanging around Gareth's neck.

"She is in danger. Cesare is on his way to Edinburgh."

"Then let's get you out of here." Baudoin trudged forward despite the obvious pain. He reached for the crystal.

"You can't touch it," Gareth warned.

"If I don't touch it—" Baudoin began, but his words turned to a shriek as his fist closed over the talisman. He tore it from Gareth's neck and flung it across the room before sinking to his knees with a whimper, clutching his sizzling hand. "—how will I save you?"

Gareth reached for the reeling Baudoin, but the chains held him back. He tested them again, but his heavy arms still couldn't tear metal free from stone.

Amazingly, Baudoin staggered to his feet. "That hurts."

"Yes. Can you free me from these chains? I must get back to Edinburgh."

The servant rolled his eyes and patted Gareth's chest with his good hand. "I'll be fine, my lord. Don't worry about me." He walked with unsteady steps into the corridor and returned dragging a chair that he placed in front of Gareth. He climbed onto the seat, wavered for a second, and then reached up. His rough tunic rubbed across Gareth's face.

"Aren't there guards outside?" Gareth watched the servant's fingers fumble with the manacles.

"Not now."

"Did you find keys?" The prince could see the pain etched on his man's face, but even so, Baudoin kept working.

"Not necessary. The manacles are just pinned. Fortunately, living with you has given me the dexterity of a human." There was a metallic click, and Gareth's right hand dropped free. Baudoin started to work on the left wrist.

"Thank you, Baudoin. You are a marvel. This is just the sort of thing that always happens to the Greyfriar in books. When things look darkest, a miracle."

Baudoin suddenly stiffened.

Gareth glanced up. "What's wrong?"

The servant's face lowered to look at his friend. His mouth twitched and opened slowly. His eyes narrowed with great sadness. With quivering lips, he murmured, "Gareth . . . my boy."

"Baudoin!" Gareth reached with his free arm to support Baudoin as he began to drop. Behind the servant's slumping form, he saw Flay.

The war chief raised a bloody claw to her mouth. "How many others must die for you?"

"Just one more!" Gareth shouted, and grabbed for the murderous Flay. He felt a pull on his left arm as he tore the chain loose. He caught her by the coat, his wrist trailing the chain with a broken haft on the far end. He let Baudoin drop and seized Flay by the neck with his claws. He surged forward, tearing at her throat, lifting her off the floor.

Flay clawed at Gareth's face. She dug into his right forearm, trying to pry his sharp fingers from her bleeding neck. He slammed her full against the wall, and her breath flew out. Without pause, Gareth pulled her forward and smashed her into the stones again. And again. He pounded her abdomen with his fist and heard ribs crack under his knuckles.

Flay snapped at him with her teeth, latching onto the tendons at the base of his neck. She ripped, and his fingers loosened from her throat. She made to escape the close quarters, to bring her speed to bear.

Before she could slip away, Gareth pushed his right forearm against her gnashing mouth and she instinctively bit hard, tearing into his muscle. He dug his left claws into her ribs while pounding the back of her head like a piston against the wall. Her eyes rolled back and her attack slackened. Gareth drove his arm deeper into her mouth, stretching her bloody jaws wider.

Flay's eyelids flickered, and she started to refocus on him. Gareth pulled his arm free and gathered the chain in his scarred hands. The war chief started to bolt, but he looped the heavy links around her neck and pulled tight. Flay gasped and frantically grabbed for the chain. Even in his battered state, she couldn't match Gareth's fury. She turned her claws on him, tearing his face and throat. He felt the blows, but ignored them, pulling the unyielding steel chain ever tighter.

Flay's desperation turned to panic. Her eyes locked on Gareth's in a second of unfamiliar fear. She gasped, "Gareth . . . we . . ."

"There is no *we*." He strengthened his death grip on her.

Flay sank her claws into his forearms, raking flesh and tearing muscle. She dug so frantically, several claws snapped off. Gareth stared beyond her, listening to the sounds of her dying struggle. He thought of Baudoin. He thought of what Flay would do to Adele if given the chance. He pulled the chain ever tighter.

Then he heard Flay's heart flutter with its final weak beats. And it stopped.

Her form went slack, and Gareth let it drop to the floor. He watched the chain links slide over Flay's lifeless throat and follow him as he stepped back. He scrambled to Baudoin.

"I'm so sorry, my friend." Gareth placed his hand briefly against the cold cheek of his beloved mentor. "Thank you for everything."

Gareth straightened and then lurched for the door. He scrambled up the stairs toward open air. Vampire figures raced past him. He paused, ready to fight, but they ignored him and took to the sky.

Gareth vaulted out of a window. He caught a rough updraft and soared quickly. Wheeling above the palace courtyard, he saw the colossus of Ramses, or Dmitri, on the ground.

In the blue sky above London, Gareth noted a vast metal airship, unlike the sailing ships he was familiar with. The weird oblong behemoth belched smoke. Vampires rose to meet it with their usual vicious abandon. Already the gleaming, sloping hull was crawling with black figures. Even without the rendezvous, General Anhalt was attacking. Or at least attempting to.

Gareth moved toward the airship on an instinct to fight alongside the Equatorians. But no. The thought of Adele and Cesare came back to him with a horrific shock. There was nothing he could do for the humans, and he knew Anhalt would understand. One more against the thousands would make no difference now. He put the ship and its men from his mind and set his face northward with terrifying urgency.

—⁓—

Adele woke.

She felt the soft bed beneath her and listened to the remorseless wind whistling around the empty castle. Everyone was gone. Her Harmattan, save a couple of bodyguards, and even Morgana had gone north with Hariri on *Edinburgh*. She took a deep breath and shifted her leg slightly, feeling the weight of Pet sprawled at her knee. His careless snores comforted her. The cat hadn't been awakened by anything unusual.

Then why was she awake?

Adele cast her eyes about without moving her head, and lay listening for anything out of the ordinary. The peat hissed from the hearth, casting a soft glow. Nothing moved.

Just as she was about to sink back into the pillow, something hard fell on her face. She instinctively tried to turn away, but her head was locked in place. Pet leapt up with alarm and bolted from the bed. She felt a pressure on her chest, and she took a sharp breath.

Immediately her head was filled with a soft, sweet smell. She cursed herself, and she now felt the prickle of herbs pressed against her mouth and nose. Her vision began to cloud. She grasped the hand on her face, but it was too strong.

"Don't fight," came a command in a familiar voice. "I don't want to hurt you."

Adele's gaze shifted, and in the shadows she saw the face of Mamoru hovering over her. He was drawn and thin, unshaven, a bit wild. She went for her dagger that lay on the bed next to her.

Mamoru swiftly seized the weapon and slid it into his belt. "No, no. You won't need that."

Adele tried to claw at his eyes, but now her arm fell limp on the mattress and the fingers that clutched his hand slid down to her chest.

Mamoru pressed the sweet herbs tighter to her face. "Breathe deeply, Adele."

The empress struggled to hold her breath. She felt like a thrashing fish on a pier, trying to fight, but her eyes told her that she was motionless. Helpless. The cloying stench was already seeping deep into her, slowing the flow of blood from her heart far into her limbs.

"There." The samurai smiled with gentle relief and pried her eyelids wide to examine. He removed his hand from her face and then proceeded to brush the stems and leaves away like a worried mother cleaning a dirty child. "As always, you are amazing. There is no one on Earth who should have heard me approach. But you did."

Adele watched him throw back the bedclothes and felt him reach under her neck and knees. He lifted her off the bed. He looked down into her face with kindness.

"Come, Adele," Mamoru said. "Let me help you one last time."

She could do nothing as her old mentor carried her out into the night, past the bodies of her murdered guards.

CHAPTER 38

GARETH FOCUSED ON squeezing every sliver of speed from the cold blasting winds. He knew he couldn't reach Edinburgh before Cesare, but he didn't think about that. Reach Adele. That was his goal. Then he would deal with whatever he found. It seemed like months had passed since he left Baudoin and Flay dead in London when he finally saw the grey spires of Edinburgh.

From the air, buffeted by the harsh northern winds and the grey clouds obscuring the morning sun, the city looked deserted. There was no layer of smoke and no sign of movement. As Gareth descended, the castle looked normal.

Surely Adele would have had a fire if she were there.

Gareth dropped into the courtyard like a stone, leaving a heavy indentation in his wake, and he raced for the palace entrance. He shoved the door open and was overwashed with the smell of blood. His wounds were healing slowly, but his head swam with exhaustion. He couldn't make sense of the stench. It didn't have Adele's scent, but it was clearly blood.

He raced up the stairs, caution lost to fear. The door to her room was open, and Gareth ran inside.

"Adele!"

The room was empty. The hearth was warm, but unattended for some time. Her scent was faint.

He noticed with alarm that the bedcovers were thrown about. There had been a struggle of some sort here. His heart pounded and his breath grew thin.

A shadow shifted along the wall, and Gareth dropped into a crouch with claws out. He saw two small eyes reflecting near the floor. A cat. The animal hissed at him, arching its back.

"Pet." Gareth extended his hand. "Where is your mistress?"

The grey cat pressed himself against the floor, ears pricked forward. He growled low in his belly. Gareth quickly snatched the animal and stood. Pet snarled and clawed, but the vampire didn't feel it.

He left Adele's room and returned to the outer courtyard. He stood listening and scenting the air. The wind roared in his ears and carried hints of blood, but he couldn't pinpoint her. He moved toward the great hall and pushed open the doors.

"Adele!"

He saw the corpses of his cats strewn across the floor.

All the animals that had once charged out to meet him when he returned home now lay motionless at his feet. Pet struggled wildly in Gareth's arms, no longer growling with anger but howling in terror. He dropped the frenzied animal, who scurried into a dark corner.

Gareth knelt over a mound of stiff bodies. He saw one that he recognized and reached down to lift the small white kitten that gazed up with round sightless eyes. He stroked the cold matted fur. This was the small refugee he had named after Adele. Pet trilled from the corner, and Gareth turned to see the poor animal nudging a motionless companion with an uncomprehending paw.

Then Gareth heard the sound of paper tearing.

At the far end of the hall, he saw a figure seated in a chair.

Cesare.

His brother had his feet on a trunk. Gareth's library. In Cesare's hand was a book, and in the other hand was a page, freshly torn out. The younger prince smiled as he dropped the loose leaf onto a pile of pages beside the chair. He looked up pointedly at Gareth as he slowly ripped another page from the book.

"Hello, Gareth," Cesare said. "I must say I'm surprised to see you."

"Where's Adele?"

Rip. Another page went into the pile. "From your dreadful appearance, I'd say it wasn't an easy escape at least. I assume Flay is dead?"

"Where. Is. Adele?"

Cesare held up the mutilated book and tossed it aside. "Please tell me you just have these things as an affectation. You haven't sunk so low as to try to read?"

Gareth remained silent, gathering his strength.

The king-to-be reached down and lifted objects from behind the trunk, a rapier and one of Greyfriar's scarves. It was the one Gareth had given to Adele. Cesare took an exaggerated sniff of the scarf with a smile, and then he spread it out to conceal his lower face. His cold blue eyes shone over the edge of the cloth. "Does this make me look human?"

Gareth laid the little cat's body aside with a gentleness that belied the rage he felt. "I'm going to ask you one more time before I kill you. Where is Adele?"

"You won't be killing anyone. You can barely stand." Cesare inspected the sword curiously. "It's too bad Greyfriar wasn't here to save her, because I drank her blood and threw her onto the rocks."

"You're lying."

Cesare shook his head. "If only I had gutted her when I first saw her last year. Ah well, life would be tedious if I always made the right decisions."

Gareth leaned on a chair, gripping the wood until it cracked, imagining it was Cesare's neck. "And I should have killed you on your airship."

"Yes. That was stupid of you." Cesare chuckled at his brother's frailty and dropped the sword and cloth to the floor. He sat forward lazily, eyeing something in the back of the room. "Hm. I missed one."

Gareth glanced over his shoulder to see Pet hunched at the door. He moved to block the cat from Cesare's sight.

The younger prince came to his feet. "Well, I had hoped you would see my coronation before you died, but that isn't possible now. I'm afraid, my prince, I must execute you here before the eyes of your last remaining subject. And then I'll kill it too." Cesare raised his snarling face slowly to his brother. "Just like I killed our father as he lay in his own filth."

Gareth charged, fueled by sudden flaring wrath. He impacted Cesare, who fell back against the chair, throwing up his arms in defense. Gareth's claws struck home on his brother's face and chest. Cesare grunted from the force.

Gareth screamed, "Tell me Adele is alive! Tell me!"

Cesare managed a callous sneer even while taking savage blows, but stayed silent. This enraged Gareth further, and he seized his brother by the throat to crush the breath out of him.

"You couldn't have killed her," Gareth growled. "You're no match for her."

"Then where is she, Greyfriar?" Cesare whispered. "Where is she?"

Gareth threw his brother against the wall. Cesare slammed into a polished shield and dropped to the floor. Gareth was on him, claws deep in his neck.

Then Gareth felt pressure against his wrist, and watched in shock as his hand was pulled away in the grip of Cesare's claws. The younger prince laughed as he stared at his own remarkable feat. He was besting Gareth in strength, something that would've been unthinkable before. Gareth knew with desperation that this was no fluke. Cesare had calculated it. The young king-to-be would never have allowed himself to fall into combat with Gareth if he didn't know he could beat his battered older brother. Cesare kicked Gareth in the stomach and threw him across the room.

Gareth struggled to his knees and started to rise, but he felt Cesare fall on him like a terrier, plunging claws into his head.

Cesare's triumphant voice came close to Gareth's ear. "I've dreamed of this moment so long I almost don't want it to come. But it must. Now there will be nothing to stop me from becoming the greatest ruler our kind has ever seen. No Dmitri. No Gareth. No Greyfriar. No Adele."

Gareth tried to hold himself up. His arms trembled with effort. His legs quivered. He saw a stream of his blood striking the floor and pooling beneath him.

"Stop struggling," Cesare crowed. "It's all over, Greyfriar."

Gareth's mind drifted away to thoughts of Dmitri as a young father, so brave and wise. The sounds of the wind across the Highlands and the smell of heather. The pure pleasure of battle. Watching Adele make tea in a bronze helmet in the British Museum, her delicate fingers moving together in ways he could never master. Her contrary eyebrow raised. The vision of her dancing in the colored sunlight of this very room. Her laughter. Her distant touch as he lay wounded. Her welcoming smile before the fire.

Cesare's voice wafted into his visions. "Never fear. I'll tell Adele how you died."

Gareth now felt the claws in his back. His gaze slipped around the great hall. He heard the wind howling outside. His right hand inched forward through his own blood until his fingers touched a blunt shape and curled around it.

With a desperate heave, Gareth pushed up, catching Cesare by surprise and throwing him back. The Scottish prince whirled with steel flashing, and Greyfriar's rapier sliced clean across his brother's throat. Cesare started to mock, then realized with alarm that he couldn't speak. His hands went to the deep gash under his chin.

Cesare staggered back a few steps before he bared his sharp teeth and flashed his bloody claws. He gurgled the pronouncement, "I'm the king."

"I'm the Greyfriar." Gareth drove home the rapier through his brother's heart and twisted the blade.

The younger prince's eyes went blank.

"And now, I am the king." Gareth released the pommel of the sword and watched it topple back with Cesare's body.

He staggered to a seat and collapsed. For a long time, he stared at his motionless brother, soaked in blood. After so long, it was finally over. He whispered, "Damn you, Cesare."

Now to find Adele. She had to be alive. Perhaps she had gone off with her soldiers when Baudoin came to London. He felt a pang at the thought of his lifelong friend lying cold. Baudoin deserved better for his sacrifices.

Gareth felt a buzzing in his head. He blinked and doubled over. He was weak and needed to feed, but there were probably no humans left in Edinburgh. He had to keep moving. If he stopped, he might never rise. He pushed himself to his feet, and the throbbing behind his eyes grew worse. Suddenly a wall of heat slammed him to one knee. He smelled silvery fire in the air, and a bubbling heat rolled beneath his feet.

"Adele," he moaned.

Gareth crawled to Cesare's inert body. He needed the witchfinder's talisman; something that might weaken the brutal energy surging around him. He pulled back Cesare's blood-soaked shirt. Nothing. Gareth ran his shaking hands over the inert body with his brother's dead eyes staring at him. Finally he felt something sharp in the pocket of Cesare's once-immaculate coat and reached inside. The minute he touched it, a wave of cool air washed over him and he was able to draw a deep breath.

Gareth stepped over his brother and used the wall to keep himself upright. He reached the door and stumbled out into the blustery court-yard. The air shimmered around him. He dragged himself up the stone wall to reach the roof of the great hall. He squinted his eyes.

A geyser of argent fire blasted up from the trees south of Castle Hill. Gareth knew it was Adele's doing, but there was something different about it. It tasted odd in his mouth. It was wild and unrestrained.

He concentrated on standing. When he tried to lift into the air, the cyclonic fire slammed him off the northern edge of the castle mount. He crawled up the wall back onto the ramparts and took flight, shuddering as new waves of heat cascaded over him.

He tacked back, sliding along the gales, using the fiery waves to push him. Even with the talisman the brewing energies crushed him. He struggled forward, taking punishment for every foot he gained. He could only imagine how bad it would be without the talisman. The energies slipped across his flesh and burned his lungs with every breath. Gareth didn't stop. Adele was at the center of the eruption.

And she was in Greyfriar's Kirk.

CHAPTER 39

The fires of the Earth rose in front of Gareth's eyes as he plummeted toward Greyfriar's Kirk. The sheer weight of it pushed back against his body. His muscles strained to continue even though he knew the suffering it would bring. All he wanted was to sink to the ground and curl up into a ball, and let the weight and the heat finish him. Every agonizing second brought him closer to the eye of the maelstrom.

Through the haze of pain, he saw two figures in the trees below him. Adele was laid out on a crypt of stone next to the kirk. She was as still as any of the dead in the churchyard. A stone image of a skeleton with a book, frozen on the kirk's wall, looked down on her. Mamoru stood over her supine form. The traitor had found his student again. Crystals lay around her like candles for mourning, but Gareth knew they were for a much more deadly purpose.

He dove, but Mamoru sensed him and glanced up. The priest made an adjustment with the crystals, his lips moving ever so slightly. The Earth flinched, and Gareth screamed as a burst of silver fire erupted, sweeping up and over him. He slammed hard to the ground. The impact drove the air from his lungs. It felt as if a searing anvil sat upon his shoulders. The ground beneath him boiled, blistering his chest and face. The smell of his burnt flesh filled his nostrils.

He struggled to rise, even just to his hands and knees. In his fingers, he still clutched the talisman. A hoarse shout slipped from his lips at the effort. Mamoru ignored him, calmly continuing his ministrations.

Adele remained oblivious, lying deathly still on the stone. Her eyes were wide open, her face to the sky, but only the barest rise and fall of her chest indicated she was alive, bathed in a sheen of sweat. Tendrils of smoke slithered over her still form.

"Adele!" Gareth's voice came out as a desperate cry.

With each adjustment Mamoru made to the crystals around the empress, the heat increased tenfold and her breathing labored. Gareth crawled toward her. His hands crackled and burned, pale flesh transforming to black.

The ground around him was a violent thing to see. Torrents of silver magma pushed up from cracks in the surface. Tombs were shuddering as the smoke coiled around them. The stone skeletal faces on the head-stones watched him in silent judgment, their hollow eyes cold and black. Shoving himself upright with one final effort, his shoulders hunched over against the pain, he dragged himself the last few feet. His gaze remained fixated on Adele.

He was mere paces away when Mamoru looked at him. The priest narrowed his eyes and aligned the final crystal. Gareth's world exploded. A wall of liquid heat rained down on him. He screamed as it engulfed him. He was going to die, but he would do so at Adele's side.

—◦◦◦—

The eye of the Earth opened and pierced Adele with its stare. She was lost. The air around her formed intricate patterns, colors swirling like a cocoon, hot and constricting. They were carrying her someplace, as if she were trapped in a turbulent river. The water was sparkling silver, washing over her, although she never got wet.

Everything screamed, and she couldn't shut her ears to it. Such power could transform the world if only it was free, but she knew it wasn't right. Her chest constricted, again and again. Her heart con-vulsed and then beat once more, wildly, painfully. Her body flushed as if she were ill. Heat was building beneath her.

A different scream cut through the chaos. She jerked violently, and the kirkyard snapped back into focus. She recognized the anguished voice and tried to turn to see, but she couldn't will herself to move. She let her rage fill her, and her attempts to escape from the rift's hunger intensified. Finally her head flopped to the side and the kaleidoscope of energy faded from the corner of her vision. She saw two figures. One she recognized as Mamoru, his back toward her. Her Fahrenheit dagger was shoved into his silken sash. Then beyond him, she saw Gareth, his skin half burnt black. His body was shuddering and shimmering as if the colors were bleeding out of him.

Adele strained to sit up. Her fury welled up inside her. She managed to roll to her side. Her limbs were heavy, her head spinning and her body flushed nauseatingly with the power. The rift beneath her was wide open; its energies screaming through her, flooding into the lines of the Earth, spreading out into the distance.

Adele shoved herself upright and weaved precariously onto her feet. She took a palsied step toward where Mamoru stood over the figure of Gareth writhing in the grass.

"There is no pain too excruciating for you." The samurai placed a foot on the vampire's chest. "If I could prolong your agony for my lifetime, for *your* lifetime, I would do it."

Gareth reached feebly for Mamoru's leg, barely strong enough to tighten his fingers around the cloth of the samurai's robe.

Mamoru slapped Gareth's weak hand away. "You thought you had beaten me, hadn't you? You were so proud of how you twisted her against me. Where's your pride now? You're nothing but a filthy animal rolling in the dirt. And soon you'll be nothing but a pile of ashes. All your kind will be gone. Forever."

"Adele," Gareth gasped.

"You can stop pretending you care for her." Mamoru stomped down onto the vampire's chest, nearly crushing his rib cage with the pressure. "You've won one small victory, if that satisfies you. You've killed her. Did you want to force me to do it? Is that why you didn't just murder her when you first saw her? You thought I wouldn't do it. You were wrong. There is no sacrifice I wouldn't make to destroy you. Even Adele."

The sight of Gareth's agonized face tore at Adele as she staggered in reach of Mamoru. She grabbed for the khukri in his belt. As she pulled the dagger free, the samurai looked down and then back at her. Shock filled his eyes as if he was seeing the person he had least expected in the world.

"Adele?" Mamoru reacted in strange academic curiosity. "How—?"

She struck out with the blade and stabbed Mamoru deep into his heart. The knife went in easily and her mentor shouted, arching back. He merely continued to stare at her with a look of wonder, even admiration. The samurai staggered past Adele and dropped heavily onto the slab, his arms scattering the crystals.

Then he rolled over and smiled. He mouthed the word, "Tomiko."

Mamoru slumped dead.

Even with the ritual shattered, the flow of the energy didn't stop roaring around Adele. It was free now, and she had no idea how to stop it.

Gareth fell against her and she held him. He was a terrible sight. His hair aflame and his skin burning and blistering, but his eyes were open and fixed on her, at peace, ready to die.

"No!" Adele screamed.

She looked back into the cold glare of the rift. Adele refused to be just some mote in God's eye. She would do anything to save Gareth, to protect him from herself.

Silver smoke covered her, boiling forth from every pore, touching her, pulling her, forceful and vulgar in its demands. It was consuming her from the inside out as if someone had opened a valve to the molten core of the Earth and all the energies were gushing through one tiny funnel—her. The power was too great, stretching her to the point of agony. The glow of the bubbling energies blinded her.

When at last Adele's vision cleared, the world looked suddenly different. The earth was no longer green. It was immersed in a furnace of white, and she stood alone upon a pillar of rock set in a silvery, molten sea. The wisps of flame danced all around her. She bit back a shriek of terror.

Adele's hands reached out tentatively and shoved against the shimmering heat. It undulated and darted from her will, celebrating its freedom. She let out a wail of frustration and then remembered what she had been taught. She concentrated, and went back to her first lesson. She came en garde in five.

If the Earth consumed her, so be it, but it would not consume Gareth.

She knelt before the rampaging Earth and flung her hands into the white lava at her feet, ignorant of any harm to herself. Every nerve within her came alive. She saw the entire world. The infinitely complex web of lines spread through every rock, every tree to form shapes and structures. Her body sang with its power. She tasted the sand in Alexandria, hundreds of miles to the south. She smelled the ice of the Arctic. She languished in the molten core at the world's center. The maelstrom had joined with her, and she reveled in it.

Her arms tingled and she looked down. The liquid coating her hands was turning to what seemed to be crystal at first, but she perceived it on a deeper level. She saw millions of threads of life. The effect cascaded to the far horizon and slowly began to crawl up her arms. With a panicked shout, she struggled to pull her arms out, but they were held fast. She grew frantic.

Then Adele remembered how easily she had shaped the facets inside her mother's crystal. Perhaps this was no different, just on a more massive scale. Swallowing her fear, she stopped fighting and embraced it, staring into the grasping, thriving fibers. She could feel them, touching and pushing.

The lines were fraying with excess energy, like something far too large was thrashing in the delicate strands of a web. Soon it would fly apart, completely unrestrained and unguided. This, she realized, is what her mother had dreamed about in her journal. Adele needed to be the spider weaving new silk lines into a web. Healing. Strengthening. Changing. The revelation that her mother's faith was with her, even now, brought new power. Her determination swelled.

Adele seized one strand that was heaving this way and that in a chaotic motion. It shivered violently, but then subsided at her touch. With a gasp of effort, she blended it together with a more stable line. The manipulation produced a new pleasing pitch.

She continued to weave, her fingers fluttering over countless channels of life. The unrestrained torrent that Mamoru had unleashed was slowly brought under her hand, unified into recognizable flowing dragon spines. The wild escape of power from the rift had been slowed, but now it had to be stopped.

Adele arced the lines back toward her. The shattering tones of the Earth wailed with power returning on itself. Sounds and colors stormed around Adele, threatening to break loose again. The new web she had spun could not long contain the energies piling up around her. The lines trembled and showed signs of unwinding as they surged with unspeakable heat.

So Adele herself absorbed the excess, preventing it from escaping into the world. Her body writhed with pain, but she didn't care. She felt as if her flesh was flying apart. Her bones shattered. Still, she calmed her mind, listening to the tones she was making. She gathered the energy within her, and though her first instinct was to cast it out, regardless of direction, in order to save herself, she steeled her resolve and forced it back into the well of the rift, placing each ley line carefully, one by one, so the screeching became merely a hum.

The eye of the Earth stared at Adele and for the first time recognized her. She was no longer just a speck of dust. The world shifted and the eye blinked. The power came to a complete stop.

Adele felt beaten and worn thin. Every nerve in her body pulsed and throbbed against her skin. She wanted to collapse, but the silvery wisps caressed her, easing her pain. They murmured to her now, reminding her of what she could do. Her body relaxed, and the glow of the world brightened. The Earth held her fast in its warm grasp, supporting her. Power still arced from her fingertips, sparking the air in front of her. She watched the wisps dance among the energies of the Earth. With a whim, she wondered if she could make the deserts bloom and erode mountain peaks with a violent nudge. The strands stretched to the horizon like an enticing distant road. She longed to follow it.

Something soft and unintelligible kept calling to her from somewhere distant and vague—calling her name. Over and over. She stopped looking out into the vastness of the rift and looked back at herself.

Adele focused on the noise speaking softly in her ear. She rallied her strength and struggled to wade out of the rift, ignoring its pleas to stay. Her arms slowly pulled out of the resilient mire. It took such effort. She stood swaying, staring at her feet. Beneath her, the great eye closed, asleep at last, content, but the darkness dragged her with it.

Gareth knew only suffering. His body was burning up. He was dying. Adele was rigid against him, holding him upright, but she was gone too, lost to the rifts of the Earth. Lost too was his eyesight, consumed by the flames.

He had struggled so to save her, but he had only succeeded in finding her. His head rested on her shoulder. He had no strength to lift it, but he kept repeating her name over and over, his cracked lips brushing her ear.

The ground was still pulsing with intense energy shooting up from the tombs, washing over him again and again. The silver smoke had receded, but the heat remained. His pain crested to unimaginable heights. This was on a scale beyond anything he had ever experienced. He couldn't see his skin, but he knew it would be as black as night. Perhaps he was merely bleached bone, akin to the marble skeletons that surrounded him.

Adele's heart beat wildly but still strongly under his cheek. She was still alive and fighting somewhere. He continued to whisper to her. If all he could do was awaken her and give her enough time to fight free, it was enough.

Suddenly, she dropped to the ground as if she were a marionette with the strings cut. They fell together, still clutched in each other's arms. She didn't move, but she was breathing, steadily, not racked by pain like him.

"Adele," his tortured lungs continued to rasp out. His lips were against her throat. He knew she still radiated power even if he could barely feel it. He could sense faint drops of cold slipping through his fingers as the stone in his hand liquefied. He was dying slowly, his organs almost gone now, burned through. He longed to see Adele's face again, touch her hair, but all that was lost to him. He was slipping away. He tried to swallow, but there was nothing but cinders in his mouth.

"Adele," he whispered one last time, his voice barely audible now. Her blood flowed just beyond his ears. There was no life there for him, but perhaps it would hasten his demise and end his suffering. He could taste her one last time and be consumed, wash the ash from his throat with her gentle spice. And he would be able to tell if she was going to survive. A final union. It would be quick and joyous all at once before it took him.

"I love you," he told her. And with that he bit her.

—◦◦◦—

Blinking her eyes against the new light, Adele realized she was back in Greyfriar's Kirkyard. She was alive, even though her stomach was twisting this way and that. Her neck hurt. The world spun, and the only thing that grounded her were the arms wrapped around her.

Gareth!

She turned her head, and her mouth opened in a scream of silent horror. His face was charred almost beyond recognition. His fangs protruded cruelly through lips that were burnt away.

"No, oh God. Please no!" Tears streamed, her throat convulsing as she choked on her wrenching sobs. "Gareth!"

This wasn't supposed to happen. She embraced him, not caring what he looked like, rocking him back and forth.

"Don't leave me. Please come back. Just open your eyes."

But he did not stir.

The graveyard was serenely still except for her terrible weeping. There wasn't another living soul around them for miles. There was no one to be strong for anymore. Hours passed. Eventually, her tears dried on cold cheeks. Sounds came softly to her: a small bird's cry, a gentle wind rustling a tree branch. Life was returning to the kirkyard, all life but one.

Her fingers touched his blistered cheek. "Wake up, Gareth," she begged him. "I need you." But he didn't. He lay curled on his side, his terribly blackened head in her lap.

Baudoin had been right. She had been the end of Gareth.

No.

Mamoru had. His body still lay near them, a swath of blood pooled at his side. He was dead. He had once meant so much to her. He had always been there for her and this was how he showed his affection, controlling her like everyone else, everyone except Gareth. And now Mamoru had taken him from her also.

"You will never control me!" she shouted at the lifeless body. Tears were falling again, hot trails bleeding across her cheeks. "You think I'm weak. I'm not. My power belongs to me!"

There was such anger in her along with the anguish, but it had nowhere to go. She was alone. She hunched over Gareth, weeping. Her strength had fled from her, and she could do nothing but hold him.

"It isn't fair. We could have been happy."

She fumbled for his hand, and she felt something soft. Her eyes widened. Charred skin was peeling away, leaving healthy pink flesh beneath.

His hand was healing.

Her body flinched when he took his first shallow breath. "Gareth!"

He stirred, unfolding from a fetal position, ash falling from him.

"Gareth! Wake up! Open your eyes!" Her body trembled so hard she thought she would fly apart. "Can you hear me?"

His eyes slitted. He blinked repeatedly as if trying to focus. His left hand lifted. "A-Adele?"

"Yes. Yes." She choked and squeezed his hand. "I'm here."

"Are we dead?"

"You were."

His breathing quickened. "I was burning." His other hand touched his face, where his skin had almost completely healed.

"I don't know how, but you're alive," she told him.

"I drank your blood," he whispered.

"What?" She reached up and touched her neck. There was dried blood on it.

"When you were gone. I wanted to be one with you before I . . . I thought it would . . . end my pain."

"It should have. I don't understand. All the other times my geomancy almost killed you."

"You tasted different. Like wind and rain. Clean. You've changed."

"No. The Earth changed." She swallowed hard. "All I remember is that I had to save you. I rearranged the ley lines to stop the flow of energy."

"You did more than that. I'm different. I shouldn't be able to touch you." Gareth shoved himself to a sitting position with her help. He touched his chest with a frightened expression. "Have I become human?"

Adele embraced him, her sobs now a joyful noise. His arms lifted around her as well. She laughed with a hiccupping breath as she pinched him as hard as she could. "Can you feel this?"

"No."

"Still a vampire, I'd say."

"Oh."

"Don't sound so disappointed."

Gareth held her head against him and whispered gently, his voice thick with uncustomary emotion. "I'm not. I just didn't expect to see you again."

Her arms tried to clutch him, but she couldn't make them respond any longer. Her breath started to shudder as the shock of the last few hours captured her. She was too exhausted to speak, but she drank in the sight of him.

Gareth lifted Adele and carried her into the church beside them, away from the body and the blood on the ground. The sun shone in through the shattered windows, creating honey tones along the length of the building. Gareth found a small alcove under one of the intact arches. The dark timber in the ceiling was like the wings of a protector spread over them. He laid Adele gently down, kneeling over her as if she were the only icon he would ever pray to.

Hours later, they remained cradled together within the quiet solitude of Greyfriar's Kirk.

EPILOGUE

AFTER ENDLESS DREARY clouds and misty rain, the day was bright and clear. The sky above Greyfriar's Kirk was tinted an azure blue. Adele set the bouquet of highly scented wildflowers on the stone tomb bearing Baudoin's name. The townspeople had carved the headstone with great care. Gareth's eyes had been shining when they presented it. It didn't look as ancient as others in the cemetery, but it would eventually. There were mounds of flowers, almost cloying in their sweetness, around the headstone, left there by the citizens of Edinburgh for their fallen.

Adele stepped back with Gareth's help and clasped his waist, holding him close to her. Her body still felt drained, but she was more alive than ever before. When she glanced up at him now there were no tears in his eyes, although there were some in hers.

"Do you think he'll mind?"

"Mind what?"

"The flowers. It's a custom. A human one."

Gareth regarded her with a puzzled expression. "Why would he mind? He's dead."

Adele cuffed him and then tried to explain. "Humans like to think people who have passed on can still hear us. It comforts us. Hopefully, Baudoin sees how beloved he was."

"Yes."

"I miss him."

"Yes." Gareth stood staring at the tomb.

Adele noticed Gareth was growing morose at the sight of his friend's grave, so she tugged him gently to lead him through the kirkyard. The surrounding monuments with their stone lamentations reminded her just how close she came to losing Gareth. Her chest tightened, so she held onto the joy all the tighter.

They passed a recently opened crypt, now a mausoleum for the cats of the castle, and Adele paused to remember them, her eyes misting with tears. She thought it only fitting they have a place here at Greyfriar's Kirk. Their rambunctious presence in the castle had given her the first hint of the humanity dwelling inside Gareth.

A wide shadow passed over them. Looking up they saw *Edinburgh's* hull fly over toward a landing zone at the castle.

"They're back!" Adele shouted. She wanted to run, following the descending airship, but a rapid walk was the best she could manage. By the time they climbed up Castle Hill, she was gasping for breath and hanging on Gareth for support. On the gangplank from the moored airship, Adele noted the flowing robes of Captain Hariri, and then behind him came the figure of General Anhalt.

The sirdar walked with halting steps, leaning heavily on a mahogany cane. His left sleeve was pinned armless to the front of his tunic. His dark face showed the pallor of exhaustion and sported horrific scarring from savage burns. Adele struggled to keep the pain from her expression at the sight of her beloved Anhalt, who had been so brutalized in his endless service to her.

Broad smiles spread over both men as they caught sight of the approaching couple. For the benefit of her station, she should have greeted them formally, but Adele was so overjoyed to see them again, she couldn't help but press into them with as strong a bear hug as she could manage. She breathed in the spicy scent of Alexandria.

"Dear General Anhalt." She put a hand on his arm and kissed his cheek. "Why are you exerting yourself with these travels so soon? There are many others who are in better condition."

He appeared confused by her concern and said, with slightly slurred speech, "I am well enough, Majesty. And there is much to do."

It had been only three months since the consecration in Greyfriar's Kirk. After healing their terrible wounds enough to travel, Adele and Gareth had raced to London on *Edinburgh* to discover what had happened there. On the journey south, they had seen thousands of vampires, all dead. Cadavers burned to ash, lying black and flaking in the wind. In London, they found the crash site that had once been Buckingham Palace. The burnt wreckage of *Bolivar* spread over the ground and, to their amazement, they found a few survivors in the hands of kind Londoners. General Anhalt had lived through the conflagration, but just barely. As soon as he could be moved, the general had taken *Edinburgh* at her best speed back to Equatoria. Now he had returned, bringing ships and troops to occupy London.

"How was Alexandria?" Adele asked eagerly as they proceeded slowly across the castle grounds.

"Warm. Dry." Hariri angrily drew his coat tight against the damp. "How could there be a land where it rains so much? It's unnatural."

She raised an eyebrow at the usually more affable captain.

Anhalt leaned over to the empress to explain. "The admiralty tried to promote him. Offered him an office."

"Would that not be a great honor?" Gareth asked.

Hariri huffed. "I don't need their pity or their daily schedule."

Adele laughed and slipped her arm through Hariri's. "I love you just the way you are."

"But I will still receive a raise in salary? Yes?"

"Of course."

"Then the matter is settled!" Hariri beamed, and the small group strolled toward the palace buildings as Anhalt related the news from Alexandria in a strained voice.

"Prince Simon has made his triumphal return to the capital, much to the delighted surprise of the populace. He is in fine form and has taken to wearing copious amounts of leopard skin and sporting all manner of wicked African blades."

"Are the people disturbed by the ruse?"

"No. As usual, they are quite taken by the bold strategies of Your Majesty. There seems to be no sense of anger that they were hoodwinked by the prince's death. And you may be at ease that there are men around His Highness who are assisting him to manage the situation there, while you supervise in the north. Prime Minister Kemal has been amazingly upright, and Foreign Minister Doreh is growing into a force to be reckoned with. Fortunately, she is a great loyalist of yours."

Adele asked, "You came by way of London, yes?"

"Yes," he told her. "A fleet of six airships is now anchored over London. We have at least two divisions dispersing into the city and its environs."

"Can we spare the troops from the front?"

"For now. The vampire counteroffensive stalled, and we are gaining ground thanks to their confusion and the warm weather. Field Marshal Rotherford took Lyon in May. The clans are still dangerous, of course. The Danube Front remains static. But the creatures are not nearly so well organized, with Cesare dead."

Gareth grunted with satisfaction.

Adele asked her commander, "Any sign of vampires in Britain?"

Anhalt shook his head. "No, Majesty. Britain seems cleansed, although they continue to thrive in their former habitats. As we flew in, *Edinburgh* passed a wall of vampires off the cliffs of Dover. Quite extraordinary. The creatures flitted along some invisible barrier that denied them access to the island. Any that dared approach, burned and fell into the sea. Whatever you've done it seems to be permanent."

"I think you may be right. But still, I've learned to distrust the word *permanent*."

"You have worked a miracle," Hariri crowed. "I tell you, there are no vampires in all Britain, present company excepted."

Adele glanced sidelong at Gareth's impassive face. He remained immune to the geomancy effect. She didn't understand it. There were times she was terrified that it could end at any moment and he'd die in front of her eyes again. Her nightmares were filled with such grisly fears, but they were fading as time passed and he remained safe with his arms around her.

The quartet entered the castle accompanied by some wheezing from both Adele and Anhalt. The silence that greeted them in the dim interior made Adele's heart ache. Gareth reached for her hand and gripped it tight as they traversed the now-empty castle.

He intoned, "There are rooms for you, gentlemen. Morgana will see you settled. There should be a meal in the great hall. Will you join us?"

Hariri rubbed his hands eagerly. "Excellent! That woman can cook my meals anytime."

Pet suddenly bounded down the hall toward them and Adele knelt to scoop him up. He smelled musty, and she knew the cat had been exploring the recesses of the castle, still searching for his absent companions even after these long months.

As the group entered the great hall, Morgana was just placing a large platter with a glistening roasted chicken on the table. She looked up expectantly at Adele and Gareth, then with surprise at their guests.

"My dream come true!" Hariri exclaimed with an exaggerated sniff. "I've flown through day and night, through storm and sun, through vicious hordes to reach this table. And you." He gave a brazen kiss on Morgana's cheek and hugged her. She blushed but didn't pull away.

"Aye, it is only my skill in the kitchen that you love, you pirate."

"Nay, miss. You have so many fine attributes I can scarcely name them all. But at this hour, it is indeed my empty belly that dictates my affections. But who knows where the day may take us." He winked at her.

Such simple flirting brought warmth to the room, and everyone settled down to eat. The conversation and ale flowed freely, but Adele noticed Gareth said little. His attention had drifted to the high windows.

General Anhalt leaned in his chair, making it creak. "Gareth, are you ready to go to London and become king of Britain?"

The vampire turned slowly to regard him. "King of Britain? What would be the point of that? I would be no more effective there than I am here."

"We'll need something there. The situation in London is fragile. No doubt, the same across the land. The humans are in wretched shape, both mentally and physically. There are still Undead about, and they attack without discrimination. And there are freed humans who seek retribution against collaborators."

"How are the people themselves?" Adele asked tentatively. "Do they seem happy to be liberated?"

"They are in shock, I think. Some are aware they are free; others are just stupefied. There are some who see us as the new occupiers."

"To them, we are."

"Would they prefer the vampires?" Hariri quipped.

"Of course not, but these people have been under a vicious regime for generations now. They've known one way of life, meager though it was."

"The eyes of Alexandria will be on you, ma'am," Anhalt said, stabbing a piece of chicken with a knife.

"This is the first test of imperial ambitions." Adele tapped a thoughtful finger on the table.

"It will be a delicate affair, I grant you."

"Hospitals and other needs of the people must be met first and foremost."

"Construction is already under way on a hospital."

"Good. Christen it the Miles Clark Memorial Hospital." Anhalt raised an eyebrow, so she added, "For our fallen American brethren, General."

"Of course." Then the general said, "Perhaps you should make a trip south soon, Your Majesty."

"Yes, I intend to. I need to see to affairs in London for myself."

"London, yes. But farther south as well." Anhalt shifted his aching legs with a grimace. "When do you intend to return to Alexandria?"

Gareth stood. "Excuse me." He walked out of the room.

Hariri stared after him. "Pardon me saying so, but he doesn't seem too concerned about the future of his people."

"He has no people," Adele stated solemnly. "He's the king of ashes. I killed them with a wave of my hand." She glanced at the door before saying, "I want to discuss my plans with you in greater length soon, General. It will be difficult, but I hope to establish some sort of court here in Edinburgh, as well as maintaining my presence in Alexandria. There will be arrangements with the court and Commons, and Simon, to ensure a smooth government there, and here. Furthermore, on the grand issue of our liberation of Europe, it is my intention to seize control of Mamoru's cabal of geomancers, and to unite them with Greyfriar's network. I will do what Mamoru should have been doing all along: create a corps of geomancers who will venture into occupied Europe and train humans to resist their vampire masters."

General Anhalt huffed appreciatively. "Arming a man's food against him. Cunning."

"There are difficult and exciting times ahead." Adele nudged Pet to the floor and rose. She ran a soft hand over Anhalt's shoulder. "I can't express how grateful I am to still have you beside me to see it."

"No need, Majesty." The sirdar glanced up at her with a gleam replacing the fatigue in his dark eyes. "It has been my honor. Always."

"Now, gentlemen, I beg your pardon, but I must step away."

Hariri took a deep breath and set down his chicken leg. He studied his companion. "I am in awe of you both. After all you've been though, you still won't stop. How long do you think you can maintain your strength, my old friend?"

Anhalt watched his beloved Adele depart. "As long as she needs me. As long as she needs me."

—◦◦◦—

Adele hurried the halls looking for Gareth. The castle was so large she doubted she'd find him if he truly intended to hide from her. All the rooms were empty, so she searched outside on the ramparts and found him near the remnants of a gigantic iron cannon.

She didn't say anything, but merely stood beside him. Even though the day had been warm, the winds gusting off the coast brought a nip to the air. After a silent moment, he pulled off his cloak and wrapped it around her shoulders. His arms slipped around her waist and drew her against his chest. The warmth of his body warded off the remainder of her chills. Together they stared out over the city, watching the smoke from chimneys curl skyward. Neither spoke for a long time. Adele's insistent patience finally wore him down.

Gareth said, "I'm just trying to decide my place in this new world."

"It's right beside me," Adele answered softly.

"Of course. But there is more to me than that."

Her head settled against his shoulder. "I know. What do you want to do?"

"I don't know, but it appears neither Gareth nor Greyfriar are needed anymore."

"Rubbish!" she declared with a trace of anger in her voice. She turned in his embrace to face him.

He looked down, his blue eyes melancholy. "Gareth is king of the dead. He has no clan to rule."

"Perhaps Greyfriar could go to London and assume the throne. The people know him. They would accept him."

"And if they found out who he is? Remember when you discovered it? I doubt I'd be able to charm everyone in Britain with my feeble library."

Adele took an exasperated breath, but he was right.

Gareth worked his long fingers deftly as if holding a sword. Then he let his hand drop to his side. "Greyfriar has no place. Should he keep rescuing kittens in the midst of global slaughter?"

"That's ridiculous and you know it."

"Do I? When Flay destroyed Riez, I accomplished nothing. In the trenches of Grenoble, thousands of your soldiers died around me while I saved one boy. You're the inspiration to your people now. My time playing masked hero has passed."

Adele laid a hand upon his chest, feeling his steady heartbeat. "Do you remember what I told you in the castle the time I discovered you writing?"

"That I was free to use your alphabet? Are you rescinding that now?"

A small laugh pushed through Adele's serious demeanor. "No. Not that. I told you that it takes only one man to bring about change."

"What's one man in a world ruled by armies?"

"You don't see it, do you? The Greyfriar was never about saving the world."

He regarded her quizzically.

"He was about saving only one." Adele picked up his hand and placed it on her chest. "Me."

Gareth straightened and breathed deeply as he considered that thought. "You're right," he said. He kissed her slowly and then wrapped his arms around her once more. She turned so they were both facing the same direction again.

Pet padded along the stone battlement and bumped up against them. Instinctively, Gareth's hand reached out to stroke the cat's back, and Pet stretched up to meet his warm palm, purring contentedly. Adele gathered the feline in her arms and stared at the dark-stoned city beneath them.

On the farthest spire of the waking city she imagined a man cloaked in grey with his face obscured by a scarf and mirrored glasses, watching over the people slumbering in their beds. That figure projected hope and sanctuary to so many, and particularly to her. It wasn't right for his story to end. She tilted her head back to look at Gareth.

He glanced down at her curiously. "What?"

"You should write a book."

His face betrayed genuine shock. Then he chuckled and tightened his embrace, gazing once more into the distant sky. "What would I possibly write about?"

"Write about Greyfriar. You could write his true tales. Not the silly stuff his books are filled with now."

"Like riding elephants? Or saving the world single-handedly?"

"Yes, exactly." She turned his chin so he faced her again, her expression serious. "Only you can tell us how it really is, tell us about the people you save, and the sacrifices you make."

"Tell the truth," he murmured.

"As much as you want to tell anyway," she said. "This is your chance to speak out. A book penned by the Greyfriar himself."

There was a pause before he said, "The sum total of my writing life is two notes. It seems a great stretch to jump straight to a book. I don't have the ability."

"You'd be perfect. Who knows a good story better than you? I can help you with small things like grammar. Simon's very good with that also. He'd be thrilled."

"He'd have me riding an elephant."

Adele laughed. "Well, one should always make time to ride an elephant or two."

"Perhaps." His gaze again tracked toward the south, perhaps toward far distant London. "Perhaps I should write my story . . . as Gareth."

Adele's breath hitched. "My God. You're brilliant. A book written by a vampire about his own life."

Gareth shrugged hesitantly. "Oh, I don't know. Who would read that?"

"Every human on Earth."

The furrows in Gareth's brow faded completely, and he stared into Adele's glowing face. He drew her close again. They held each other until shadows gathered in the stones around them.

A soft faint scrape sounded behind Adele, and she turned along with Gareth and Pet to spy a shape moving against the far grey wall. A feral white cat slinked past and disappeared inside the dark doorway behind them. Pet wrestled free from Adele's grasp and loped after the newcomer.

Gareth smiled and swept an arm around Adele's shoulder.

Life was returning to their castle.

ABOUT THE AUTHORS

CLAY AND SUSAN GRIFFITH were married at Greyfriars
Kirk in the shadow of Edinburgh Castle.
That's why these books exist.

Follow the Vampire Empire trilogy online:

http://clayandsusangriffith.blogspot.com
www.facebook.com/vampireempire